Alex Gray is the *Sunday Times* bestselling author of the Detective William Lorimer series. Born and raised in Glasgow, she has been awarded the Scottish Association of Writers' Constable and Pitlochry trophies for her crime writing and is the co-founder of the international Bloody Scotland Crime Writing Festival.

To find exclusive articles, reviews and the latest news about Alex Gray and the DSI Lorimer series, visit www.alexgrayauthor.co.uk or follow Alex on Twitter @alexincrimeland.

Alex Gray

THE RIVERMAN

SPHERE

SPHERE

First published in Great Britain in 2007 by Sphere
First published in paperback in 2007 by Sphere
This edition published in 2022

1 3 5 7 9 10 8 6 4 2

A CIP catalogue record for this book is available from the British Library.

Grateful thanks to Faber and Faber Ltd for permission
to quote from *The Waste Land and Other Poems* by T. S. Eliot.

ISBN 978-1-4087-2609-9

Typeset in Caslon by M Rules
Printed and bound in Great Britain by Clays Ltd, Elcograf S.p.A.

Papers used by Sphere are from well-managed forests
and other responsible sources.

Sphere
An imprint of
Little, Brown Book Group
Carmelite House
50 Victoria Embankment
London EC4Y 0DZ

An Hachette UK Company
www.hachette.co.uk

www.littlebrown.co.uk

This novel is dedicated to George Parsonage, Glasgow Humane Society Officer, to the memory of his father, Ben, and all rivermen before them.

PROLOGUE

April

THE RIVERMAN

The riverman knew all about the Clyde. Its tides and currents were part of his heritage. His father and others before him had launched countless small craft from the banks of the river in response to a cry for help. Nowadays that cry came in the form of a klaxon that could waken him from sleep, the mobile phone ringing with information about where and when. It wouldn't be the first time that he'd pulled someone from the icy waters with only a hasty oilskin over his pyjamas.

This morning, at least, he'd been up and doing when the call came. The body was over by Finnieston, past the weir, so he'd had to drive over the river towing a boat behind him on the trailer. He was always ready. That was what this job was all about: prompt and speedy response in the hope that some poor sod's life could be saved. And he'd saved hundreds over the years, desperate people who were trying to make up their mind to jump off one of the many bridges that spanned the Clyde or those who had made that leap and been saved before the waters filled their lungs.

George Parsonage had been brought up to respect his river. Once it had been the artery of a great beating heart, traffic thronging its banks, masts thick as brushwood. The tobacco trade with Virginia had made Glasgow flourish all right, with the preaching of commerce and the praising of a New World that was ripe for plucking. The names of some city streets still recalled those far-off days. Even in his own memory, the Clyde had been a byword for ships. As a wee boy, George had been taken to the launch of some of the finer products of Glasgow's shipbuilding industry. But even then the river's grandeur was fading. He'd listened to stories about the grey hulks that grew like monsters from the deep, sliding along the water, destined for battle, and about the cruise liners sporting red funnels that were cheered off their slipways, folk bursting with pride to be part of this city with its great river.

The romance and nostalgia had persisted for decades after the demise of shipbuilding and cross-river ferries. Books written about the Clyde's heyday still found readers hankering after a time that was long past. The Glasgow Garden Festival in the eighties had prompted some to stage a revival along the river and more recently there had been a flurry of activity as the cranes returned to erect luxury flats and offices on either side of its banks. Still, there was little regular traffic upon its sluggish dark waters: a few oarsmen, a private passenger cruiser and the occasional police launch. Few saw what the river was churning up on a daily basis.

As he pushed the oars against the brown water, the riverman sent up a silent prayer for guidance. He'd seen many victims of despair and violence, and constantly reminded himself that each one was a person like himself with hopes, dreams and duties in different measure. If he could help, he would. That was what the Glasgow Humane Society existed for, after all. The sound of morning traffic roared above him as he made his way downstream. The speed of response was tempered by a need to row slowly and carefully once the body was near. Even the smallest of eddies could tip the body, filling the air pocket with water and sending it down and down to the bottom of the river. So, as George Parsonage approached the spot where the body floated, his oars dipped as lightly as seabirds' wings, his eyes fixed on the shape that seemed no more than a dirty smudge against the embankment.

The riverman could hear voices above but his eyes never left the half-submerged body as the boat crept nearer and nearer. At last he let the boat drift, oars resting on the rowlocks as he finally drew alongside the river's latest victim. George stood up slowly and bent over, letting the gunwales of the boat dip towards the water. Resting one foot on the edge, he hauled the body by its shoulders and in one clean movement brought it in. Huge ripples eddied away from the side as the boat rocked upright, its cargo safely aboard.

The victim was a middle-aged man. He'd clearly been in the water for some hours so there was no question of trying to revive him. The riverman turned the head this way and that, but there was no sign of a bullet hole or any wound that might indicate a sudden, violent death. George touched the sodden coat lightly. Its original camel colour was smeared and streaked with the river's detritus, the velvet collar an oily black. Whoever he had been, his clothes showed signs of wealth. The pale face shone wet against the pearly pink light of morning. For an instant George had the impression that the man would sit up and grasp his hand, expressing his thanks for taking him out of the water, as so many had done before him. But today no words would be spoken. There would be only a silent communion between the two men, one dead and one living, before other hands came to examine the corpse.

George grasped the oars and pulled away from the embankment. Only then did he glance upwards, nodding briefly as he identified the men whose voices had sounded across the water. DCI Lorimer caught his eye and nodded back. Up above the banking a couple of uniformed officers stood looking down. Even as he began rowing away from the shore, the riverman noticed a smaller figure join the others. Dr Rosie Fergusson had arrived.

'Meet you at the Finnieston steps, George,' Lorimer called out.

The riverman nodded briefly, pulling hard on the oars, taking his charge on its final journey down the Clyde.

PART ONE

February

CHAPTER 1

D uncan Forbes knew what he had to do.

He pulled the camel coat onto its hanger as he did every winter morning, felt the brown velvet collar under his fingers, then hung it over the old wooden coat stand. Like so much in this room the coat stand seemed to have been there for ever, its worn varnish a dull yellow against the dark wood-panelled walls. The faint scent of furniture polish lingered from the earlier ministrations of the cleaning staff, a whiff of lemon sharpening the air.

Duncan allowed a small sigh to emanate from his chest. He frowned. As one of the older partners of Forbes Macgregor, Duncan was not known for indulging in sentimentality, yet, as he stood quietly facing the corner of the room, he felt as though all his senses were heightened. For the first time he wondered how many more days he would be able to come here and hang up his coat in its customary place. Somehow that small action mattered more than all the consequences to come. He'd already faced the idea of losing one half of the house and the cottage in Argyllshire. Night after night he'd forced himself to picture the aftermath of the firm's collapse, sweat beading his forehead as he lay on his back, images of the future dancing mad patterns on the ceiling. He'd come to terms with all of that, though what Liz would make of it God alone knew.

It was always something that happened to other people, other firms, those modern ones that sprang up like weeds only to be pulled out and chucked on the compost heap of progress, not an old, respected establishment like Forbes Macgregor. And this cover-up must have been going on for years, maybe even before the firm had become one of the Big Six . . .

Duncan looked around the room that had been his father's office and his father's before him. A family firm of accountants, established nearly a century ago, was a matter of some pride, especially when it was now a player on the international stage. He'd never resisted the gentle push towards continuing in the family tradition. On the contrary, he'd welcomed the chance to step into a job with such a secure future. His mouth twisted at the thought. Security. Nothing would be secure once he'd set things in motion. His eyes fell upon the frame that held his practising certificate. When he'd first hooked it on to its place on the wall, Duncan had looked upon it as an achievement; the guarantee of a substantial career. Now he saw it as only a piece of paper caught behind a fragile sheet of glass.

He turned slowly, surveying the place where he'd spent the last thirty years, then walked across and sat down heavily in the captain's chair behind the leather-topped desk. Photographs of the children stood in silver frames: Janey on the beach in Arromanches, Philip standing solemnly with his first violin after a school concert, their graduation pictures, Janey with the baby, Philip grinning from under a bush hat somewhere in Kenya.

Philip. Duncan's mouth straightened in a hard line as he thought of his only son. There would be no job in the firm for him after all. Would he mind? Suddenly Duncan realized he had no earthly idea how his son would respond. When had he last talked with him about such matters anyway? Had he ever? Or was it something they'd all taken for granted?

For a moment Duncan Forbes was smitten by a strange hollow sensation.

What he was about to do would affect so many lives, so many careers, yet all he could think about was how much he would miss the daily routine of coming into this room with all its memories.

CHAPTER 2

The woman smiled lazily as she stretched her arms above her head. That extra half-hour in bed made all the difference at this time of year. Duncan had slipped away earlier than usual, but that was all right. She'd learned a long time ago that his absences meant he had more work and that more work gave her the kind of freedom afforded to few women these days. The years of jumping out of bed in response to the alarm clock's strident ring and all those city-bound trains with their crushed cargo of heaving bodies were long behind her. Thank God. Or maybe that should be *thank Duncan*, a little voice reminded Liz Forbes. He was the one who'd enabled her to stop working when the children were born, after all. How many years ago? She'd lost count now.

From time to time there had been a flicker of discontent. Janey had once called her a dinosaur, complaining that other girls' mummies had careers as lawyers and doctors. They managed to raise families and do all the things that Liz did, her daughter had complained, so why didn't she go out to work? There was a time when Liz had missed the camaraderie of office life with all its gossip and nights out, especially when the babies had been fractious and sleepless nights had seemed endless. Hugging her dressing gown around her exhausted body, she'd watched the smartly dressed girls pass her window each morning on their way to the railway station. Then she'd yearned for the familiar routine of making up her face and choosing which outfit she should wear. But those days had passed. Besides, Liz loved her house, her garden and her daily habits.

Now Liz couldn't imagine how she'd fit even a part-time job into her busy day. For a start there were the demands of her charity work. She sat on various committees as well as organizing an annual fundraising ball. Once a month, from May until September, she and Duncan opened their garden to the public, again to raise funds. It was the focal point of the community for the Christmas carol service, when they strung thousands of fairy lights from the trees and provided mulled wine and Christmas pies for the locals. That counted for something, surely? People were always telling her how much they loved it.

Most of Liz's own friends were working women: some through the necessity of making ends meet post-marriage, others because it was simply what they did. She couldn't imagine Sally not being a primary headmistress, for instance. It was something that defined her oldest friend, just as being at home and tending to her large garden was the image her friends had of Liz Forbes. It was hard work and kept her slim and fit, but there were times like now when she could snuggle under the duvet, watch the grey streak of cloud shift above the brightness on the horizon and listen to the blackbird in the pine trees.

The sound of the doorbell signalled the arrival of the morning's post and Liz rolled out of her warm cocoon, toes wriggling in anticipation of the sheepskin rug that lay on her side of the bed. A second ring made Liz scurry through the hallway, buttoning her dressing gown. Quick fingers tugged the snarls out of her hair as she glanced at the grandmother clock. Was it that time already?

'Thanks, John.' She flashed a smile at the postman as he handed her the day's mail. As usual there were several A4-sized envelopes that were too large for their antique letterbox. A flick through the bundle revealed that the bulk was for Duncan, with two bills and a letter for Liz plus a postcard from Kenya addressed to them both.

Dear All,

Having a great time here. Saw the most amazing herd of elephant yesterday. Our ranger, Leonard, took us pretty close. Weather still hot but the nights can be surprisingly chilly. Met a group of Aussies who are off to Scotland next month. May meet up with them when

I'm back. Only three more months to go. Can't believe how the time's passed! Hope you're both well.
Love, Philip

Liz smiled. It had been her idea for Philip to take a year out after university. 'He'll be in a nine-to-five routine for the rest of his life,' she'd argued when Duncan had objected. 'Give the boy some space before he settles down. He's worked hard enough for his degree, after all.' And that was true enough. Philip had achieved an upper second after a year when he'd sacrificed his social life on the altar of constant study. Duncan had grudgingly acknowledged this, adding that his studies weren't over yet. There would be the Chartered Accountancy exams for a couple of years at least, once he'd joined the firm.

She placed the card on the glass shelf above the radiator in the hall, where Duncan would be sure to see it on his return home, then took the rest of the day's mail into the kitchen. As Liz waited for the kettle to boil she sorted out her husband's post and put her own into a smaller pile. The two bills were from Marks & Spencer and Frasers, she noticed, turning them over. The letter addressed to Mrs D. Forbes was typewritten on a long blue Basildon Bond envelope. She glanced at the reverse, hoping to see a self-addressed label but there was none. It would be something to do with one of the charities, Liz decided, reaching out for the paper knife she kept on top of the bread bin. But it wasn't.

The two sheets of paper typed in single spacing danced before her eyes. *Dear Mrs Forbes,* the letter began. That was right. She was Liz Forbes, wife of the highly respected Duncan Forbes, CA, partner of Forbes Macgregor. But the rest of it? No. The rest of the letter was all wrong. It had to be. And the signature? Well, there wasn't one, just a typed line: *from a friend.*

Liz slumped against the kitchen chair, hands trembling. Her first instinct was to phone Duncan and tell him of this horrible thing that was happening to her. A poison-pen letter, wasn't that what they called them? She bit her lip. What if it was true? How would Duncan respond to her calling the office? Liz took up the letter again and read its contents. It was about Duncan, the writer explained. It was from a sense of duty that the letter was being written to Mrs Forbes, he went on. *He?* Liz thought suddenly. Or *she?* Somehow it sounded like a man: the wording was formal, educated. There was nothing spiteful in the language, no sneering at Duncan for what he was supposed to have done, the tone almost apologetic, as if the writer had had no alternative but to reveal the horror that was causing Liz's mouth to dry up.

If there had been even one word of malice she would have torn the letter to shreds and binned it, she knew. But the unheard voice was so reasonable, so matter-of-fact, that Liz continued to read the closely spaced lines until the phrases were indelibly fixed in her brain.

Her husband was having an affair, she read. Had been

16

having an affair for several years, if the letter was to be believed. With someone in the office.

Liz looked at the letter and the envelope. It wasn't office stationery, that was for sure, but it must have come from somebody in the firm. Her mind buzzed with several possibilities. One of the partners? But even as she tried to picture Duncan's closest colleagues, Liz could only call to mind the various women who peopled her husband's working life.

But this was absurd! Duncan wasn't the type to have a fling! They were *happy* together. He *loved* her. Wasn't he always telling her so? Then why did she feel as if someone had punched her in the stomach? Why was she having any doubts at all? Why was her mind frantically running through the faces of Forbes Macgregor's female members of staff? Was this what the writer had intended? Was this some insidious ploy to throw Liz Forbes into confusion? To make mischief between Duncan and herself?

Liz let out a huge shuddering sigh that ended in a sob. Whatever the intention behind this letter, it was making her feel as though she had been hurled into the bottom of a deep dark well. There was nowhere to go, no discernable way out. She couldn't tell anybody about it in case it was true. Especially Duncan. But she couldn't ignore it either. It was there in front of her, its words and sentences starkly telling her of her husband's infidelity. Or telling her a pack of filthy lies, more like, Liz's more robust, sensible voice asserted. What to do? Bin it and forget it ever arrived? That was the wiser course of action, wasn't it?

But even as Liz Forbes' trembling fingers folded the letter back into its blue envelope she was thinking of a place where she would keep it hidden.

CHAPTER 3

'Thank you for seeing me at such short notice,' Duncan began. 'Sorry you had to put off your client, Alec,' he added, noticing the frown above the managing partner's rimless spectacles. Duncan sat down, straightening his back from the tweed of the chair as its coarseness rubbed against his shirt. He was uncomfortable enough as it was, the managing partner's large bulk looming across at him. The man's unsmiling expression suggested a barely concealed impatience, his jaw firm under layers of flesh, his hazel eyes assessing Duncan coldly. Alec Barr had become head of the Glasgow office by dint of his personality as much as by his expertise in tax matters. There had never been any bitterness on Duncan's part when their paymasters in London had seen fit to bypass him for the senior post; Alec was undoubtedly the right man to run the Glasgow office in this twenty-first century. Yet he had had some misgivings since then, more due to the man's style than anything else. These regrets, he'd persuaded himself, were simply nostalgia for a family firm that no longer existed.

'Now what's all this about, Duncan? Your email came over pretty strong.' Barr was already flicking papers on his desk as if whatever lay there took precedence over his partner's request for an immediate meeting. Suddenly Duncan felt an angry warmth suffusing his cheeks and he stared at the man opposite until Barr was forced to look up and meet his eyes.

'It's bad, Alec,' Duncan began, his tone deliberately sombre.

'Someone been putting their fingers in the till, eh?' Alec gave a mirthless smile but his lips tightened when Duncan nodded slowly, his expression inscrutable.

'Who the hell . . . ?' Barr whipped off his glasses, glaring at Duncan in disbelief. For a moment the managing partner's discomfiture gave Duncan a fleeting spark of pleasure. Under any other circumstances he would be glad to have unsettled the man who now held such major control of his family's firm. But not now, he realized as the moment burned down into a sudden cinder. Not now.

He took a deep breath. 'Michael Turner came to me last week. With this.' Duncan fished out a sheet of A4 paper that had been secreted in a pink file. He watched as Alec Barr read its contents, noting the man's frown deepening. At last Alec looked up. His face seemed to have fallen in on itself, the fleshy jowls slack, the mouth part open in disbelief. For the first time since

Duncan had known him, the man appeared exposed and vulnerable. Then the lips closed again and he replaced the half-moon glasses on his nose. Silently he read the contents of the paper once more then looked straight at Duncan, waving the paper between them.

'And what have you done since then? Nothing stupid, I hope.'

Duncan raised his eyebrows. Whatever Alec expected him to do, surely he could rely on his integrity?

'I told Michael I'd deal with it, not to worry and to keep it to himself for the moment.'

'For the *moment*! For God's sake, man! Something like this could blow us all sky high!' Barr's voice barely rose nor did he thump the desktop, but his eyes had darkened and twin crescents of red were flushing his cheeks.

Duncan said nothing. Seven sleepless nights had given him enough time to work out the implications of young Michael's discovery. It was interesting to have seen these same implications flitting like shadows across Alec Barr's florid face.

'Have you spoken to anyone else about this? Liz?'

Duncan shook his head. 'Not even Liz.'

'But why didn't you come to me straight away, man?' Alec seemed genuinely perplexed. 'Why wait a whole week?'

Duncan resisted a smile. Alec Barr might be the managing partner of Forbes Macgregor and have the biggest stake in the firm north of the border, but it was Duncan who had invested most of his life in this accountancy practice.

'To think it all through,' he replied at last.

'And what conclusions have you come to?' Barr growled.

'There's only one option as I see it,' Duncan sighed. 'We have to find out who's behind this . . . discrepancy . . . and then be as open as we can about it. That way we'll at least salvage some of our reputation.'

Alec Barr narrowed his eyes but said nothing, nodding at the man opposite. Duncan sighed again, more in relief than anything else. It was going to be okay. At least Alec appeared to agree with him on this.

'Any idea who . . . ?' Barr asked at last.

Duncan shook his head. 'Hadn't got as far as that, I'm afraid. It's obviously one of us. Nobody else but one of the partners has the kind of clout to sanction something like this.'

'Well, it isn't me!' Barr growled again.

'D'you think I'd be here now if I thought that, Alec?' Duncan asked quietly. For a moment both men stared at one another and Duncan Forbes felt a flicker of misgiving. The managing partner had been very quick to leap to his own defence. Too quick, perhaps?

'No. Of course not. Look, Duncan, you've obviously been through a hell of a week, keeping this to yourself, but this is what I want you to do. Just go about your affairs as normal. Don't try to track down this person by yourself.'

'What are you going to do about it?'

'I'll put things in motion. It might not be a lost cause. Yet,' he added grimly, seeing the doubt on Duncan's face. 'Give me a few weeks to have an internal investigation set up, maybe under the pretext of a routine review. I'll think of something. Then I'll get back to you. All right?'

'I can't see how we can salvage anything. Once word gets out it'll be a rerun of the Enron disaster. There are almost three hundred partners in the UK alone. We're all collectively liable, you know, Alec,' he added gently.

'I know,' Barr replied testily. 'And that's why I'm not going down without a fight. Just keep your mouth shut, Duncan. This conversation never took place. Right? And maybe you'll be able to thank me in a couple of months' time if I succeed.'

Barr looked keenly at Duncan once more. 'And you're sure young Michael hasn't said a word?'

'I trust him,' he said simply. But, even as he spoke, Duncan wondered just how often he'd put his trust in his fellow partners over the years. And now one of them had betrayed that trust in the biggest possible way.

Alec Barr stared into the distance, blind to the view across the river that his office commanded, his fingertips pressed sharply against the flesh of his lips. All thoughts of his client waiting downstairs were now forgotten. Michael Turner was uppermost in his mind. What to do about him? The young accountant's previous assessment

23

had brought him to Barr's attention as having partnership potential. Who had made that observation? Barr suddenly recalled. It had been Duncan himself. He'd thought it typical of Forbes that he'd been ready with praise for a youngster who might easily present competition to his own son, Philip, in years to come. Barr's face grew dark. There *would* be years to come in this firm, he told himself. There was too bloody much to lose.

But first he had to deal with Michael Turner.

That young man was not going to go down in the annals of Forbes Macgregor history as the whistle blower who brought about the demise of the company. Not if he could help it.

CHAPTER 4

The bartender smiled to himself as he turned away. A little harmless flirtation was the spice of this job, he reckoned, and the female customers always seemed to respond to his Aussie charm. It was the accent, Eileen had told him when he'd boasted a little. Not his good looks and what remained of his surfer's tan, then? He'd laughed when she'd given him a playful shove. The women over here weren't in the habit of paying compliments to their men, he'd found. They were more likely to insult than flatter you. But this woman had smiled at him in a knowing sort of way and he'd responded by turning on his charms full blast. She was a bit older than the usual clientele who patronized the City Cafe. Her clothes looked expensive: black suit, white shirt, the uniform of the office worker, except hers were fine wool and silk. He glanced over his shoulder to see if she was still looking at him but her eyes were on her glass of wine, thoughtful and brooding. She was a good-looking, classy woman, her dark hair expertly cut, make-up discreet except for those vampish red lips that had curved into a smile.

'Michael! Over here.'

The bartender watched as a young man strode towards his new customer. Now this was someone he did recognize. This fellow was a regular after office hours: someone he'd seen among the younger set that frequented the smart wine bar, with the view across to Pacific Quay. Was he her son, perhaps? He waited a moment, watching their body language: the handshake, the deferential way he moved as he sat down beside her when she patted the seat of the booth. Not her son, then. A toy boy? No. Not from the nervous expression on his face. A colleague, perhaps. The bartender caught the woman's eye and was by her side in three easy strides.

'What'll you have, Michael? A G-and-T?'

'Oh,' the young man seemed suddenly uncomfortable. 'Em. Just a Coke, thanks.' The bartender smiled wryly, caught the woman's eye for an instant then sauntered off to fetch the order. Couldn't handle his lunchtime drinks then? Right enough, he was only a one-pint-and-then-I'm-off customer, now that he remembered. Never came in at lunchtimes.

The barman laid the glass of Coke carefully beside the woman's white wine (an Undurraga Sauvignon Blanc that he'd specially recommended), his smile bland enough to encompass them both.

It was a matter of a few minutes, a tiny episode in

an otherwise busy day that he'd probably forget before the afternoon was out. He'd never have guessed that two months from now he would be quizzed repeatedly for information concerning the meeting between this pair. Or that it would have such profound repercussions.

CHAPTER 5

The ball ricocheted off the wall with a whack and came back satisfyingly at an angle within the man's reach. He tipped the edge of the squash racquet and hammered the ball home for the final point.

'My game, I think.' Graham West smiled, trying not to show the exhilaration he felt at his victory. Three weeks in a row now and Frank hadn't come near to beating him.

Their eyes met briefly and West tapped his racquet lightly on the other man's sweating back. 'Same time next week?'

'Oh, why not? Though I must be a glutton for punishment,' his partner protested.

Under the shower's warmth West succumbed to the needle-like jets revitalizing his body. After a few minutes his skin took on a pleasant numbness and he let his head and shoulders slump beneath the hissing spray. Life wasn't at all bad. Maybe this time next year he'd be in a London gym and living in one of the newer properties by the Thames. And maybe have a boat moored near by? Still, he'd want to keep both his penthouse flat on the south side of the river Clyde and his boat out at Inverkip Marina. A foothold in both cities, he mused. If things got too heavy down south he could always come back here for a break.

There was something about Glasgow that never really let you go, Jennifer had told him, when he'd asked why the pretty redhead had never left the city of her birth. He'd shrugged in compliance with her point of view, but was glad that it didn't apply to him. Glasgow might have a hold on him but it was business, not personal, he thought, grinning as his mind dredged up the *Godfather*'s famous cliché. He could be at home anywhere he liked and having a place either side of the border might be fun.

Graham West turned off the shower and towelled his dark hair into untidy spikes then stepped out, surveying himself in the mirror. The reflection grinned back at him: a lean, tanned body, the epitome of vigorous manhood. He slung the towel across his shoulders and headed towards the sauna. No need to dash off to work just yet; a nice interlude to dry off and relax, then he'd think about it. That was the beauty of being a single man in the city, he often told himself. There was no significant other demanding that he keep to a routine, throwing him out of bed at the sound of an alarm and expecting his return with the advent of rush hour. No, that was for the likes of Malcolm and old Duncan. They could keep their staid little lives.

As he settled back on to the hot boards, West closed his eyes and thought about the future. Already his hat had been thrown into the ring; it couldn't be long until they decided on the next UK deputy head of Forbes Macgregor. Peter Hinshelswood was retiring in June and rumour had it the names were being put forward before Easter. Alec had as good as promised him that the post would be his. He couldn't wait to move to London and the money he'd made already would easily cover a more expensive flat. He grinned. Ach, the job was his for the asking! No other office had results like theirs and no other aspiring partner had the charisma that had taken Graham West on his journey to the top. It would mean new challenges but, even as he contemplated what these might involve, West felt a tingle of excitement. There was nothing like the whiff of a complicated case to arouse his interest. It was as good as sex, he'd told himself more than once. The thrill of the chase, the danger of losing a quarry and the feeling of triumph when it all came right, just as he'd planned: how like the conquest of a woman!

Graham West gave a smile. There was one particular woman he had in mind right now who would benefit from a long, lingering farewell.

Catherine Devoy did not meet West's glance when he came out of Alec's room, her eyes apparently on a document she seemed to be examining closely. He moved swiftly along the corridor, his shirt sleeves brushing against the wall's cool surface, before she raised her head from whatever had taken her interest and saw him vanish into his own office.

West closed the door and leaned against it, aware of a pulse throbbing in his temples. For a time he simply stood as if protecting this, his own designated space that had suddenly become a sanctuary from the world outside. His was a large corner room looking out over the river and beyond towards the suspension bridge. The high walls were painted a pale salmon colour, the ornate cornicing picked out in dazzling white; crystal droplets from a chandelier cast their fragments of light across the dark oak furniture and the blood-red carpet. It was a room West loved to be in. Sometimes his fingers stroked the velvet curtain fabric by the side of his desk or he would simply breathe in the smell of well-polished old wood. All the partners' rooms had similar furnishings but each of them had personalized their own office. West had purchased several pictures from the Glasgow Art Club's exhibitions and two of those, one standing figure and one reclining nude, were displayed to the right of his desk. The early morning light often made the skin tones seem to come alive as a rosy glow came from the east of the city.

But right now the man was blind to the seductive charm of his surroundings. A feeling of lassitude suddenly overwhelmed him and he walked unsteadily towards the chair behind his desk. What he'd heard behind those closed doors meant the end of all his plans. It couldn't be true. This wouldn't happen to him, surely? With a rising sense of dismay, Graham West sunk his head into his hands and wished an impossible wish.

'He'll do what I ask him to,' Alec Barr growled. 'And so will you!'

Catherine sat still, hands folded tightly on her lap, breathing deeply. Would this be the day she took a risk and told him what she really thought? Could she throw over the traces that held her here in this job and this fruitless relationship? She could say a great deal to this man across the desk from her but they would be words wasted. Alec had decided on their fate and she must comply with his decision. As she always did.

A familiar feeling of self-loathing swept over her and she clenched her hands so hard that the tips of her fingernails left small indentations of crescent moons on her skin when she eventually made herself relax. Breathe in for four, breathe out for eight. Funny how she'd never forgotten the ante-natal exercise and yet the whole process of giving birth to that poor creature had been long erased from her memory.

'It has to be done, Catherine. I don't like it any more than you do, but it will all work out in the end, you'll see.' Alec removed his half-moon spectacles and rubbed his nose. The eyes staring at her from across the desk willed Catherine to trust him just once more. Her heart sank. Trusting Alec Barr had been her undoing all those years ago.

Catherine watched as his hand came across the desk, searching for her own to respond, and she saw her treacherous fingers reach eagerly across and be enveloped in his grasp. Any thoughts of rebellion died in that moment, the strength of his clutch and the depth of his stare into her own eyes stilling her into submission.

'Same time next week, Mr Adams?' The woman behind the raised desk smiled at Malcolm and held his gaze. She knew, he thought suddenly. Maybe they all knew. Did the consultant gather them together to brief them on how to treat their terminally ill patients? Possibly. Malcolm had never come into contact with any of those softly-softly people: therapists, counsellors, whatever. Up until now he'd had no need for them and no patience for those who chose that sort of path. But now, as the woman's eyes gleamed with genuine sympathy and unspoken words, and he nodded his agreement for the next appointment, Malcolm wondered if he'd simply shut himself off from other possibilities.

His life consisted of compartments, boxes into which he'd file troublesome things as 'pending'; but to be truthful they should be marked 'no intention of going there'. Malcolm bit his lip, uncomfortable with this self-revelation, but the idea had caught hold of him and would not let go. It was the same whenever he read the papers. A trite remark about the latest wave of terrorism sufficed then he could turn to what really mattered: the business section of the morning papers. It was all a matter of perspective, wasn't it? If you had a relative involved in the armed forces then each and every inch of news about the conflict in the Middle East would be scanned with a growing eagerness to know what was happening and if any danger could touch the person involved. He'd learned to shut off any possibility of acrimonious discussion during his university years. The debating-society types were anathema to Malcolm, his preference had been for the film theatre whenever accounting lectures allowed. There he could indulge the perspective of others for a quiet hour or two before returning to his own much more satisfying existence.

Malcolm Adams found he had walked all the way past Charing Cross and up Sauchiehall Street before he realized. He'd meant to call a passing taxi to take him downtown and across the river but now he stopped, considering whether he could manage to walk the rest of the way. The very act of thinking about his strength seemed to make it ebb away and Malcolm felt the pain in his head pounding as if there were something actually inside striking against his skull. He swayed slightly then took a deep breath. It would never do to collapse in the middle of the street. Just then a black cab appeared round the corner of Elmbank Street and he raised his hand as the 'for hire' light shone out like a beacon.

'Carlton Place, please,' he told the cabbie, sinking back against the leather seats. None of the staff knew that Mr Adams was attending a consultant on a week-to-week basis. When the echelons of partnership were finally reached, such things could be concealed from even the most eagle-eyed secretary. Random or even regular meetings were up to each individual and breakfast meetings were now a popular norm in the city's business life. If Shirley thought Malcolm had such calls on his time, then that was up to her and he did not see any need to enlighten his secretary further. His diary simply noted that Mr Adams was not available at certain hours. Some of the others abused this privilege, he knew; Graham West being one of them. How that fellow got away with his trips to the gym and long weekends sailing he never knew.

The taxi rounded the corner of Blythswood Street, past the bijou galleries and then over the hill towards the river. Malcolm watched, detached, as the people streamed across the street in obedience to the traffic lights. They were all going somewhere on their own personal journeys, no doubt, but just now they seemed like ants scurrying at the prompting of some collective inner will. The feeling of being small and unimportant made him shrink further into the corner of the cab. He would pass out of this vehicle, just another fare, and then be immediately forgotten as the driver scanned the streets for custom. Would it be like that a year from now when he was dead and buried? Some other audit partner would be sitting in his place at Forbes Macgregor, well-meaning friends of Lesley might even be thinking to encourage her out of widowhood and back into the marriage market. The thoughts passed Malcolm by as if he were considering the fate of one of his clients, not his own place in the scheme of things. The sudden realization of his own unimportance had been revealed the first time he had seen the X-rays. Now his days were spent planning for Lesley and the kids, his best achievement and the only part of his life that deserved a good inheritance.

'Just here,' Malcolm leaned forward as the taxi slowed down outside the elegant Georgian building. 'Thanks. How much?'

Standing on the kerb, Malcolm breathed in the cool air with its faint smell of the river and was suddenly and unreasonably grateful for the work that awaited him.

CHAPTER 6

Elizabeth Forbes put down the telephone, her hand cold and trembling. She couldn't even trust her own voice, she realized, as the conversation played over in her head. Jennifer Hammond had been chatty, groaning about Monday mornings and wasn't Mrs Forbes lucky to be out of the rat race. Pleasant, inane phrases that meant nothing, not even a barb of resentment that Liz had such freedom to live her life as she pleased, something that she had sensed from a few of the younger women in the firm. But of course Jennifer revelled in her career, everyone knew that. She sighed for a moment, thinking about the vibrant redhead who was always so full of energy. And mischief, a little voice reminded her. Ah, but harmless mischief, Liz countered. Jennifer was *fun*. Surely she would never send such a horrible letter to Duncan's wife? Everyone respected her husband, she believed, and she had always thought that respect extended to herself. But somebody had sent it.

Liz's eyes were drawn towards the hall bureau with those contents now hidden from view. She'd placed the letter in the tiny compartment of a musical box and shoved it behind the lowest drawer: the box had tinkled half a bar of Mozart as she'd pushed it away, reminding her of the birthday when Duncan had given her the gift. It had taken extra resolve to jam it under an old sheaf of papers and Liz had heard the sob catch in her throat.

What to do now? Her earlier intention to speak to some of the women in Duncan's office had shrivelled with that meaningless conversation she'd had with the human resources manager. Just get on with your day's work, she told herself briskly, her usual common sense pushing down the rising panic she'd felt all morning. That was a good thought. There was plenty to be done. The Scouts were coming at the weekend to collect jumble for their annual sale. That would keep her going, sorting through stuff and taking cartons from the attic out to the double garage. The sound of a blackbird scolding out on the lawn reminded her that she still had to refill all the bird feeders.

Liz straightened up, pulling in her stomach muscles and letting her shoulders slide down her back as she did at Pilates every week. Taking a deep breath, she resolved to forget the contents of the bureau and to think about other, more pleasant things. But, despite her best intentions, her hands slid across the polished surface of the bureau. For an instant she fancied the shelves and drawers were made of glass that she could look through right to the bottom where that envelope lay, its contents visible for all to see.

CHAPTER 7

The heads of the mourners were bowed towards the grave, obscuring his view, but DCI Lorimer knew from the priest's clear voice that the coffin was slowly being lowered into the ground. He had chosen a place by the path, far enough back not to intrude into the crowds that circled round the family but reasonably near so that he looked like a genuine mourner. Today Lorimer was wearing his new winter coat, its thick black softness surprisingly light over his suit. Cashmere, Maggie had told him smugly, proud of her Christmas gift to her husband. He'd never possessed such a fine garment before and had almost protested at the price she must have paid for it, but one look at the glow in her eyes had stopped him and he'd kissed her instead. Now he wished he could tell her how it felt as he stood there sheltered from the blast of icy wind that swept across the cemetery, snug within its folds.

Anyone glancing his way would never have taken him

for a policeman. His early studies in history of art had been an unusual beginning for the man who was now a familiar figure in Strathclyde CID. Yet those who knew him remarked on that still, steady gaze. It was the gaze of one who could see hidden depths whether within a work of art or into the very heart of a man. Detective Chief Inspector William Lorimer made most people look twice, thinking perhaps they had seen him somewhere before. His height alone marked him out and he had an air of authority that was shared by those accustomed to contact with television cameras: an actor perhaps? Or was he a sportsman? He stood with feet apart, hands held behind his back in an almost military stance, but his was the sort of face that looked used to issuing commands, his piercing blue eyes alert to what was going on around him.

The man's death had made front-page news, given his status in the city as well as the bloody nature of his killing. Tony Jacobs had been in the Sunday supplements just weeks before, his lucrative chain of bookmakers catapulting him into the ranks of Scotland's Rich List, his distinctive thatch of grey hair above a still-youthful face a trademark in the glamorous circles he'd frequented. Sadly for him, it had also been an easy mark for the guy with the shotgun. They had hauled in a variety of known thugs, some of them Jacobs' own hard men, until the identity of the man's killer had finally been established. A contract killing with a confession; Lorimer should have felt some satisfaction that the case was done and dusted, but he knew that the ripple effect in Glasgow's underworld could still prove troublesome. Shug McAlister might be safely locked up in Barlinnie for now, yet his paymasters were still out there and the man wasn't talking. At least Tony Jacobs' family had some sense of relief now that the Procurator Fiscal had finally released the body for burial.

A sudden flash made Lorimer turn and he saw, to his irritation, that the press had arrived at the cemetery gates. In swift response, a couple of burly men peeled themselves away from the group around the grave and headed towards the cameramen. They had no sooner moved than the journalists hastily shouldered their gear and legged it. Shelley Jacobs had insisted on privacy when Lorimer had offered a police escort for the family and so he had come alone. It had been too much to expect that the media would have respected the wishes of a young widow.

Tony Jacobs had managed to avoid any brushes with the law but there had always been a suspicious whiff of something unsavoury about the man. Digging deeper into the case, Lorimer had found himself curious about Jacobs as more and more faces of the bookie's colleagues expressed a sympathy that was obviously feigned. The man who'd owned Jacobs Betting Shops had been universally fêted and just as universally disliked. Only Shelley had seemed genuinely distressed when Lorimer had spoken to her following the shooting at Jacobs' Clyde Street office. *My Tony*, she'd kept saying over and over, *my Tony* . . .

Lorimer saw the movement of the crowd and made to leave the cemetery before any of the mourners realized who had been standing in their midst. He would observe them from the sanctuary of his car as they filed out, noting who had come to pay their last respects and storing away the thoughts of those who had, for reasons of their own, failed to attend. As he turned from the graveyard, Lorimer saw a flock of crows wheel over the fields and he heard the rumble of a tractor beyond the hedge of yew trees. He stopped for a moment, watching as the birds dipped in a sweeping motion towards the sound, their black shapes vivid against the grey February skies.

Ploughing, seedtime and harvest, he thought. Life goes on.

Life was certainly going on in the division as he returned to the city. The station car park was busier than usual and Lorimer had to reverse the Lexus into a corner space next to a wall, causing him to squeeze his way out to avoid scraping the door. Not that a few more scratches would have mattered; the old car had seen better days. For an unsentimental man he was still inordinately attached to his ancient Lexus. Mitchison had dropped hints to him on several occasions about replacing it with something more suitable but this had simply served to strengthen Lorimer's resolve to hang on to the car until it was ready for the great scrapyard in the sky. His superintendent might look on its faded glamour with disdain but Lorimer had no intention of trading in the old girl.

Given its age and mileage it was practically worthless anyway.

Lorimer hung the cashmere coat carefully on the stand by his office door. He'd meant to bring in a coat hanger but had forgotten again in the rush to leave the house. His mouth creased in a smile as he remembered why he and Maggie had had to skip breakfast and hurry towards their cars. A sigh of contentment escaped him. God, but it was good to have her back!

His reverie was interrupted by the telephone ringing and soon the DCI was immersed in conversations that would keep him occupied for the rest of the morning.

'That's it! Well done, Robbie. *Empathize*. Like *sympathize*, only the poet puts himself into the place of the bird . . .' A strident bell signalled the end of the period and Maggie Lorimer stood back as desks banged and feet shuffled towards the door. Robbie Ross caught her eye and grinned at her, still pleased to have cracked the idea behind Keats' poem. Pleased, too, to have gained her enthusiastic praise.

Once the classroom was clear and the last sounds of laughter had disappeared down the corridor, Maggie tidied the papers on her desk and filed them carefully into her bulging briefcase. It had gone so well, that lesson on 'Ode to a Nightingale'. Her sixth years were the icing on the cake in a timetable that was really pretty decent, given that she had been away in the States for half a year. Another head of English might simply have given her the dregs as a way of reminding her that others had worked hard while she'd been swanning it in Florida but Kara Steele wasn't like that, thank God. The woman had made a real impact on the English department in the short time she had been there. And she had no problem communicating with her staff. They pulled along really well as a team and as a result their classes responded by giving of their best. It was not something that could be said of other subjects in the school and Maggie knew she had a lot to be grateful for. Kara had missed her, she'd said. Nice to have a different perspective on things while the American exchange teacher had been there, but not the same as having Maggie Lorimer around. Not too sorry her replacement had been forced by family circumstances to finish earlier than intended, either, Kara had added.

Maggie smiled as she locked her cupboard door. It had not been an easy decision to up sticks and leave Scotland for all those months but the break seemed to have done her career no harm. In fact she knew the job was more enjoyable than ever, even if she still groaned at the weight of marking that had to be done. She sat down for a moment, savouring the peace and quiet of the lunchbreak, then switched on her mobile and saw that she had three messages. Her smile at the recipient faded as she read what he had to say: *Late tonight. Don't wait dinner. Love you X*

Maggie sighed, remembering the days when such messages would have built up in a mountain of discontent. Never again, she had resolved. Never again would she let her feelings spiral out of control. She had her job to do and he had his. Both mattered and both should be respected; still, there were times when her resolve might falter and Maggie knew better than to let any resentment simmer. She didn't have such a huge marking load that a wee drive over to see Mum for an hour or two was out of the question. Anyway, there was always tomorrow morning, she told herself with a wicked grin, as her stomach rumbled reminding her of what she'd preferred to breakfast.

The glass tipped over almost with a will of its own, the red wine pooling on the white linen in a sudden stain.

'I'll get that,' a voice at Shelley's elbow told her, and before she could reply another glass of wine was in her shaking fingers and Craig's hand was under her elbow, steering her towards a vacant chair by the hotel window.

'Here. Drink it. You look like you need it,' Craig's voice was stern but his usually hard eyes contained a glimmer of sympathy for the boss's wife. Shelley Jacobs nodded her thanks and sipped the wine. It was good stuff, not the gut rot in boxes that she'd tasted at her father's funeral. God! That had been a trial. Joseph had insisted on footing the bill: insisted that this was a Reilly funeral.

Shelley glanced up, trying to see her brother through the crowd of people who had come back to the wake. Had he left already? Surely even Joseph would have sought her out before he'd gone home? His bitter dislike of Tony should be kept hidden today of all days. Shelley thought with a sudden sadness that the two men she'd loved best in all the world had never tried to resolve their antipathies. Now they never would.

'Hi.'

Shelley looked up and there he was, pint in hand, his tie already loosened from its restrictive knot. Part of her wanted to rage at him for his slovenly appearance. Could you not have made an effort just this once? It's my husband's funeral, for God's sake! But something in his expression stopped her.

'I'm sorry,' Joseph said and suddenly all her pent-up emotion gave way and Shelley found herself sobbing into her brother's shoulder, hearing his soothing words whispering in her ear. He'd look after her. She'd be okay. He'd not let anything happen to her.

Shelley drew back, fumbling in her handbag for yet another tissue. Joseph had said sorry, that was all that mattered. The other things were platitudes, stuff she'd heard for weeks from the lawyers. But his final words didn't make sense. Nothing was going to happen to her. Was it?

CHAPTER 8

The man turned his collar against the sudden wind that knifed his face as the ferry sailed across the Clyde's choppy waters. It was a perfect morning, the air crisp after an early frost, the sky above the Cowal Hills icy blue. He breathed in the familiar smells of diesel and sea tang, feeling the throb of the small engines under his feet. It was a short crossing over to MacInroy's Point and he could easily have stayed in the warmth of the car but he preferred to stand outside for those few minutes, like an intermission in his day. Eddie let his mind loiter as the waves splashed against the sides of the boat, mesmerized by the curving patterns of water repeating their shapes over and over. It was with a sense of reluctance that he came to, as the voice on the tannoy requested drivers to return to their vehicles.

The ramp made a grinding sound beneath his wheels as Eddie drove off and turned left towards Gourock. It was a fine time of day for his business; the school run from Dunoon had left an hour ago and now the roads were pretty clear of commuter traffic. He switched on the radio and listened to the news as he navigated his way through the narrow curves of the town centre and headed along the coast. He'd turn off the main road at Port Glasgow, he decided, and take the back roads instead. The music from the radio began again and the man found himself humming along to it; a quick glance at the clock told him that he was in perfect time for his rendezvous. There was no hassle to these assignments: in fact, if it hadn't been for the frisson that came with the risk of being caught, he might have stayed in that boring nine-to-five job. Glorified delivery man, Connie had called him once, but he'd soon settled *her* hash for her. Deliveries of the stuff he dropped off were lucrative and she'd better remember that instead of whining at him.

The first drop was in one of Eddie's favourite places, well off the beaten track, up a narrow country lane. He'd already passed Gleddoch Country House and now he slowed down as the road darkened, flanked by trees on either side. The car splashed through surface water swilling from the edges of a rain-soaked field and Eddie changed gear again to make the sharp turn left and down into a sudden valley. Through the leafless beeches the gaunt shape of a house emerged, Gothic and sinister even on this cloudless March day. The car park was opposite the lodge house and he turned into it, immediately spotting the grey Porsche. So, the buyer was here first, was he? Eager for the stuff, Eddie laughed to himself, suffused with the sudden power that came from a control of supply and demand.

Eddie had just got out of the car and grinned to the driver of the Porsche when the sound of another vehicle slowing down made both men turn their heads. As the red estate wagon curved around the corner he threw himself back into his white car and, with a nod to the buyer to follow him out, he reversed then accelerated past the new arrival, leaving a bemused pensioner and a barking retriever in his wake. He caught a glimpse of the Porsche in his rear-view mirror and nodded to himself with satisfaction. It was okay. He'd find a quiet lay-by where he'd exchange his goods for the other guy's cash. He smiled to himself. This was the life! It was worth wee risks to see the baffled looks on folks' faces whenever he had to scarper suddenly. Like being in a movie or something.

Usually Eddie didn't give a thought to what would happen to the stuff or how it was used. That wasn't his concern. All he was interested in was the bulging brown envelope that he'd receive at the end of the day. The thrills were an additional perk of the job. Still, there were times when he wondered about some of these punters. Take this guy, for instance, with his flashy car. He was a handsome guy, too; didn't look like he'd have any bother pulling the women. So why go to all the bother of buying large quantities of a date rape drug? He shrugged absently. Other people's tastes were none of his concern.

The man in the Porsche shivered as he left the shadows

of the railway bridge. He disliked all this cloak-and-dagger stuff. It felt demeaning to have to act as an errand boy, and the near-miss with the red estate had given him his first intimation of just what sort of dangerous game he was playing. Up until now the whole thing had been anonymous, but as he drove slowly through the Renfrewshire villages he realized there was at least one more person involved who could identify him if anything were to go wrong.

He took one hand off the steering wheel and fingered the package by his side. What if he were to open the electric window and toss the thing over a hedge? But what would he do then? He had already considered the consequences of such an action and knew with a sinking heart that he would carry out his part of the scheme. Even when he was aware of the lives that it would ruin.

PART TWO

April

CHAPTER 9

'Yes!' The champagne cork popped to the sound of corporate laughter and there was a general clinking of glasses as the waiters made their rounds.

'Here's to you, Michael,' Alec Barr raised his voice, momentarily causing the people in the room to turn his way. 'On behalf of the partners and staff of Forbes Macgregor I'd like to wish you every success in your new venture.' Barr held his flute aloft. 'To Michael,' he added, a smile of satisfaction on his face as the toast was repeated on everyone's lips.

Michael Turner, flushed with drink, beamed at his superior. 'Thanks very much. Thank you. I'll miss you lot.' He grinned again, sweeping his glass in a wide gesture to encompass the friends and colleagues gathered around him.

'Aye, sure,' someone commented. 'You'll be too busy spending all those dollar bills to think about your old mates!' More laughter rang out, then a tall redhead came forward and linked her arm through his, leading Michael away from the throng.

'Ah, what it is to be young and starting out all over again,' Duncan Forbes nodded his head and smiled warmly in his young colleague's direction.

'Some champagne, sir?' the waiter offered, the napkin-swathed bottle already tilted towards Duncan's empty glass.

'No thank you. Orange juice, if you have it, will be fine.'

'Not even tonight, Duncan?' Alec Barr's tone was a mixture of amused benevolence and gentle persuasion.

'Not even tonight,' Duncan Forbes replied.

'Ah, Duncan, can I have a quick word?' Catherine Devoy had glided towards her two fellow partners, her pink suede heels noiseless on the executive carpeting. Duncan inclined his head and followed Catherine who led them into a quiet corner of the room. Alec Barr watched them move away, his eyes following them closely as if he needed to imprint their images upon his memory. 'Duncan and Catherine,' he murmured to himself. 'Duncan and Catherine.'

Outside the hotel, the row of lime trees swayed as the wind caught them, their branches heeling over in a medley of creaks and groans. Even the tall grey lamp-standards rattled under the onslaught of the storm, causing the lights within the white globes to flicker nervously. Deep shadows fell across the entrance to the hotel, contrasting with the lozenges of light from the hospitality suites on the first floor. Below, the water churned black and cold, the occasional reflection glittering on the wind-whipped crests. Cars passing between the river and the shadowy glass building were forced to creep slowly over the speed bumps on their way towards the hotel car park.

Liz Forbes turned off the ignition and shivered inside her sheepskin coat. What the hell was she doing here? The decision had been a moment of utter madness. At first she'd told herself it would look like a good wifely gesture to arrive late in the evening on the pretext of driving Duncan home, but now it simply seemed idiotic. There was no need for her to be here at all; Duncan had his own car parked in the Crowne Plaza car park and there were always taxis laid on after a party.

The woman unbuckled her seat belt and contemplated the lines of darkened vehicles parked on either side of her. Inside they'd be laughing and drinking, having fun on young Michael's last night. Her mouth tightened as she had a vision of Duncan chatting companionably to the women. They'd all be smartened up for tonight, a bit of glitter relieving their ubiquitous black office suits. Liz craned her neck to see her reflection in the rear-view mirror: a tired-looking woman with wisps of wind-blown hair gazed back at her, the hastily applied lipstick already smudged at the corners of her mouth. Her heart sank. It wasn't really so difficult to imagine

Duncan preferring one of the younger, sexier females to that face, now was it?

That second letter had really clinched it for Liz, its reasonable tone reminding her of Duncan's continuing infidelity, suggesting times and places too. She'd been frantic in her search for his desk diary, checking the dates against those nights when she'd supposed her husband working late in the office. They'd all tallied. Was it another sign of mischief-making? Or was the writer of the letters really telling her of something already known to others within Forbes Macgregor? The thoughts seemed to stifle her and Liz opened the door, gulping in the cold air. A short walk would help, maybe, she told herself. Then she'd drive off home and Duncan would never know she had been there at all. The lights flicked twice as she pointed the remote to lock the doors then, taking another deep breath, Liz Forbes made her way out of the car park and headed along the grey ribbon of cycle path that bordered the river.

She stopped beside the swirling waters, looking down into the inky depths. Some might see this as a romantic place, the lights dancing across the black surface, but Liz found herself glancing fearfully over her shoulder as if someone might loom up at her out of the night.

Her steps quickened on the walk back and she paused only once to look up at the glass-fronted windows where the party was taking place. A figure moved towards the window as she glanced upwards. Had she been seen? Liz moved into the shadows again, almost tripping in her haste to regain the safety of the car. At last she was sitting in the Mercedes once more, fingers fumbling the key into the ignition. As the long sleek shape of the car glided past the hotel, Liz knew only a sense of relief. Nobody would ever know how close she had come to making a complete fool of herself.

Behind her, the angled head of a CCTV camera continued to follow Liz's progress, having already recorded her brief but visible walk along the river.

The last car door slammed shut, the doorman waving the revellers off before stepping inside the warmth of the hotel, the glass door closing behind him silently. At last he could knock off. That party had been going on for hours, folk wandering outside and back into the corporate area all blooming night. All the lights were still on in the mezzanine and would be until the cleaners came on duty. It was a right waste of electricity but none of his damned business. So long as the pay cheque kept on coming he'd keep his mouth shut.

The doorman did not turn to look out at the night or the faint mist that was rising from the river. There was no one to see the empty path or the wind catching the dead leaves and casting them upwards. Not a soul moved downstream or looked over the cold railing to where the river's detritus bobbed darkly. There were no eyes to discern the shape that floated away from the embankment or watch its progress into the swirling waters of the Clyde. It was as if nothing had happened to disturb the ebb and flow of the waves moving between the banks of the river.

But there had been eyes to see that shape tumbling downwards and ears that had heard the muffled splash below. And somewhere in the city there was at least one sleepless soul replaying that moment over and over again.

CHAPTER 10

'You know who it is, then,' George Parsonage said. It wasn't a question. DCI Lorimer wouldn't be here with Dr Rosie Fergusson and the Procurator Fiscal without a good reason.

'Had a tip-off,' Lorimer muttered, his eyes upon the sodden corpse lying on the quayside. The examination tent had been erected so that no passers-by could catch sight of the body, especially the press who would only add to the problem the DCI now faced.

George nodded. There would be a name and a history to this man lying dead on the banks of his river. Lorimer would let him know in due course if he asked. But George didn't always want to know. Now that there was nothing more he could do for the victim his thoughts turned to Glasgow Green where his small fleet of boats awaited his attention and from where he might be called out again.

He cast off and let the boat drift with the tide, the

figures on the bank becoming less significant as he plied his oars upstream.

'D'you think it's him?' Iain MacKenzie, the Procurator Fiscal, looked at the senior investigating officer, intently waiting for a reply. Rosie Fergusson glanced up from where she knelt by the body.

Lorimer nodded at them both. 'Certain. Fits our caller's description to a T. Aye.' His mouth formed a tight line against his unshaven face. 'It's Duncan Forbes all right.'

'Looks like he's only been in the water a few hours, maybe eight, or so,' Rosie said.

'Did he drown, though?' the Fiscal asked.

Rosie raised her eyebrows. 'Million dollar question, isn't it? Need to see what the PM shows. There's no other obvious sign of injury though, is there?'

'And the caller told us we'd find his body here,' Lorimer mused slowly to himself. 'Said there was something we should know.'

'I wonder just what that was,' the Fiscal remarked.

'That's what we'd like to know. The line went dead before the caller had time to finish speaking. At least that's what it sounded like on the tape.'

'And?' Iain MacKenzie fixed his eyes on Lorimer's face, waiting for him to elucidate.

'It was a woman. Said we'd find Duncan Forbes in the Clyde near the Crowne Plaza Hotel. Gave a full description of his appearance and what he was wearing.'

'Is that all? I mean, he could have fallen in. Jumped in, for that matter.'

Lorimer shook his head. 'There was more to it than that. She was crying. Saying she was sorry. She didn't mean it to happen.' Lorimer looked up the Clyde towards Bell's Bridge. High above the river a skein of geese flew eastwards, their cries muted by the morning traffic's roar. He watched them until their flight became almost invisible against the pale grey clouds. They would come and go every morning, prompted by some ancient impulse to follow the same route between the estuary and their chosen feeding grounds. What, he wondered, had prompted the early morning telephone call that had them standing here over the body of Duncan Forbes?

'Sudden, suspicious and unexplained,' MacKenzie broke into his thoughts.

Lorimer nodded. 'It might be a straightforward fatal accident but we wouldn't have come down here unless we'd thought the call was genuine, would we?' he replied, nodding towards the officers who were presently unfolding a body bag.

'Or me.' Rosie grimaced. 'Who's playing silly buggers with us, Lorimer?'

'Well, not his wife anyway. When she was contacted she was beside herself. Said her husband hadn't come home last night. Wanted to know what was going on. And, no, before you ask, Mrs Forbes has a completely different voice from our mystery caller.'

'Well, let me get back to the mortuary. I'll have this chap seen to as a matter of priority.' Rosie smiled wanly, picked up her bag and fell into step beside Iain MacKenzie, away from the tall policeman who seemed in no hurry to leave the quayside.

Lorimer stared into the swirling waters of the Clyde. What had the riverman pulled out? A murder victim? Or some unfortunate soul whose last moments had been seen by the woman who'd called them? His reverie was disturbed by the sound of a zip encasing the corpse in the watertight bag. He looked down at the dark shape on the ground. Only hours before, this had been a living, breathing human being. What had happened to bring him to this?

Glasgow City Mortuary had the appearance of a small museum, dwarfed by the taller buildings of the High Court. Apart from the plaque fixed beside the entrance, a passer-by would never attach any morbid significance to the modest Victorian building.

Elizabeth Forbes hardly noticed the steps up to the entrance or the hand on her elbow, steering her gently into the place where her husband lay. Inside she had the impression of being closed in, the grey walls encircling her as she moved through the corridor. Then they were in a waiting room and several people introduced themselves to her in subdued tones.

Somebody spoke her name; they were trying to tell her something but she couldn't hear the words. As if in a dream she allowed herself to be led out, her eyes fixed straight ahead to where they were taking her.

It was a small room with a large glass window obscured by pleated pink curtains and a potted palm in one corner. A small print of Monet's garden at Giverny caught her eye, the long reeds obscuring the water below the bridge. They need cutting back, Liz thought, staring at the painting, reluctant to take her eyes off the green swirl of brushstrokes. She felt her arm being squeezed and her name spoken once more, as the family liaison officer gently eased her into a chair. On a table directly in front of her were two small television sets, side by side.

'Just take your time. It's the right-hand screen,' the officer murmured. Liz turned anxiously to face this girl who was looking at her with such compassion, then swallowed hard as she turned towards the television.

The black and white image showed a bare room with a hospital trolley in the middle. Under its swathe of white lay the body of a man. Someone had lifted the sheet off the top end of the makeshift bed, revealing the man's face. For a moment Liz felt pleased that the bedding was so clean and neat, the fold precise and square on the turned-back sheet.

It was Duncan. And she was looking down at him through this absurd television.

Liz smiled. It was all right. He was only asleep. She felt a sigh come from her chest as she looked at his familiar face, the eyelids closed, his mouth a straight line, the way it always was as he slept.

But there was something wrong. Duncan never slept on his back like that.

Liz frowned and glanced at the girl who was still holding her arm.

'Mrs Forbes? Can you confirm that this is your husband?'

A tight feeling constricted Liz's throat, making it impossible to speak. She nodded instead and then looked at the television again as someone stepped in and began to cover Duncan's face.

Immediately Liz struggled out of the policewoman's grasp and staggered towards the image of her husband, trying to call his name.

As she grabbed the edges of the television set, the figure beneath the sheets seemed to disappear, leaving an empty white space filling the screen.

Liz recoiled suddenly, whimpering.

Taking a step backwards into the arms of the girl behind her, Liz's eyes were fixed to the screen. It was there again, the body of her husband. Of Duncan.

Then a single scream of 'No . . . !' was torn from her throat.

CHAPTER 11

Dr Rosie Fergusson twisted the ring under the two layers of gloves, feeling the diamond below the soft material. She should have taken it off but as usual she had forgotten. Since Christmas, her engagement ring had become a part of her and she only removed it for surgery. When she remembered. For a brief moment Rosie allowed herself to think of Solomon and how she would feel if it were his corpse lying on her slab, then immediately banished such thoughts. The poor woman who had been in earlier to identify her husband was inconsolable. Rosie had caught a glimpse of her as they left by the rear of the mortuary. It was not a good idea to encounter relatives before you cut open their loved ones, she thought. The police liaison officers had done their usual excellent job with Elizabeth Forbes. Now it was up to Rosie to do her bit.

*

As she threw the outer gloves into the pedal bin, Rosie gave a sigh. 'So far there's nothing to show that Duncan Forbes has died from any other cause than drowning,' she remarked to Dan, her fellow pathologist who had been the note-taker while she had performed the post-mortem. Victims of drowning were given post-mortems as a matter of routine; those that might carry the suspicion of being other than accidental required two pathologists in attendance. The double-doctor system that Scottish law demanded had the added advantage of pathologists being able to bounce ideas off one another.

'He was certainly alive when he entered the water,' Dan replied. It was true. His lungs had breathed in water from the Clyde.

Rosie frowned. 'There are no injuries to his hands which would suggest he's not struggled against any rocks. Haemorrhaging in the inner ear is in keeping with no immediate cardiac arrest. No, this chap's drowned all right.'

The toxicology tests were still to be done and so they'd know more in a few days, if she chased the results. Maybe the poor sod had simply had one over the eight and stumbled at the river's edge. They'd seen drownings like this before where little struggle had been the result of intoxication.

Rosie washed her arms under the tap. Pity. She'd like to have something more to tell Lorimer, but he'd just have to wait.

*

The Crowne Plaza Hotel sat on the banks of the river Clyde, its glass walls a shimmering reflection of sky and water. On one side of the hotel lay the humped back of the Armadillo, one of the city's most popular concert venues, with the newly built Clyde Arc (the 'Squinty Bridge', as it was fondly known by Glaswegians) angled across the river to Pacific Quay. On the other side was Bell's Bridge, the footpath that had spanned the Clyde since the Glasgow Garden Festival of the eighties. Behind the gleaming block of mirrored glass stood the 'Big Red Shed' or Scottish Exhibition and Conference Centre, to give it its full title. Everyone who was anyone had stayed at the Crowne Plaza, from pop stars to members of the royal family. Functions were booked up months and sometimes even years in advance, the huge ballroom a perennial favourite for gatherings such as Burns' suppers and New Year's Eve celebrations.

Lorimer bumped the car gently over the speed humps, slowing almost to a standstill to allow a white van to pass him by. The barrier to the hotel car park lifted and he drove in, making a mental note to find two pounds in change for the way out. The DCI sat for a moment and glanced at the names in his notebook. All five of the Forbes Macgregor partners had been there the night of Duncan Forbes' death, along with many of the staff. He was here to talk to the duty manager but first he wanted to wander along the path that ran beside the river.

Lorimer leaned against the white painted railings

that overlooked the Clyde. They were just above waist height, not difficult for someone to vault over if they'd a mind to do it. Looking down, he could see the yellow tops of safety ladders spaced along the river wall; on the water's black oily surface were numerous bits of detritus including a Drambuie bottle and an upturned blue plastic basin. There was no sense of depth to the murkiness below him. It would certainly be a shock to fall in water like that, he thought. And it was still icy cold. Lorimer turned towards the Millennium Bridge that spanned the Clyde. From here he could see the hotel and the walkway more clearly. There was a considerable amount of tree cover and shrubbery screening the walkway from the hotel itself, probably designed to give a modicum of privacy to the guests. But had it also served to hide the manner of Duncan Forbes' death?

He walked further along, noting the buds on the lime trees. Not so much cover here, then. And these white globes on the streetlights would have illuminated the entire path. Or almost, he told himself, walking round a curve that opened up into a quiet area hidden from view. Here the shrubbery was thicker, a mixture of rhododendrons and berberis, and the bare lime trees had given way to a stand of scrubby pines. There were several benches constructed from black metal mesh, their surfaces spray-painted with white graffiti. Above him towered the immense height of the famous Finnieston crane, the last relic of Glasgow's shipbuilding past, the words CLYDE BUILT etched clearly on its side. The path narrowed at this point and the wall dropped directly into the river with hardly any ledge to the other side of the railing. Lorimer tapped his fingernail against his teeth. Could Forbes have fallen in at this spot? George Parsonage had warned him of the river's notoriously unpredictable currents. The tides had certainly taken the body upriver.

The DCI turned on his heel and walked away from the spot just as a cyclist free-wheeled off Bell's Bridge towards the city centre. It made him look up and across to the farther bank, to where the Scottish Criminal Record Office stood on Pacific Quay: a square of dull green glass whose windows looked directly towards the walkway. Beside it, the BBC's new premises rubbed shoulders with the Scottish Media Group. CCTV cameras were dotted round the whole area, but they were like those at the Crowne Plaza: fixed heads looking inwards to protect their own. Still, it would do no harm to ask if anyone had seen an incident late at night. Security guards, perhaps? Lorimer gave a sigh. It was all so bloody nebulous, this inquiry into a fatal accident that might turn out to be no more than that. If that caller hadn't given them all the idea that Forbes had been deliberately killed, he'd be doing something a bit more useful than sniffing around the Clyde on a cold April morning.

The black words printed along the walkway railings made Lorimer grin suddenly. He'd been thinking it was just for pedestrians but the words 'cycle path' immediately made him think of all the old psychopath jokes.

He shivered suddenly in spite of himself. Was that a premonition of some sort or just a cold gust of wind coming up from the slithering waters?

Inside the hotel, Lorimer approached the reception desk and held up his warrant card.

'DCI Lorimer to see Mr Wotherspoon,' he told the blonde receptionist. She smiled brightly at him and lifted the telephone at her side. Lorimer could hear her ask the duty manager to come to reception.

'Just take a seat over there. He won't be a second.' She smiled again, indicating a row of squashy seats opposite the main door. Lorimer nodded and gave a sigh. A second in her language would more likely be ten minutes, he thought, sinking into the soft leather. But he was wrong. He'd hardly time to stretch out his long legs when a youngish man in a tweed suit approached.

'Andrew Wotherspoon,' the duty manager announced, hand outstretched. 'Good to meet you, sir,' he addressed Lorimer. 'Perhaps you'd care to come through to the office,' he added. Lorimer nodded, rose to his feet and followed Wotherspoon across the foyer and into a side room.

'Terrible business, this,' Wotherspoon began. 'Have you any idea how it happened?'

'It's being investigated,' Lorimer remarked blandly. 'We hope to learn a bit more once we know Mr Forbes' movements on the night he died.'

'Of course. What can I tell you?'

72

'Where he was, for a start.'

'Actually,' Wotherspoon nodded, 'I can do better than that. I can show you, if you like. The Forbes Macgregor party was held in one of our meeting rooms on the mezzanine. Staffa, I think it was,' he added, checking a paper on his desk. 'Yes, it was. Staffa. These rooms are all named after Scottish islands,' he explained. 'Like Staffa, Barra, Jura and so on. The whole hotel has a nautical theme running throughout. Perhaps you'd noticed that?' he asked eagerly, hoping for some reaction from the detective chief inspector.

But Lorimer had already risen to his feet.

'This meeting room?'

Wotherspoon walked him back across the foyer and up a narrow staircase that led to a mustard-yellow corridor. Lorimer glanced absently at the decor, wondering if the decorator had eventually tired of sea blues.

'Here we are,' Wotherspoon announced. 'All the rooms are identical actually, and of course they all look out onto the river.'

Lorimer strode across to the window. Below him the hotel's conservatory jutted out, its wall of windows stretching up, parallel to the mezzanine.

Seeing him look down, Wotherspoon explained, 'The conservatory's for the business delegates or guests using our meeting rooms. They can wander down for a coffee whenever they like.'

'Or a fag break?'

'Well, not really,' Wotherspoon frowned. 'They have

to go outside for that, but there's a side entrance to the conservatory where most of the smokers tend to gather.' As the duty manager brushed an invisible speck from his trousers, Lorimer grinned.

He'd bet Wotherspoon would have been happier with a total ban on smoking even outside the hotel.

'Can you give me a list of everybody who was here last night?'

'Of course. There were only about thirty in the Forbes Macgregor party—'

'No,' Lorimer interrupted him. 'I mean *everybody*. All the guests in each of the meeting rooms, downstairs in that conservatory bit, anywhere you have a record of someone, in fact.'

'Oh, but—' Wotherspoon began.

'Someone might have seen Mr Forbes from up here,' Lorimer insisted. 'Look. You can see the cycle path for quite a distance on either side. Almost as far as the Squinty Bridge. If he did *walk* that way . . . ?' Lorimer shrugged, leaving the question hanging in the air.

'Oh, I see what you mean. Right, I'll try to find lists of names for you, Chief Inspector.'

'I particularly want you to ask for anyone whose room had a clear view looking down towards the Finnieston crane. Okay?'

Wotherspoon jotted down the DCI's request on a thin hotel notepad then looked back solemnly at Lorimer.

'And your CCTV tapes. We'll need to see them too, of course.'

'Ah, yes.'

'What areas do they cover? I only spotted the ones at the car park and at reception.'

'We have all the entrances covered,' Wotherspoon told him, 'including the delivery entrances. The tapes are changed on a daily basis.'

'Exactly when are they changed over?'

'At midnight. By the security staff. We have seven twenty-four hour tapes that are then recycled for the following week.'

'So if I wanted to see what happened a week ago last night . . . ?'

'You couldn't, I'm afraid.'

'Okay.' Lorimer turned away from the window. 'I think that's all I need to see up here for now, Mr Wotherspoon. Once we have the particulars of your delegates we can begin to ask some more questions. Nobody on the night staff mentioned anything untoward happening last night?'

Wotherspoon shook his head. 'First we knew about it was your officers turning up here this morning. Bit of a shock. Not the first drowning there's been near the hotel, mind you, but it's hardly an everyday occurrence.'

'Had one recently then?' Lorimer asked as they left the room and walked to the far end of the yellow corridor.

'No.' Wotherspoon grimaced. 'There was a young boy who fell in a few years ago. Not one of our guests,' he hastened to add. 'Chief Inspector,' Wotherspoon hesitated, 'may I ask what exactly this is all about? We didn't expect an officer of your rank to be making inquiries about an accidental drowning.' The duty manager's face was turned up questioningly to Lorimer's, but there was no trace of indulging his human curiosity. The man was justified in asking something that impinged on the business of his establishment.

'I'm afraid I can't comment on that just yet, sir,' Lorimer replied. 'And I'd be grateful if any speculation were to be kept away from the press' He looked at Wotherspoon who nodded gravely. He'd trust the duty manager but it would be impossible to prevent the rest of the staff from whispering among themselves if the inquiry gained momentum.

'We'll walk down this way, just to let you see the other stairs,' Wotherspoon said.

Lorimer passed the lift and pointed at it enquiringly.

'For disabled guests,' Wotherspoon said briefly, making his way round the end of the corridor and down a carpeted flight of steps. The stairway turned onto a half-landing and Lorimer stopped suddenly, struck by the view. From here he could see the entrance to that lonely spot with its empty black benches. Had anyone wandered down this way last night? Duncan Forbes, maybe? Well, the CCTV footage would surely tell some of that story.

The DCI hardly heard Andrew Wotherspoon as he rattled on about the famous mural that covered a whole wall of the hotel. It depicted the Clyde's heyday with scenes from celebrated launches and three generations of royalty, as well as the men who had laboured to produce the world-famous *Queens* who'd taken their names. His eyes flicked over the mock art deco Mariner Restaurant to the bar with its tent-like canopy, a visual simile for sails, no doubt. But Lorimer's inner eye was trying to see beyond all that, to a darker scene altogether where a man had crossed to the railings and then fallen to his death in the waters below.

CHAPTER 12

'Right, an afternoon at the movies.' DS Alastair Wilson leaned back, hands behind his head and winked at his colleague. DC Cameron sat up straight in his chair, arms folded, an expression of annoyance across his face. It seemed an inordinate waste of time to spend on a drowned man who'd simply fallen into the Clyde, all because some hysterical woman had called the station. They'd listened to the recording of her voice a few times now, at Lorimer's insistence.

'Oh God, I'm so sorry. It's Duncan Forbes. He's been killed. I mean he's drowned but I didn't mean it to happen. Truly I didn't.' There was a pause, then a sound like a smothered sob. 'He's over by the Finnieston crane. Near the Crowne Plaza. Oh God . . . There's something you should know about—' Then the line had gone dead. As if another hand had cut off her voice, Lorimer had observed.

Cameron screwed up his face as the CCTV footage

showed black and white figures coming and going from the hotel's main entrance. It was the obvious tape to begin with, Wilson had told him. The next one in the pile would be the tape covering the mezzanine corridor. Cameron yawned and tried to concentrate. It was a tedious but important part of the initial investigation. Should anything criminal come to light, they'd both be up in court giving any evidence these tapes might reveal.

There were several photographs of the deceased on the table in front of them. But it would be a darned sight easier if they had someone here who'd actually known the guy. Wilson grinned at the younger officer as he tried to stifle another yawn. They were in for a long session in front of the video screen.

Lorimer switched off the ignition and gave a sigh.

'Hellish, isn't it?' WPC Annie Irvine shook her head. Meeting the relatives of the deceased was never easy, no matter how often you'd done it before. She'd made countless pots of tea in her years in the force. Annie Irvine liked to think it was her sympathetic manner that made her the usual choice for these jobs, but it was more likely that everyone else seemed to disappear into the woodwork whenever Lorimer was looking for a female officer to accompany him.

Lorimer didn't reply. That was par for the course, Irvine knew. Yet he would open up to his officers whenever there was something to say. You just had to be a bit patient with DCI Lorimer; that usually reaped rewards.

As they stood together on the doorstep of Manse-wood, Irvine glanced around. They had parked next to a sweeping lawn that lay opposite the wide driveway with shrubberies that screened the property from prying eyes. The owners probably paid a fortune for a gardener to keep it so neat and tidy. All the gardens they had driven past in this part of Bearsden looked well tended. The policewoman's eyebrows were raised in admiration. It took Irvine all her time to remember to water the plants on her windowsill.

In answer to the shrill note of the doorbell they heard footsteps thudding down the stairs. The door opened and a young woman stood looking at them uncertainly. Her brown hair was scraped back into a ponytail and she was wearing a baggy shirt over a grubby pair of jeans.

'You're the police?' she asked, glancing at the WPC's uniform, her sharp question delivered in a refined accent.

Lorimer held out his warrant card. 'Detective Chief Inspector Lorimer. WPC Irvine. We've come to see Mrs Forbes. She's expecting us.'

'You'd better come in,' the girl said, holding open the door reluctantly. 'Mum's not feeling too great and I'm not letting anyone visit. But I suppose you people are different.' Her face showed a defiance that Lorimer recognized as a mask to hide emotions that were not too far below the surface.

'Thank you, Miss . . . ?'

'Mrs,' she replied shortly. 'Mrs Collins. Jane Collins.'

The girl saw Lorimer look pointedly at the space where a wedding ring should be and the faintest of smiles appeared on her face. 'Can't wear it just yet. Haven't lost the post-baby flab.' Jane Collins turned and led them through to the back of the house and into a pretty drawing room that looked over gardens that rose in a gentle slope ending in a row of leafless beech trees.

Elizabeth Forbes did not rise as they came into the room. She was seated on a cream-coloured recliner chair, her legs crossed on the footrest. A beige fleecy rug was wrapped around her body.

'Mum, this is Chief Inspector Lorimer to see you.' The girl had dropped to her knees and was stroking her mother's hand.

Elizabeth Forbes raised her eyes to the strangers in her drawing room and nodded. Eyes puffy from hours of weeping looked blankly at Lorimer and Irvine. She opened her mouth as if to speak, then turned her head towards her daughter.

'If it's too much for you . . .' Lorimer tailed off.

'No.' The word came out hoarsely. 'No. It's all right. Please sit down.' She lifted a weak hand towards the easy chairs opposite.

'Tea?' Jane Collins asked, rising to her feet. Lorimer nodded. It would be better if the girl was occupied with something while he spoke to her mother.

'Oh!' she exclaimed as the sound of an infant crying came from another part of the house. 'Looks like I'm needed upstairs.' As the girl headed for the door, all thoughts of tea forgotten, Elizabeth Forbes caught Lorimer's eye.

'First baby,' she confided in hushed tones, then gave a smile. 'You know what it's like, Chief Inspector.'

Lorimer returned the smile politely. He didn't know and never would know what parenthood was like. If Elizabeth Forbes wanted to assume he understood about babies that was fine by him. The grandmotherly pride in the new infant had at least brought some colour to her ashen face.

'We wanted to talk to you about your husband,' Lorimer began.

The smile disappeared like a cloud obscuring the winter sun as Elizabeth Forbes dropped her gaze.

'The sooner we can piece together Mr Forbes' last movements, the more we'll make sense of just what happened to him,' he explained gently.

The woman nodded her understanding but still looked down at her hands, one fingernail working away at another. Lorimer's eyes followed her small action, noting the well-trimmed, capable fingers devoid of any nail enamel. These were hands used to manual work he realized, and was surprised at the observation.

'When did you last see your husband?' he asked, the routine question sounding annoyingly clichéd as he spoke.

'Yesterday. No. What day is it today?' she asked, looking at Annie Irvine as if only a woman could keep track of such things.

'Friday,' Annie replied. Duncan Forbes' body had been washed up on the shores of the Clyde the previous morning following that odd telephone call. They waited until the woman had worked this out for herself.

'Duncan left for the office on Wednesday and was due to go to some leaving party that evening,' she began.

'At the Crowne Plaza?' Lorimer prompted.

'Yes. He said he might come home first to change but he didn't.' The woman considered for a moment before continuing. 'So I suppose I last saw him that morning before he left for work.' Her hand threw back the rug and it fell to the carpet. 'He said he'd be home before eleven.' She looked up at Lorimer accusingly. 'He *said* he would.'

'Mr Forbes didn't contact you at all then after Wednesday morning?'

'No. I was out for most of the day anyway.'

'Did he leave you a message, perhaps? From the office or from his mobile?'

Elizabeth Forbes shook her head and looked down again. When she raised her face Lorimer could see her cheeks wet with tears.

'Oh, if only he had!' she cried. 'At least I could listen to his voice on the tape. But now I've got nothing, nothing at all!' And she sank her head into quivering hands, sobbing heavily from a throat already exhausted by too much weeping.

Lorimer watched as Annie Irvine knelt by the woman's side, holding her arm and making shushing noises as though she were calming a child. At last the sobs gave way and Elizabeth Forbes took the proffered tissue, blowing her nose noisily.

'All right?' Lorimer asked, his body bent towards the widow so that their eyes were level. She nodded, still too full to speak.

'I have to ask you this, and I'm sorry if it upsets you, Mrs Forbes, but could you tell us if there was anything worrying your husband recently? Was he anxious about anything, do you know?'

The moment Lorimer saw the woman's face stiffen, he knew he'd hit a painful spot.

'What was troubling him, Mrs Forbes?' he continued, his voice gently inviting her confidence.

Elizabeth Forbes glanced down into her handkerchief, deliberately avoiding his eyes.

'We have to know what your husband's state of mind was, you see,' Lorimer told her. She shook her head as if trying to push away the implication of his words.

'He wouldn't . . .' she began. 'We were happy . . .'

'Wouldn't what, Mrs Forbes?'

She looked up again. 'Duncan would never have taken his own life,' she said, sniffing loudly. 'He had far too much to live for. Janey, the baby . . . oh, everything.'

'But there *was* something on his mind?' Lorimer persisted.

Elizabeth Forbes nodded.

'Can you tell us what that was?'

'No. No, I can't.' She gave a shuddering sigh. 'He

never told me but I knew all right. I knew something was wrong. He was, well . . . preoccupied. More so than usual. And he was home late a lot more often from the office.'

Lorimer saw her bite her lip. To keep from weeping again? Or to stop herself from sharing her own thoughts on what might have troubled her husband?

'That's all I can tell you, Chief Inspector.' The woman's shoulders sagged under the weight of Lorimer's gaze.

'Are you certain?' Lorimer asked. 'Could there have been a reason behind this accident?' he asked smoothly, giving no inflection to the word. It was not up to him to suggest that Duncan Forbes had died at his own hand or that of another.

Elizabeth Forbes shook her head again, but this time it was as if she were trying to reconcile herself with a sudden thought. 'He . . .' She looked away, biting her lower lip, then returned her gaze towards Lorimer. 'He used to be an alcoholic, Chief Inspector,' she said slowly. 'But that was years ago. He *never* drank any more!' she exclaimed. 'That's not how it happened. I assure you!'

Lorimer looked at her. The voice had no tremble now and her eyes were bright with anger as well as unshed tears.

'We received a 999 call from a woman. She told us where the accident had taken place. You wouldn't happen to know who that caller might be, Mrs Forbes?'

Lorimer saw her face as she sank back against the

recliner chair. It was like watching the shutters coming down on a window.

'No.'

The silence that followed hung heavily between them, the ticking of the clock on the mantelpiece unnaturally loud.

'I think I need to rest now, Chief Inspector,' Elizabeth Forbes told them, her voice suddenly firm.

'If we need to call on you again, we'll let you know, Mrs Forbes. We'll see ourselves out. Thanks. Don't get up,' Lorimer said, rising to his feet.

As they crossed the hall a voice could be heard singing somewhere in the house. Janey Collins was with her new baby, her father's death temporarily forgotten in the need to comfort her child.

'What d'you think?' Wilson asked.

'It's him, all right. Looks a bit the worse for drink, too, if you ask me.'

Both men looked intently at the screen where the figure of a man weaved his way out of the Crowne Plaza and headed left, disappearing out of the frame.

'Let's see it again.' Wilson pressed the rewind button and then stopped. Once again the dark shape of a man crossed the screen, coat flapping around his knees as if a sudden gust of wind had caught him unawares. Wilson pressed another button and the figure froze in wavy lines, forever stepping out of the shadows into a pool of artificial light. The man's face was in profile, staring ahead as if he knew his destination. Then the DS released the captive image, letting Duncan Forbes step into the night and towards whatever fate had befallen him.

'Aye. You're right on both counts. Looks as if he'd had a skinful. Reckon he'd needed a bit of fresh air. Seems like he's heading over towards the railings.' Wilson shook his head in a world-weary manner. 'Gets blotto, makes for the side of the river, spews up and falls in. Poor sod,' he added.

'You couldn't just fall in like that,' Cameron reasoned. 'You'd have to climb over the rail, surely?'

'Know that part of the river, then?'

'Aye. I do. Cycled over Bell's Bridge and the Millennium Bridge plenty of times,' Cameron told him.

'Oh, well. I'll take your word for it. We'll still have to record the way he was moving. It's consistent with drunkenness and that's what a court will ask for. If it comes to that. Personally I think we're dealing with an accidental death.'

'What about that phone call?'

'Och, some woman sees the guy fall in and gets over-hysterical.'

'The call was cut off rather abruptly,' Cameron persisted.

'Someone decided she shouldn't be involved,' Wilson answered, then, realizing what he'd said, he looked at the younger detective and both men raised their eyebrows in a speculative silence.

*

There was silence in the car as Lorimer drove back. He was thinking about what Elizabeth Forbes had eventually told them. That her late husband was a reformed alchoholic; that he'd never touched the stuff for years. There had been an angry insistence in her voice that worried the DCI. It was as if the lady did protest too much. When Lorimer had spoken of the 999 call, she had become tense and quiet again. Had it been the mention of a woman caller that had made her clam up like that? Or did she really suspect her husband had gone on a bender that had resulted in his death? She was in denial about something. And who could blame her? Lorimer felt a sudden pity for the woman they'd left behind in Bearsden. Whatever had happened to Duncan Forbes, there were other victims still suffering.

'Okay, let's leave this meantime. The toxicology report will no doubt give us the usual tale. Too much alcohol in the blood. Bad accident. End of story.' Lorimer looked round at the officers who had spent no little time following up the mysterious telephone call. 'Sorry about all of this. Our dear leader will probably blow a mild fuse but at least he can't fault us for not following correct procedure.' Lorimer grinned slightly as some of the officers shook their heads at yet another waste of time. Superintendent Mitchison was a stickler for going by the book and generating multiple reports for each and every bit of investigative work. In the few months that Lorimer had been acting superintendent during Mitchison's sick

88

leave, they had enjoyed a return to the old freedoms that certain European directives threatened to curb, as well as a rest from the endless paperwork.

'What about the tapes?' DC Cameron asked testily. His head ached from sitting in front of a VCR all afternoon and now the boss was telling them it was all a waste of time.

'We retain them until the tox. report comes in. You can send them back after that. Sorry,' Lorimer added, raising his eyebrows at Cameron's scowl.

There were mutterings as the officers left the room and Lorimer couldn't blame them. A suspicious death was just that until proven otherwise and it would be more than their jobs were worth to ignore the signs. Still, that was one of the frustrations about police work. He closed his desk drawer and sat back with a sigh. Tomorrow would bring other crimes, other lines of inquiry, but it looked as if he'd heard the last of Duncan Forbes.

CHAPTER 13

The plane nosed up into the air and that familiar sinking feeling in the pit of his stomach made Michael Turner grin with pleasure. He was off! The roar from the aeroplane seemed to mirror the excitement he felt, as if he too were screaming with the engines, his whole body vibrating with joy.

Since the news of his promotion, Michael hadn't stopped for a moment: packing, sorting through his affairs and leaving the flat in the hands of the property agent. Then last night he'd spent some sweet hours with Jenny. He'd made promises they both knew would never be kept, but he'd made them anyway, between kisses that spoke only of here and now. He'd woken alone, the empty space beside him a sobering reminder of all he was leaving behind. No voice had disturbed him these past few days with the grim news about Duncan Forbes. Even the answering machine in his flat had remained strangely silent, though Michael had been far too busy to notice.

As the seat-belt sign blinked off, Michael pressed the recliner button and settled back to enjoy the flight. He'd tucked a paperback and the *Gazette* into the seat pocket in front of him and now pondered which of the two to choose first. The paperback won. The *Gazette*, with that little news item about a man drowned in the river Clyde, remained folded between the in-flight magazine and a bottle of Highland Spring.

It would be several days before Michael Turner learned about the death of his mentor and by that time he would be in no position to reveal the secrets he knew.

CHAPTER 14

'Liz, it's me, Catherine.'
There was a sound of heavy breathing, then a click as the line went dead.

Catherine Devoy held the handset at arm's length, puzzled, as if it had performed some obscene trick. Then she shrugged, replaced the telephone and lifted it again. Just as she was about to press the redial button, she paused. Maybe she had misdialled. Maybe that wasn't Liz on the other end of the line. Just to be on the safe side, Catherine redialled the number and waited as the phone rang on and on. She sighed. There was no one home. That first call must have been a wrong number. Oh, well, she'd try again later on. There was no way she was going to duck out of being supportive to Duncan's widow. No way at all. Alec had been adamant on that point.

Liz sank back into her chair, trembling. What had she done? Catherine was just trying to be friendly, wasn't she? Then why on earth had she bottled out of speaking to the woman? She caught sight of the photograph on the table by her side. It was a holiday snap of Duncan and herself up at the cottage, his arms full of brushwood for the fire, her hair blowing in the wind, both of them laughing. Her eyes filled again with the tears that just kept on coming. He *had* loved her; she knew it in her heart. So why was she feeling such pain, such terrible doubt? And why had she just cut Catherine off? Was every other woman in Duncan's life going to be a potential mistress? Liz dropped her head into her hands, weeping freely through her fingers. Not Catherine, surely not Catherine, a voice drummed in her head.

'Miss Devoy.' A voice at her door made Catherine look up. It was Zoe Nicholl, Duncan's secretary.

'We've had a message from Kirkby Russell,' the girl said.

'Oh?' Catherine cocked her head to one side. Kirkby Russell was Forbes Macgregor's US partnership. Things had come a long way since the days when the practice had been run by Duncan's father. Nowadays there were offices spread across the globe and Forbes Macgregor was a serious player on the international accountancy stage.

'Anything interesting?'

'I'm not sure,' the girl began. 'It's about Michael. They want to know when he's arriving.'

Catherine Devoy frowned. 'Are you sure?' she asked,

then, realizing how foolish the question sounded, added, 'There must be some mistake. Michael was being met . . .' she looked at her slim gold wristwatch, 'yesterday afternoon about three o' clock their time.'

'Maybe there's been a hold-up of some kind. Isn't there a baggage handlers' strike on?'

'Yes, but that wouldn't affect Michael's flight. He was flying BA. There must be some mix-up,' she said, dismissively. 'Check our emails to them with the ETA and flight numbers. They should have been sent within the last week.'

'Okay. Will do.' Zoe turned on her heel, closing the door behind her.

Catherine stared at the door. Something churned in her stomach. The acid reflux had worsened recently, a sure sign of stress. But Catherine Devoy was adept at hiding anything that would reveal her inner turmoil. She'd had to be, particularly in the last few months. Still, there was something disquieting about this little incident. Why had Kirkby Russell failed to make contact with Michael Turner? Surely he had arrived? And if not, what the hell would they all do about him now that he was out of their reach?

CHAPTER 15

I t had not gone according to plan.

JJ swore softly under his breath as he lugged the heavy bag of groceries up the concrete steps to the loft room. Carting food for a mark wasn't in his job description: blowing him away, yes, but keeping him here, whining every time he showed up, no siree. If only he'd kept his mouth shut, then none of this would have happened. JJ recalled the conversation in the limo after he'd picked up the Scotsman from JFK.

'Which part of the country you belong to?' he'd asked. An innocent enough question, surely? It was just one little hike up from discussing the Yankees, which he usually did when softening them up before the kill. The guy had gone on at length about the beauties of Scotland until JJ changed the conversation.

'What line a business you in?'

Now the talk was all about the guy's new job. JJ listened, prompting only when he needed to hear more.

What had brought him out here? Why hadn't he stayed on in Bonnie Scotland?

Then the story had come tumbling out, the confession that didn't matter a damn, you were only telling it to some dumb ass of a taxi driver you'd never see in your life again. JJ knew that was how their minds worked.

Then JJ had found himself having to take out the folded bandana that he kept in the top pocket of his blue uniform jacket. The sweat trickled down the side of his face and as he dabbed at it, he took a surreptitious glance at the passenger in the back of the limo. He could take a risk or he could carry out his orders as usual. The thought of the consequences should his plan fail made him shudder. This guy was his passport to the good times, that was for sure. And nobody would suspect him. All they wanted was a body.

The rest of the journey had passed in a blur as JJ turned the limo away from Jamaica Bay along the highway that led into the city. He'd faked a grin as the guy exclaimed over his first sight of Brooklyn Bridge and even given him a spiel about what a great place he was coming to. His passenger had never batted an eyelid as they'd driven through Holland Tunnel then into the maze of city streets; the guy had been too busy turning his head this way and that, everything new to him, everything unfamiliar. JJ had kept that smile on his face; it was all one to the poor sap whether he was in downtown Manhattan or in any one of the ghettos that could conceal them until the driver had decided what to do.

JJ's instructions had been, as always, to do the job quickly and efficiently. A clean single shot followed by a trip out to the backwoods with a sack and shovel; that was the customary procedure. He'd pick up the rest of his fee when the limo was dropped off at the valet service depot and that would be that. No remorse, no questioning a conscience long-dulled by routine executions. JJ was a consummate businessman when it came to dispatching his victims.

The man grumbled to himself as he reached the top step and put down the grocery sacks. Below him the sounds of distant sirens mingled with the screams of kids playing in a waste lot on the corner. He searched in his trouser pocket for the key then fitted it into the padlock, conscious of a stirring from within the room as he pushed open the door.

Michael Turner lay on a bed next to the wall, his hands bound behind him, the red patterned bandana binding his mouth.

'Feedin' time,' JJ told him, kicking shut the door with one foot as he carried the bags towards a table in the centre of the room. There was a moment when their eyes met and JJ hesitated. Then the older man turned away and busied himself emptying the groceries onto the table.

Michael's nostrils twitched with disgust as he peered through the stifling half-light of dusk. There was no air conditioning and the smell of recently cooked burgers and rancid fat lingered in the room. The driver had gone and he was once more on his side, tied firmly to the bed. There was one window set high in the roof, its glazing criss-crossed with wire mesh. Occasionally a crow would scratch its way over the glass, claws sliding on the surface until it squawked away. There was a constant sound of traffic buzzing outside, sometimes the shriek of a siren. But no emergency services ever came to release Michael from his cell.

At first he had tried to struggle out of his bonds, but as the days passed he became aware of a lethargy coming over him, weakness, he guessed, and muscle fatigue from lack of movement. Self-pity washed over him now as the utter loneliness of his position set in. He'd been astonished at how much he'd welcomed the infrequent visits of his captor, though on reflection he realized that the man represented a chance to sit upright, to eat and, most importantly, to talk.

This time the questioning had been preceded by the man washing his prisoner's face and hands, tending to his rope burns with a tube of ointment that looked like Savlon. He'd been handed the food and watched carefully as he made some attempt to eat it, his jaws sore where he'd chafed against that stinking red neckerchief. Michael had given up asking why he'd been imprisoned. His questions only met with a stony silence.

At first he had protested, had threatened to invoke the wrath of all the gods at Russell Kirkby and Forbes

Macgregor combined, then, as time had passed, he had begun to fear his silent captor and had begged for release. But now there was only a weariness and bewilderment as he sought for answers as to why he had been whisked away from JFK to this stinking hole.

It had been several days since he'd emerged into the cold sunlight of the airport, his face turned up to the patch of sky above the buildings, his blood racing with anticipation. He remembered how he'd felt, proud to be driven in that limo along those massive highways, through the streets with their colourful video screens and flashing lights, buildings towering above him on either side. This was to be his city! He'd be a partner within two years, he'd been assured by Alec Barr. Even Catherine Devoy had taken him aside to give him some friendly advice about his career path. That seemed like another lifetime, that brief glimpse of a future that now looked so remote. Michael shivered despite the cloying warmth of the room.

Today the limo driver had asked him what he was doing in the city, who had sent him, what his bosses wanted of him. Michael had answered everything as truthfully as he could, assured, as only the innocent can be, that the truth would set him free. The man had asked more sinister questions. What had he done to upset his bosses? Then that chilling final question today: who would have wanted him killed?

CHAPTER 16

'You're not going to believe this,' Rosie's voice told him.

'Try me,' replied Lorimer.

'There's no trace of alcohol in the bloodstream of the deceased.'

Lorimer was silent for a moment, absorbing the pathologists's words.

'So, what—?'

'So I told them to run a few more tests. There was something unusual in the print-offs that I thought worth following up. So they did, and guess what we found?'

'Tell me.'

'Gamma-hydroxybutrate.'

Lorimer whistled through his teeth. 'How much? Enough to kill him?'

'Enough to make Duncan Forbes appear very drunk fairly quickly. He'd have experienced physical disequilibrium and perhaps feelings of illness.'

Lorimer nodded as she spoke. Gamma-hydroxybutrate, or GHB, was a street drug that had been filtering into Glasgow all too often in recent years. There had been several cases of date-rape: one such had resulted in a fatal accident inquiry when a young woman had died as a result of being given an overdose of the drug.

'Would he have been able to jump over the railings?'

'That's for your lot to find out,' Rosie retorted, then added, 'but it might have been difficult for him to get over them by himself. He was a big man and the effect of the GHB might have taken longer to achieve. He'd be bleary-eyed and unsteady on his feet, given the quantity we found.'

'Would you stand up in court and say that?'

'If I had to. Why?'

Lorimer tapped a pen against his teeth. He'd dismissed the death as accidental due to excess alcohol in the bloodstream and was expecting the report to the Fiscal would say just as much. Now Rosie Fergusson's revelation had turned this into something quite different.

'Maybe we will be looking at this as a murder inquiry,' he told her.

'Hold on to those Crowne Plaza tapes.' Lorimer nodded to DC Cameron as he passed his desk. 'We're not done with this case yet.'

The Lewisman looked up at his boss, eyebrows raised in an unspoken question.

'Cause of death unknown. For *now*.' Lorimer stressed

the last word deliberately. 'High doses of GHB in the bloodstream. No alcohol,' he added tersely. 'So we're still treating this as a suspicious death.'

'Not suicide?' Cameron asked.

Lorimer shook his head. 'Can't see it somehow, unless he was trying to dull his own senses by taking the drug before he tipped himself over the edge. Doesn't seem likely from what little we know of him. But that will have to change, won't it? We need to know a lot more about Duncan Forbes.'

'So you want me to do a background check?'

Lorimer nodded. 'Find out what you can about the firm, Forbes Macgregor. See if there was anything dirty going on. Anything that would have him desperate enough to take his own life.'

'But you don't really think he did, do you, sir?' Cameron looked Lorimer directly in the eye.

'No. I think there was someone else involved.' He shook a small object in his hand. 'That's why I'm having this analysed,' he said, glancing towards the sound tape that held the voice of their mystery caller. 'See what our other experts can come up with,' he added wryly.

It was after eight when Lorimer eventually locked the car and strolled up towards his own front door. As he turned the key in the lock he could hear music coming from the sitting room. Maggie was home. He grinned to himself. Coming home since that wonderful day when his wife had arrived back in February had been a joy compared to the long months when she had been teaching overseas.

'Hello?'

'Hey, how's my man? Ready for some dinner?'

Lorimer chuckled. Maggie looked out from the kitchen and waved a wooden spoon in her husband's direction. Something smelled good.

'You bet. Haven't had anything since breakfast.'

'Not even time for one of Sadie Dunlop's famous Danish pastries in the canteen?'

'Nope. Too busy working.'

'Hm. Why does that not surprise me? Mitchison making you decimate what remains of the rainforests, then?' she asked wryly.

'Actually, no.' Lorimer had made his way to the kitchen where Maggie was stirring spices into what he hoped was chicken curry. His arms encircled her waist and gave a squeeze. 'Working on a possible murder case,' he murmured, nuzzling her neck. He felt her sigh as she leaned back against his body, a gesture that held the promise of good things to come.

'Don't tell me. At least save the gory bits for when it's all over.' She stepped out of his grasp and laid down the spoon. 'Ten minutes and it's ready. Okay? Just let me re-heat this rice.'

Lorimer smiled and wandered through to their sitting room. There was the usual mess of books and folders, waiting for his wife's red marking pen, beside her favourite armchair and several days' worth of newspapers. The place had become a total shambles during Maggie's absence until Lorimer had sought the services of a cleaning woman. Jean still came in twice a week and was a godsend as far as they were concerned. Lorimer sank into the chair opposite the television, stretching his long legs in front of him.

'How was your day?' he called through. 'Any horror stories?'

'Yep. This was our day to take the fourth years on a trip to the local youth theatre. All very cultured except when Jo-Anne Dury was sick on the bus home and Raymond Flannigan started dropping hints that she might be pregnant. What a shower! I tell you, these kids can be really nasty sometimes.'

'Not like the angels back in Florida, then?'

'Don't start. "You know I've got certain misgivings about this exchange programme, but on the whole I really think it was a positive experience."' Maggie put on what Lorimer called her 'please miss' voice. She'd had to give several talks about her time in the US and had tried to be honest about her stay overseas, but admitting that she'd been terribly homesick was not what the exchange programme's organizers had had in mind. Lorimer smiled to himself. Maggie had taken the decision to work in the US for an academic year after a period of restlessness. It had been caused in no small way by his own horrendous working hours and the resulting lack of a decent social life. He'd spent Christmas with her in Florida, and after the holiday, the parting had been even harder than when she had first left. But that, thank God, was behind them now.

'Okay. That's it ready. Come on through.'

Wiping his lips with a napkin, Lorimer gave a sigh. 'That was great. Best ever.'

'Glad you liked it. Listen, while I've got you in a good mood, any thoughts on a summer holiday?'

'Actually I've put in for leave the first two weeks of July. Where do you fancy going? Portugal again?'

'Oh, I've missed Scotland so much this last year. I can't bear the thought of flying off anywhere else. Skye, maybe? Or Wester Ross?'

'Wherever you want,' Lorimer told her. 'But don't forget it'll be midgie season!'

'Hey, after all those months of mossies, our wee midges will be a doddle.' His wife put on a mock-Highland accent that made him laugh. She was good at voices. He could imagine her pupils being enraptured whenever Mrs Lorimer read to them.

'How about looking on the Net to see what I can find? A cottage somewhere, maybe. Or would madam prefer a posh hotel?'

'A cottage. I'm not sharing you with anything but the midges, William Lorimer.'

After he had cleared the supper dishes away and his wife had disappeared into the study, Lorimer sank back in an armchair with a smile on his face. Maggie had that rare talent for making him see the world through different eyes. They'd have a wonderful break together, he was sure. Maybe he could plan things this time as a surprise for her, he told himself, a twinge of guilt reminding him of how it always fell to his wife to book the holidays. Suddenly the picture of Elizabeth Forbes swam unbidden into his mind. What holidays had she planned with her husband that would now be cancelled?

The warm satisfied feeling shrivelled up inside him as he remembered her stricken face and the way it had closed when he'd mentioned the female caller. Lorimer frowned. What if Duncan Forbes had been given GHB in his drink? Had someone set out to seduce him? Or had the intention been much more sinister than that? Thoughts of the Hebrides faded from his mind as he sat there in the darkness, the only light coming from a flickering television screen. Now he was trying to see through those last few days since George Parsonage had brought the man's body ashore; if only he could make some kind of sense of them.

Maggie sat at her desk staring into space. Funny how a day could change things, she thought. One minute you're up in the air, the next your wee bubble of self-satisfaction has burst. It had been the kids on the bus who had started it all. She'd overheard their whispering and strained to make out what was being said once the name 'Mrs Lorimer' was mentioned. Then she wished she hadn't. It was only kids talking, surely? But was there any substance to their gossiping? 'Bet he's been having a bit on the side when she was away,' one of them had sniggered.

'Aye, just like what goes on in *The Bill*,' another had laughed, her voice just raised enough to ensure that Maggie had heard. It was just some nasty-minded wee lassies trying to get her back for something, she told herself. Nothing to lose sleep over, nothing at all.

CHAPTER 17

'The police will be paying us a visit later this week. It will probably be just a routine affair but I want us to be prepared.' Alec Barr looked over his spectacles, his bushy eyebrows almost meeting in the middle. There was an edge to his tone that brooked no opposition. Catherine Devoy crossed then uncrossed her legs. She desperately wanted to catch the others' eyes but, as Barr pinioned them with his glare, there was no hope of any silent communication going unnoticed. She thought she heard Malcolm give a sigh but maybe it was just the sound of traffic several floors below. Looking down she caught sight of their feet: Graham's well-polished black Italian shoes next to Malcolm's Oxford brogues. You could always tell something about a person from their choice of footwear, Catherine thought absently, suddenly realizing with a pang that she could not remember a single thing about what sort of shoes Duncan had worn.

'We've had several meetings about our problem over

the past two months, none of which have been minuted, naturally.' Barr smiled sourly, staring into the eyes of each of his partners. This time Catherine did sense Malcolm shifting uneasily. Her eyes flicked to the man by her side. Malcolm Adams sat bolt upright, his arms crossed in front of him as if his body would fall apart should he let them go. His pale blond hair was cropped short to hide the receding widow's peak, revealing a pulse throbbing visibly at his temple. Catherine took in the skin stretched tight over high cheekbones. He'd lost weight, she realized with a start. Why hadn't she noticed that before now? What had been the cause of that? she asked herself. Something on his mind that he'd been unable to share with the others, perhaps?

'I want us all to be quite clear about this matter.' Barr was tapping his finger on the edge of his desk, drawing her attention back to the senior partner. 'No one is to mention anything about the firm's . . . difficulties.' He smiled a crocodile smile that failed to reach his eyes and Catherine shuddered in spite of herself.

'We're all implicated by this. And we'll simply have to stick together. For *all* our sakes,' Barr added, giving Catherine a gimlet stare. She tried to return his smile but failed, recognizing the senior partner's threat for what it was.

Their futures were supposed to be safe now, but she had never felt so vulnerable, nor so afraid.

CHAPTER 18

'What about the funeral?' Janey asked. There was a pause before her brother's voice came back, muted by the airport noises around him. 'I'll be home tomorrow, then we can make plans.' There was another silence, then, 'How's Mum?' Philip asked.

'How d'you think?' came the retort. 'Not sleeping, not eating, cries all the time. I'm at my wits' end what to do for her. If it wasn't for the baby I'd be worried that she'd do herself some mischief.'

'Don't say that.'

'Well, it's true. Wait till you see her.'

'How are *you*, Janey?' her brother asked, more softly this time.

'Okay. Colin's bringing over more stuff tonight. We're staying here with Mum for as long as she needs us.'

'Good. At least you've got him around, and the wee one.'

'Look, I have to go now. Betsy's awake and I don't

want Mum to have to go up and fetch her all the time – she's worn out enough as it is.'

'Okay, see you the day after tomorrow.' Philip Forbes hung up and turned back into the heat of the airport.

It seemed totally unreal. Here he was killing time in this sweltering part of Africa, his recent safari adventures already receding into the background, and his father was dead. Drowned in the Clyde. What on earth had happened in Glasgow to cause such a terrible tragedy? Dad was the best swimmer he knew. Had he fallen and hit his head on something? Janey had been very cagey about it all and now that the initial shock had worn off, Philip found himself questioning her reticence. Was there something he wasn't being told? As the younger sibling he was accustomed to being fobbed off, and normally he didn't mind, but this was different. Now he needed to know every detail for himself to try to recreate the awful thing that had happened to his father. The young man wiped the sweat that beaded his forehead. The air conditioning inside the terminal building was erratic and his shirt was already showing patches of dampness.

Maybe Catherine would know more, he thought suddenly. After all, she was his godmother. Cheered by the prospect of talking to his father's business partner, Philip Forbes sat up straighter and walked back to the telephone kiosk. He glanced at his watch. There was plenty of time before his flight and Catherine Devoy was likely to be in the office just now.

*

Ten minutes later the young man slumped back into the line of bench seats, his backpack by his side. She'd been there, all right. But what little his godmother had told him made Philip Forbes feel even more helpless and remote. Catherine had spoken gently to him, but that had only made it worse. As far as they could tell, the signs all pointed to Dad having gone on a bender and falling into the river after a late-night party. The boy's fists clenched. How could he? After all his promises and years of abstinence; how could his father have thrown it all away? Tears pricked the back of his eyes and he had to swallow hard. It wouldn't do to come over all emotional in a public place. He should be furious with his father: spoiling life for them all, making his mum a quivering wreck, cutting short his own time in Africa. He should feel angry, he should be picturing the final staggerings of a drunk man tipping himself over into a dark and sinister river.

Yet, try as he might, all Philip could see in his mind's eye was a man laughing as he ran up a grassy hill hand-in-hand with his little boy, pulling a home-made kite behind them.

CHAPTER 19

The background report on the late Duncan Forbes, CA, made interesting reading for DCI Lorimer. It was now a full week since that early morning by the riverside and the man's body was quietly stored away in the mortuary, awaiting a decision from the Crown Office. They were at that in-between stage trying to correlate the post-mortem and toxicology results with what else they knew.

Duncan Forbes had been fifty-seven years old when his life was cut short. A large, fit man, he'd had no real health problems unless you could count the difficulties of alcoholism that had dogged him twenty years before. A recovered alcoholic was how his GP had described Forbes, emphasizing that the man's adherence to the straight and narrow had been absolute. His AA meetings had continued right up to the week of his death and he was a model for others to follow. Lorimer chewed the end of a pencil. So Forbes had shown strength of character, after what had been a lapse in his thirties. What had caused his alcoholism in the first place?

Lorimer considered the papers in his hand. The Forbes family business had been merged with a bigger accountancy firm in the eighties when Forbes senior had still been at the helm. Following the new partnership, the old man had retired and left his son to shape the firm that would one day become one of the Big Six, as these world-renowned companies were known. That was the time when Duncan Forbes had gone on those drinking binges that were to mark him for the rest of his life. Lorimer made some calculations. Forbes' kids would have been very young, the boy a mere toddler. What kind of trial had it been for Elizabeth Forbes coping with an alcoholic husband? Yet she'd stood by him then and, if he'd read the woman correctly, she'd genuinely loved her husband.

There was more in the report that Lorimer skimmed over: Duncan Forbes' membership of the local golf club, his involvement in Rotary International and some dealings with charities. He had been a good solid citizen, the report was telling him, a man who had over-come his weakness and gone on to make something worthwhile of his life. Who would want to kill a man like that? The thought came unbidden into Lorimer's head. There was no evidence of murder yet, although the GHB in his bloodstream suggested something sinister had happened that night at the Crowne Plaza. And that weird phone call? Someone had seen the man fall into the river, someone who knew it was Duncan Forbes.

Lorimer tried to imagine the dark night, the lights from the conference rooms shining across the river, the trees mere shadows at the water's edge. Forbes had staggered out of the side door and across to the railings and then disappeared, hidden by the evergreen shrubbery. Whoever had seen this must have been close enough to the man to know his identity. So why had they not alerted the security staff at the hotel? Why wait until the early hours of the next day to make that hysterical call? It didn't make sense. Unless the mystery caller had not wanted the man to be found until it was too late to save him. And the abrupt ending of that call? Another hand had been at work there, Lorimer believed. Someone had cut off the woman's emotional outburst just as she had been on the point of telling the police something significant. Lorimer shuddered suddenly, despite the warmth of his room. It was all in his imagination, wasn't it? Yet an image persisted of a man's hand closing on the woman's wrist, forcing it away from the telephone, pressing the button that would cut her off from the police.

No. What he should be looking at were the reasons for the man to have taken his own life. Something had been on his mind, his wife knew. Something to do with the firm? Yet, as far as he could tell from the papers before him, Forbes Macgregor was not only a highly successful firm but one that attracted all the right sorts of clientele. In short, it was a respectable firm of accountants.

Lorimer's eyes ran down a list of major companies that were audited by Forbes Macgregor's Glasgow office. An oil company and all its subsidiaries, a major supermarket and a well-known publishing company were among the household names. It looked safe and sound, but perhaps the facts and figures required a more expert analysis.

Turning a page, Lorimer recognized a familiar name. So Forbes Macgregor handled the accounts of Jacobs Betting Shops, did they? That was interesting. He shrugged. Someone had to do it and one of the bigger accountancy firms was bound to have landed an important client like that. And it wasn't the only bookmaker's business they handled; The Pony Express, a chain of newer, flashier betting shops, was also a client. It was probably one of those bizarre coincidences he came across every week of his working life, and most DCI's would dismiss it as such, but the more Lorimer stared at the lines of figures, the more uneasy he felt. He'd been looking for a clue to the death of Duncan Forbes. Could this be it? The murder of the bookmaker had caused shockwaves across the city and there was still an ongoing investigation into the case. They had a good idea who might be behind the contract killing but with Shug McAlister still refusing to give them names, there wasn't much that could be done. He'd pass this onto Forensic Accounting if the Crown Office deemed it necessary. And maybe the Fraud Squad would have something to offer. It was always a good idea to put feelers out with cases like this. It would only take one more shadow of doubt over Forbes Macgregor for Lorimer to recommend to the Procurator Fiscal that this suspicious death should be treated as a murder inquiry.

'Chief Inspector,' Alec Barr stood up and offered Lorimer his hand. 'Please take a seat.' Barr came round his desk and waved a hand at two blue armchairs that were placed strategically, angled towards one another. These were for intimate chats, Lorimer guessed. The more functional seating opposite the senior partner's desk was strictly for business.

'We're investigating the circumstances surrounding your former partner's death, Mr Barr,' Lorimer began, swinging one leg easily over the other.

Alec Barr did not reply, but merely stared at Lorimer as if willing him to continue. The man's bushy eyebrows were drawn down in a frown but beneath them the DCI could see a pair of keen eyes regarding him with interest.

'We received an anonymous telephone call early on the morning following Duncan Forbes' death. Checks on the call have shown that the person's accent is local. I wondered if I could speak to your human resources people, sir. Ask them to listen to the tape of this call to see if anyone recognizes the voice.'

'Why our people?' Barr blustered. 'If the call was made the morning after Duncan . . . ?'

'It was also the morning after a Forbes Macgregor function, sir. The last people to see Duncan Forbes were probably your own colleagues.'

Barr considered this for a moment and Lorimer could see he was thinking hard.

'The senior human resources manager is Jennifer Hammond,' Barr said suddenly. 'She's been with the firm for longer than anyone else in that department. Would you like me to call her in?'

'Please,' Lorimer replied, clasping his hands over his bent knee and leaning back into the folds of the armchair. The more relaxed he appeared, the less he would give away to the senior partner whose own body language was displaying high levels of stress. He watched Alec Barr as the man dialled the extension and asked for Jennifer. Barr had turned his back on his visitor and Lorimer could not see the man's expression, but beneath the snow-white shirt the DCI could have sworn those shoulder muscles strained with tension.

Jennifer Hammond was a tall, leggy redhead whose smile immediately made Lorimer uncross his legs and stand up to greet her. She smoothed back her long russet hair as she took the seat beside him. Her dark brown suit was immaculately cut, the skirt just above the knee, showing a pair of slender legs. The severity of her clothes simply drew attention to her face, however, and to a pair of green eyes that were looking at Lorimer with something like amusement. It took him only a heartbeat to realize that this young woman was appraising him not as a visiting policeman but as a possible conquest. Was this a device she used with all her colleagues and clients? he wondered, as Alec Barr made the introductions. Or was it designed to disarm him? If so, it was certainly working as Lorimer realized that he was holding her outstretched hand for just a fraction too long.

He cleared his throat. 'Miss Hammond,' he began.

'Jennifer, please.' She smiled. 'Everyone calls me by my first name. It's much friendlier, don't you think?'

Lorimer suddenly found himself wondering how a judge might respond to such a request in court. 'Just call me Jennifer, my lord. It's much friendlier.'

'Jennifer,' he began again, 'I would like you to listen to a tape recording of a call that was made to Strathclyde Police. It was the call that alerted us to Duncan Forbes' whereabouts following his death.'

'Really?' The carefully plucked eyebrows were drawn up in twin arches of surprise. She glanced briefly towards Alec Barr who had perched on the edge of his desk, then looked back at Lorimer. 'Why do you want me to listen to this, Chief Inspector?'

'To see if you might be able to identify the caller,' he told her. 'Just on the off-chance that it was made by one of Mr Forbes' colleagues.'

'Well, of course. How odd. Why would someone tele-phone the police and not leave their name?' she asked, the smile dropping from her face as she gave the matter some thought. 'Do you have the tape here, Chief Inspector, or would you like me to listen to it at a police station?'

'It's at Pitt Street,' Lorimer answered, not revealing that a voice analyst had been working on the tape at police headquarters.

'Now?'

'If it's convenient,' he replied. The sooner this was over the better. And if Miss Jennifer Hammond could identify their mystery caller, they would be some way down the line in discovering what had really happened to Duncan Forbes.

Lorimer felt a slight awkwardness as he walked along Carlton Place. Jennifer Hammond had donned a loose raincoat but it swung open as she walked beside him, her long legs matching his own stride. She gave him a little smile as they set off, a smile that made him feel distinctly hot under the collar. It was as if he'd asked her out for a date, not for assistance into a police investigation. He tried to concentrate on the traffic coming off the George V Bridge, looking for a likely place to cross the street. Instinctively he took Jennifer Hammond's arm as a gap appeared in the line of cars, hurrying them over towards the Lexus parked on the other side. Once across the road he let go of her, that small courtesy satisfied as far as he was concerned. She waited until Lorimer had opened the passenger door then slipped inside in one easy movement.

'Were you at the function at the Crowne Plaza the night of Duncan Forbes' death, Miss Hammond?' Lorimer began, as they rounded the corner and began the short journey across town.

'Jennifer,' she reminded him. But when he ignored her, she continued, 'Yes, of course I was. It was Michael's last night before he set off for New York. We were very good friends. There was no way I'd have missed that party.' She laughed.

'A good night, was it?'

'Yes, great . . .' she paused, suddenly aware of what she had said. 'Oh, God, of course it wasn't. Poor Duncan. What a thing to say!' Jennifer Hammond looked at Lorimer, a question in her green eyes. 'You wanted me to say that, didn't you?'

'Perhaps I wanted to find out what sort of evening you all had before it became a tragedy,' Lorimer replied quietly.

Jennifer Hammond nodded. The flirtatiousness had suddenly disappeared from her face. It was as if she had only just begun to realize that the policeman by her side was a senior officer who was conducting an investigation into something altogether more serious than an accidental death.

'It was a good party,' she began. 'There were about thirty of us: all the partners and Michael's friends, mostly managers from tax and audit. We had the usual drinks and nibbles, some folk drifted off in the middle of the evening but most of us stayed till the bitter end.'

'And Duncan Forbes?'

'Can't remember what time he left. It was late-ish, certainly. I think most of the partners left around the same time. Sorry. We had a fair bit to drink that night. With taxis laid on to take us all home, I might add,' she said, a twinkle appearing back in her eyes.

Lorimer tilted his head. 'What happened to the one that was supposed to be taking Duncan Forbes home to Bearsden?'

Jennifer Hammond shrugged. 'Sorry. Couldn't tell you. But if you check with our office manager, he'll be able to give you the name of the taxi company we always use.'

Lorimer listened to the musical quality in the woman's voice. There was no tremor to show grief for a colleague's sudden death or any expression of how awful it really was.

Most women, in Lorimer's experience, would have made some remark like, 'Isn't it terrible?' or 'Who would have believed it?', trite clichés that were still an expression of their genuine feelings of sorrow. But not this lady, he thought. Why? Well, there was one way to find out.

'How did you get on with Duncan Forbes?'

'What a strange question to ask!' Jennifer Hammond answered sharply, a look of annoyance on her face as if Lorimer had actually insulted her.

'Maybe, but I'd like to know just the same,' was his mild reply.

'Fine. He was a good partner to work for. Everyone liked him. He'll be a great loss to the firm, I assure you.'

Listening to her, Lorimer could hear not Jennifer Hammond, but the voice of a human resources manager. It was as if she were rehearsing a press release on behalf of the firm. The insincerity might be lost on anyone else, but DCI Lorimer's ear was more finely tuned than most to take in all kinds of emotional nuances. She didn't like him, he told himself. Then, I wonder why?

Perhaps that was something he might have to find out before much longer.

Inside the red-brick building of Strathclyde Police HQ, Lorimer left Jennifer Hammond to the attentions of the desk sergeant. Once her security badge was fixed on, he led her to an upstairs office where the tape recorder had been set up. It was a soundproof room with no windows. At once Lorimer felt his scalp prickle with unease, the old feeling of claustrophobia making itself manifest. He took a deep breath as if he were about to plunge under-water then exhaled slowly. Sitting just to one side so he could see her face, Lorimer waited while the sound engineer explained to Jennifer Hammond what was required and then fitted on their earphones.

As the caller's voice began speaking, Lorimer could see the woman's pupils dilate, then she swallowed hard. She blinked quickly a couple of times, almost as if she were trying to clear her vision.

She knows, Lorimer told himself, experiencing a sudden moment of triumph. He continued to study her as she sat, immobile, while the message continued.

'. . . but I didn't mean it to happen. Truly I didn't.' The pause allowed Jennifer Hammond a moment to respond but, apart from a sniff then a pursing of the lips, she remained silent.

'He's over by the Finnieston crane. Near the Crowne Plaza. Oh God . . . There's something you should know about—'

Jennifer Hammond remained sitting still, as if expecting something more, then, hearing the click, she removed the headphones and looked questioningly up at Lorimer.

'That's it?'

'Want to hear it again?'

The woman shrugged. 'If you think it's necessary.'

'You recognize the voice?'

She shook her head, putting on the headphones again and deliberately avoiding his enquiring gaze. They listened together twice more, Jennifer Hammond not reacting in any way but simply concentrating hard as if just to fulfil her part of the bargain. She sat staring at the whirring machine as it rewound the tape then spoke without turning her head in Lorimer's direction.

'Sorry. No idea who that is. Certainly nobody at Forbes Macgregor. And I should know.' She smiled and looked at the DCI at last, adding, 'I know everybody.' Then, tilting her head, she added, 'Pity the phone line went dead. It sounded as if she was about to tell you exactly where to find him. Doesn't it?'

Funny, thought Lorimer, she's deliberately misinterpreting the final words of the message to make it seem as if they were totally innocuous. Whereas the reality was that the anonymous voice on the other end of that line sounded hysterical.

'You're quite sure you don't recognize that voice, Miss Hammond?' Lorimer asked, his tone serious.

She made an impatient gesture. 'Looks like having me here's been a waste of time, Chief Inspector.' Jennifer Hammond was on her feet and gathering up her raincoat.

As they shook hands and he showed her out of the room, Lorimer was not so sure about that. She hadn't identified the caller, but he was fairly certain that Jennifer Hammond knew quite well who the mysterious woman really was.

CHAPTER 20

'Solly?'

'Mm?'

'I think Lorimer's stumbled onto something rather nasty,' Rosie looked up from the floor where she was drying her hair in front of the fire.

'What kind of nasty?'

'Pond scum. Or rather something dredged from the bottom of the Clyde.'

Dr Solomon Brightman turned away from the screen of his laptop and regarded his fiancée silently. A few moments passed until Rosie made a face at him and he smiled in reply. 'What do you want me to say?' he asked mildly.

'Oh, I don't know. Just thought you might be interested. You see we've found traces of a date-rape drug in the victim's bloodstream and there's this weird tape of a phone call made hours after the guy landed in the river . . .' she trailed off as Solly smiled his enigmatic smile and shook his head.

'Did he jump or was he pushed? Is that the question?' he teased.

Rosie sat up, running fingers through her still-damp hair. 'Sort of. It's one of those cases where the death is suspicious but there's absolutely nothing to hint that the guy's been murdered. He could've taken the GHB himself, after all. Or even if some idiot spiked his drink it could still have been an accident.'

'What does the Crown Office think?'

'It's to be treated as a suspicious death, possibly a murder inquiry,' she answered. 'Lorimer was finding out about that today.'

'And you say he has a bad feeling about this victim,' Solly mused. 'Do you think he'll make a murder case on the strength of his policeman's instinct?'

'Actually, no,' Rosie replied. 'At the end of the day, I think a verdict of accidental death is the likeliest outcome.' She moved over to Solly, her breath soft and warm as her lips brushed his dark curls. 'But I wouldn't mind if you were to take a wee look at the file. Just out of interest,' she coaxed, her hand finding Solly's own, winding his arm sinuously around her waist. For one delicious moment his grip tightened then he rewarded Rosie's efforts with a playful pat on her bottom.

Solly extricated himself with a chuckle and turned back to his laptop. 'No thanks. I've plenty to occupy myself right now, thank you. Another trip into the world of investigative psychology can wait until there's real evidence of foul play.' He glanced back over his shoulder. 'Then I might be interested.'

Rosie gave a shrug and settled back towards the glow from the fire. There were plenty of times when a body had been brought in under suspicious circumstances and no action had been taken. The law stated that there had to be sufficient evidence of a crime before a thorough investigation could take place. But, as Rosie knew well, Lorimer usually followed his own instincts anyway. She was certain he had followed up the taped telephone message for a start. And she knew for a fact that he'd been asking some difficult questions of the victim's family and friends. Routine, he'd tell them, but really a bit beyond the requirements of an accidental death. Sometimes they joked about Lorimer's nose for trouble but he was invariably proved correct, a fact that disquieted the pathologist as she fluffed out her hair in a gesture of annoyance. Better for the poor widow to think it was an accident, wasn't it? She looked across at Solly, that glossy black head that she loved so well bent over his computer. Who'd want to have the memory of their husband forever bound up with a murder inquiry?

Maggie Lorimer stretched her arms high above her head and yawned.

'Time for bed?' Lorimer asked.

'I wish. Just let me finish this lot of S2 marking. If the wee blighters had just done what I'd asked them then

I wouldn't have all this correction to do!' she moaned. 'Some of them have written at least double the amount I asked for.'

'You're complaining about that? Thought it was like getting blood from a stone with your second years.'

'That's the other section. This lot are eager beavers. Trouble is I keep finding stuff that's obviously copied straight off the Net. It's a nightmare and I haven't the time to source it all.'

'You should have a school technician to do that for you,' Lorimer told his wife.

'Aye, and the day that happens there'll be two blue moons in the sky!' She stood up and stretched again. 'Fancy a cup of tea?'

Lorimer nodded, looking up from the pile of papers on his lap. 'Love one. Want me to make it?'

Maggie shook her head. 'No thanks. Been sitting too long. Need to move myself.'

A few minutes later Maggie paused, the tea tray in her hands as she caught sight of Lorimer's good coat. It was hanging over the banister, its hem caked with mud. Where on earth had he been? With a sigh she laid the tray on a side table and picked up the cashmere coat. A quick brush might be all that it needed, she told herself, examining the garment.

'Damn!' Maggie swore softly. There were dark stains above the mud. Whiffy stains, too. This would be a job for the cleaners. Making a face, she bundled the coat into the hall cupboard and shut the door. It would have to wait till the weekend and his nibs would just have to wear his old jacket. Picking up the tray, Maggie Lorimer dismissed the coat from her mind; she couldn't be bothered making a fuss. Tonight had been so pleasant and relaxed. Why spoil it?

Lorimer smiled. It was good to sit for a bit with Maggie. How long that would last, though, was anyone's guess. Iain MacKenzie had given him the go-ahead and Duncan Forbes' death was now being treated as a possible murder inquiry. Between the taped phone call and the toxicology report, the Fiscal reckoned there was enough to justify Lorimer and his team digging deeper. Part of him experienced that old restlessness that wanted to be up and off, asking questions, seeing people and places. Then again, he was reluctant to let go of the comfortable routine that had been established since Maggie's homecoming. Somehow Lorimer felt that this case would prove both tricky and time-consuming.

Tomorrow, he told himself, it could wait until tomorrow. Then he'd have the team primed and ready to begin a full-scale murder inquiry, starting with the accountancy firm on the banks of the Clyde.

CHAPTER 21

JJ raised the gun and trained it upon his victim. He felt the kick on his shoulder as the bullet was fired straight into the man's chest. He'd used a silencer, but the body made a muffled sound as it hit the forest floor and a scattering of crows took off from the trees, screeching their protest.

He stooped to retrieve the shellcase then walked calmly towards the spot where the dead man lay, hearing the crunch of oak leaves beneath his boots.

There was an acrid smell in the air that mingled with the earthy scent that rose from the damp ground. JJ took a deep breath then pushed the man once with his foot, hard. The body tumbled into a large hole and JJ stooped over the grave, looking for a moment at the sight below him.

The man's face was turned towards the sky, his astonished eyes now for ever sightless. That was another problem taken care of, he thought. No ghosts would haunt him from now on, not if he could help it.

JJ gave a satisfied grunt then began to shovel earth back into the hole. A scattering of winter leaves and the grave would disappear into the forest floor, its newest inhabitant lost for good.

CHAPTER 22

'Are you sure?'

Jennifer Hammond stood in the senior partner's room, one hand clutching the edge of the desk to steady herself.

'His body was found this morning.'

'I can't believe it.' The woman staggered into a vacant chair, her legs no longer able to support her.

'We had a call from Strathclyde Police. The New York Police Department informed them last night.'

'And they're sure it's Michael?'

'Seems they found his credit cards and other stuff,' Barr replied. 'I'm sorry, Jenny. This has come a shock hasn't it?' The senior partner sat watching the young woman as she stared at him, her expression one of total disbelief. Then, as if it had only just occurred to him, he came round the desk and put his arm around her shoulders.

'Don't!' She shook off his embrace and stood up,

white-faced and shaken. 'Don't touch me!' She glared at Barr then straightened up as if mustering some remnants of her dignity. 'Don't ever touch me again!'

Alec Barr stroked his chin as he watched the redhead slam out of his room. It was only natural that she would be upset, he told himself. Michael had been the latest in her string of office conquests, though, to be honest, she had seemed genuinely fond of him. You don't know what you've got till it's gone, he reminded himself wryly. Well, Michael Turner was gone and there was no bringing him back now. Jenny would just have to get over it. Give her time, a little voice told Alec, time to recover her usual, playful self. Maybe suggest some leave; a few days in the sun, perhaps? The villa was not occupied at present. Once she'd had a chance to calm down, his offer of a week in the Cyprus sun might be just the thing to bring his human resources manager back to her senses. And it would not be a bad idea to have Jenny out of the office while the police were nosing around.

Lorimer listened as his superintendent spelled out the choices.

'The vacancy won't be there for ever, Lorimer, and I really think you should consider it. Staying here is an option, of course, but we both know your promotion chances will be limited if you do.' Mitchison nodded as he spoke.

'What can I say?' Lorimer began.

'You can say you'll think about it,' was Mitchison's

reply. 'But not for too long. I'm happy to recommend you for the post. I really think it's something you would enjoy.'

'Thank you, sir.' Lorimer stood up, gave the superintendent a brief handshake and left the room, his thoughts in a whirl.

He was under no illusion about why Mitchison had put him in this position. Having a DCI who had once coveted his own job wasn't all that easy for the super. They'd never rubbed along since Mitchison had been promoted over Lorimer's head, though, God knows, it had been less to do with the disaffected officers than the manner in which Mitchison chose to run his department. The paperwork was stifling them all to begin with but it was the man's arrogant attitude that got under their skins, especially Lorimer's. Now Mitchison had found a way out for his second-in-command. A job in the newly formed Unresolved Case Unit had come up, one that required an experienced officer of at least the rank of DCI. And Mitchison had as good as told him it was his for the asking. He felt a frisson of excitement: notorious cases that were unsolved when he'd been a wee boy might yet come within his reach. It was something . . .

Back in his own room, Lorimer sat contemplating the painting on the wall. Van Gogh's *Père Tanguy* gazed back at him, his barely concealed eagerness to be up out of the sitter's chair and back to work was, for him, the most appealing aspect of the painting. If he stayed here the paperwork alone might drive him mad. The new unit would offer him new challenges and more chances to be out and about, which was what Lorimer enjoyed most about his job. Then there was Maggie to consider. She'd made it only too clear how much she wanted his career to advance, not out of her own ambition for him but from an enthusiastic loyalty that he found hard to resist.

Well, he would consider it but right now he had some questions to ask the NYPD about a certain Michael Turner. The accountant's body had been found in woodland in upstate New York. A hunter with his three hounds had found the grave. Lorimer read over the details again. A white male, shot once in the heart at close range. Identification in the form of credit cards found on the body showed it to be a British citizen, Michael Turner. The victim's hands had been tied behind his back, leaving no room for doubt that this was a deliberate homicide. Turner had been missing for several days, following his departure from the UK. There had been no trace of the young man since his arrival at JFK airport. Flight lists confirming his departure from London Heathrow and Passport Control showed he had indeed made his way onto American soil but after that, nothing. The NYPD were asking for next of kin so that arrangements might be made for the transfer of the body back to Scotland. There was no immediate family as far as they could ascertain from current immigration records. Both his parents had been killed in a motoring accident years ago, Lorimer read. Then he frowned as the details took shape. His mother had been an American citizen and Michael Turner might have opted for dual nationality. But he hadn't.

Perhaps he'd been too young when the choice could have been made, he thought. Still, even such a tenuous link with the United States might throw something up.

His mind wandered fleetingly to Florida and his holiday there with Maggie the previous Christmas. Lorimer glanced at the calendar on his wall. Just ten more weeks and she'd be finished for the session. Ten weeks and he'd whisk them both off to a cottage in Mull. He'd made tentative plans for that already. There was a remote place called Fishnish Bay, several miles from the nearest village. The views across the Sound of Mull to the Morvern hills were spectacular, if his source was to be believed. Three weeks of peace and quiet, and maybe a trip to Iona for good measure. It was a place of ancient pilgrimage with gravestones by the abbey dating back many hundreds of years.

He gave a sigh as he contemplated that other grave, in woods far across the Atlantic. Michael Turner. Strange that he should meet his end in such mysterious circumstances so soon after Duncan Forbes' death. And could the two possibly be linked? Lorimer shook his head ruefully. Not a chance, he told himself. That was the stuff of Saturday night TV detective fiction. Still, there was something odd about it that made him unsettled.

'Mr Barr.' DS Wilson reached out and shook the senior partner's hand. The firm handshake gave him reassurance that the man was perfectly in control of the current situation.

'A dreadful tragedy, gentlemen. We can't begin to tell you what a shock this has been, and coming so hard on the heels of Duncan's accident.' Barr shook his head. 'We hear all about the violence over in the States but never really think anything can happen to someone we know. But that's the way of things, I suppose,' he added, looking at Wilson and DC Cameron for assurance.

'Yes. It always happens to somebody else, doesn't it?' Wilson agreed blandly. 'Now, Mr Barr, what we need to get are some details of Michael Turner's family. The New York Police Department will naturally be anxious to transfer his remains back home.'

Barr raised his eyebrows and exhaled loudly. 'I don't know offhand about any family, but this should soon tell you what you need to know.' Barr turned to his computer and tilted the screen so that his visitors could watch as he brought up a list of personnel. He highlighted Michael Turner's name, clicked the mouse and both men watched as the screen produced a blank page. Barr frowned, scrolling down then up again, cursing softly under his breath as he tried to locate the dead man's file.

'I'm sorry, Sergeant. Seems to have been deleted: some over-zealous admin assistant, no doubt, clearing up records.' He cursed again. 'I'll have their necks for this! Michael Turner is still technically a Forbes Macgregor employee. Oh, hold on,' he clicked back and forth, trying different files. 'Maybe he's simply been transferred to the Kirkby Russell site. That's our

US arm,' he explained. 'Where Michael was supposed to be working once he'd left us.' Barr's eyes were on the screen but Wilson exchanged looks with the DC, wondering if the senior partner's eagerness to find the dead man's details was genuine or not. Would Barr be so conversant with such matters, anyway? Wasn't this a task for a lesser mortal to deal with: Jennifer Hammond, the human resources person, perhaps? Why all this fuss?

'I'm sorry.' Barr turned the screen a fraction more in their direction. 'This is rather embarrassing. There's not a thing about Michael anywhere.'

'Almost as if he's ceased to exist?' Cameron suggested quietly, regarding Barr thoughtfully. The other man did not reply but simply stared at the detective constable. 'Maybe there is a written record?' Cameron continued.

Barr seemed to come to with a jolt. 'Yes, of course. Let me show you through to the filing room. Someone there will no doubt be able to help you.'

The filing room consisted of row upon row of pull-out cabinets on wheels. A young woman stood flicking through different drawers, a pencil pushed behind one ear and a sheaf of papers clutched under her arm. She glanced up nervously, her dark fringe almost hiding her eyes as Barr approached.

'Emma, find Michael Turner's personnel file for our friends from Strathclyde CID, will you, please?' Barr took a quick look at his watch then turned to face Wilson. 'Sorry, Sergeant, must leave you in Emma's capable hands. Duty calls.' Then with a quick handshake and a fixed smile, the man was striding back towards his office. Wilson looked after him. Business as normal, he thought. One partner drowned and another employee murdered in suspicious circumstances and yet Alec Barr simply forged ahead with the day-to-day running of his accountancy practice. Was it sheer callousness or did he really have an overweening sense of responsibility?

'Looks like you're stuck with us,' Wilson heard the tall Lewisman say to the young woman.

She smiled back ruefully as if the request was just one more harassment in an already busy day. 'See what I can do for you. Shouldn't be too difficult to find.' She replaced the papers, slammed shut the cabinet that she had been searching through and walked them both around a corner, stopping at a different cabinet with pink legal ribbons threaded through the handles. They watched as she found the staff files from P to T, her fingers walking through the names.

'Here we are,' she said at last. 'Michael Turner.' She drew out a buff-coloured file and handed it to Cameron. But even as her fingers felt the slim file, her expression changed. 'It's empty,' she said, face reddening. 'Mr Barr will kill me!'

'Really? Why? It's not your fault,' Cameron spoke reasonably as they regarded the open folder.

'But he asked me to find it for you!' The girl's voice rose in a wail.

'So? How can that be a hanging offence?' Cameron joked.

Emma muttered something under her breath that sounded like 'You don't know Mr Barr.'

'We weren't meant to hear that,' Wilson murmured to Cameron, composing his features into a deliberately neutral expression. 'I'll take it anyway, Miss . . . ?'

'Emma. Emma Rogers,' the girl replied. She handed over the empty file, looking at it with something akin to despair.

'Any idea where I might find out about Michael Turner's personnel details, Miss Rogers?' Wilson asked.

The girl shrugged. 'Computer records. Or try human resources. They might have a duplicate of this somewhere,' she replied. 'I'll take you along to that department, if you like,' she offered, leading them away from the filing systems through an open-plan area that looked out over the river and into an adjoining office. 'Jennifer . . . oh. Where is she?' Emma Rogers stood at the office door, the two policemen by her shoulder. 'God, this place is mad this morning,' the girl muttered, then walked to the office next to Jennifer Hammond's.

'Anyone seen Jennifer?' she asked. A grey-haired middle-aged man looked up at her from his seat behind a desk.

'Gone home,' the man replied shortly. 'Said she wasn't feeling well. Why?'

Emma hesitated then turned towards Wilson as if sensing his growing impatience.

'These gentlemen are from Strathclyde Police, Adrian. They're looking for Michael Turner's personnel records and they could be missing from filing. Seems they've been deleted from the computer system as well. Any ideas?'

The man got up and came around to where Wilson and Cameron stood in the doorway. 'Adrian Millhouse. I'm one of Jennifer Hammond's staff. Just part time, actually.' The man grinned and thrust out his hand. 'Should've retired ages ago when I gave up accountancy, but couldn't stay away from the old place,' he added. 'You're looking for young Michael's files? Can't say I'd know where to start looking if you've already tried filing and IT. Tell you what, let's have a dekko in Jennifer's office.' His eyes twinkled. 'Our Jennifer had a soft spot for Michael,' he added.

The four of them trooped back into the human resource manager's room and Wilson watched as Adrian Millhouse went straight to the desk drawer. After only a moment's rummaging, he produced a handful of papers and grinned.

'Here we are. Michael's personal stuff. Personal rather than personnel, if you get me.' He winked again.

'Are you sure you should be doing this?' Emma Rogers sounded doubtful.

Wilson bit his lip. It wasn't really his place to break bad news to Barr's staff but this was becoming farcical. 'Michael Turner has died,' he told them quietly, watching as Adrian's grin melted off his face and Emma gave a gasp of disbelief. 'The American police are treating his death as murder. Mr Barr will no doubt make an announcement to you later today and I expect you'll be reading about it in the papers before too long.' He grimaced, sensing Cameron nodding in agreement beside him. 'Meantime, I'd appreciate it if you could be discreet.'

Adrian Millhouse leaned against the desk. 'That's why the poor woman was so upset. No wonder she needed to go home.'

Wilson turned to Emma. 'Thanks for your help, Miss Rogers. I wonder if you might bring us a cup of coffee? I think we'll have a wee chat with Mr Millhouse.' His voice was deliberately kind. Making coffee for them would give the girl something to do and an opportunity for Millhouse to tell them more about the relationship between Jennifer Hammond and the late Michael Turner.

An ache was beginning to nag at the top of Lorimer's skull as he reread the papers in front of him. Michael Turner had left his flat in the Merchant City in the hands of estate agents. It would fetch a pretty price, thought Lorimer, looking at the particulars on the schedule. But to whom would the dead man's estate belong now? That was the question uppermost in his mind. DVLC records had thrown up some information as had Turner's medical records, but so far there was no sign of a next of kin. He had been an only child as had his father, so there were no uncles or cousins on this side of the pond. It was a can of worms, and a suspicious can at that. Could there possibly be any older relatives still living? Lorimer threw the papers down. It was time for his staff to find these things out, he thought as the telephone began to ring.

'Chief Inspector? Adrian Millhouse here. Your detective sergeant asked me to call if I remembered any details about poor Michael that might help the investigation.'

'Yes?'

'Well, it's maybe nothing, but we shared the same dentist. I just thought ... medical records and all that ...' the man's voice trailed off uncertainly.

'No, you were quite right to call, Mr Millhouse. Give me the dentist's name and number, would you?'

'It's Ian Lynch,' Millhouse replied, then reeled off the dentist's phone number. 'Michael asked me to recommend a good dentist when his old one retired. He's been going to Ian now for about four years, I think,' Millhouse gabbled on.

'Yes, thank you.' Lorimer paused then asked, 'Mr Millhouse? Is there any possibility of you coming in to HQ to listen to the same tape Miss Hammond heard?'

'Ah.' The tone of the old man told him he's hit a sore spot. ''Fraid not. Hearing's not reliable, you know, even with this digital gadget. Things tend to get a bit distorted.'

'Thanks anyway, sir. Much obliged.' Lorimer rang off. That was one witness whose testimony wouldn't stand up in court. Still, the dental records would certainly be useful to the NYPD in corroborating the dead man's identity, although there was little doubt about that, surely? What Lorimer needed now was to talk to Jennifer Hammond. Maybe the ex-girlfriend would be able to shed some light on the puzzle of why these personnel files were missing.

CHAPTER 23

The light was fading by the time Lorimer drove back through the city streets. April was a month of strange contrasts. One day it could be cold enough to snow, the next there were these lovely spring sunsets with the promise of longer days to come. What was it Maggie was fond of quoting?

'April is the cruellest month, breeding

Lilacs out of a dead land.'

Eliot's famous words, of course, that referred to the dead of a century before. April in upstate New York had not been so cold that the grave of Michael Turner had frozen over. In fact it had been amazing that it had been found so quickly after the young man's death. It was a freak coincidence that those hunting dogs had turned it up so soon after the body had been buried. Could've lain there for years, the officer in charge had told him. They usually do, the man had added gloomily. But by some quirk of fate this body was not meant to rest in foreign soil for long.

Lorimer turned out of the motorway traffic and headed towards the slip road that would take him into the leafier suburbs and the patch of peace and quiet that he called home. The clouds were darkening now, layers of nimbus showing bright against fading grey as the sun sank somewhere out of sight. The final part of his journey took him directly west towards the Kilpatrick Hills. A pall of mist obscured the outline of the hills but he could still make out their blue-green slopes with darker patches from burnt winter heather. For a few minutes Lorimer forgot the job, the meeting with Mitchison, everything, in his contemplation of the view before him. He was heading west where the hills became wilder and grander, hiding deep waters and mountain cataracts. Glasgow citizens were so lucky, he often told himself. A few miles and the streets were left behind, the open countryside there for the taking. He cruised along on the outside lane, open fields on either side. A faint tinge of green had begun to show on the hedgerows now. Soon there would be a quickening of the blood as the sap rose and birds began their seasonal couplings.

The image made Lorimer's thoughts turn to Jennifer Hammond. A close friend of Michael Turner's: she had a soft spot for him, Adrian Millhouse had said. Wilson had not been slow picking up on that titbit. She'd certainly reacted badly to the news of his murder, according to her colleague. Well, tomorrow he'd make it his business to speak to her, to find out just how close she had been to the dead man. And, he told himself, whose name she had held back on hearing that tape; the voice of a hysterical woman who had witnessed what might have been a murder.

The morning dawned grey and still, a fine drizzle covering the hills as Lorimer drove back along the motorway towards the city. It was early enough to miss the traffic jams that would hold up lines of commuters trying to make their offices for a nine o'clock start. Since Maggie had come home Lorimer had found himself spending more sensible hours at work. That was one of the few things he'd agreed on with Mitchison following his wife's return, he thought wryly, though police work never really kept to a nine-to-five schedule, despite European directives about working-time practices. There was always the pressure to push on with the latest job and always a shortage of manpower to achieve it. Public perception of the police was not as good as it used to be, especially since the Soham case down south. The Home Secretary hadn't made any of their lives easier in the wake of that scandal. Now every 'i' had to be dotted and every 't' crossed, something in which his superintendent seemed to revel. He could see the point of it, but sometimes he felt as if all the administration got in the way of the real job of catching criminals and bringing them to justice. Would the cold case unit be any better? That was something he'd have to find out.

Lorimer slowed down and took the exit that led south of the river and to the complex of flats beside Kingston Bridge. Jennifer Hammond's flat was one of a modern development that had been resurrected from the site of the famous Glasgow Garden Festival. The DCI drove directly under Kingston Bridge, glad for once to be free of the usual early morning log-jam on the three lanes that straddled the Clyde, and slowed down as he made his way around the perimeter of the complex. There were bright swathes of daffodils blossoming on the landscaped verges of Riverview Gardens and the patches of ever-green shrubbery were well trimmed. Given its proximity to the city centre, this place was an oasis of calm.

Lorimer found the block of apartments where Jennifer Hammond lived, right at the end of a curving road close to the water's edge. He locked the car, turned his jacket collar against the now heavy rain and hurried towards the main door.

'Yes?' The voice over the security entrance system sounded sharp.

'DCI Lorimer, Miss Hammond. May I come up?'

There was a pause then a buzzer sounded to admit him and Lorimer entered a square hallway with pots of leafy plants placed where they would catch the sun. The hall was carpeted and clean and the small lift free from any sign of graffiti, he noticed, as it glided upwards to the fifth floor of the building. There was no doubt that the human resources manager lived in some comfort and style. It probably cost the tenants a fortune in service charges. The days of taking your turn to clean the stairs simply didn't apply to owners of modern apartments.

Lorimer had barely pressed the doorbell when Jennifer Hammond pulled open the door. Today her green eyes were cold and distant; it was hard to imagine that they had regarded Lorimer with such flirtatiousness on their first meeting. Michael Turner's death had made an impact on her, he was sure.

'I suppose you'd better come in,' she said at last, opening the door wider. Lorimer stepped into a long, narrow hallway, almost stumbling over a suitcase against the wall. Its sides were bulging and an identity strap was secured across the case.

'Going somewhere?' he asked, eyeing the case then directing his gaze at the redhead.

'Yes,' she replied shortly. It was still early yet the woman was dressed in a dark-green trouser suit and was wearing high-heeled shoes, as if she were preparing to leave the flat. Just where was she going? Not work, he thought, glancing once more at the suitcase. Her name and a destination in Cyprus were scrawled across the luggage label. Jennifer Hammond turned on her heels and led Lorimer down a passage to a light and airy sitting room with picture windows that overlooked the river. Lorimer took a deep breath. The name Riverview Gardens was entirely apt. The view was positively pan-oramic. Towards the west he could see many familiar landmarks, including the spire of Glasgow University and the twin towers of Kelvingrove Art Gallery. The arc of Kingston Bridge showed cars and lorries whizzing across from north to south. And was that really a cormorant he could see flying low over the water? Lorimer tore his gaze reluctantly from the window. Inside, the sitting room was comfortably furnished with pale wooden tables and open shelving, a large glass table dominating the centre of the room. The pictures on the wall were Jack Vettriano prints, placed there more for the fact that they matched the decor than for their aesthetic qualities, Lorimer surmised.

'Please sit down, Chief Inspector.' Jennifer immediately sat on the edge of an armchair covered in pale gold fabric that faced a matching two-seater settee. Lorimer had no option but to sink his long frame into the squashy cushions. For a moment their eyes met and he thought he saw a hint of challenge in the woman's expression as she waited for him to begin.

'First of all, I have to say how sorry I was to have to pass on the information about the death of your colleague, Miss Hammond,' Lorimer began. He paused but there was no pert smile and 'Call me Jennifer' this time around. 'It appears that Michael Turner has no next of kin here in Scotland and so we are anxious to see who among his close friends might help with ... arrangements.' She stiffened slightly at the euphemism, but still did not speak. 'You seem to have been good friends?' Lorimer tilted his head and waited. Surely this time she would respond? He watched as the woman's shoulders sagged in defeat.

'He was my boyfriend before he went away,' she said flatly.

'Were you sorry to see him go off to America?'

Jennifer Hammond made a face. 'We weren't that sort of couple. Neither of us saw it as a long-term thing. Especially when Michael got the chance to transfer to Kirkby Russell.'

'So there were no plans for you to join him over there? Or go for a holiday?' Lorimer asked pointedly.

The woman shook her head, letting her long red hair fall over her face.

'But you're off on a holiday now?'

'Yes. The firm has a holiday place in Cyprus. I was going to take a few days off.' Lorimer heard the hesitation in her voice.

'And now?'

'I don't know.' She looked up at him. 'What exactly do you want me to do?'

'Tell me what you can about Michael Turner. His background. His family. Anything that might help us to trace any living relations.'

'Oh, well, that's easy. He hasn't any, unless there's a wife hidden away somewhere.' She began to smile then her mouth twisted in a grimace. 'Sorry, that wasn't even remotely funny. Michael wasn't ever married and he was an only child. His mum and dad were killed in a road accident when he was at university. There were no uncles or aunts. He told me this,' she added firmly and Lorimer nodded, encouraging her to continue. 'He

152

had lots of friends, some from uni days and others from work.' She paused, looking directly at Lorimer. 'He was a nice man, Chief Inspector.' Jennifer Hammond's voice softened. 'He deserved better.'

'Is there anyone else you could suggest who would want to help sort out his estate?'

She frowned, thinking hard. 'Can you leave that with me? I'd need to ring round various people and it won't be easy once they know about the circumstances of . . . of his death.' Lorimer saw her swallowing back sudden tears.

'And Cyprus?'

She gave a self-deprecating smile. 'I'm not in the mood any more. I'll take a few days off work, though. See if I can rally some of Michael's buddies.'

'I'd appreciate that, Miss Hammond,' Lorimer told her, sensing the change in the woman's mood.

'Jennifer,' she reminded him, and he nodded as he rose, acknowledging her renewed cooperation. He was almost at the front door when he turned towards her again. 'Jennifer,' he began, 'that tape. Are you sure you didn't recognize the caller's voice?'

The eyes that met his did not flicker for an instant. 'Quite sure, Chief Inspector Lorimer.'

Lorimer hesitated then fished out a card and pen from his inside pocket. He scribbled on the back of the card before handing it to the woman.

'Here. I've added my mobile number. If you think of anything at all, please call me.'

Jennifer Hammond took the card and turned it over in her hand, one eyebrow arched in an unspoken question. Then her eyes met Lorimer's. 'Thanks,' she said, 'though I don't expect I'll use this.'

The woman breathed a long sigh as she closed the door and leaned against it. That was that, then. She turned the card over and over in her fingers, wondering about the tall policeman who was now making his way back down to the car park. There was something about him that kindled a spark within her. She smiled and moved towards the hall table where her mobile lay. Wouldn't do any harm to put in his numbers, she thought. He was a good-looking guy was DCI Lorimer. Maybe she could call him up sometime, a little voice suggested. She hadn't noticed a wedding ring on his finger, but that hadn't stopped her before, had it? Her green eyes shone with a host of possibilities as she laid down her phone, Lorimer's numbers safely logged away for future use.

CHAPTER 24

JJ whistled along to 'Little Old Heartbreaker Me' as he drove the big van along the freeway. He'd paid cash for the Chevy after settling that final job, cleared out his bank account and told his cleaning lady he was off to Europe for a long vacation. Fat lot she'd care, lazy bitch that she was. Her long face was going to miss the extra money, not ol' JJ, despite what she'd said. Once she'd left the apartment building, JJ had gone to work on his disappearing act. That final shot in the woods had burned his bridges with New York. And with his employers. JJ gave a soft laugh as he remembered the body thudding onto the forest floor. Well, he'd killed a man in cold blood one last time, as professional an execution as you could find. There were plenty who would want to thank him personally for that job, but he knew they'd never have the chance to shake his hand. Not if he could help it.

It was a good feeling to be out of the city and heading

west once more. All his stuff was loaded behind him, making him feel like one of the early settlers in their covered wagons. JJ grinned at the image. Even if they were to be held up by savages of any description he'd be ready, his arsenal of weapons safely stowed, some close at hand. He chewed the wad of gum in his mouth, savouring its minty flavour, then turned and smiled at the man sitting in the passenger seat.

'Okay, pardner?' he joked, his voice a deliberate parody of TV cowboys.

The man beside him nodded silently then looked away, regarding the passing countryside with scant interest. It was going to be a long trip and JJ could keep company with the country radio station if he wanted to. This man had other things on his mind, thoughts that would keep him occupied for many a weary mile.

CHAPTER 25

'We need to talk,' Jennifer whispered into the mouthpiece as though there might be somebody in the room who could overhear her conversation. 'Soon,' she continued, then paused to listen to the voice at the other end. 'Why here?' Her tone was petulant. 'But – oh, all right, then. Tonight?'

She listened some more then replaced the handset by her bed, slouching back against the plump, frilled pillowcases with a sigh. Truth to tell, she'd rather be on that flight to Cyprus and anticipating a week of sunshine and beachside cocktails, but it just wouldn't do. There were some things she owed Michael Turner.

The woman sat up slowly, removed her green jacket and threw it onto the chair beside her bed. It was a novelty to have a day at home all to herself and Jennifer was suddenly at a loss as to quite how she would spend it. That DCI had only taken half an hour at the most and her phone call had only lasted a matter of minutes, so

157

Jennifer had the prospect of filling the entire day any way she wished. She rolled lazily onto her side and reached for the remote control, pressing buttons as she fixed her attention on the TV screen. A bit of breakfast television would pass the time while she decided just what she most wanted to do. There was no point in contacting any of Michael's friends until later this evening, probably just after six o'clock when they were most likely to be at home.

Jennifer Hammond smiled to herself. This time tomorrow she'd have it all sussed out. Then she could take off for Cyprus and stay there for as long as she wanted.

Malcolm Adams put down the telephone, his hand trembling. He'd had nothing to eat since yesterday and hunger was making him nauseous. But it wasn't just hunger. The dull ache in his belly was a constant reminder of that insidious shadow he'd seen on the X-rays. Six months, the specialist had told him. Six months during which he would become weaker and weaker until the cancer eventually overtook his entire abdomen. It was quite inoperable, being so advanced. 'Take a long holiday while you can still enjoy it,' the oncologist had advised him. 'Let the office go. They'll understand.'

Malcolm had not relished the prospect of telling anybody, especially his colleagues. Things were fraught enough. If he could hold out a bit longer, have his affairs transferred as he'd planned, then at least Lesley and the kids would be all right. His wife had been so anxious, making him tasty little meals to tempt his appetite, urging him to go back and see their GP. But Malcolm had brushed off her attentions, saying that the ulcer wasn't responding quickly enough to the medication Dr Downie had given him. Lesley had looked at him questioningly but had taken his word for it. She believed him so implicitly, Malcolm thought, her wifely innocence so at odds with his own sordid secrets.

He leaned forward, putting his head in his hands with a groan then sat up suddenly, the pain shooting through him as his stomach felt the sudden pressure. There was hardly any way he could be comfortable these days. He'd taken to going for gentle strolls along the banks of the river during his lunch hour. Watching the traffic criss-cross the bridges or feeding his sandwiches to the numerous water fowl that populated the river gave Malcolm a strange sort of respite from the rest of his day. It was an interlude that he found especially soothing; sometimes ducks bobbed their way to the edge of the river bank below his gaze, caring only for what they could gobble up. To them he was a source of food, that was all, not a man under the torture of a life sentence. Their small acts of selfishness offered Malcolm another perspective of himself. They didn't give a damn about his cancer, and their indifference seemed to rub off on him. There were days when he could have stayed looking down into the river all afternoon but of course he was always back at his desk, fearful of drawing unwanted attention to himself.

Sitting down and walking slowly eased the constant torment and the sedatives helped at night. Lesley had begun to bring him a hot water bottle now, sensing his increased discomfort. Did she guess? Or was she practising the sort of denial which those close to a cancer sufferer indulged in? He wasn't being particularly brave by keeping this a secret, Malcolm admitted. It was more that he was terribly afraid of what consequences might follow if he were to reveal the truth of his illness.

He looked out of the window of his third-storey office, distracted by the man whistling outside. For a moment he watched as the window cleaner rubbed the long glass panes with a cloth then swiped them clean with his scraper. The man's denims were frayed at the knee and his plaid bodywarmer had seen better days but he stood there on the trolley, whistling as if he hadn't a care in the world. Malcolm Adams knew a sudden pang of envy. This bloke probably took home a meagre pay packet each week and spent it on booze, fags and the occasional cheap holiday to Spain. He'd never have sampled the kind of fine wines that Malcolm had amassed over the years, or visited such exotic locations. His kids wouldn't be at private schools. His wife wouldn't be able to afford the latest in designer fashions. Yet, as he listened to the whistling, Malcolm knew he would give anything to exchange his own life for that of the man outside his window.

'Malcolm? Are you busy right now?' Catherine Devoy was in the doorway, her face tilted anxiously in his direction.

He shook his head and she came into the room, closed the door carefully then sat down, smoothing her skirt over neatly crossed legs.

'Malcolm,' Catherine looked intently into the eyes of the man behind the desk. 'I think it's time we had a talk, don't you?'

'I don't believe her,' Lorimer told his detective sergeant. 'I'm certain she knows whose voice is on that tape.'

Alistair Wilson raised his eyebrows but said nothing. Lorimer's intuitions were usually spot-on in his experience. It was as if the man were possessed of an invisible antenna that caught all sorts of nuances that were lost to other mere mortals. Maybe it was his background in the study of art, the cultivation of a kind of perception that senses more than is simply visible to the eye.

'In fact,' he continued, 'I'd go so far as to say she's covering up for one of the staff at Forbes Macgregor.'

'Any point in making tapes of them all?' Wilson asked.

Lorimer made a face. 'Our voice expert reckons the hysteria would have altered the woman's voice considerably. You know what it's like when we're interviewing someone under stress and their tone of voice goes right up the scale? Well, our guy tells me the same sort of thing was happening here. The caller was genuinely frightened, probably in a state of shock, when she spoke into that telephone.'

'Distorted her usual voice, then?'

'To some extent. But not so that Miss Hammond couldn't recognize it.'

'Maybe she's heard the same voice having hysterics before?'

'Could be. But unless we put extra pressure on her she's not going to tell us.'

Alistair Wilson shrugged. 'What now, then?'

'Now we keep digging around at Forbes Macgregor.'

Jennifer Hammond was humming along to the television's jingle when the doorbell rang. Her visitor was early, but that was okay. She'd been ready for ages. The wine was cooling in the fridge and she'd put out some low calorie nibbles on a Chinese dish on the glass table. She flicked her red hair back from her face as she walked along the corridor, aware of a new spring to her step. Some serious retail therapy had lightened her mood after that policeman's earlier visit and now she was going to compound it with her well-thought-out scheme.

'Hi, come on in. Let me take your coat.' She smiled at her visitor, noting the water droplets on the raincoat as she took it through to her bedroom. 'Make yourself at home,' she called. 'Help yourself to some Chablis. It's in the fridge and I've left glasses on the worktop.'

Jennifer glanced at her reflection in the mirrored wardrobe. Her face was flushed with excitement and anticipation. Nothing could go wrong, surely? She'd thought out all the angles. With a sidelong smirk at herself, the redhead flicked off the light switch and sauntered back into the sitting room. Her visitor had drawn the cork and filled two long-stemmed glasses already, Jennifer noted with satisfaction.

'Cheers,' she said, raising a glass and swallowing a welcome mouthful. 'Happy days,' she added, sniggering inwardly at the irony of her words. If all went according to plan there would be plenty of happy days for Jennifer Hammond, but she was not so sure that the same would apply to the person who sat opposite watching her thoughtfully.

The nausea hit her when she tried to stand up. Okay, she'd managed to polish off the best part of two bottles of wine. Her visitor had been more abstemious, having to drive, but Jennifer was used to a few glasses. Shouldn't be feeling like this. Maybe coming down with a bug, she thought as she tried to steady herself. She sat down again heavily, her hand brushing the edge of the coffee table.

What if . . . ? The sudden thought made her grab her mobile. The names blurred as she scrolled down the list. Blinking hard, Jennifer saw his name and pressed the green button. For a moment the ringtone was all she heard then another wave of nausea came over her and the mobile dropped from her fingers.

The Jack Vettriano print on her wall seemed to be moving as if a wind had caught it from behind, its very shadows seeping out of the frame as Jennifer swayed on her way to the bathroom.

Light smashed against her eyeballs as she pulled

the light cord and she just made it to the wash basin in time as her stomach contents heaved their way upwards. Staggering now, she turned on the cold tap then put out her hand to swish away the disgusting mess blocking the basin. But at that very moment a different sensation swept over her and she felt her legs give way.

There was no sudden intimation of mortality, simply a fading away of her senses as Jennifer Hammond closed her eyes on the world for the last time.

CHAPTER 26

Davie McLaren was furious. Why couldn't the factor have sent someone round immediately? God knows they charged enough in monthly service fees. Meantime he'd had to wait over an hour while his bathroom carpet became more and more sodden underfoot and the ceiling threatened to give way. Knocking on the door of upstair's flat had met with nil response. The silly cow had gone out and left her bath running, by the looks of things.

The footballer banged his fist against the telephone table, making the instrument jump with a sudden tinkle. Damn and blast! He'd wanted to soak in a bath and ease away all the sore places that hurt after today's training session but couldn't risk even stepping into the bathroom lest the whole ceiling came crashing down. At least he could use the loo in the ensuite and have a shower if he really felt like it. But Davie McLaren had wanted to have a bath and the young midfielder had become used to having what he wanted at the click of his fingers. He'd give that stuck-up redhead a real piece of his mind when she came back.

'What's wrong?' Davie opened the door a little wider to admit the woman he recognized from the factor's office. She was chalk-white and trembling.

'Can I use your phone?' she asked, not waiting for Davie's reply but walking straight towards the telephone on the hall table. 'My mobile's on the blink,' she added, quickly dialing three numbers.

Davie started to speak but shut up immediately as the woman shot him a look, waved her hand at him and spoke into the telephone.

'Police, please, and an ambulance as well. Eighty Riverside Gardens. Yes.' She paused and her eyes met Davie's as she continued to talk to the emergency operator. 'Linda Roberts. I'm here from Treeby-Willis on behalf of the downstairs tenant. Water was coming from the flat above. I . . . I found a woman's body in the bathroom.' There was another pause as Davie stood, mesmerized by what he was hearing. 'Yes, I'm sure she's dead.'

Lorimer watched as the photographer flashed shot after shot of the mess in Jennifer Hammond's bathroom. The woman's body was slumped between the bath and the wash basin, her red hair falling over her face. Someone had turned off the tap and made a start at clearing the vomit into evidence bags. The smell emanating from the tiny room was sweet and rotten. The stench of vomit was infectious; you couldn't help but want to add your own stomach contents to those already splattered by a victim. The scene of crime lads were impervious to it all, going through the motions of collecting traces and investigating the woman's last physical movements with nary a qualm.

Lorimer retreated into the sitting room. It was only this morning that he'd stood here contemplating the scenery from this window. Now the midnight view was all stars of brightness and blinking headlights as the traffic still sped over the black arc of the Kingston Bridge. He could see the reflections on the water in a pattern of pale crescent moons as the river continued to move below his gaze.

He turned back and looked intently at the room. It was much the same as it had been earlier; a stylish, comfortable room with its central table and that single wine glass that would be taken away for examination. He wandered into the small galley kitchen. Two empty wine bottles sat on the counter beside a bottle opener. There were scraps of dark green foil pushed to one side that matched the necks of the wine bottles. So she'd been on a binge, had she? Lorimer tried to imagine the red-haired woman drowning her sorrows about Michael Turner, but somehow the scene refused to equate with several designer carrier bags that he'd found shoved in a hall cupboard. The receipts were still inside, showing that Jennifer Hammond had enjoyed a shopping spree a few hours before her death. Binge-drinking herself to the stage where she lost control was not the impression he'd had of this young woman. She was much more sophisticated than that. Much more. Drugs, then? a little voice suggested.

Her bedroom was past the bathroom and Lorimer had to squeeze his way carefully past the white-suited officers. Like the sitting room, the walls were decorated in pale gold with a rich amber fleur-de-lis pattern bordering the plain coving. But there any resemblance to the other room ended. Jennifer Hammond's king-sized bed was swathed in a rich, dark red satin. Tasselled and frilled pillows embroidered with red and gold oriental designs had been grouped at the head of the bed below a sweeping canopy. Lorimer looked up at the ceiling, almost expecting to see an oval mirror but there was none. Despite this, the room still had the air of a bordello. An ancient hookah stood in one corner of the room, several small brass bowls placed artfully around its base. Lorimer sniffed the air but could detect nothing. The old pipe was purely for decorative purposes, then. Like the silk shawl that was fastened to the wall opposite the window, pinned somehow to make its pattern of peacocks fan their tails in three perfect arcs. Its fringes whispered in the draught of air coming from an under-floor heating vent.

Lorimer continued to look at the contents of the room, trying to see past the lavish furnishings for the more mundane things that might give him a clue to what had happened that evening. The bedside cabinet, a queer, carved affair on spindly legs, had only one drawer. Lorimer opened it carefully with gloved hands. Inside there was the usual detritus of female existence; a packet of contraceptive pills, a black-handled hairbrush with red hairs entwined in its bristles, a calf-skin address book, a Filofax and two pens bearing the name of Forbes Macgregor. A half-empty jar of Clinique night cream and a small wooden pill box completed the drawer's contents. Lorimer unscrewed the box but the white pills could have been anything. That was a job for the lab. On top of the table was a pseudo-antique telephone, enamelled with flowers in shades of pink and red and finished in gilt.

For a second, Lorimer could imagine the dead woman lying there in splendid opulence, the satin sheets drawn up around her pale skin, telephone in one hand, smiling coquettishly as she flirted with her latest admirer. He experienced a sudden feeling of loss that the woman's vivaciousness had been snuffed out in such a sordid manner. Lorimer sighed. He wouldn't be here if he hadn't written that earlier report about his visit to the flat. Maybe Superintendent Mitchison's paper trails had some uses after all. And a sudden death in the midst of a murder inquiry was reason enough for the DCI to impose his authority.

Maggie sank gratefully into the armchair. It had been a long day and being all alone this evening had made it longer. Ah, well. Some things never changed, she thought wistfully, wondering what it was that had kept her husband late tonight. The demons of doubt began to whisper in her ear. Was he seeing someone else? That blonde DI who had been an undercover officer was part of her husband's team. Maggie recalled the girl from a party they'd been at. She'd been there with Mark Mitchison, as she remembered. A pretty girl, DI Josephine Grant, smart too. Maggie forced down the picture in her mind of her husband with another woman. An overactive imagination, that was what was wrong with her, she scolded herself. Think of something else.

Maybe she'd give Mum a quick ring; see what she'd been up to today. Her hand idled over the arm of the chair to where the telephone lay on the floor. She wriggled sideways then caught sight of the red flashing light. Damn! The buzzer had gone again on the answering machine. How many missed calls this time, she wondered? There was just one from Bill, telling her he'd be late. There was nothing unusual about that, Maggie told herself, so why was she unable to banish these treacherous thoughts about a certain blonde DI who might also be working overtime?

CHAPTER 27

On the other side of the Atlantic, Officer Biegel stared at the medical report and then looked again at the most recent fax from Glasgow. He frowned and read them both again. That didn't make sense. He shook his head as if trying to shake off an irritating blowfly, then gave a sigh. It might be more trouble than it was worth, but his own curiosity as well as the knowledge that he ought to dig a bit deeper stopped him binning the fax. The NYPD officer swivelled around in his chair.

'Hey, Curt! Take a look at this.' Biegel waved the papers in the air. 'Think we've got a problem.' He waited until the other man loped across to his desk and read the two papers studiously.

'Surely they've made some mistake?'

'How do we tell? Want me to ask them to double-check their records?'

'S'pose.' Curt yawned and strolled away. It had been a long enough day and if eager Biegel wanted to correspond with Strathclyde CID at some ungodly hour of a Scottish morning that was up to him. He had a wife and kids to go home to.

Jeff Biegel considered the two documents then nodded. 'Yeah. Why not?' He glanced at his watch. It was way out of office hours, but maybe there'd be someone who'd be able to check this out for him. The policeman lifted the telephone and dialled the number at the foot of the page. There was no answer, which wasn't totally surprising, then, just as he was about to hang up a voice stated 'Strathclyde CID.'

A few minutes later the New York policeman was out of the building and weaving his way between the mass of humanity that coursed along the streets. The Glasgow cops had his cell phone number. And it wouldn't be the first time he'd been woken from sleep in this job of his.

Suzanne put down the telephone. How strange for Strathclyde Police to ask for another copy of that man's records. She'd already photocopied one set and sent them off by next-day delivery. What on earth could they want with another lot? She'd see to it during her coffee break and maybe mention the call to Mr Lynch whenever he came out of surgery. That police officer must really want them in a hurry, insisting on picking the records up later this morning. Odd, Suzanne thought, then dismissed the incident as the door buzzed to admit the next patient for their nine-thirty appointment. She would never know that several thousand miles away Officer Jeff Biegel was

172

catching a few hours' sleep while he waited for the young receptionist to carry out this one simple request.

The police officer scratched his head wearily. It was true, then. This second fax had supported the first one. There was no mistake about these dental records after all. No cock-up by the Brits. He screwed up his face. If what he was reading was true, then there had been a total mix-up on this side of the puddle.

That body in the woods was not Michael Turner. And now they had the additional problem of a missing person on their hands.

'Who was she, Bill?'

Lorimer did not reply for a moment, his mind on the vivacious redhead whose life had been so suddenly snuffed out. He remembered her green eyes and that come-hither look she'd given him the first time they had met.

'Her name was Jennifer Hammond. She's dead,' he replied.

Maggie realized now why his face was so white and drawn. It wasn't just lack of sleep, then.

'She was the human resources manager at Forbes Macgregor. Michael Turner's girlfriend.'

'The one who was killed in New York?'

Lorimer nodded, his mouth a thin hard line.

'And she tried to contact you?'

Lorimer looked across to see another question in his

wife's eyes. 'I gave her my card. Hoped she'd see sense and tell us who made that anonymous phone call.' He sighed heavily. 'They reckon she was trying to call me just before she died.'

'But why?'

Lorimer slumped back on the pillow and shook his head. 'My guess is whoever was with her made sure she would never reveal their identity. Now we'll never know,' he added bitterly.

Maggie took her husband's arm and squeezed it lightly. 'I'm so sorry,' she whispered.

'Me too,' he replied, wrapping his arms around her and holding her tightly against him. 'Me too.'

'I don't want to tell them,' Lorimer said in a tone that made Superintendent Mitchison raise his eyebrows.

'And why not?'

Lorimer pulled his chair a little closer to his senior officer's desk and leaned towards him. 'We have two suspicious deaths on our hands and one case of mistaken identity, all beginning the night of Michael Turner's going-away party. Duncan Forbes is found dead, drowned, but with enough gamma-hydroxybutrate to make us suspect that his death was deliberate. Plus we have a hysterical caller that simply adds credence to this line of inquiry. Then Turner's girlfriend dies in her own flat with a pack of GHB tablets in her bedside table. Aren't these reasons enough? Who knows what's happened to Turner, but he's certainly not going to get rid of his own credit cards for no good reason, is he?'

'We don't know for certain how Jennifer Hammond died, though, do we?'

'The lab reports should be in fairly soon. The tox. tests will show if she's ingested the drug,' Lorimer replied. 'One thing we do know though, is that no finger-prints were found on that pill box.'

Mitchison raised his eyebrows. 'Someone cleaned them off? Hm. That would seem to rule out a self-induced dosage, then.' He frowned and sighed. 'Have you come up with any new information about Michael Turner yet?'

Lorimer bristled inwardly. What on earth did the man expect with faxes flying to and fro across the Atlantic; a sudden miracle? But he kept his cool as he replied 'No. Maybe once NYPD identify the victim we can put more of the pieces together. He was expected to join Kirkby Russell nearly two weeks ago. There must be some reason why he failed to show up there. We do know he entered the States, but after JFK airport there's been not a trace of him.'

'Except for those credit cards.' Mitchison steepled his fingers thoughtfully. 'Do you think he's dead?'

'I think there's a strong chance of that. It wouldn't astonish me to hear that New York police find another body out in their backwoods.'

'And meantime?'

'Meantime, as the senior investigating officer in this

case, I don't want any of Forbes Macgregor's personnel knowing that Michael Turner might still be alive. We can slap a D notice on the press, too. There's something distinctly odd about the whole thing. It smells bad. And until we know a bit more I'd rather leave these Glasgow accountants thinking he's dead.' Lorimer fixed his blue gaze on the superintendent. 'There was no trace of the man's records when Wilson and Cameron went to their office. It was almost as if somebody had expected him to be eliminated,' he said, unconsciously echoing his detective constable's words.

Mitchison's eyes widened and he nodded. 'All right. But it'll be your responsibility to keep the lid on the New York end of things. I don't want anybody pointing the finger at us for misleading them.' He picked up a stack of papers and tapped them sharply on his desktop as if to intimate that the meeting between them was over, but his DCI remained seated.

'Was there something else, Lorimer?' Mitchison tilted his head in an imperious gesture. For a moment Lorimer was tempted to report on the dead woman's last call but that could wait until a more auspicious moment. For now, he was more concerned about pushing this case forward and it was just possible that he knew how that might be achieved.

'Yes,' he replied, folding his arms across his chest and leaning back, 'I want to use the expertise of Doctor Solomon Brightman.'

*

'Told you so!' Rosie crowed triumphantly. 'Now it's official, you can put your mind to solving Lorimer's case!'

Solly passed a hand over his eyes. A loyal fiancée was one thing but even Rosie's faith in him couldn't produce magical results just like that. Still, now that he'd been officially asked, the psychologist found himself interested in the deaths of those people from Forbes Macgregor. Apart from Michael Turner, the two Glasgow deaths had similarities, not least in their locations. Solly was big on locations. It made sense to look at the areas in which victims had been found, to trace a pattern. So often the perpetrator of multiple killings could be hiding somewhere in the circle of a map, especially if its radius was not too wide. And here, he told himself, the river impinged on the locations. Even the accountancy firm itself was situated by the banks of the Clyde, in the elegant Georgian buildings of Carlton Place.

But two deaths, related or not, were going to be insufficient for any sort of geographical profile. Still, other factors could be brought into the equation like those sources supplying the drug. The Glasgow bridges had long had an unsavoury reputation as meeting places for pushers, addicts and, of course, the homeless who could sometimes be counted in the latter category. Yes, there were other areas he could look at. However he would need to ask a lot of questions about the victims and about any previous crimes involving GHB before he could be confident that some pattern might emerge.

Rosie smiled fondly. The room was silent but it was

a busy silence, as she knew from past experience. The cogs would be whirring in that clever brain of Solly's and he'd be immersed in this case before bedtime, she was sure. Fixing her reading glasses onto the bridge of her nose, the pathologist returned to the paper she was reading. It would need a few tweaks here and there but the essence of her lecture was pretty sound. Still smiling, Rosie sank down into the armchair by the fire. To the outside world theirs might seem an unusual relationship: the pocket-blonde pathologist whose outgoing manner contrasted with Solly's quiet seriousness. How odd that fate should have thrown them together. And yet, was it really so strange? After all, weren't they both involved in probing deeply within the hidden recesses of death? Rosie gave herself a little shake. It was good to have her lover involved with a case again. If anyone could come up with an idea about these two GHB deaths then surely it was Dr Solomon Brightman.

CHAPTER 28

G eorge Parsonage drew up a chair nearer the fire. 'Tea or coffee, Dr Brightman?' The man opposite smiled back at him, his dark eyes twinkling under their luxuriant lashes. 'That would be lovely, thanks.'

The riverman shook his head slightly. He'd make tea, then. This chap seemed so vague that he probably wouldn't notice what he was drinking. Another glance at the man took in the full beard and pale complexion that gave him a slightly exotic appearance but George was a shrewd enough observer of humankind to notice the intelligence shining at him from behind those horn-rimmed spectacles.

Solly had carefully considered the deaths of Duncan Forbes and Jennifer Hammond; he had been asked to give any rationale as to whether their deaths were related. He had decided to start with this man who was known to Glasgow folk as the riverman. Lorimer's report was full enough in its own way, but here was a man to whom the tides and currents of the Clyde were an every-day language and Solly had an urge to see where the man's expertise might take him. There was something about the river Clyde that gnawed away at the edges of his mind. If its water could tell tales . . .

It was almost two hours later that the psychologist walked through Glasgow Green. It was the first time Solly had been in this part of the city and he looked around at the large expanse of grass, trying to imagine what it had been like in centuries gone by. Women from all over had brought their laundry to dry here, George had told him. On a windy day it must have been like the sails of ships blowing madly across the green, he supposed, a picture forming of a place full of people, full of bustle.

His mind shifted to all the other stories the Humane Society officer had spun around the Clyde, some tragic and others spiked with undeniable humour. But Solly had gleaned what he had wanted: a picture of the river's ebbing and flowing and its gathering of one man's body into its cold arms. George had photocopied charts of the tides and times as well as his own report of the day that he'd pulled Duncan Forbes from the river, and these were now stowed safely in Solly's battered briefcase for further perusal. The background report on the dead man suggested that there was no good reason for him to have deliberately ingested the drug, nor was he a typical suicidal case. What Solly wanted now was a picture in his own mind of what might have taken place after the man had disappeared from the range of that CCTV camera.

The taxi deposited him at the Crowne Plaza Hotel and Solly shrugged his coat closer around him as the wind cut across the river and blew directly into his face. Despite the April sun it was bitterly cold. What on earth must it have been like on that fateful night? Solly imagined the sudden splash of a man's body entering the icy water: surely he'd have flapped about, calling for help? He'd been a strong swimmer, but that may have counted for nothing given his heavy winter clothing and the strong currents. And if the GHB had so dulled his senses that he'd been unable to make himself heard? There had been a howling wind that night too, according to the riverman's minutely detailed logbook.

The psychologist walked slowly towards the bushes next to the cycle path. At one point the pathway curved out of sight of the hotel, its strip of pale concrete running all the way along the north side of the riverbank towards the city. Already many eyes had scoured the area in a search for clues as to the exact place where Duncan Forbes had fallen into the river. Did he fall or was he pushed? Solly's own words came back to him, now utterly devoid of humour. The path wound around the Crowne Plaza shrubbery and took him to the main road leading out of the Scottish Exhibition and Conference Centre complex. For a few moments the psychologist stood pondering the ways in and out of the area, then he made up his mind and strode towards the City Inn, a more modest hotel but one that intrigued Solly. From where he stood he could see that there was an extended deck reaching out from the restaurant and jutting right over the river. Above it, the Squinty Bridge traced its white arc against the grey skies.

The revolving glass doors admitted Solly into the bright hotel foyer. To one side he could see a figure behind a coffee machine, its hiss of steam creating a halo around the man's head. A few people sat at tables drinking coffee and talking in lowered voices. It was close enough to the various offices that surrounded this part of Finnieston for people to choose the hotel's coffee bar for their afternoon break, he supposed.

The barman looked up as Solly approached: his smile switched on like an automatic sensor but the psychologist could see that the man's eyes were glazed with boredom.

'One pot of tea, please. Do you have any herbal?'

'Sure. Green tea, camomile and ginger, strawberry, peppermint or blackcurrant,' the man replied, his Aussie accent rolling over the choices of teas as if they were all so tantalizing that Solly might have difficulty in making his choice.

'Camomile, please. And can I take it outside?'

The Aussie's eyebrows lifted. 'Pretty cold for that, mate,' he shrugged, 'but it's okay with me. Chairs and tables are there if you want.'

Solly glanced at the exterior deck that was not entirely

empty; one person at least had braved the April winds, muffled and hooded in a pale-blue fleece.

'Does the hotel keep this section open all year round?' he asked, looking towards the river as the man fetched a small silver teapot from a shelf at his side.

'Yeah, it's kind of our trademark, y'know. Ever since the *Gazette* did that big piece on waterfront restaurants everybody seems keen to venture out there.'

'Even at night?'

The man grinned. 'Especially at night. We've overhead heaters and canopies to keep the worst of the weather off. Folk seem to like it, y'know, the glitter on the water and all that.'

Solly nodded his thanks and ventured out onto the bleached wooden decking that stretched out around the restaurant area, tray in both hands, briefcase under his arm. The figure on the deck did not move as he paused behind her, wondering which table to select. He took in her polar fleece, its hood pulled over the woman's head to keep out the cold, though strands of long blonde hair obscured her face, tugged by the wind. Then he noticed her ungloved hands busy scribbling on a notepad. Solly nodded to himself. A reporter of some sort, perhaps? But why sit out here when inside would have been adequate for her purposes? As he moved nearer, curious to see what she was writing, he caught sight of a fragment of a sentence that might have been poetry, but at the same moment the woman looked up. For an instant she frowned as if trying to place Solly in her mind. Had she recognized him? Then, giving her head a tiny shake, she returned to her writing, ignoring the psychologist completely.

Solly placed his tray on a table far enough away to give the woman some privacy then sat down to contemplate his surroundings. From here he could see the pathway and the line of bushes that broke the worst of the river's breeze. Anyone sitting on this deck had a good view of the river. Had Lorimer's team come here to ask questions? Solly did not recall a mention of the City Inn from the bulk of notes that comprised the senior investigating officer's reports. If anybody had been here that night . . . Solly sipped his tea then turned and looked back into the coffee bar. Perhaps a few words with the bored Australian might liven up both their days.

'Yeah, read all about it. Poor bloke. Drunk, wasn't he?' The barman shook his head as Solly gave a non-committal shrug. 'We had some people staying here. There are always the stragglers who check in for the night. Been to the Armadillo and it's too far to go home. Can't afford the Crowne Plaza prices so they come here.' The man polished a row of wine glasses absently as he spoke.

'Did Strathclyde Police ask you anything about the incident?' Solly enquired politely.

'Me?' The Australian looked surprised. 'Why'd they ask *me* anything?'

Solly smiled benignly. 'Perhaps to confirm if any

of the residents had been at the Crowne Plaza earlier? Maybe some of your guests had been there earlier in the evening? Checking out accommodation?' Solly replied, following up the barman's own line of thought.

'Oh, you'd need to ask at reception. That's not my bag. What's your interest in this anyway, mate?' A frown appeared between the man's dark eyes and Solly detected a hardening in his expression. With a small sigh of resignation he drew a business card out of his coat pocket and handed it across the counter.

The Australian's lips moved imperceptibly as he read the card.

'I help the police with their investigations from time to time,' Solly explained, shrugging again as if to say it was no big deal.

'Doctor Brightman, eh? Psychologist.' The man nodded then pursed his lips.

Solly smiled. The card could be useful. It allayed any suspicions and gave him a little bit of authority to ask questions. And he could see that this man was suddenly impressed by the letters after his name. Still, he would have to return with one of Strathclyde's officers in tow if he wanted to find out about the hotel's guest list *and* whether it included anyone who had seen Duncan Forbes walking unsteadily along that footpath several nights ago.

It had been a long day. Solly pulled the cupboard door open and hung his coat carefully on its customary hanger.

His stomach had been rumbling noticeably for several hours, reminding him of a missed lunch and a belated dinner. He really should make the effort to prepare a meal even if it was only a can of soup and some bread.

Eventually Solly was wiping the soup mug with the final bit of crust and savouring his last mouthful. With a sigh he put down the mug and cleaned his mouth and beard with a checked napkin. That was better. The intense cold that had penetrated his bones for most of the day was finally loosening its grip. For a while the psychologist simply stared into space. An observer might have thought that he was practically asleep, the long eyelashes half-covering his dark eyes, but Solly was not falling into a dream. He seemed to be staring into the night sky beyond his room but what he was actually trying to see were pathways up and down the river Clyde; pathways that made sense to a killer.

From Forbes Macgregor's offices it was a fifteen-minute walk along the river to Jennifer Hammond's flat and less than that by car (or cab, in Solly's case) to the Crowne Plaza Hotel. The psychologist had walked the pathway all the way back to the city centre, his eyes absorbing each and every aspect of the riverside. Much of these banks had undergone a regeneration process since Solly had made Glasgow his home and he was intrigued to see so many cyclists and dog walkers in this part of the city. There was something prestigious nowadays about owning a property that had a view over the river and Solly could see the attraction. Foxes had been spotted regularly along the walkways, and cormorants were a familiar sight. Graham West's own residence was in the penthouse flat of what was known as the Butterfly Building. Its two triangular shapes looked like a butterfly from the air, the riverman had told him. Solly had passed several other modern blocks of apartment buildings before crossing the Squinty Bridge to the river's south bank to the complex of flats where Jennifer Hammond's body had been found.

George Parsonage had told him stories about the bridges and the several attempted suicides that he had saved from drowning. His job was not just about fishing sodden corpses from the depths of the Clyde. An April night might have seen any number of people wandering around the bridges including the usual derelicts who tended to doss down under the Kingston Bridge; Solly had looked upwards at its concrete span as he'd stood by the gateway to Riverside Gardens. Traffic filled the busy link between north and south, a constant dim roar above his head.

The offices at Carlton Place were secured at night by an elderly janitor, but every member of the senior staff could access the building at any time if they had a security pass. There were at least thirty people who might have been in and out of that office after hours on both the night Duncan Forbes had died and the evening Jennifer Hammond had been murdered, Solly had discovered. All the partners and managers could come and go as they pleased: staying late was a common occurrence and the managers were well paid for over-time. Solly had looked into the taxi fleet that had taken members of Michael Turner's going-away party to their homes afterwards; its records showed a surprising amount of Forbes Macgregor's staff had not availed themselves of the taxis' services. Michael Turner had gone back to his own home by taxi with Jennifer Hammond. But he had noticed that none of the partners had been driven home. Possibly they'd taken their own cars, whether drunk or sober, he thought grimly. Solomon Brightman had never known any desire to drive. The attraction of fast cars was simply beyond his comprehension, but he did understand the prestige many attached to owning and driving a luxury car. Even Lorimer's old Lexus had some cachet in that department, though its enormous mileage rendered it of little value in monetary terms. Some potential eye witnesses to Duncan Forbes' death could be ruled out from the staff that had been at Michael Turner's party then, as they were well on their way home, but not all.

The last dregs of soup congealed in the mug as Solly's mind turned round and around, following a shadowy figure along that pathway by the Clyde.

CHAPTER 29

'That's all, is it? An officer to accompany you to the City Inn and a search warrant for Forbes Macgregor's offices? Oh sure.' Lorimer's sarcasm came thickly over the line. 'I don't think so. Well, not the warrant at any rate. That's for the Fiscal to provide.' There was a pause as the two men remained silent, one waiting for a response, the other trying to figure out what he had achieved by asking for more than he actually required. If Lorimer had guessed the psychologist's simple tactic he was not showing it. Maybe Mitchison was breathing down his neck? Solly grinned. That wouldn't affect the senior investigating officer's decision, he told himself.

'So who do you want to ask the questions at the City Inn?' Lorimer asked shortly.

Solly's grin widened. The DCI wasn't happy that this particular line of inquiry had been overlooked, that was all. 'Oh, anybody,' Solly answered airily.

'Tell you what,' there was a pause as Lorimer

considered, 'why don't we meet there in, oh, about an hour, say? You don't have any classes today, do you?'

'No.'

'Okay. I've some stuff to clear up here then I'll see you.'

The Australian barman was replacing empty bottles above the optics when Lorimer and Solly strode into the City Inn's coffee bar.

'Hi.' The smile appeared instantly on the barman's face. 'What can I get you gentlemen to drink?'

His smile fell a little as Lorimer placed his warrant card on the counter, asking, 'May we have a quiet word, please?'

Rick Murray sat between the two men, glancing at each of them in turn. Luckily the coffee bar was empty at this time of day but it wouldn't be too long before he'd need to set up the tables for lunchtime.

'What's this all about, guys?'

Lorimer took out a photograph and placed it on the table. It was a photocopy of a page from *Accountants' Magazine* showing various members of Forbes Macgregor's staff, including all their Glasgow partners.

'I wondered if you had ever seen any of these people before,' he began. 'We particularly want to know if any of them checked into the hotel on the night of 7 April this year. Take your time,' he added as the barman opened his mouth to speak. One look at Lorimer's steely glare and Rick's mouth closed again. It would be the easiest thing in the world to deny having ever seen anyone, heard anything, said anything like the wise monkey he should be. But that pair of blue eyes was fastened on him, forcing the barman to look at the paper on the table. Rick scanned the faces smiling up at him. Some of the people in the photos were standing outside a building, others were seated around a large table. He looked intently, wondering which of them had ended up in the Clyde. Finally he met Lorimer's gaze and shook his head. 'Not sure about any of the men there, sorry,' he shrugged, then hesitated. 'But there's one face I do recognize,' he said, pointing to a dark-haired woman in the middle of one photo. 'Her.' He looked up and grinned. 'Don't usually forget the lookers, do you?'

'A regular, was she?'

'Nope. In fact I only saw her the one time, but I do remember her.'

'When was that?'

'Oh, couple of months back. More towards the beginning of February, I'd say.' He frowned as if trying to remember. 'See, she was meeting this younger guy for lunch.' Rick glanced at Solly to catch his eye. 'I like to watch the couples, y'know, see how they interact, watch their body language.' He nodded towards the psychologist. Solly's impassive expression yielded nothing so he turned back to Lorimer. 'Gets a bit boring in here otherwise.'

'And did you recognize this younger man?'

'Hey, let me see these pics again.' The barman picked up the photocopy and turned it to the light. 'Yeah, that's him there. The one at the back. Not such a great photo of him, but I'd seen him in here a few times after office hours.'

Lorimer froze as the barman chattered on. 'Never came in for a drink with the woman, though. Just lunch that one time. Don't know who the guy was though and, come to think of it, haven't seen him in here recently.'

'Did you think he might be her boyfriend?' Solly asked.

Rick grinned. 'No chance. He was way too polite to her. No, I reckoned she was his boss. But I tell you what. He was pretty excited after she'd gone. That's something I do remember.'

Lorimer resisted the urge to meet Solly's eyes. There might be nothing in this, but he would be intrigued to know just why Catherine Devoy had come across the river to lunch with Michael Turner.

'We'd also like a look at your guest register, please.' Lorimer kept his tone neutral, though he could feel his heart thumping with excitement. There was something worth investigating here after all.

It was late by the time Lorimer reached home. The hotel's register had revealed nothing at all. No members of Forbes Macgregor's staff had elected to stay over on that April night. At least not under their own names, he thought, his naturally suspicious mind ferreting into dark corners.

'Hey, Mags. I'm home,' he called out, opening the door of the living room to the brightness and warmth within.

'Hey yourself.' His wife smiled up at him. 'Had anything to eat?'

Lorimer ducked his head and offered a sheepish grin. 'Curry with Solly, actually. Sorry.'

Maggie rolled her eyes to heaven. 'Just as well I hadn't cooked anything special then, isn't it?' But her words became lost as Lorimer scooped her into his arms in a hug. Maggie felt the cold of his jacket sleeve as she stroked it in response to his hands circling the small of her back, a ploy guaranteed to weaken her defences.

'Oh, that reminds me.' She looked up, the smile dying on her lips. 'I took your cashmere coat to the cleaners after school. How on earth did it get so mucky?'

Lorimer opened his eyes wide in feigned innocence and shrugged.

'Och, you! Anyway, I found something in the pocket.' Maggie leaned over and retrieved the tape from a side table.

'Ah.' Lorimer took the tape from his wife. 'That's a copy of the voice Jennifer Hammond said she didn't recognize—'

'And you didn't believe her,' Maggie finished for him.

'Well, maybe we'll never know now.' He paused for a moment, turning the tape over and over in his fingers. 'Don't suppose you'd like to hear it?'

'Is it scary?'

'Not especially.'

'Okay.'

Maggie watched as Lorimer slotted the tape into their machine, and sat back against the warmth of her husband's shoulder. The machine whirred in silence then suddenly a woman's voice uttered the panic-stricken words that had led Lorimer to look at Duncan Forbes' death in a new light.

'Play it again, would you?' Maggie asked, her eyes fixed on the tape recorder.

Lorimer rewound the tape then watched his wife's face as she listened once more. A tiny frown formed on her brow as the voice repeated the unfinished message. 'She's scared, isn't she?' Maggie remarked at last, moving closer. 'A well-educated lady, by the sounds of her, not an old person either . . .' She shivered suddenly, and laced her fingers through Lorimer's. 'What on earth did she really see, I wonder?'

The tape whirred silently in the machine as Lorimer felt her body rigid with tension; Maggie had a rare gift of empathy with people that could be a blessing or a curse. She could be reliving the unknown woman's terror he thought, gently caressing her hair as if to erase the images inside her head.

'I wonder where she is now,' Maggie murmured. 'Poor woman.'

'Let me get you a drink,' Lorimer suggested.

'Sure. A whisky'd be grand,' she replied, eyeing the decanter on the sideboard.

He dropped a swift kiss on the top of her head as he rose to fetch them both a glass. 'What're you going to do now?' she asked.

'We've set up another house-to-house inquiry, this time asking the neighbours if they saw anyone the same night as the Forbes Macgregor party. Don't know if it'll do much. People get sniffy when there's a repeat visit. Think the police don't believe whatever they told them the first time.'

'What about the neighbour?'

Lorimer frowned. 'Aye, we got a lot of grief from that guy downstairs who reported the water coming through his roof. Wee toerag. Thinks he's God's gift to the SFA.'

'Who's that?'

'Davie McLaren,' he replied, handing her the glass of whisky. 'Heard of him?'

Maggie screwed up her brow. 'Wasn't he the boy wonder who was sent off five minutes after the kick-off when Scotland played Norway?'

Lorimer grinned. 'Very same. Hasn't learned anything from that incident either by the looks of it. Full of himself.' Lorimer sipped his drink thoughtfully. Davie McLaren had appeared to be in shock, babbling on about wanting his agent with him, as if the young footballer needed a grown-up to hold his hand in a crisis. Which he probably did.

'What we want is for someone to positively ID a visitor to Jennifer Hammond's flat,' Lorimer said. 'On either of the nights,' he added thoughtfully.

'Don't the flats have CCTV cameras?'

Lorimer shook his head. 'No. There's a security man around during the day but he's only there to stop non-residents parking within the grounds. He goes off at five o'clock every night.'

'So,' Maggie began again slowly, 'unless you have a witness who saw someone go into Jennifer's flat, you're not very much further forward, are you?'

Lorimer shrugged. 'Solly's nosing around a bit. And we're running a check on the accounting firm itself.'

Lorimer drained his glass and stared into space. Wheels had been put into motion now that this was effectively being treated as a double murder. Someone had wanted Jennifer Hammond out of the way. Was that why she had been preparing to leave for the firm's holiday villa in Cyprus? Well, he was due to see the Forbes Macgregor partners tomorrow. Maybe one of them would be able to enlighten him. And there was still the matter of an employee missing somewhere in the United States, an employee whose credit cards had been found on a dead man. Michael Turner's farewell party had stirred up something murky, Lorimer mused to himself. But like the bottom of the river being scraped by a dredger, silt that had been disturbed was now fogging up the clearer waters.

CHAPTER 30

'So how do we know that Othello has reason to feel jealousy?' Maggie looked around the class of sixteen-year-olds. A few tentative hands were up, but still she let her eyes roam over the others, giving them time to think through a response.

'What d'you reckon, James?' she finally asked a thin teenager slouching at the back of the classroom.

'Don't know. Maybe he was just like that?' James shrugged and resumed chewing whatever he had in his mouth. Maggie ignored the exaggerated rhythm of his jaws. She'd had one confrontation too many with this lad and wasn't about to let him disrupt her Shakespeare lesson.

'What do the rest of you think? Yes, Lewis?'

'He'd been warned by Brabantio though, hadn't he Miss?'

'Good, Lewis. What was it Desdemona's father said again?'

There was a rustle as the students looked up the pages of their textbooks.

'Yes? Kirstine?'

'He says, "Look to her, Moor, have a quick eye to see: She has deceived her father, may do thee." Is that it, Miss?'

'Does that mean she'll gie him a doin', Miss?' James called out to an undercurrent of sniggering.

Maggie shook her head, more in despair at the boy's deliberate misinterpretation of the text than at his cheek.

'Ah'd gie anyone a doin' if they tried it oan wi' ma burd. Know whit ah mean?'

Maggie sighed. The nature of Othello's jealousy was rapidly going downhill, but maybe she could salvage something from the boy's insolence.

'You've got a jealous nature too then, James?' she asked.

'Oh, aye, Miss,' he replied, then looked slyly at his neighbour before asking, 'D'you not feel a bit thon way yourself?'

Maggie stood motionless. What the hell did he mean? She felt the redness suffuse her cheeks and continued to stare, quite unable to form a coherent reply.

'Eh, Miss? Did ye no' kinda' wonder aboot Mr Lorimer when ye were away?'

There was a sudden collective intake of breath from the rest of the class. James Kerrigan had gone too far this time. Mrs Lorimer would give him a real telling off or even sling him out of the room.

But Maggie did neither of these things. Instead she continued to gaze at the boy. Had other kids in the school been asking the same question? A murmur among the girls made her aware that she had to speak or be condemned by her very silence.

'Is that what you think the normal reaction is between people, James?' she said, trying hard to control her voice. Then, turning to look over the whole class, she asked, 'What do you all think? Is it reasonable to become suspicious of one's partner?'

The relief within the room was palpable and a few hands shot up.

'Desdemona's younger than him, Miss, and she has lots of admirers,' one of the girls piped up.

'And Iago makes him think like that, Miss. He's pure evil, by the way,' another added.

Just then the bell shrilled out and Maggie watched as each student began to pack up hurriedly and head for the door.

'Walk!' she called automatically as the boys began to run along the corridor towards the canteen. Last period in the morning was a good slot for teaching, but Maggie rarely had any pupils hanging back to discuss the finer points of Shakespeare in their rush to find lunch.

'A'right, Miss?' James looked back over his shoulder at her as he turned away from the door, an insouciant grin of mischief on his face.

Maggie waved him off. James was a pain and she should have dealt with him more severely. He knew it too, she thought, as she watched him kick an imaginary football into an equally imaginary goal. God! That had been close. She'd nearly made a right fool of herself. Next time he'd be given a reprimand for insolence and made to stay behind. So why hadn't she done that today? Maggie asked herself, gathering in the textbooks that had been rapidly thrust down to the front row of the class. Was it because she was frightened to hear what he might tell her?

She piled the books into her cupboard shelves and locked the door. Outside, the corridor was silent, the last sound of rushing feet having died away. With a huge sigh, Maggie turned and headed towards the staffroom. A cup of coffee, she thought, then a sit down.

The staffroom was a pleasant cacophony of noise, the hiss from the coffee machine and the sound of voices talking and laughing. A few faces turned her way and smiled as she passed them. Maggie smiled back feeling, as she sometimes did, that this was her real home among these people who shared her way of life, her grouses about certain pupils, her frustrations with aspects of the system that seemed utterly pointless; things that Bill would never really understand. There was that lovely solidarity with folk like Sandie, who was already beckoning her over to sit next to her.

'Hard morning?' Sandie asked as Maggie slumped into the chair by her friend.

'Sort of. That James Kerrigan. He's a cheeky wee so-and-so.'

'Oh, him! I've given up expecting much of James. His computing assignments are way behind. Can't think what on earth we'll do without him after the summer,' she added, her voice laden with sarcasm.

'Is he leaving, then?'

'Yep! Doesn't want to be bothered with school, he tells me. Doesn't need any grades for what he's going to do.'

'And what might that be?' Maggie asked darkly. 'Dealing at the school gates with big brother Tam?'

'Wouldn't surprise me,' Sandie replied, 'but he said he was starting with his pal's father in his joinery business.'

'Ah, well, so long as he keeps his nose clean. Those Kerrigans have been nothing but trouble,' Maggie grumbled, rising to her feet in search of a cup of coffee.

'Come and see, come and see!' Stephanie, the probationer in Maggie's English department, sat opposite them and placed a pile of wedding magazines on the table with a flourish.

'Tell me what you think,' she prattled happily, turning a page and pointing at an advertisement for wedding stationery. Several of the women leaned in towards the girl and examined the magazine. Maggie sat back and sighed to herself. Steph, with her long glossy dark hair and impossibly tiny waist, was just like a wee girl at times. Her voice rose in a squeal of excitement as she showed off her choices of wedding invitations and orders of service. Had she ever been like that before her wedding to Bill? Maggie wondered. Memories came flooding back of standing at the church door, rose petals whirling in the spring air and Bill grinning at her like an idiot. The happiest day of my life, she thought. But there had been other moments too, like being whisked off her feet and carried over the threshold.

Suddenly she was back there again in Glasgow's West End, seeing herself as she must have been at Stephanie's age. Their flat had been two flights up a dark staircase that smelled of late-night curries and mouldering vegetables. The front door was a home-made job, flat brown formica nailed across whatever had been there before in a vain attempt to give the place some class. That had been an utter failure, but at least it had served to distinguish their wee place from all the rest. Some time previously the apartment must have been a fine building, since traces of cornicing could still be distinguished on the ceiling of the tiny hallway. Theirs had been one room with a shared communal kitchen and a long cold bathroom with an enormous bath. It had taken hours to fill and far too many of their precious coins in that greedy meter. Maggie smiled to herself remembering the time she and Bill had clambered, giggling, into that huge tub, hoping their collective weight would make the water level rise sufficiently to give them a decent soak. They'd made love then, careless of the presence of other folk just through the thin partition walls, careless of anything other than their own fervent desires. She'd trembled beneath her young husband's touch as he'd dried her skin, as much from passion as from the cold air that had swirled around that Gothic excuse for a bathroom. The wooden floorboards were worn and shiny from countless pairs of feet, she remembered, and those green tiles with their black trim just had to have been the original decor.

Now it was all gone, felled by the wrecking ball that had cleared that whole section of Gibson Street. She had gone back once, before the heavy plant had moved in, seeing the blank windows with their dingy lace curtains and the rubbish that had piled up inside the closes. How had she felt? Had it been nostalgia for the days they'd spent in that wee nest or gratitude that their home consisted of far more than a single rented room? She couldn't remember. Stephanie had got onto the subject of her new flat and all the Ikea furniture she wanted to buy but Maggie was barely listening. In her mind's eye she was seeing Bill loping along Gibson Street, his dark hair shining under that street lamp just below their window and remembering how her heart would lift at the very sight of him.

Had they lost something of that along the way? The lonely nights spent in hospital beds after yet another miscarriage had perhaps served to make her grow up or grow away from the person she'd been. Would a family have made any difference to them? Or was this a condition that came to all married couples in time? Would young Stephanie still have that magical sparkle ten years from now?

'What's up with you?' Sandie asked, making Maggie

aware of the huge sigh that had escaped from her chest.

'Och, nothing. Pity we all have to grow up, isn't it?' she whispered, nodding towards Stephanie.

'Aye, sure is,' her friend replied dryly, 'but at least you've still got a man to go home to. When he's there, that is.' Sandie grinned, digging Maggie in the ribs.

Maggie smiled. This was true. Sandie's messy divorce had left her a bit jaded about men but she had never sought to be other than supportive whenever Maggie moaned about Bill's long hours in the force. Or was that what she really meant? Was she maybe trying to tell her something quite different?

For a moment Maggie Lorimer sat and thought about the possibility of her husband being unfaithful to her. It happened to other couples. Look at poor Sandie. But that would never happen to her and Bill, would it? A cold worm of fear wriggled somewhere in the pit of her stomach. And with it came a small voice asking the question; how was she ever to find out if he had cheated on her?

CHAPTER 31

JJ pulled the van door shut and clicked the remote locking device. Giving a sigh, he flexed his shoulder muscles and yawned. On the overhead power lines birds swayed in the late-afternoon heat as the breeze lifted them to and fro. A faint mist of brown dust blew over the scrubland on either side of the road where JJ had left the van. Shading his eyes from the sun he gazed out across the prairie grass that stretched for miles until the heat haze made the red hills seem to rise out of a shimmering sea. It was a long time since he'd been out here shooting rabbits and crows, away from the city that had become his natural habitat and erstwhile hunting ground. He was finished with all that now. One last throw of the dice and he could slip away to retire in comfort: somewhere in Florida, maybe. He'd buy a nice beachside property, do a little fishing, watch the sunsets.

His reverie was broken by a voice behind him.

'Is *this* where we're spending the night?'

JJ turned sharply, frowning. He followed the other man's gaze towards a single storey house at the end of an overgrown path. It was shaded by several live oaks but even through the shadows the place had a beaten, neglected air.

'Sure.'

'Not exactly a home-from-home, is it?'

JJ spat onto the dried ground. 'What d'ya expect?' he snarled. 'Five-star hotels or sump'n?' Then, picking up the bags that he'd dropped by the van, he motioned for his companion to follow him.

'Every home comfort, wait till you see.' He nodded, and headed up towards the house.

Behind him the other man hesitated. They'd travelled a long, long way already and his body was aching. A bath and a meal were what he needed right now. Tonight he'd go along with the older man's wishes, but tomorrow might be a different matter.

Owls screeched outside as the two men settled down by the empty fireside. JJ had proved as good as his word, cooking a scratch meal from stuff he'd emptied out of a grocery sack and finally producing a bottle of Jack Daniel's from a cupboard in the main living room. He'd not spoken a word about the house, but from his easy familiarity with all the kitchen utensils it was obvious to his companion that he knew the place well. The darkness outside and the light from the tablelamp made the house feel as though its walls were wrapping themselves around the two travellers, protecting them from the world outside.

'Reckon we should make a start,' JJ began, pointing at the laptop on the table between them. 'Boot it up, pal.' He grinned.

Michael Turner blinked as the screen was illuminated. How many days ago had it been since he had sat in his Glasgow office staring at these images? He tried to calculate but his mind slipped into a grey indifference. Being alive was what really mattered now. He risked a glance at the man sitting opposite him. Staying that way might be another thing altogether.

CHAPTER 32

'Tony Jacobs,' Lorimer said. 'That's right, the bookie.' He paused, listening to the voice on the other end of the line. 'No, there's no reason to suspect anything illegal,' he said. 'Not at this stage, at any rate.' Lorimer listened then laughed as the voice protested that he had a dirty mind. 'That's what they pay me for,' he retorted and hung up, grinning. He clasped his hands, index fingers resting on his lips as he thought about the process that was now in motion. Forbes Macgregor's accounting services might be white as the driven snow as far as the Jacobs' company was concerned but he wasn't in the business of making assumptions like that. The client records would be examined in detail to see if there had been anything that might link the murder of the bookmaker to Duncan Forbes and Jennifer Hammond.

Solly hadn't come up with a preliminary report, but that was okay. His methods were slower than those of the police. Lorimer thought of Rosie and Solly. An unlikely couple in many ways, yet their respective jobs demanded the same quality of patience and perseverance. Where the DCI was more inclined to put things into action, the psychologist had a different perspective, his maps and statistics making pictures he could follow in his mind. The first few days of any murder case were crucial before the trail grew cold and the traces were overlaid by numerous contacts.

Today Lorimer was meeting the partners of Forbes Macgregor. He'd toyed with the idea of asking them all to meet here but had decided on balance that their own territory was better: they'd be more inclined to relax in familiar surroundings, if they could relax at all after the events of the last few days. Lorimer nibbled his fingernail. Should he let them know about Michael Turner? Or would his hunch about the missing man being found dead come to pass sooner than he imagined?

Graham West scrolled down the list of emails and stopped as his eye was caught by a familiar name. It couldn't be. This was surely someone's idea of a sick joke. Or a virus, maybe? No, they had all the firewalls IT could provide. Nevertheless, his fingers trembled as they moved the mouse and clicked on the line of text.

He read the message three times before printing it off. Somehow he needed to have the thing in his hand, tangible, before it would seem real. Now should he delete it? West felt sweat begin to dampen his palms. He wasn't that au fait with computer technology to know if this message could be retrieved once he'd sent it spinning into oblivion. Nor was he certain if he should obliterate it. That would prevent any reply, wouldn't it? And the message very plainly demanded some response.

As West sat staring at the screen his mind was whirling. Was this a hoax? Should he turn it over to the others? Was his passport up to date? This last thought crept in unbidden and Graham West realized he was shivering badly with shock. Not only was he looking at a demand that could break his career but that demand seemed to be coming from beyond the grave.

At last he took a breath and pressed the reply button. With shaking fingers he tapped out the words: give me time.

'Got a minute, Graham?' Alec Barr's head appeared beside the door so suddenly that West's hand caught the sheaf of papers that had been balancing on top of his in-tray, sending them tumbling to the floor. Hiding his confusion, he scrambled below the desk, retrieving the scattered documents then stood up, looking at Barr.

'Something wrong?' the managing partner asked, his eyes narrowing shrewdly. 'You look as though you've seen a ghost.'

West's jaw dropped. How could he – had he been emailed too? 'I . . .' Words failed to issue from his lips and he found himself sitting down, the bunch of papers still clutched in both hands.

'What's up, Graham?' Barr was standing over him now, his brows drawn down.

'Nothing. I just felt a bit faint when I bent down, that's all. No breakfast. Probably low blood sugar, shouldn't have worked out at the gym so early . . .' he gabbled. 'Did you want something, Alec?'

Barr frowned as if he were about to speak, then gave his head a tiny shake. 'Just to let you know the police will be in at two-thirty this afternoon. We're meeting them in the boardroom. Okay?'

Graham West swallowed hard. Police. He'd forgotten about them but as Barr's eyes bored into his face, he replied. 'Fine. Fine. Thanks.'

Barr nodded then, turning at the door, he paused. 'Sure you're all right, Graham? Anything troubling you, you just need to come to me. Okay?'

'Of course. Thanks.' West felt the moisture trickle down the back of his shirt as Barr finally left the room. What had he done? Why hadn't he taken the opportunity to tell Alec about the message that lay mixed up in all these papers?

Sinking back into the chair, he knew the decision had been made. He'd follow up this poisonous demand and this time he'd do it on his own.

'Ha! We've landed a fish!' JJ chuckled and rubbed his hands with the sort of glee that reminded Michael of the pantomime villains of his youth. Only this man wasn't playing a part. His antics were for real. 'One of your old bosses, isn't it?' he asked.

The two men were sitting side by side, gazing at the laptop between them. Graham West's reply had appeared on the screen: give me time, it said. A short response but one that told Michael Turner plenty. He was scared, that was one thing. And he'd probably have to involve other people. But would he come up with the sort of money JJ was demanding? Michael Turner's head was spinning. JJ had revealed the price that he'd been paid for Michael's execution, chuckling, 'Who wants to kill you that bad, son?'

Who indeed? Michael wondered. Duncan Forbes had assured him that everything would be fine. And he'd believed him. But after the last few days anything was possible, even the thought that Duncan had sent him into the arms of an assassin.

So why hadn't *he* returned this email? Why had the answer come from Graham West? Michael glanced at his companion who was busy tapping away on the keyboard. There were things JJ wasn't telling him.

'Just how much do you know about all this?' Michael asked.

The older man tapped the side of his nose. 'Enough,' he said, then smiled to himself as his attention was taken up once again with the information on the screen.

Michael sighed. He'd dropped out of the world days ago, or was it weeks? No newspapers or radio had come his way, only that endless stream of country music that JJ had insisted on playing all the way down from New York. A hunger to know what was happening on the other side of the world was gnawing away at him. There was a land line here. The laptop was plugged into a wall socket so there had to be a telephone but so far he'd been unable to find any trace of a handset or even a mobile phone, though he was certain JJ had one somewhere. One call, that's all he wanted to make, just one call to see if there was any way out of this crazy mess.

CHAPTER 33

Detective Chief Inspector Lorimer and Dr Solomon Brightman stepped into the foyer and hurried across to the lift just as it was closing. A young woman carrying a bundle of buff-coloured files avoided making eye contact with these two strangers who had so abruptly invaded her space. Lorimer pressed the button and felt the lift shudder a little as it ascended. It was an old building and not every attempt at modernization had succeeded, he thought, stepping out as the lift doors opened again. Solomon, glancing behind, caught her curious stare before the young woman dropped her gaze.

Forbes Macgregor's reception area consisted of a wide lobby flanked by a pair of two-seater settees and an easy chair on one side with a pair of half-glass swing doors on the other.

'Chief Inspector Lorimer,' he announced to the woman who was sitting behind a modern reception desk bearing the name Forbes Macgregor and the company's logo, a combination of the letters F and M. 'And Dr Brightman,' he added, indicating the figure standing to his right. 'Mr Barr is expecting us,' he said, though that was not strictly true. Solly's presence had been an afterthought and the DCI had deliberately left him out of the picture until now. He didn't want any of them to think too much about a psychologist sitting in on their meeting. The woman smiled at them and came round from her place behind the desk.

'Please take a seat. Can I take your coats?' she asked, lifting Lorimer's off his arm before he could reply and hanging it on a stand behind her desk. Solomon smiled and shook his head, but unravelled his enormous knitted scarf from around his neck, letting it fall in two garish strips either side of his shoulders. The receptionist frowned at Solly then pursed her mouth in disapproval. 'I'll let Mr Barr know you're here then,' she said firmly, motioning the visitors towards the seating area.

Lorimer listened as she spoke into the telephone, noticing how her Glasgow accent changed to a more formal tone. The woman caught his eye to let him know their arrival had been dealt with and he smiled back at her. She reminded him of someone, but for the moment he couldn't think who it was. Lorimer studied the receptionist as she continued to answer calls. She was a slightly built, middle-aged woman whose sharp features and determined mouth brooked no nonsense. Her short grey hair and olive cardigan were neat but unprepossessing. Most receptionists nowadays seemed turned out from the same sleek mould of perfect make-up, sharp suits and long, straightened hair so it was interesting to see that Forbes Macgregor had deviated from that image. It showed something like confidence, Lorimer thought, as they waited for the managing partner to appear. Perhaps it was a deliberate attempt to show their clientele that this was an old-established firm with traditional values. He smiled to himself at his attempt to read something into a seemingly insignificant situation. Maybe it was Solly's influence. They were probably short-staffed and the woman was merely filling in.

The movement from the swing doors alerted Lorimer and he looked up to see the managing partner coming towards them, the smile and outstretched hand tokens of welcome.

'This is Dr Brightman from the University of Glasgow. He's helping us with our investigation,' Lorimer explained. The two men shook hands briefly and then Barr turned abruptly on his heel.

'Good to see you, Chief Inspector . . . Doctor,' Alec Barr began. 'We all hope this dreadful matter can be resolved as soon as possible.' The man's voice lowered in deference to the dead woman, reminding Lorimer of the first time he had seen Jennifer Hammond. Her red hair and winning smile suddenly flashed through his mind. Following Barr into the main office area, Lorimer was aware of his fists clenched in anger at whoever had taken away the life of such a vibrant woman. He took several deep breaths. This was going to be a difficult meeting and he required clarity, not passion, in order to focus on each of Forbes Macgregor's four remaining Glasgow partners.

'After you, gentlemen.' Barr stepped aside and ushered Lorimer and Solly into a wide room with double windows that faced out onto the river. Around a massive oval table sat three people who all looked up as he entered the room. There was a certain wariness about each of them, Lorimer thought, noting the two men on either side of the table, one rising from his chair to shake the detective's hand, the other sitting motionless, following the action with eyes that seemed sunk into his head.

'Graham West.' The man let go of Lorimer's hand and attempted a smile.

'Catherine Devoy,' Barr said, indicating the woman who now stood near the head of the table, her hands clasped in front of her. Lorimer made towards her but she merely inclined her head in greeting. 'And Malcolm Adams,' Barr continued, his hand on Lorimer's elbow.

The man across the table did not attempt to stand but simply nodded. 'Chief Inspector,' he said in a voice that was barely a whisper. Lorimer took in the gaunt face and pallid complexion. Unless he was much mistaken, Malcolm Adams was one very sick individual. Had he come in especially for this meeting? Lorimer wondered, but he had no more time to reflect as Barr was now taking his place beside the Devoy woman and indicating that the chief inspector should chair the meeting from the top of the table.

Solly was introduced briefly to the others then took his place to one side in a shadowy corner behind Lorimer where he could observe the proceedings without actually taking part. The woman had stared at him curiously for a moment then looked away as if he was of no significance to this meeting.

Lorimer sat down, wondering where to begin. He'd prepared several versions of an opening preamble in his mind, but now that he was under the scrutiny of these people he wanted to get straight to the point.

'As you know, there is an investigation under way into the deaths of Miss Hammond and your former partner, Mr Forbes. I'm afraid to have to confirm that this is now being treated as a murder inquiry.' He paused just long enough to observe their reaction. Barr's face did not alter at all but the two other men showed signs of agitation. Graham West sat back in his chair, hands out of sight, but Lorimer could almost sense the fingernails pressing into the soft flesh of his fingers. Malcolm Adams had opened his mouth in dismay, his eyes staring at Lorimer before looking at each of the others in turn.

'Are you sure, Chief Inspector?' Catherine Devoy shook her head slightly as if there was some mistake. 'We thought Duncan's death had been . . . an accident,' she said.

Lorimer noticed the deliberate pause in her voice, the subtlest of innuendos. Duncan was drunk, she was telling him. Duncan was an alcoholic. Lorimer looked more closely at the woman who had not simply been one of Forbes' colleagues, but a family friend, godmother to his son. Her well-plucked eyebrows were arched in a question above a pair of eyes that stared straight at him. Catherine Devoy was an attractive woman in her forties, slim and neat, her dark hair fashioned in a modern cut. This was not the sort of person who would command attention like the Jennifer Hammonds of this world. Rather, she held herself in as if more might be revealed, but only on her terms. Given her relationship to the Forbes family, Lorimer had expected a warmer response from the woman. Her apparent lack of emotion made him curious. How would Solly be assessing her?

'Duncan Forbes was a good man,' Adams whispered breathily, his voice weak but insistent.

'We all took it for an accident, Chief Inspector,' Barr put in gruffly. 'Can't think of anything other than that. Tragic accident. Of course it was,' he insisted. Lorimer did not reply for a moment. That was what anybody would want to think, he told himself. People always needed a reasonable explanation. Murder was never going to happen on their doorstep.

'I'm afraid our investigation shows that Mr Forbes and Miss Hammond were murdered,' Lorimer told them quietly. 'Probably by the same killer.'

'No! Not Jennifer!' Graham West's face registered a look of horror. Then Adams' hissing intake of breath made all of them turn to look at him, but he merely shook his head, as if the news were too shocking for words. Barr's frown roamed round each of the partners in turn. Was he, too, suffering the disbelief that so often followed such dramatic news?

'How can we help?' Barr said suddenly, his hands open in a gesture of resignation. Lorimer nodded slightly at the man. He'd been swift to endorse the authority of the police and now he was moving on to the next stage. Lorimer was impressed. It was not surprising that Barr had risen to the top in what was a competitive profession, Lorimer thought. He might mourn the passing of his colleagues but there was no sentimentality in Alec Barr, just a steely determination to put things right. It was a relief that at least one of them was trying to see things from the police point of view.

'First of all I'd like you to tell me about the night Duncan Forbes died. I know it has not been an easy time for you all and I would appreciate your help here.'

'Well, where should we begin?' Barr asked, folding his arms.

Lorimer smiled thinly. 'At police headquarters, Mr Barr. We would like to speak to every one of you in private.'

'So why bring us all in here?' Graham West protested but stopped as Barr turned a disapproving look his way.

'To let you all know what is happening in the case,' Lorimer replied, as politely as he could. 'It's rather odd, don't you think, that three people from the same firm should suddenly meet their fate in a short space of time?' He looked intently at each of their faces as he spoke. Barr stared at him with the same unchanging expression, but Catherine Devoy had turned away and was searching in her handbag. Malcolm Adams was shaking his head and Graham West sat with his mouth pursed, as if afraid to say any more.

They're terrified, Lorimer thought, wondering if Solly was sharing his impression.

'Is there any reason to think that somebody is stalking members of our firm, Chief Inspector?' Barr suddenly asked.

A good card to play, Lorimer thought, mentally approving the man's strategy.

'Surely we're not in any danger?' West blurted out.

'The inquiry is still in its early stages, sir,' Lorimer replied, answering West rather than the managing partner. 'We do have several means of determining the sort of person who carried out these acts,' he added, stifling a grin as he thought of the bearded individual who was sitting in their midst. 'I would like to ask for your cooperation at every level. While we are not yet certain of any links to the firm itself, there is every possibility that we may need to look more closely at this building and the staff.' Lorimer paused again. Catherine Devoy was blowing her nose. Maybe her outward calm was simply a veneer? He looked for signs of red-rimmed eyes but could see none.

'Michael Turner . . .' He paused; the temptation to reveal the truth about that corpse in the woods was growing ever stronger. 'It was after his party that Duncan

Forbes died. That's something we have been examining very closely,' he told them.

Barr nodded, his face creased in frowns, 'Terrible business that, just terrible.' He looked up, 'And you think his death might have something to do with this case?'

Lorimer inclined his head but said nothing. An ambiguous gesture, it was designed to let them all think what they liked. But one thing was interesting. Alec Barr might present a gruff exterior but, unlike the others, he was finding it far from easy to refer to his dead colleagues by name.

'What about the press?' West asked suddenly.

'We've put things into motion so there will be minimal coverage of the case,' Lorimer told them. 'But it will leak out eventually. Given a large firm such as yours, it's inevitable. But we are trying to contain information as best we can,' he continued smoothly. 'Meantime I suggest you give every cooperation to any of our investigating team who may be visiting the firm.'

Lorimer watched the effect of his final words. Barr remained quite still, his gaze on the policeman's face, but Graham West glanced around anxiously at the others who refused to meet his eyes. Malcolm Adams seemed even more tense and drawn and the woman had sunk back into her chair, half hidden by the managing partner's bulky figure.

'That you away, sir?' The receptionist helped Lorimer into his coat, holding it up high. He smiled as he bent his knees to let her slide it over his shoulders. 'Mind how ye go, now,' the woman added sternly, her eye suddenly on Solly who was occupied with winding his scarf back around his neck. There was a fearless quality about this wee person, Lorimer thought as he walked out of the office. She'd be polite enough but stand no nonsense from anybody, even a senior officer from Strathclyde Police.

'That's who she reminds me of,' he told Solly. 'Put her in a white overall and pull back that grey hair from her face and she'd be a dead ringer for Sadie Dunlop,' he exclaimed.

'Ah yes,' Solly's eyes twinkled in recognition, 'the scourge of the police canteen.' He looked at his companion. Lorimer seemed animated suddenly. Had he seen all the signs Solly hoped he had? Back in that room there had been enough material to create a whole term's worth of seminars on behavioural psychology. Some of the partners had said little but their unspoken language had told the psychologist much, much more.

CHAPTER 34

Glasgow on an April evening was not the grey post-industrial city many people might imagine, thought Solly as he turned from Great Western Road towards the park that would lead to his home. Music floated out from the open doors of a church on the corner, something hymn-like, he thought. Then the sounds were overlaid by the liquid notes of a bird, making the psychologist look upwards. The bird sat on a rhododendron branch, its neck stretched out as the song emanated from its throat. A thrush, Solly decided, noting the creamy yellow breast with its pattern of dark-brown speckles. He passed two schoolgirls who were deep in conversation, utterly oblivious to the free performance being given from the branches above. Each of them wore a black cotton skirt and T-shirt, no sign of a jacket or cardigan to cover their bare arms. Young ones never felt the cold, his mother used to say. He smiled, remembering her voice. A Jewish mother who had never scolded, always encouraged her brood, Ma Brightman's home had been the magnet for all their friends. Solly smiled again. She'd have stopped to listen to that bird, too.

There was something in the air, Solly told himself as he left the thrush singing its melody over again. Now that the days were lengthening and there was enough warmth to allow these girls to cast off their winter garments, there was a sense of impending pleasures to come: summer was only a few weeks off now that the final term had begun. In London the deckchairs might already be out in Hyde Park. April was a strange month up here. One day could be warm enough to encourage those clouds of mayflies that hovered over the river Kelvin, Solly thought, observing their mad dance. The next day could see snow or hail blotting out the hills he loved to see from his windows high above the city. It was a place of many contrasts, Solly had found, and he liked that.

The psychologist stopped by the front door of the elegant terrace and glanced down at the park below. Already the spring flowers were carpeting the edges of Kelvin Way and the formal beds beside the Art Gallery. He breathed in deeply, glad to be alive on a day like this. Anyone seeing the beatific smile half-hidden below his beard would have known that this was a man at peace with himself.

Rosie was singing along to something on the radio as he stepped into the flat and he watched her for a moment before she turned and came swiftly towards him and flung herself into his arms. Solly sighed happily as he enveloped her in a hug, her blonde head snuggled neatly against his shoulder. Wasn't it funny how he had never missed having a woman in his life? And yet now he could not imagine his world being complete without Rosie in it.

It was dark outside, the uncurtained windows showing a starless sky, as Solly lay on his back, pondering the events of his day. Beside him Rosie's warm body snuggled under the duvet, an invisible but vital presence. After his meeting with Lorimer he had been to see the factor of Riverside Gardens, asking to see the flat where Jennifer Hammond had lived and died. There he had stood, silently watching the cars go by across the bridge, a never-ending stream of humanity on endless journeys. The flat itself had depressed him. Empty of any life, the leftovers of her existence seemed to be mocking the world that the young victim had enjoyed. As he lay in the darkness, Solly recalled the sleek kitchen with its functional machines. The fridge was still to be emptied of its pitiful contents: a solitary croissant shedding its crumbs onto the bare shelves below, a half-packet of butter past its sell-by date and a couple of ready meals. Solly had looked intently at the dead woman's choice of foodstuffs. Salmon in a white wine sauce and a pack of sushi: what did that tell him? he'd shrugged. A predilection for fishy foods wouldn't reveal much in the way of her character, but it did show that she was someone who probably ate out a great deal and enjoyed the finer things of life. Twin circles on the bottle container of the refrigerator made Solly look closer. The ridged patterns resembled the underside of champagne bottles. There were traces that looked like dried spilt milk, yellowing under the darker patterns, and bits of greenery had been caught between the glass shelving and a grubby salad basket. Jennifer Hammond had not been a domestic goddess.

Looking through the dead woman's wardrobe had revealed numerous boxes of high-heeled designer shoes; he'd seen others shoved in a jumble of handbags and hatboxes below the rows upon rows of clothes that hung uselessly from their double rails. She'd had a love for colour, a zest for living, he could see that easily from the bedroom's decor alone. But she'd been a woman in a hurry, never spending enough time on her own to tidy or sort things out. Rosie was inclined to be messy around the flat, rushing off to work and leaving their bed unmade, but this woman's flat had been a temporary refuge, not a home. Even the exotically furnished boudoir (for there was no other word for it, Solly told himself) had the appearance of a carefully designed place to make love rather than somewhere to rest and relax.

She'd been careless with her possessions but had she also been careless with herself? Solly thought not. There was a lavishness in her home that spoke of a person who had relished her life, not discarded it in an impulsive moment. No. Jennifer Hammond had been murdered, of that Solly was certain. But as he looked into the patches of cloud that were scudding across the night sky he could not begin to imagine who would have wanted to kill the vivacious redhead. Nor why.

'Right, any feedback from yesterday's meeting?' Lorimer's voice could not hide its eagerness, a fact that amused the psychologist. The DCI would love an instant answer if it could be somehow magically conjured out of the air. But Solomon Brightman did not work like that.

'Not yet.' He chuckled, imagining the detective's crestfallen expression. 'But I do have some observations written down about each of those four people.' He paused, reflecting on their responses to Lorimer's revelation about the double murder case. Some interesting things had been noted but he was not ready to draw any firm conclusions about them. 'No profile, though, not yet,' he repeated. 'When will you bring them in for more questioning?'

'Soon. I'll let you know. You can be there, I presume?' Lorimer asked, a new edge to his voice.

'Oh, yes. Just let me know when, so I can rearrange my timetable,' Solly told him politely. He could hear the frustration in Lorimer's voice as the telephone call ended. Smiling to himself, Solly nodded. So much could be gleaned from the disembodied human voice. He would be interested to know how a sound analyst might interpret the DCI's conversation.

The psychologist sat staring into space. Before him

the computer screen showed a map of the river Clyde with several large dots placed at strategic points. Those dots indicated the places around the river associated with the murders and just this morning a new circle had been added, that of Graham West's penthouse flat. It was close to the human resource manager's home, perhaps less than a ten-minute walk through the car park at Springfield Quay and past the cinema. According to their information, Jennifer Hammond had left the party with Michael Turner and had later gone back to her own flat. Where had West been? It would be interesting to find out what had happened to the members of Forbes Macgregor's party as they'd made their various ways home. And what Graham West had been doing the night of the woman's murder. He recalled the horror in the man's voice as he'd blurted out, 'No! Not Jennifer!' That had given something away. He'd not wanted to make a connection between the death of the woman and his partner, Duncan Forbes. But did that mean he knew nothing about their deaths? *Duncan Forbes was a good man,*' Malcolm Adams had insisted in that throaty voice. So good that he didn't deserve to die, he might have added. Or was he trying to tell them that within that boardroom there was one among them who was the perfect antithesis of goodness?

CHAPTER 35

Graham West raised the lid of the laptop and pressed the 'on' button.

What on earth was going on here? That policeman had referred to Michael Turner's murder. He was dead; of course he was. Watching the screen flick through the preliminaries, West chewed his lip nervously. Would there be another message for him? Could a dead man really make contact from the other side? He shuddered as the thought washed over him, then gave himself a mental shake. This was just silly. Michael was gone and someone was playing games with him. But they were dangerous games and he'd be a fool to ignore them.

There were several emails but none from his mysterious correspondent, West noted with relief. A glance at his wristwatch told him it was two-thirty in the morning New York time. But why should he assume the messages were coming from across the Atlantic? Just because the guy used Michael's name didn't mean he was over there, did it? The return address was so encrypted that it would be impossible for an amateur like him to trace. But would it be beyond their own IT experts? Graham West drew a deep sigh. It was far too risky. Nobody could be party to what had been going on in his life these past few months, nobody. And yet someone out there had revealed that they had enough information to make him pay dearly for it.

The door creaked once and the man stood still, holding his breath. The silence was so intense it was almost tangible. Back in the city he had wept with frustration at the constant wail of police sirens and loud shouting from the streets. For a moment he remembered his own flat in Glasgow's Merchant City. There the night noises were friendlier: happy drunks staggering past after closing time, the sound of pigeons scratching on his windowsill, the woman downstairs singing to her wee baby. The tenement where he'd lived contained a hotch-potch of people, from student rentals to the newer residents like Michael who had invested before they were priced out of the market. And he'd been so keen to get away from all of that, he thought. Going to seek pastures new, the Big Apple. God! What he'd give to turn back the clock and be in Glasgow now.

Unbidden, Michael gave a sob then stopped in horror as the sound seemed to fill the space outside the room. To waken JJ might be more than his life was worth. Literally. The bathroom was at the end of a narrow corridor. All he needed to do was have a swift look around for another telephone point somewhere down low near the skirting board. Then he'd flush the toilet and JJ would assume he was taking a leak. Michael blinked, peering through the darkness. There was no artificial light outside in this remote hideaway but he could see a pale stream of moonlight wash through the bathroom window. He hunkered down, trying to make out any tell-tale crevices along the wall but there were none that he could see. Might as well have a piss, he thought, realizing that nerves had made his bladder full.

The trickle of water into the bowl sounded suddenly loud and he wondered if his captor would come running along the corridor, gun in hand. For a moment the image made him want to giggle, it was so absurd. But the moment died as he pulled up his trousers. This was mad, but not in any way funny. What he had found out in Glasgow was having serious repercussions in this back-woods shanty. Duncan Forbes had said it would be all right, but he had lied. It was most definitely not all right and now he was somewhere in the southern states of America with a hired killer who was trying to blackmail one of Duncan's partners.

He pulled the chain and heard the water thundering from the cistern.

'Feelin' hungry?'

Michael jumped at the voice behind him, then turned to see JJ's unshaven face grinning at him from the corri-dor. The moonlight glinted off the weapon in his hands.

232

'Fancy somethin' myself. How about it?'

Michael hesitated, his eyes on the gun.

'Go fix us a sandwich and a beer,' JJ commanded, watching as Michael backed out of the bathroom and felt his way back up the corridor in the dark.

Michael made his way slowly towards the kitchenette, hand trailing against the wall. JJ had to go to the toilet some time and now was the best chance he'd have to locate a telephone point. Switching on the light, he eyed the counter where the bags of groceries had been. There was an old-fashioned Dualit toaster and a stack of crockery under the overhanging shelves. Frantically he searched the entire room, but there was nothing.

Hearing the sounds from the bathroom, he whipped open the refrigerator door and began pulling out the makings of a snack. The bread rolls were in the salad compartment and as he bent to pull them out it dawned on him that he couldn't see where the appliance was plugged in. He shuffled on his knees, craning his neck around to see the space behind the fridge.

For a moment he was disappointed, but then he saw it. Under what must have been years of dirt and thick layers of cobwebs, the electric cable was plugged into the wall at the back. And right next to that was an empty telephone socket.

JJ's footsteps brought Michael to his feet and he threw some salad into the sink and turned on the cold tap, first rinsing the dustballs off his fingers. He sensed the man standing in the doorway but did not turn around, making a show of running each lettuce leaf under the water. Michael realized that he had been holding his breath as he heard JJ grunt and move on down the corridor. He finished making up the rolls, pulled out a couple of cans then carried the lot back through to the main living room.

The older man had lit the paraffin lamp next to the window, creating a reflection of the interior. One false move on his part and JJ would see him. Best to play dumb for now, Michael thought, sitting back into the chair where he had fallen asleep some hours before. He had found one thing that might bring him closer to escaping this gunman. A little more patience and he might just find the handset that had been plugged into that disused telephone socket.

'You're slipping, pal.' The man slapped Graham West on the shoulder as they left the squash court. West mustered a grin to Frank who was whistling cheerfully on his way to the locker room, but his expression changed to one of anxiety as soon as the other man was out of sight.

He *was* slipping. It was true. West had to admit that he wasn't able to concentrate on anything, especially at work. The deadlines for reports had come and gone and still they sat in his desk drawer. He wasn't sleeping at night, despite the large amount of brandy he'd consumed; alcohol might dull the senses but it only seemed to keep him in a state of permanent half-wakefulness. A bad conscience, his granny would have told him. And she'd be right.

West towelled his hair slowly, feeling the ache in his skull. He hurt all over these days. It was as if his former level of fitness had suddenly deserted him, leaving him with a body that seemed unfamiliar, alien. Was this what happened when insanity took a hold of you? Did your physical self disintegrate along with your mental faculties? Get a grip, he told himself fiercely. This will all go away in time. Just ignore it. No one can hurt you. It's only words.

But the words had become more and more menacing and West no longer knew whether he could take the risk of refusing to meet the demands of this person who used the name of a dead man.

'He's bitten!' JJ's glee could not be contained.

'What d'you mean?'

JJ looked over his shoulder, a cigarette dangling from the corner of his mouth. 'Your pal back in Scotland. He's coming up with the goods.'

'How?'

'Banking on the net. Simple as taking candy from a baby,' he crowed. 'My account'll show a certain . . . increase in funds, then I take off for the good life,' JJ told him.

What about me? Michael Turner wanted to ask, but the words stuck in his throat. That was a question that didn't need any answer. Now that his usefulness was at an end, why should this thug bother to keep him alive?

CHAPTER 36

'Aunty Cath?'

'Is that you, Philip? Are you home?'

'I've been home for a few days, actually. Just got round to calling you, that's all.'

Catherine Devoy listened to the catch in her god-son's throat. He was trying to sound grown up, be the man of the house, but the gruffness failed to mask the yearning in his voice. Whenever things went wrong Philip had always called her: exam results, the problems with Duncan over this gap year. Once he'd even asked her advice about girls. Catherine's face softened as she imagined the boy standing in the hallway of Mansewood. She'd always been fond of Philip, especially as a baby. She had been happy to babysit for them in the days when Liz and Duncan had been enjoying themselves at all those corporate bashes, and the two Forbes children had always called her 'Aunty' as if she had really been one of the family.

That had been part of the trouble, Catherine acknowledged to herself; having a ready-made family and none of her own. Had that been the underlying reason why she'd never come to the marriage bed? Had her life been too convenient; a lover who was inaccessible and a career that gave her so much satisfaction?

'Aunty Cath? Are you still there?'

'Yes, sorry, Philip,' Catherine Devoy sighed. This was going to be difficult. 'What can I do for you?'

There was a silence, then, '*Do* for me? I didn't ring you to ask for anything.' The boy's voice rose in irritation. 'I just wanted to talk to you. About Dad,' he added finally.

Catherine sighed again. 'Of course you do, dear, but the phone's maybe not the best way to have a discussion like this. How about meeting up? Can you come into town or would you like me to come over after work?' She crossed her fingers. Say you'll come in, she begged silently. Say you'll come in.

'Don't mind, really. Mum and Janey are here all day with the baby. Wouldn't mind getting out for a bit, to be honest.' His voice dropped to a whisper. Catherine smiled. Philip wouldn't want to offend his mother or sister by letting them hear his last words. How like Duncan he was in that respect: a decent, nice young man who only wanted to make his family happy and proud of him. Duncan had been just the same in the old days when she'd first known him.

'Well, how about this afternoon? We could meet up town somewhere.' She thought quickly. It would have to be somewhere private where the boy could open his heart to her. 'Do you know Tchai-Ovna?'

'Oh, that wee place off Gibson Street? The one where we heard that old poet?'

'That's the one. See you . . . about three o'clock, say?'

'Okay,' the boy replied, a new jauntiness in his tone. 'It'll be great to see you, Aunty Cath.' There was another pause. 'I've missed you.'

The woman put down the phone then slumped over her desk. God, she was weary! It took all her reserves of strength just to get up in the morning, go to work and remember that she would never see Duncan Forbes again. Now she had to face his son. How on earth would she find the answers to any questions he might ask when she was too afraid to confront them herself?

The different scented teas and home baking gave the place a warm and comforting feel, thought Philip Forbes as he ducked his head under the low entry. Tchai-Ovna had been a regular student hang-out for many of his female friends at Glasgow University; Philip could recall nights gathered around the mismatched tables and oriental couches where they'd spent hours putting the world to rights. And there had been that time with Aunty Cath when he'd listened to recitations from Edwin Morgan. He'd not understood everything but had picked up the gist of what was being read. Some of it had been unsettling and, remembering that, Philip suddenly felt the same emotion of unease wash over him.

There were several people in the tea room already so Philip chose an empty corner-table where he could watch the doorway to see his godmother arrive. His eyes drifted around the room, taking in the posters advertising literary readings and musical events. Behind him was an elevated area consisting of squashy cushions. It had probably been a bed recess before the old tenement flat had been pulled about to make it interesting to its present-day clientele. The tiny kitchen was out of sight from where Philip sat but he could hear dishes clattering and voices taking orders for tchais of all descriptions. When Cath arrived they would sit here and drink from some of the weird cups and containers that the owners had accumulated over the years. That was part of the place's charm, he admitted. His mother, with her preference for Royal Doulton china cups and side plates that matched, would have hated it.

'Philip.' Suddenly Cath was sitting opposite him and smiling. He wanted to stand up and hug her but he'd wedged his long frame behind the table and she was already reaching out for his hands.

'Thanks for coming,' he said gruffly, squeezing her fingers. 'Good of you to leave work and all that.'

'Oh, you rescued me from a very tedious afternoon, I can assure you, Philip. It should be me thanking you,' she retorted, noting how her words made him grin. 'Well, tell me everything about Africa,' she continued, releasing his hands and brushing back a stray lock of hair that had been blown forward in the wind outside. 'I'm sure you've had lots of adventures.'

Philip Forbes smiled again, 'Yeah, you could say. I'll have some great photos when they're developed. Though I didn't take my digital camera in case it got nicked,' he added. 'I can tell you all my stories then and you'll see the places and stuff . . .' he tailed off. His eyes dropped from her gaze. 'I really wanted to talk to you about Dad,' he mumbled.

Catherine suppressed the mounting feeling of panic that was rising in her chest. Breathe in, breathe out, she told herself. Forcing a smile, she picked up the menu. 'How about ordering first?' she asked. 'Then we'll have peace to talk.'

Across the table Philip Forbes nodded then watched as his godmother scanned the choices of exotic teas and cakes. There was something wrong. Her face bore signs of strain; lines that he'd never noticed before were etched deeply into her brow. The boy pressed his lips together. Nothing would ever be the same with Dad gone: Mum was in pieces, Janey went about like a cold hard icicle that might shatter if you pushed it too hard and now even Aunty Cath had changed. What had he expected? That she'd be untouched by his father's death? She'd seen him day and daily, though, hadn't she? Worked with him for years, been part of all their lives, so why had he expected Catherine Devoy to have been immune from all of this awfulness? Studying her face, Philip wondered. Had his father ever been more to Cath than just a good friend and colleague? There was something darker in her manner, he thought, something that told of a deeper sorrow.

'You're staring at me, Philip,' Catherine said evenly. 'What is it? Have I a dirty mark on my nose?'

Philip blushed and hung his head but was rescued from the moment by the waiter coming to take their order.

'Shall I be mother?' Catherine asked lightly. Philip nodded as he watched her pour their tea into deep earthenware bowls. The steam rose, making him shiver as he realized how cold it was inside the room. But then he'd been feeling the cold ever since his return.

'About Dad,' Philip began. 'He didn't really go on a binge did he?'

The woman opposite shook her head and he was pained to see a single tear trickle down her cheek. 'Cath?' he said, not quite sure what to do.

'I'm sorry, Philip. It's just horrible talking about it,' she sniffed. 'No, I don't think your dad ever touched the bottle again,' she continued. 'In fact I remember he was drinking orange juice on the night that . . .'

'The night that he died,' Philip finished quietly. 'Cath, what really happened? Do you know? Nobody's telling me anything,' he burst out suddenly. 'I'm not a wee boy any more and I've a right to know what's been going on. Haven't I?'

Once more he felt his fingers being held in hers.

'Of course you do, dear, of course you do,' she murmured soothingly. 'At the moment the police think that Duncan was killed by somebody, but I'm not convinced they're right,' she rushed on, 'I think it must have been a terrible accident. Don't you?' she added, looking directly into his eyes.

'Well, yes, I suppose so ... I mean who would've wanted to kill my dad?' Philip felt the threat of tears and pulled his hands away to fumble in his pocket for a hanky. Dad had always made him carry one when he was a child and the habit had stuck.

Remembering his dad's face and the way he used to run his fingers through his thatch of hair made Philip bury his face in the handkerchief and choke back a sob. For a moment he closed his eyes, then he turned aside and blew noisily into the crumpled hanky.

'Sorry,' he mumbled, glancing across at his godmother.

Catherine Devoy was shaking her head, her eyes bright with tears. 'No need to be,' she whispered. 'If we can't cry now, when can we?' She smiled tremulously at the boy.

Philip sipped his tea then cupped the bowl in his hands, blowing across the surface to cool it down.

'Too hot?'

'A wee bit. But it's better without milk, isn't it?'

Catherine shrugged. She'd always liked her tea with a good splash of milk, even Earl Grey. But Duncan had been a purist about tea, she remembered. Like father, like son, she thought sadly.

'Aunty Cath,' the boy began and hesitated.

Catherine steeled herself for more probing questions but was surprised when he asked, 'What shall

I do now I'm back? Shouldn't I be coming into the office?'

The woman simply stared at him, a look of utter blankness on her face. It was only natural that Philip Forbes would want to begin his career as an accountant. It had been Duncan's intention for years to bring the boy into the firm and none of them had objected, especially when he'd obtained such a good degree. On the contrary, all the partners had agreed it would be right to continue a thread of the family line. So why had she forgotten about this?

'Aunty Cath?' The boy prompted her. 'What do you think?'

Catherine Devoy swallowed hard. This was going to be difficult.

'I think,' she began gently, 'that you should look elsewhere for employment, Philip.'

'But why? Forbes Macgregor was Dad's firm and his father's and grandfather's before him!' Philip's eyes were angry and puzzled.

'Things have changed, Philip,' the woman began. 'Listen,' she said firmly, 'you've always trusted me, haven't you?'

The boy nodded.

'Well, I think you might as well know that things aren't great in the accountancy world right now and Forbes Macgregor may not weather the storm that some of the financial pundits tell us is coming.' She leaned forward and lowered her voice. 'This is absolutely confidential, do you understand, Philip? Word of this in the financial press would be disastrous for the firm.'

She watched the boy as he sat back, frowning. This was hard for him to accept. And, anyway, did he believe her? A slight shake of his head told Catherine that he was stunned by this news but the look he gave her showed more supplication than scepticism.

'What should I do, then?'

Catherine sat back, relieved. He was accepting her at her word as he always did, thank God. 'Go into industry. And spread your wings, Philip. No need to stay in Glasgow to work. There are greater opportunities south of the border. Or beyond,' she told him, trying to sound enthusiastic. 'And,' she breathed hard, hating herself for playing this trump card, 'it's what your dad would have wanted you to do.'

'But what about Mum? We've not even had a funeral yet.'

'No need to worry your mother, Philip. Just begin to look in the papers, register with a few of the better agencies. I'll even see what I can find out on the grapevine, shall I?'

The boy nodded slowly. 'Okay. I suppose.' His mouth was turned down in a sulk.

'Philip?'

He shrugged. 'Bit of a surprise, that's all. Suppose I should've kept in touch more with what's been happening.'

'Not many people are aware of all this,' she answered him grimly. 'Take my word for it.'

'Right. And thanks,' he said, his young face looking up at her. 'Knew I could trust you to sort things out. Dad always said you were the best brain in the place.' He smiled.

Catherine Devoy returned her godson's smile but inwardly a voice was crying out, Dear God! What have we done to you, Philip?

CHAPTER 37

Philip sat back on his heels and sighed. They weren't in any of the likely places. He'd tried his own room and the downstairs study but nothing had come to hand. The certificates had been put into a blue folder, he remembered. He'd been so certain they'd be in his desk drawer but when he'd opened it everything was neat and tidy, but there was no folder. Okay, he'd been away for months and Mum was a stickler for keeping things in order but surely she wouldn't have shifted all his SCE certificates and his degree parchment?

'We'll need to have this framed.' His dad's words came so suddenly to mind that Philip found himself fighting back the tears. It seemed just like yesterday they'd all been sitting around a table in Stravaigin toasting his health and his future. What sort of future would he have now? The bitter thought dried his eyes and he stood up, looking down the length of his father's study. He ran a finger over the bookshelf behind the huge oak desk. The resulting smear of grey bore testament to the fact that nobody had been in here to dust in weeks, not even their cleaning lady. Dad's old desk looked exactly the same as it always had, the family photos angled so he could glance at them as he worked. Philip slipped into the chair, drawn by a sudden urge to see what his father had seen, feel what he might have felt as he'd sat here night after night, working on stuff for the office.

He'd never heard his dad complaining about the hours he'd put in: never heard him moaning about work at all. Forbes Macgregor had been such a big part of his life, all their lives, that it seemed wrong that Philip wouldn't be continuing the family tradition of working in the elegant red stone building by the Clyde. He stared into space, willing some vision of his father to come to him then, to explain whatever had happened, but all Philip could see was his godmother's face smiling at him.

Right, that was it, he thought, rising from the desk. He shouldn't be wallowing in self-pity; Dad would've hated that. He'd really have to find that folder if he wanted to take Cath's advice and look for a job. Maybe Mum had put them in the hall bureau. With another sigh, he slouched along the corridor, sunlight from the study window following him.

The bureau was always full of stuff that his parents liked to keep. Philip sat down heavily on the carpet and opened it up. Here things were a lot less tidy, he thought as a bundle of papers tied in pink legal ribbon came to hand. A faint smile dawned over his face as he recognized the school reports and the daft hand-made Easter cards he and Janey had made all those years ago. Fancy Mum keeping all that stuff! Philip flicked slowly through the bundle then laid it aside. No. It was definitely a blue folder he was looking for. Opening the drawer wider, he began pulling out what looked like architect's drawings on squared paper; a project for the extension to the kitchen that had never happened. Maybe his certificates were underneath this lot? Yes! He lifted the envelope bearing the University of Glasgow crest and drew out the paper proclaiming that he, Philip Kenneth Forbes, was now a *Magistrum Artium cum honoribus secundae classis*. For a second he regarded the parchment with a wistful pride then put it to one side as he continued his search for the other certificates.

Aunty Cath had reminded him he might need more than just his degree when he went for interviews. Some companies liked to know what you'd achieved at school, she'd said. It gave them an insight into your other skills.

Philip pulled out the remaining papers but his certificates were nowhere to be seen. Had they fallen down the back of the cabinet? Kneeling down, Philip peered into the space beyond the back of the drawer. There *was* something there, he realized, his hand feeling around. But it didn't feel like papers, it was something hard and square in shape. His fingers closed over the object and he drew it out carefully, the narrow space causing the drawer frame to graze the back of his hand.

It was a music box. He turned the thing in his hands. It was made from heavy green china with a gold lyre embossed on its lid. He remembered this old box. Hadn't it used to sit on Mum's dressing table? What tune had it played? Squatting down before the bureau, Philip instinctively turned the key. Nothing happened. Puzzled, he turned the box upside down and shook it gently. A dull tinkling sound came from within. There was a small drawer above the mechanism. Carefully he pulled it open.

There! No wonder it wasn't working. Those folded letters were obviously jamming up the works. Philip pulled them out then turned the key once more. Strains of a Mozart waltz tinkled out. Sitting back, he listened as the tune played over and over until the notes slowed down and finally stopped. He'd played with that musical box as a wee boy; he remembered the effort of winding the metal key then the sheer joy of dancing round the room with his mother holding onto his chubby fingers. She wouldn't be doing any dancing now, he thought, putting the musical box back into the drawer. He'd need to find somewhere else for these letters, he told himself, absently picking them up and straightening their creases. They were addressed to Mum, both of them typed on blue envelopes.

A sudden curiosity made him pause. Why on earth had they been secreted away like that? There was a moment of reluctance when all his instincts told him this was none of his business. Glancing towards the front door, Philip listened. Everyone was out and he didn't expect them back for hours, so why was he so edgy? With a shrug he took the letters out of their envelopes and began to read.

Less than a minute later Philip Forbes sat back against the bureau. All the power seemed to have drained from his body and he felt sick. His brain whirled with possibilities. Mum was being targeted by someone: someone who was stating the most obscene and damning things in such a matter-of-fact way. Had she confronted Dad with them? He looked at the letters in his hand with disgust. No. Not if she'd hidden them. Why hadn't she just binned these horrible lies? he thought angrily. Then another idea came to his mind, an idea so awful that his whole body trembled with fear.

Detective Constable Niall Cameron leaned back. They'd been over and over these tapes until he thought he'd be seeing them in his sleep. But that was when he'd drawn himself up. What if this repetitive viewing had dulled his senses? What if he'd missed the obvious? The very idea made him go cold. Lorimer would have his guts for garters. So that was why he was sitting yet again facing the television screen, hours after he could have packed up and gone home.

The tape of Duncan Forbes staggering out of the Crowne Plaza had been played and replayed, particularly the actual sighting of the victim, the last recorded image of him alive. Cameron had decided to look elsewhere on the tape, just to satisfy himself that nothing had been overlooked; and now he'd found it. According to the video recorder a car had passed by the entrance of the hotel eight minutes and thirteen seconds before the figure of Forbes had appeared on the screen. Cameron couldn't identify the colour from the black-and-white film but it was a light shade, maybe pale grey or blue metallic, easily identifiable as a Mercedes SLK Roadster with a registration number that was now written down on the pad in front of him.

The DC lifted the telephone. A quick enquiry and he'd be a little bit wiser.

Fifteen minutes later DC Cameron was staring at the name he had written beside the registration number. A frown creased his brow then cleared as the significance of his discovery dawned on him.

'Sir.' Cameron stood in the doorway of Lorimer's office. He saw the senior investigating officer's head come up wearily and pale-blue eyes regarding him with barely concealed impatience.

'You working late, Niall? What is it?'

'Sir, I think you should see this.' Cameron handed him a sheet of paper. 'I ran the Crowne Plaza tapes again and found a car belonging to Duncan Forbes. It was being driven by a woman, by the looks of the tape, though there's only a back view.' He hesitated, watching the DCI's reaction.

'Who do you think it might be?'

Cameron shrugged. 'Mrs Forbes, perhaps? We do know that there was a regular taxi service for all the senior staff and partners, but did Duncan Forbes usually drive himself home? We know he wasn't a drinker.'

Lorimer nodded thoughtfully. Jennifer Hammond had told him as much, implying that Duncan would have taken a taxi anyway. Mrs Forbes had expected that too, hadn't she? So what had she been doing driving from the Crowne Plaza car park shortly before her husband had left the party?

'Had she been in the building at all?' he asked. 'Do we have any tapes that give us another sighting of her?'

Cameron's sigh was so audible that a smile twitched around Lorimer's mouth.

'Look, why don't we go through them together? I'm just about finished up here.' He closed the file on his desk.

'If you're sure.' Cameron brightened immediately.

'Aye, I'm sure,' Lorimer replied. Maggie was out at the theatre with a bunch of kids so there was no problem about putting in a few more hours. 'Let's see what we come up with.'

'What d'you think, sir?'

Lorimer frowned at the screen in front of him. They'd gone over this part of the tape several times now, yet he didn't want to put into words what both he and his detective constable were thinking.

'Sir?'

Heaving a sigh, Lorimer shook his head. 'Can't think why she'd do it. But we'd be derelict in our duty if we didn't investigate the possibility, now wouldn't we?'

'I never actually met her.'

Lorimer gave the ghost of a smile. 'I did. And I'd have backed my instinct that she was a genuinely grieving widow. But then we can't afford to take chances on something as flimsy as instincts, can we?'

Niall Cameron smothered the desire to laugh. Lorimer's instincts were pretty legendary. He was the sort of man who seemed to home in on situations with a kind of moral radar, one reason why the Lewisman had plenty of respect for his DCI. 'Spouses are often the perpetrators of murders,' he ventured carefully.

'Aye and clichés aren't wrong because they're so obvious,' Lorimer countered sardonically. 'Och, we'll have to go and see her.' He sighed wearily. 'Even if it's just to eliminate her from the picture.' He jerked his thumb in the direction of the video screen. 'But not tonight. How about making an appointment for us to visit first thing tomorrow?' Lorimer stretched back in the chair, hands clasped behind his head. He could do with some exercise after all the sitting. Maybe he'd still make it home before Maggie and have time for a run?

'Want me to pack this up for the night, then?'

'Aye.' Lorimer stood up and nodded to the DC. 'See you in the morning.'

*

Philip Forbes opened the door immediately after the doorbell rang. Two tall men stood there, solemn faced and regarding him with what he took to be suspicion rather than curiosity. But after a sleepless night he really couldn't be sure.

'Detective Chief Inspector Lorimer, Detective Constable Cameron.' The older of the men was holding out his warrant card for Philip to see.

'Come in,' Philip replied distractedly, opening the door wider and standing aside.

'Thank you, Mister . . . ?'

Philip was suddenly aware of a pair of keen blue eyes scrutinizing him. They made him feel awkward and guilty like a ten-year-old kid who'd tried to cover up some misdemeanor.

'Forbes,' he replied hastily. 'I'm Philip Forbes,' he added, holding out his hand in a belated attempt at civility.

The hand that took his was warm and strong and somehow reassuring. Or was it the gentle look of sympathy that had taken the ice out of that blue gaze? The nod he received from the other man was brief but his expression too showed a kindliness that Philip hadn't expected from the policemen.

'We're here to see your mother, Philip,' DCI Lorimer began.

Philip felt a shiver run down his spine but before he had time to reply a voice came from the half-landing upstairs.

'Here I am.'

All three turned to look up at the woman slowly descending the stairs. Lorimer watched as she held on to the banister for support, her eyes on each step as if she might stumble. Elizabeth Forbes was a shadow of the person he had seen only three weeks before. Her hair, thin and unkempt, was straggling about her face and her fingers seemed devoid of flesh as they clutched the wooden rail. In the silence, Lorimer could hear her breath coming in spasms as if the very effort of coming downstairs caused her pain.

'Mum.' Philip had stepped forward and was holding out his hand, ready to take his mother's arm.

'In the sitting room, Philip.' She motioned, as the final step was taken.

The two policemen followed Philip Forbes and his mother into the brightly lit room where a fire was burning in the grate. The woman sank into the same chair that she'd taken on Lorimer's previous visit but that was the only thing that seemed familiar. Her whole appearance was altered and Lorimer was curious to know just what had turned Duncan Forbes' wife into an old woman as well as a widow.

'Philip, fetch some tea for us, will you, darling?' Elizabeth Forbes touched the boy's arm gently. Lorimer caught the look of anxiety that flitted across Philip's face as he looked from his mother to the visitors. 'It's okay, I'll be fine,' she added.

Only when her son was out of earshot did the woman turn to Lorimer.

'Well, Chief Inspector. What is this about?'

'There are one or two things we would like to clear up, Mrs Forbes,' Lorimer began. 'It has come to our attention that you were in the vicinity of the Crowne Plaza Hotel on the night of your husband's death,' he said quietly.

There was no response from her but Lorimer could see her stiffen so he continued, 'You were seen on the hotel's CCTV camera leaving the car park shortly before your husband was seen coming out of the building. Perhaps you'd like to tell us why you were there? And why you failed to inform us of that before now?' Lorimer's voice remained low but there was no mistaking the gravity of his manner.

The woman looked from one man to the other, an expression of disbelief on her face. Lorimer saw the hollow eyes widen as if in fear. She remained motionless for a time, unable to take in his words, her terrified gaze fixed on Lorimer. Then Duncan Forbes' widow lowered her eyes and began to weep, her quiet sobs becoming cries of distress as she covered her face with her hands.

Lorimer glanced at Cameron, who appeared to be visibly embarrassed by this show of despair, then rose to his feet as Philip Forbes rushed into the room, his face stricken.

'Mum!' He turned wildly to the policemen. 'What have you been asking her? Why can't you leave her alone?'

'It was . . . it was . . . the . . . letters,' Liz Forbes gasped between sobs that racked her thin chest.

'Letters?' Lorimer began.

'It's nothing to do with those letters!' Philip screamed.

There was a horrified silence as Elizabeth Forbes suddenly stopped crying and looked at her son, an expression of anguish in her eyes. Lorimer took a step forward, his hand on the boy's arm. 'What letters, Philip?'

He watched as the boy turned towards his mother and in the same moment heard her groan, 'Oh, Philip!'

Lorimer saw the colour drain out of the boy's face as he realized his blunder.

'What letters, Philip?' he repeated, in a firm tone that sounded harsh even to his own ears.

'The ones in the musical box—' he faltered.

'Letters addressed to me, Chief Inspector,' Liz Forbes interrupted. 'Letters nobody was ever meant to see.' She paused and turned suddenly towards her son who winced under her glare. 'They were anonymous. Poison-pen letters.' She gave a harsh little laugh. 'God only knows why I didn't throw them out.'

'And their contents?' Lorimer persisted.

Liz Forbes shook her head, the wisps of hair falling over her ears. 'They were about Duncan,' she began, then her face crumpled again and she began to weep softly.

'Mum, oh, Mum, I'm so sorry. I didn't mean to be

257

nosy. I was only looking for my certificates.' Philip Forbes was crouched down at his mother's side, his hand stroking her arm. She patted the hand distractedly.

'That's all right, pet. You weren't to know, it's my own silly fault for keeping them.'

Lorimer cleared his throat in an effort to recapture their attention.

'I'm sorry, Chief Inspector,' she said, fumbling for a handkerchief to blow her nose. 'Phil, go and get them, will you?'

'Okay,' the boy mumbled and stood up, casting a baleful look at the two policemen.

A sigh escaped Liz Forbes as she watched her son leave the room.

'Oh, God, what must he be thinking?' She turned towards Lorimer again, 'He worshipped his dad,' she explained simply. 'This will hurt him so badly.'

Lorimer watched as she sank back into the armchair, her face tired and resigned but oddly calmer as if relieved to have this sordid little secret out in the open.

Philip returned and approached his mother, the blue envelopes in his hand but Liz Forbes motioned that he should give them to Lorimer instead.

'Thank you,' he said as the boy handed them over with obvious reluctance. 'Perhaps we need a cup of tea now?' he added and Philip nodded and left the room once more.

Lorimer's brow was furrowed as he read the contents

of the two letters. Stuff like this often came to the attention of the police: usually it was the work of some spiteful malcontent getting something off their chest.

'You believed this?' He looked directly at the woman opposite as he held the two letters between his finger and thumb like pieces of garbage.

Her look of total misery was answer enough.

'But why?' Lorimer's tone was gentler. 'Had you any reason to think badly of your husband?'

Liz dropped her gaze, shaking her head and sniffling into her handkerchief. Then she looked up again. 'It was just a feeling. He'd been hiding something from me and I thought—'

'You thought he'd been unfaithful?'

'No . . . I don't know. I didn't know what to think. Duncan and I, we've always been so close. He'd never looked at another woman.'

'But you thought these letters might be true?'

She shook her head again in despair. 'I don't know. Really I don't. I wanted to think he was always faithful. I want to remember him that way.'

'You didn't think to ask him?' The look Elizabeth Forbes shot him was answer enough. Lorimer stifled a sigh. 'So it was the letters that made you drive to the Crowne Plaza that night?'

'Yes.' She sighed deeply. 'I wanted to see for myself if there was anyone else, if it was someone in his company. I was going to go in and pretend to be there to take him home, see who was there with him.'

'And?'

'I lost my nerve.' She shivered suddenly. 'I just couldn't bear the thought that some woman in there might be laughing at me. So I just went home again.'

Lorimer believed her. It made perfect sense to him. And the woman's grief had been so genuine that first time they'd met that he could not bring himself to think she had had a hand in her husband's death. Still, the fact remained that she had been in the vicinity of the hotel.

'Mum.' Philip had returned with a huge tray full of tea things clinking together. Lorimer's eyebrows rose at the sight of the delicate china tea service being laid on the table and the young man earnestly pouring tea into cups. This one was well trained in the niceties of refined living, he thought. After a spell in the African bush he'd have expected a few mugs of tea from the young graduate rather than the best Royal Doulton or whatever it was.

'Is there anything else you want to tell us, Mrs Forbes?' Lorimer asked, once the woman had taken a few tentative sips of the hot tea.

The cup and saucer rattled as Liz put them down. 'I don't think so, Chief Inspector. I've thought and thought every night and every day since that trip to the Crowne Plaza. If I'd gone in, if I hadn't chickened out, would Duncan still be here?'

'Mum!' Philip protested. 'It's not your fault! You can't blame yourself for not doing something.' He gave her arm a little shake.

'Oh, but I do, Phil,' she replied, a tremble upon her

lip. 'I do,' she repeated in a whisper that told of yet more weeping to come.

'And you definitely didn't see your husband that night?' Lorimer asked, the question designed to focus the woman's attention back to the matter in hand.

She gazed at him for a moment without speaking. 'No. No, of course I didn't. What are you suggesting?' Her voice peaked in a note of disbelief.

Lorimer risked a glance at Niall Cameron. The detective constable's face told him everything. Cursing inwardly, he ploughed on. 'Somebody killed your husband that night. It's our job to ensure that everyone who had a reason for being in the vicinity of the hotel can account for their actions.' He paused. 'While I am happy to accept your explanation about why you were there, you must see that your previous failure to tell us about it puts you in a compromising position.'

Beside him he could sense Cameron nodding in agreement. There were certain procedures that had to be followed and, whether he liked them or not, Lorimer was duty-bound to carry them out. 'I'd be grateful if you would give a written statement of all that you've told us,' he began, trying hard not to respond to the woman's open-mouthed expression. 'It would also be helpful if you could let us know where you were on the evening of April the twenty-first,' he added quietly.

Liz Forbes turned towards her son as if for guidance, struck speechless by this last demand.

'She's been here ever since Dad died,' Philip Forbes

protested. 'Can't you see how shattered she is by all of this? Mum can't even go out by herself to the shops, never mind anything else,' he ended lamely.

'Mrs Forbes?'

Liz shook her head, 'Phil's right. I've been here all the time, except when I had to go to the mortuary,' her voice faltered.

'What's so special about that date anyway?' the boy demanded.

Lorimer looked at them both, pity in his eyes. 'That was the night Jennifer Hammond was found dead,' he answered.

'This is becoming absurd!' Philip retorted. 'Just because Mum's been the victim of some poison-pen letters you start to think she's had something to do with these . . .' He stopped suddenly, unable to complete his sentence.

'Murders, Mr Forbes,' Lorimer finished for him. 'We have to investigate all possibilities *and* eliminate any possible suspects from our inquiries,' he added. 'Surely that makes sense?'

Philip hung his head in embarrassment. 'Yes, I suppose so.'

'Chief Inspector, you don't really think I did any of these things, do you?' Liz Forbes appealed to him, a catch in her voice.

'No, Mrs Forbes, I don't think that for one minute, but I'm trying to investigate this case and I'll have to demonstrate that you are the innocent party in all of this. You do see that, don't you?' he asked gently, turning to take in Philip and his detective constable in one sweeping gaze.

Cameron hesitated for a moment then looked away. Whatever his superior decided he would just have to follow, for now. But that didn't stop him having ideas of his own.

'Maggie?'

'Hm?' Her murmur from under the duvet was sleepy. Maybe he shouldn't bother her but that interview with Elizabeth Forbes kept playing over and over in his mind.

'You know the chap that drowned?'

The huge sigh that came from the other side of the bed told Lorimer he had his wife's reluctant attention. 'Well, we saw his widow today.'

There was a silence, but he could tell she was listening. 'Seems the poor woman suspected her husband of having had an affair. Rotten poison-pen letters.'

Beside him Maggie sat up suddenly and Lorimer put his arm around her, sensing her shivers.

'Can you imagine her anguish?' Lorimer continued, 'Never knowing if he strayed or not. I mean, why didn't she just ask him? That's the bit I can't get my head around.'

Maggie did not answer, but her stifled yawn told him he was on his own as far as this was concerned. He let go of her shoulder and tucked the edge of the duvet around her body as she sank back down to sleep.

It wasn't fair of him to disturb her like this, he scolded himself. She probably had loads on her mind too. Problem kids, parents' nights, all sorts of stuff that kept deepening the lines on her pretty face. Lorimer lay back, feeling her warmth next to him. He was one lucky sod. She could still be out there in Florida.

Maggie lay as still as she could, trying to measure her breathing to simulate sleep. What a question! She felt her face hot against the cool pillow as she thought about that woman. Why hadn't she asked her husband? That was something that the DCI's wife could have answered herself. Elizabeth Forbes didn't *want* to know if it was true. And neither did Maggie Lorimer.

CHAPTER 38

'Milk money.' The boy looked up at Maggie, his face devoid of any kind of expression. She resisted the impulse to add 'please' and turned away to find her handbag.

'How much?' she asked, throwing the question over her shoulder.

'Five-thirty.'

It was the same amount every week but the boys who collected her money changed with amazing regularity. Only once had she been ripped off, waiting like an idiot for change out of a tenner. The boy had never returned and the next night she'd opened the door to the same request, only realizing her mistake when a different lad asked for her money. She'd felt such a fool: she was a policeman's wife, for heaven's sake, she should have known better. Now Maggie asked the same question every week, ignoring the rolled eyes of the boys who thought she must be a bit thick not to remember how much she paid.

'Just a minute, don't have any change,' Maggie muttered, scrabbling in her purse. 'Can you come back in five minutes?' she asked, only to be met with a grunt that was meant to indicate assent.

Maggie closed the door, seething inwardly. There had been no time to get to the bank and Bill wasn't home yet. She'd have to rake through the wardrobe to find any loose change he might have in his jacket pockets. Once upstairs she opened Bill's side of their wardrobe and began to feel about for any coins. He had the habit of tucking folded banknotes into his top pockets so she tried there too. A quick trawl produced some silver and a worn fiver folded up with a piece of paper. She yanked them out and clattered downstairs just as the doorbell rang.

'Here you are.' Maggie thrust the money into the boy's hands, some extra for a tip. With another grunt, the boy was off.

It was only as she turned to close the door that Maggie realized the bit of paper was still in her hand. Unfolding it, she looked to see if it was something Bill would need to keep.

Remember to ask Jo about going away.

Maggie blinked at the note. It was certainly written in Bill's scrawl. She turned it over. There was nothing else written down.

Maggie slumped down on the bottom stair as if she'd been winded. Jo? There was only one Jo she could think of and that was Jo Grant, the attractive blonde DI who was so much a part of Bill Lorimer's life these days. *Going away?* Maggie's fingers shook as she looked again at the note. What the hell did that mean? Surely they hadn't gone away together while she'd been in Florida? A wave of nausea came over her, leaving her weak and trembling. No, surely not. With an effort, she rose to her feet and staggered upstairs once more.

She stared at the open wardrobe where Lorimer's jackets hung from their rail. Which suit had this been in? It was only minutes ago she'd been searching through his things, yet she hadn't a clue where she'd found the note. Some detective she'd make, Maggie told herself wryly. Then, with a cold certainty, Maggie Lorimer knew that was exactly what she was going to have to be if she really wanted to know the truth behind her suspicions. The image of that poor woman who'd lost her husband came into her head. The anguish of not knowing, Bill had murmured. Oh, God! The irony of it all!

'Get a grip, woman,' she said aloud, sitting down heavily on the edge of the bed and smoothing the cover with her fingers, remembering the way he'd cuddled her into his shoulder. 'He's never been seeing anyone else. He loves you! Don't be so daft!'

Yet even as Maggie conjured up the glorious hours they'd spent in bed since her homecoming, she was wondering who else might have consoled him in the lonely months she'd been away.

*

'Daddy? Can we go to Disneyworld again this year?'

Mandy had crept up on his knee and was snuggled into his neck, holding onto his sleeve and jiggling it to catch Malcolm's attention. He smiled at his little daughter and ran one hand over her soft blonde curls. 'Like a child out of Mabel Lucie Atwell,' Duncan had remarked once on a rare visit to the Adams' household. It came flooding back now, Duncan's face lit up with pleasure as Mandy had sat on his knee, bouncing her up and down as if the older man was her real grandpa. How proud he'd been when his daughter Jane had given birth! They'd all been treated to sticky cakes in the boardroom that afternoon, he recalled. Now Duncan's little grandchild would grow up with the knowledge that someone had taken her grandpa away.

'Can we, Daddy? Please?' Mandy's voice implored. 'I'll be a really good girl and save up all my pocket money. Promise.'

Malcolm hugged the child's warm body to his chest. Her hair smelled so sweet and fragrant, the smell of baby innocence. A deep sigh escaped him and he felt the breath upon her hair. Mandy snuggled in tighter, her little hands clasped around his neck, her whole weight against him. How trusting children were! And how ready she was to believe that Daddy could make anything possible. Malcolm wanted to weep. She was so sure of her world, what on earth would she do when he was gone from it?

'We'll see, darling,' he whispered into her hair, 'we'll see.'

Malcolm closed the bedroom door and stepped quietly away. The *Tale of Peter Rabbit* was told over and over each night but Mandy never tired of hearing Daddy reading to her. He'd left her yawning as she turned over onto her side, one thumb stuck into her mouth. It was a habit Lesley hated but tonight he hadn't had the heart to admonish the little girl. There was so little time left for cuddles and stories. Perhaps he should take the therapist's advice and simply jack in his work. An intense longing to be with his family threatened to overwhelm him. He stood outside the pink-and-white room with its hanging mobiles and flowered wallpaper, imagining the rise and fall of his daughter's shoulders as she drowsed her way to sleep. If only he could hold onto this moment for ever: the quietness, the peace of knowing that she slept contentedly, his only wish.

Downstairs the telephone rang, shattering the silence, and Malcolm made his way towards the sound, holding onto the banister for support. Lesley was out fetching Gayle from Brownies. It was probably one of his wife's friends.

Already rehearsing what he was going to say to Janette, Lin or whoever it might be, Malcolm picked up the telephone. A puzzled frown crossed his brow as a man's voice whispered in his ear.

'Michael?' He sank to the floor, his shaking body no longer able to support him. 'Michael? Is that really you?'

*

JJ had gone out, locking the doors behind him. He'd grinned at Michael as he'd left, an expression of devilry in his eyes. He wouldn't be long, he'd said. Had to see to something. Whatever that was seemed to necessitate taking the laptop and his overnight gear, a fact that was not lost on the man left behind.

Michael had waited by the window listening to the van as it disappeared out of earshot. The dust swirled from the spot where the van had stood, then gently blew back onto the grasses on either side of the road. Heart thudding, Michael raced through to the kitchen. For hours he'd eyed a large walk-in cupboard opposite the entrance from the living room. Not once had JJ tried to open it in all the time they'd been in the house, an omission the younger man had found significant.

There was no door handle, just a ragged hole where a lock might once have been. Sticking his middle and index fingers into the gap, Michael felt for an edge to grip and tugged. Slowly the door pulled towards him, then stuck, its lower edge jammed against a bulge in the thick vinyl floor covering. He looked at the floor in dismay. Maybe water had seeped under the vinyl at one time leaving the surface so uneven. Yanking the door harder made no impression so he eased himself into a position where he could peer into the dark recess of the cupboard. With one arm he held the door open as far as it would go while he thrust in the other to search the shelves. Vague shapes of boxes and polythene bags were jumbled together as if someone had stored their rubbish in a hurry and left. His vision became keener as he peered into the gloom, picking out a set of ancient tableware still in its original cardboard container, a stack of different narrow boxes that he recognized as children's jigsaws and a bundle of cloth wrapped into a roll. Digging deeper, Michael felt the shapes of jugs and vases. His hand caught the handle of something and he jumped back in horror as the smash of glass rang out in the kitchen, shards scattering out of the door. Quickly he pushed them back into the cupboard with his shoe, looking behind him and listening for the noise of an engine that would signal JJ's return.

Once more he edged into the opening and began his search. Then his fingers closed on a cold familiar shape. Almost weeping with relief, Michael clasped it tightly. The telephone was inside a plastic carrier bag and as he tried to draw it out, the handset jangled as it hit the door. There was barely enough room to manoeuvre it through the gap but at last it was out.

Speed was important now and Michael set about heaving the refrigerator a few inches from the wall so he could insert the jack into the empty socket. His hands trembled as the plastic plug refused to go in. He couldn't see what he was doing, trusting to touch alone, feeling around the socket's shape. There seemed to be a flap covering the entrance to the socket. Carefully Michael pushed this up with his thumbnail. He held his breath then let out a sigh as the jack plug slid sweetly into the socket.

Trembling, he took the handset and hesitated before he pressed out a number. Should he telephone the police? JJ had warned that they were hunting for him. A body had been found in the woods: his passport and other ID with it. They'd sling him into a penitentiary soon as look at him, his captor had crowed. It had to be someone he could trust, he told himself; someone whose name hadn't come up in those documents he'd shown to Duncan Forbes.

Michael dialled a long string of numbers quickly. The events of the past days hadn't dulled his memory, he thought with something approaching triumph as he listened to the ringtone. Numbers had always been his thing. Jenny had teased him about his ability to recall so many at the drop of a hat.

Michael gave a sigh of relief as the voice came over the line. 'Yes, it's really me. It's a long story, Malcolm, but there are things I need you to do for me. I don't have a lot of time and I might have to hang up fast so listen, will you?'

The radio was playing his favourite country tunes as JJ drove along the narrow ribbon of road. All it had taken was a couple of signatures to authorize the account. The money would be there in a matter of hours, and tomorrow he would be well on his way from this God-forsaken place with all his childhood memories. It wouldn't do to hang around these parts too long, he thought, else the nightmares that had driven him away would begin to surface once again. He glanced sideways at the red canvas bag that held his shotgun. If he was stopped on this lonely stretch of road, nobody would bat an eyelid at his carrying such a weapon. Every dirt farmer in the district used to have one when he was a kid. For an instant the smile left the man's face and his mouth became a thin, hard line. Don't go down that road, a voice told him.

'It's okay, JJ. Everythin's fine and dandy,' he hollered, a grin spreading over his face. Sure it was. He wiped the back of his hand across his eyes to obliterate a remembered image: his father lying in a pool of blood, his mother screaming at him as he lowered the shotgun. He shook his head as if to be free of the scene. Concentrate on what's goin' on right now, his grown-up voice scolded. With a sigh JJ focused on the road ahead. Soon he could put all the rest of his plans into motion. And they were plans that didn't include taking a passenger along this time around.

Michael put down the phone with a sigh. Whatever happened to him now, he could trust Malcolm to do what was right. Tears pricked the back of his eyelids as he thought of the terrible things Malcolm had told him. Duncan Forbes had been like a father to him. Now he was dead and the same hands that had effected his execution had undoubtedly authorized his own demise. The thought galvanized the young man into action.

JJ had locked the front door, and the windows in the

main rooms were all fixed with inside locks. To escape from this place, Michael would have to do some real damage. He prowled round the house, testing the glass of the windows, one ear always listening for that returning vehicle.

In the end it was the bathroom that provided his means of escape. The frosted window gave slightly under his fingers, its ancient putty cracked round the edges. What to use as a missile to burst through the glass? Michael's eyes lit on the metal stand that held the rolls of toilet tissue. Snatching it up and pulling off the paper, he weighed it in his hands. It seemed heavy enough.

With a roar Michael ran at the bathroom window. The base of the holder slammed against the frosted glass, causing it to quiver under his grasp. Three times he repeated the action then, in a burst of angry despair, hurled his whole weight against the window. To his amazement the glass gave way under the impact, swaying outwards from the now-damaged frame.

'Got you, you bastard!'

Michael seized a towel from the rail and pushed hard against the glass until at last it fell with a satisfying tinkle onto the sun-baked earth below.

He put his head out, breathing in the hot air with relish but also alert for the sound of a distant motor. The ground was covered in bits of the windowpane and he'd have to be careful as he climbed out, he realized. There was no room to do anything other than drop down head first. Balling his fists into the sleeves of his shirt he pushed himself outwards. His shoulder snagged against the rough edge of the window frame but if he forced his upper body out then simple physics dictated that his weight would take him forwards.

Instinctively covering his face with both sleeves, he dropped to the ground, rolling himself clear of most of the broken glass.

A swift look to left and right showed him an empty road. Beyond the house lay fields of long grass. Glancing upwards, Michael noticed that the telephone wires led away from the road and over the fields. Somewhere there had to be another house with a telephone. Not stopping to look back, Michael ducked under the perimeter wire that separated JJ's house from the fields and began to run.

'What's wrong, love?' Lesley sank down beside him. Malcolm glanced from his wife to their older daughter. Gayle was watching her favourite cartoon, a bowl of cereal on her lap. Brownies always made her hungry.

There was so much to tell but he could only remain silent. To begin to speak would open the floodgates and he doubted if he could trust himself to stop.

He had made that telephone call for Michael and now he wondered what was happening with the young accountant. Would he manage to evade his captor? The news about Duncan had obviously been a shock. He was glad that he had managed to avoid any mention of Jennifer.

'Malcolm?' Lesley's eyes showed her concern.

'It's okay, love, just feeling a bit peaky this evening.' He patted her hand.

'Ulcer playing up again? You really must go back and see Dr Leckie. Promise me you will?' Her head rested on his shoulder and he felt the warmth of her like a balm.

'I promise,' he replied, but even as his words were uttered he felt he was betraying the woman he so desperately loved.

CHAPTER 39

The noise of the garden gate banging in a gust of wind made her sit up with a start. Ever since Tony's funeral she'd been jumpy. Shelley Jacobs had been lying on the settee, watching the TV screen's flickering light, until that noise set her heart thudding. Slowly she moved across the room, edging against the wall so nobody outside could see her. She listened for a few minutes, waiting for another sound that might tell her it was only the wind outside and her over-active imagination that held her there, trembling in her silk nightdress.

The place was in darkness but Shelley could make out the sweep of lawn and the path that led to the gate. Just as she was about to move away from that corner by the window the security light flooded her garden with a brightness that made her gasp. And against that light was cast the shadow of a man.

Shelley sank down on the floor with a whimper. If she stayed here out of sight he couldn't find her, could he?

The sound of breaking glass catapulted her into action. She darted across the room, grabbed the telephone and dialled 999.

The female police constable sat opposite the woman, nursing a mug of tea between her hands. Mrs Jacobs hadn't stopped shaking since their arrival. The downstairs window of the utility room had been smashed and the small sprinkling of glass out on her patio showed that it had been an intruder all right. The hole looked as though it had been punched inwards leaving many more shards of glass scattered all over the laminate floor. But that was the extent of the damage unless you could count the nerves of the woman shivering on the settee.

'He came to get me,' Shelley whispered at last, her eyes flicking up to meet the patient gaze of the uniformed officer. 'I know he did.'

'Who came to get you, Mrs Jacobs?'

But Shelley dropped her eyes and began weeping silently. The shadow, the man who had intruded on her, was out there somewhere. What did it matter if he had a name or not? Tony was dead and she'd be next. But why that should be Shelley couldn't answer.

She'd never understood what had really happened to Tony. A hired assassin had blown him away, the papers said. The police had got him, though. He was inside, wasn't he? The police had asked so many questions about his enemies, his rivals. Shelley had been bewildered by it all, not knowing what to answer them. So many innuendos had been made both by the police and Tony's own staff, hinting at a side to Tony she didn't know, didn't want to know. His business had been successful; they'd been a golden couple out on the town, photographed for all the best magazines. What had been wrong with that?

The police had probed insistently. What had been happening prior to his death? Had he been threatened at all? Shelley remembered angry telephone calls and Tony's rage afterwards. Someone had wanted him to do a deal, that was all she'd known. And it had made him so furious that she'd been slightly afraid of him. But Tony had never laid anything but a loving hand upon her. After the funeral, Craig, Tony's manager at the office, had told her things. But it was just things about the business, and how her husband had resisted any idea of his precious chain of betting shops being merged with a bigger conglomerate. At the time it hadn't seemed important but later when the overtures were made to her, Shelley sensed that seemed to be at the root of it all and she'd refused to speak to any of their representatives about it. Tony hadn't wanted it so she didn't want it.

Her sobs turned to a huge sigh. She was so tired and too cowardly to fight. It was simply a matter of time before they would browbeat her into signing their agreement. The terms of Tony's will had left her as the major shareholder. Would she be prepared to sell out?

'Is there anyone you'd like us to phone, Mrs

Jacobs?' The policewoman's voice penetrated Shelley's thoughts.

Shelley shook her head then bit her lip. 'Yes. My brother. Could you get Joseph for me, please?'

Lorimer frowned. He was reading a report about the break-in at the Jacobs place. It included a statement from Joe Reilly, Shelley Jacobs' brother. Reilly seemed to be dishing the dirt on Tony Jacobs. Was this another of the coincidences he didn't believe in? Maybe it would be a good idea to probe a bit deeper into the bookmaking firm's accounts. This time he'd make sure there was no warning before certain paperwork was lifted. Jacobs Betting Shops had an unwelcome visitor this morning: unwelcome but not unexpected after what Joe Reilly had told them. His wee sister was a sitting duck, he'd said. Should never have married that creep Jacobs.

He'd send a copy of this to Solly to keep him abreast of developments, if that's what they were. But something told the DCI that they'd find a link between the dead bookie and the unexplained deaths of two people from the very accounting firm he'd used.

Solly watched the fax machine as it regurgitated the sheets of paper. It was technical wizardry as far as he was concerned. The sort of thing he could watch for minutes at a time in wordless fascination. The completed sheet slipped into his hand, and as he read the contents the magic of the process was replaced by a concentration so intense that he was deaf to the sounds of voices in the corridor outside his room.

Jacobs Betting Shops had not failed to come into the psychologist's scrutiny when considering where the murders of two people had taken place. All aspects of this case required a careful evaluation of the geography surrounding the river Clyde. From the Crowne Plaza Hotel on the northbank, down to the bridge that led across to Carlton Place, Solly had taken note of the City Inn as well as the impressive facade of the bookmaker's main shop and office, its mock-Grecian portico with steps leading down to a paved jetty. There were boats moored there too, flashy pleasure craft for rich punters. Or alternative means of escape? Maybe George Parsonage could tell him more about that sort of river traffic.

Jennifer Hammond's apartment had looked directly across at the betting shop and that fact alone made him stop and think. Nobody had been seen entering the dead woman's flat on the night of her murder nor had anyone heard anything sinister until that water had begun its insistent dripping through the footballer's bathroom ceiling. Could the killer have arrived and left by boat? Was there a mooring by the apartment block? Solly made a mental note to find out.

He laid the paper aside at last and returned to the map that was spread across his desk. Solly was taking his time over these two deaths, just as if they had been part of a larger case of serial killings. Red lines linked the different places along the shoreline from west to east across the George V Bridge and back along the southern side of the river. Past Riverside Gardens the line meandered until it came to another block of flats and stopped abruptly. Graham West lived there. He was the partner who had protested his shock at the suggestion that Duncan Forbes had been murdered. It was a protestation that Solly had listened to with interest. He was rattled in some way but the man's tone of voice and his body language had told a different story from that of a man unable to believe his colleague had been deliberately killed. West had interested Solly enough for him to have made some discreet enquiries about the man. And that had led him to extend that thin red line along the southbank of the river. But should the line criss-cross the river itself? His pencil hovered above the map as he wondered.

The fax told Solly that the police investigation had extended to a more thorough look at the finances of Jacobs' bookies and their link with Forbes Macgregor. Somewhere, he was willing to bet, Graham West's name would be on that paperwork.

While Solly was contemplating his map, Graham West was busy packing files into his already bulging briefcase. The shredder was on the floor above his office. He could destroy the stuff this evening once most of the staff had gone home. Then what? Whoever it was that had been blackmailing him might continue to access his email address. So West had to close that down, somehow, without alerting suspicion. Alec Barr was already watching him. He'd come into his room once too often on flimsy pretexts that didn't fool West for a moment. They were all twitchy since DCI Lorimer's visit. Catherine had taken to being out of the office on long lunches with clients and Malcolm simply disappeared at times, leaving his secretary to cover up for him. Now the shadows that had haunted them were closing in: the police wanted to see them again and that psychologist had arranged to visit.

Well, he for one wasn't going to hang around and do nothing. Tony Jacobs had paid the price for being stubborn and pig-headed over the merger. Duncan had stumbled on the whole sorry mess almost by accident, with disastrous results. But it had been the death of Jenny that had upset him most. The memory of her head on his pillow made Graham West stop for a moment, his resolve wavering. Should he simply tell them everything he knew? There was no future for him here any more. But maybe he could start again somewhere else? Canada, or Australia perhaps? His fingers strayed automatically to his inside pocket where he'd put his passport. Just in case he had to get out in a hurry. There was plenty he'd regret leaving behind and it might be difficult to convert his real estate into ready money. That bastard had all but cleaned out his partnership account.

How to disappear was not something Graham West had ever had to contemplate and it was proving more difficult with every passing day. It would make him seem like the guilty party, of course, but that simply couldn't be helped. His reputation was going to be in as many shreds as these files before much longer. But losing his reputation was a mere shadow compared to the threat that hung over him. If he didn't make a move soon, his very existence could be in doubt.

CHAPTER 40

Cindy stretched until she felt her hamstring begin to hurt, then slowly she eased her body back into an upright stance. That was better. A few limbering exercises and she could banish the aches that always resulted from sitting too long in the van. They'd been on the road for weeks now and the tour would be finished after today. Then, joy of joys, a whole month with nothing to do but compose more songs, rehearse every other day and see her mates whenever she wanted.

The ringing telephone interrupted her thoughts and she walked over to the large desk that was at present doubling as a make-up counter.

'Hey,' she spoke into the phone. Cindy never ever gave her name. You just couldn't tell who'd seen her the night before and bribed the hotel staff into letting them have her number.

'It's Josh. How are you, kid?'

'Hi.' Cindy twirled on her toes, her smile widening at the sound of his voice. 'I'm great. How're you?'

'Fine, just fine. Listen, there's something I wanted to ask you. Remember the night we were up in Glasgow? Had two nights' gigs back-to-back?'

'Uh huh.'

'See the second night after the Armadillo gig, d'you remember us looking out your bedroom window?'

Cindy giggled. The memory of her night with Josh Scott wouldn't easily be forgotten but she wasn't sure if she was ready to tell him that yet. 'Maybe,' she began coyly. 'How come?'

There was a pause on the line that made Cindy's smile slip a little. Had she been just a tad over-enthusiastic? Was Josh going to spoil things already?

'Remember that guy we saw staggering into the bushes?'

A sense of relief swept over Cindy. It was nothing to do with their burgeoning relationship. 'Course I do. He was so out of it. Just as well he'd someone to help him up when he fell over.'

'Cindy,' Josh's voice was serious now and she found herself drawing out a chair to sit on, 'that guy was drowned a bit later on the same night. I've just had a call from the Crowne Plaza Hotel. The Glasgow police are appealing for any witnesses. Well,' Cindy heard a sigh as he paused again, 'we're witnesses, aren't we?'

*

'Cindy Heron and Joshua Scott,' Andrew Wotherspoon told him. 'They were the last guests I managed to contact. And you did ask specifically for anyone whose rooms looked out over there.' He turned and nodded down towards the Finnieston side of the river.

Lorimer swung back on his chair. The Crowne Plaza manager had the beginnings of a smile around his mouth as if he were not entirely sure of Lorimer's reaction.

'It took us longer to locate them because they're on a concert tour of the British Isles. Currently in Bognor Regis,' he added.

'Well done.' Lorimer nodded. 'Any time you fancy swapping your present job, Strathclyde Police would be interested.'

Andrew Wotherspoon reddened at the unexpected compliment. 'Well, you did ask for a list of all guests and it was mostly easy to obtain, but those particular people took a bit longer. Being on the road, you see.'

'And you asked them to contact us here, I assume?'

'That's correct, Chief Inspector. I'm sure they'll be telephoning you some time today. I just wanted you to know that we had located all of our guests now.'

Lorimer nodded. 'And they think they saw something?'

'Mr Scott wants to speak to you about that. He and Cindy Heron believe that they may have seen Mr Forbes after he left the party.'

Lorimer sat up. This was something entirely new in a case that had become bogged down in a lot of conjecture. A proper witness to the victim's last movements, if not his actual murder, might make a great deal of difference. Between this and the investigation into the bookies maybe they would hit on a proper lead.

'Cindy Heron? I went to see her last time she was in Glasgow,' Cameron said. 'At King Tut's.'

'When was that?'

Cameron paused. 'Two nights before this case began. Must have been the night before Duncan Forbes died. I was off duty for a change.' He grinned at Lorimer, sensing a change in his boss's manner.

'Fancy interviewing her, then?' Lorimer smiled back. 'She'll be here the day after tomorrow.'

Cameron nodded and shrugged, both gestures belying his inner excitement. 'Aye, why not?'

'See they've got a witness to that first murder,' Rosie told him.

Solly looked up.

'Seems some pop star was staying at the Crowne Plaza and she and her road manager saw what might have been Duncan Forbes with another man,' she continued.

'Yes,' Solly said with a nod. 'That's good.' He turned his attention to the pile of papers on his lap.

Rosie Fergusson sighed. This looked like a real breakthrough for Lorimer and yet the man who sat by her side seemed almost indifferent. If you didn't know him better you'd think he didn't care, she told herself. Solly could wrap himself in layers of concentration, taking hours to come out of whatever project he was working on. He'd said little about a profile. Instead his attention seemed to be focused on the areas around the river Clyde. Rosie had seen him poring over that dog-eared map he'd drawn and her questions about it had only elicited a twinkling smile and a nod. When he was ready to tell her anything he'd found then he would. Until then she would have to rein in her curiosity.

'Damn!' Maggie skidded to a halt outside the front door. The rain, from lowering clouds that had threatened all afternoon, was coming down like stair rods. It was only a quick hop from door to car but she'd become soaked at the far end. With fifth year parents' night there was always a huge turnout and it usually filled their staff car park. Still cursing under her breath, Maggie made a dash back to the sanctuary of the house, ready to grab her umbrella from the stand near the front door. The rain rattled against the windowpanes, masking the sound of her key in the lock.

There was a familiar voice coming from upstairs. Bill on the phone, she thought, then paused to shake her hair back from her face and tuck it inside her coat collar before leaving again. Then she heard words that made her freeze on the spot.

'Can we still do it, Jo?'

Maggie listened in the ensuing silence and started as her husband's voice proclaimed, 'You're a darling!'

Not waiting to be discovered dripping inside the hallway, Maggie rushed blindly into the night, pulling open the car door. Despite her trembling fingers she turned the key in the ignition and put the car into gear.

What the hell was going on? Did he phone this woman every time she left the house? Maggie's head began to thump. To confront him with this or not? That was what she must decide. As she sped through familiar streets, Maggie Lorimer felt as though her body had become light and insubstantial with the sudden weakness of emotion. What should she do? What the hell could she do? There was no answer, just a blankness in her mind.

I mustn't let this take take me over, she told herself, trying to regain her normal composure. This evening she had a job to do and many parents were waiting for her undivided attention. Other things would just have to wait.

CHAPTER 41

T he day dawned a pearly pink against the thin line of hills in the distance. Graham West stretched and sighed. Only a few more minutes and he'd get up for work.

His arms stiffened as the dreams that had peopled his sleep faded. This would be his last day, he thought. He'd prepared everything he could. Sitting up, West saw the mess of papers and books strewn across the floor. Well, he wouldn't be here much longer to see it. He'd packed only essentials into a rucksack, his passport now in its outside pocket. The flight had cost a fortune but paying by credit card was something he could still do. He'd simply not be here when the bill landed on his doormat. Tomorrow's early morning BA flight to London connected with the long haul to Singapore. Then he would take another plane to Sydney. By the time they'd found he was missing he'd be sunning himself on Bondi Beach. But not as Graham

West. He'd decided to leave everything behind him, even his name.

He gave a frown suddenly. That wee nyaff of a dealer. Did he have his name or not? His brow cleared as he remembered. No. It had just been the licence plate of the Porsche that had identified him. It seemed so long ago now, the day that it had all started. If he'd known then what was about to happen, he'd have thrown the stuff over a hedge and faced the consequences. Or would he? The temptation had been too great and the risks had seemed minimal. Face it, West, he told himself. You did what you had to do then, and you'll do what you have to do now.

Kicking a muscular pair of legs over the edge of the bed, he threw the bedcovers on the floor and headed for the shower. He'd wear his best Armani suit today, since it was the last time he'd ever be in the office. He smiled at his reflection in the mirror. That wasn't a man who'd ever admit to failure, now was it? No. That was a man with a future.

Forbes Macgregor looked just the same as it always did, he thought, swinging his briefcase as he entered the building. It had the same solid familiarity, its sandstone facade towering over the banks of the river. He felt like whistling today and had to stop himself grinning inanely as one of the trainee CA's slipped into the lift by his side. These guys would have to start all over again too, but they didn't know that yet. He hugged

292

the secret to himself and walked out of the lift with a jaunty spring in his step.

Once inside his office, Graham West began a meticulous trawl through his personal papers, what was left of them from the previous evening's shredding exercise. There was nothing incriminating now. Only work in progress. Even the accounts for Jacobs Betting Shops had somehow found their way into the main filing system under the other partners' names. He smiled. Malcolm, Catherine and Alec would have a bit of explaining to do to the police if they ever cottoned on to that sleight of hand. Sure, his sudden disappearance would make them all point the finger at him but that wouldn't last too long once those documents were uncovered.

'Coffee in the boardroom, five minutes.' Catherine had popped her head around his door before West realized she was there.

'Aye, fine,' he murmured, pretending to be distracted by the papers on his desk. Then she was gone. Coffee at this time of the morning? What was up? Were the police back again, perhaps? West felt the sweat tingle upon his palms. Maybe he had been too quick with the self-congratulations. Hubris had a funny way of rearing its ugly head, he thought grimly.

Alec Barr was not in the boardroom when West arrived, only Catherine and Malcolm: the latter looking pale and anxious. Catherine, however, was pouring coffee from the jug on the hot plate, her back to him so that he could not see her face.

'Alec not joining us?' he asked, then coughed trying to cover up the nervous strain apparent in his voice.

Catherine turned and smiled, her expression calm. 'No, just the three of us. I wanted to talk to you both while Alec was out of the office.'

West sat down at the table, his fingers drumming on the edge of the polished wood. Malcolm glanced at him then looked away. Suddenly West was reminded of juries in murder trials. They avoided eye contact with the accused when they had found him guilty, didn't they?

'What's up, then?' he asked staring at Catherine, deliberately making her look at him full on.

'It's Shelley Jacobs,' she replied. 'She's been to see the police.' There was a pause as she let her words sink in. It was Malcolm who broke the silence.

'And?' he asked.

'And it seems she had someone snooping round her house. She's also had threatening phone calls.' Catherine looked at each of them in turn as if to assess their reaction. Finding none, she sniffed. 'Big brother Joseph Reilly's started to stir things up about Tony,' she went on. 'And that could mean trouble for us.'

'D'you mean *us* or do you mean Forbes Macgregor?' Graham West wanted to know.

'Comes down to the same thing in the long run,' Malcolm murmured.

'Yes, it does,' the woman replied. 'If one of us goes down, the whole damn firm goes down. Jacobs being killed like that should have made us more careful.'

'But Alec said everything was fine!' West protested. 'Nobody's going to pin anything on us!' He spread his hands in a gesture that was intended to look innocent but Catherine Devoy gave him a baleful look from under her brows.

'The police aren't wasting their time. With three murders on their hands they're probably looking at us as potential killers.'

Graham West gave an involuntary start. 'You are kidding, aren't you?' He glanced from Catherine to Malcolm, relieved to see the Malcolm's eyebrows drawn up in scepticism.

'Why d'you think they want to interview each of us separately?' Catherine let the question dangle for a moment, eyeing the two men. She kept her gaze fixed on them, determined to provoke some reaction. West frowned. Let her think that his cage had been rattled, he thought. Malcolm had dropped his head and seemed to be deeply engrossed in some stain on the boardroom carpet. West watched as Catherine hunkered down, meeting Malcolm's eyes, forcing him to look at her. 'What's wrong with *you*, for instance? You've been acting oddly ever since Duncan's death.'

Malcolm swallowed hard. 'It's nothing really. A stomach ulcer. Might need to go into hospital for some stuff, that's all,' he muttered, his eyes flicking hopelessly from one partner to the other.

Catherine smiled. 'Poor you! And here we were thinking you might be suffering remorse of conscience.' She gave a mirthless laugh. 'Well, that's one way to keep out of sight. Take to your sick bed.'

Graham West patted Malcolm's shoulder, a gesture of male solidarity designed to annoy Catherine.

'Look, what I'm saying to you both is be very, very careful,' she scolded. 'Someone out there is desperate enough to take lives and Jacobs worked with some funny people.'

'Well Forbes Macgregor didn't seem too worried about taking him on as a client in the first place,' West blurted out. 'They knew his reputation, didn't they?'

Catherine glared at him, 'You mean *we*, don't you Graham? Don't forget we're all equity partners. That means we *are* Forbes Macgregor.'

'And we all have plenty to lose,' Malcolm added quietly.

Malcolm watched as the others left the boardroom, then rose to his feet. With shaky hands he put the untouched cup of coffee onto the tray then clutched the back of a chair as another spasm hit him. Stomach ulcer. They'd bought it without question. Just like everyone else. It was another lie to add to all the rest. But Catherine's barb about his conscience had smitten him. If only she knew just what had been going on in his heart and mind these past few days. He hadn't heard from Michael again and with every passing hour he wondered if the young man had indeed escaped from his kidnapper. The alternative didn't bear thinking about. There had been too much bloodshed already and for what? Yes, it was ironic but Catherine's initial suspicions had been right. Malcolm was finding it hard to live with the knowledge of what had happened. Who was it that had said the truth could set you free? Now he knew what the truth really was. And it had made a prisoner of him.

CHAPTER 42

Michael sank below the edge of the ditch. Sweat gathered on his hairline and trickled in fat droplets into his eyes. The skin on the back of his neck felt hot and dry where the late afternoon sun had burned it red.

JJ was back. Through the tall grasses bordering the ditch, Michael could see the front door swinging freely. Right now the man would be going from room to room, searching for him. He imagined the curses rending the fetid air within and felt his heart pounding in his chest as he lay there. Then another thought struck him: maybe this had all been part of JJ's plan. Why had he never bothered to tie him up? Was it because this house was in such a lonesome place that nobody would find him? Or had he wanted his captive to make a run for it? Was he even now looking up towards this field, thinking to leave a corpse where only vultures would discover it?

The irrigation ditch was halfway between the two homesteads, an easy way to set the boundaries of the two properties, perhaps. Michael hoped to make it as far as the house on the horizon but the appearance of the van forestalled that idea. He ducked down lower as JJ's stocky figure appeared on the dirt path. Had he left any traces to show his mad dash across the field? Or would the swaying grasses hide where he had fled?

Hardly daring to breathe, Michael waited. All his senses seemed to be heightened. His eyes flicked to a glittering green beetle wandering across the back of his hand. It tickled intolerably, its tiny feet tracing a path over his skin. If he could only brush it off. Above him a passing crow flew through the hot dense air, its wing-beats a swish of sound. And still he lay, never daring to move. Immobility would be his saving, he knew. If JJ should come upon him then one swift bullet would make an end of him. But while he remained motionless, the sun beating on his naked head, there was still a fragment of hope.

After what seemed an eternity Michael heard the sound of an engine starting up. Still he lay, terror gripping him. What if it was a ruse to make him show himself? He could imagine JJ standing by the vehicle, the engine running and his shotgun slung over his arm, waiting to train it on his prey. No. Better to wait until he was sure. The engine note changed and he could hear the tyres rumbling down the track then the distant whine as the van took to the open road once more.

The trembling in his body made him feel as if he were in the grip of some fever. Perhaps he was? In his weakened state there was no telling what he might have picked up.

Michael looked down at his hand. The beetle was gone. He blinked once then saw its shining carapace clinging to a single stalk of grass. It could only have been minutes since it had crawled over his skin but it seemed like hours. With a shuddering sob, he pulled himself up onto his elbows and looked over the ditch. There was no one there. Even the dust kicked up from the van's wheels was drifting towards the edge of the field.

He looked ahead at the farmhouse. It seemed empty, maybe it was only a desolate shell of a place, but on further inspection he saw that the shingled roof was intact and a pile of sawn logs were stacked neatly to the side. With one fearful glance behind him, Michael raised himself up and began a clumsy run towards the farmhouse.

JJ glanced once at the petrol gauge. He'd enough to see him way beyond the county line. Things hadn't gone according to plan. Something had happened and it could only have come from that bastard in Scotland. The bankteller had looked blank as he'd demanded the money from his new account. Then everything had started to unravel. There was no account set up after all. Somehow the big money that he'd expected from Forbes Macgregor had vanished into the ether. The six hundred thousand dollars he'd extorted from the Glasgow partner were all he had to show for his pains.

JJ had driven at breakneck speed, tyres screaming on

the hot road. Then he'd arrived back to find Michael gone. The empty house had unnerved him. The Scotsman could be anywhere. Probably hitched a ride to the next town and it would only be a matter of time before the guy called the cops.

JJ didn't look back at the old homestead as he drove on. So, he'd lost out on the biggest scam he'd ever tried. Well, there was still plenty of mileage in it if he played his cards right. Knowledge meant money and what this guy had told him could still be turned into big bucks. JJ's eyes narrowed as he nodded at his reflection in the windshield. It wasn't over yet. And his expertise as a hitman would keep him free for as long as he wanted.

CHAPTER 43

'Fancy a pint?' Alec Barr stood in front of West just as he was packing his briefcase for the last time. He was about to shake his head, make an excuse, when the man's eyes bored in to his. A hollow lie might alert Alec's suspicions. It would be best to go along with him for now.

'It's a grand night. How about we take a wander over to the pub? Leave that babe magnet of yours in the garage for a change?' Alec laughed out loud as if he'd said something really funny. West shrugged. That was fine with him. He was all ready to go in the morning. A quick pint with Alec might be just the very ploy to allay any trace of guilt. He'd talk about seeing the football at the weekend, about his team's prospects for the League, something innocuous that could make it seem as though he'd be around for weeks to come.

It was a pleasant April evening and the signs of spring were already showing in the primary colours of daffodils, tulips and grape hyacinths stacked neatly into their window boxes outside the office building.

'Let's take this way round,' Alec suggested, turning right towards the suspension bridge. West smiled his agreement. That was fine with him. He liked to look up and down the river from the swaying structure. It felt like being on the bridge of an ocean liner. Alec chatted companionably as they approached it. It was empty except for one man coming towards him carrying what looked like a case for snooker cues. West glanced away, not wishing to make eye contact with a stranger. This was a funny part of town; sometimes a drug addict would stop him blearily in the street, asking for a few pennies for a cup of tea. A few pennies to put stuff in his veins more like, West always scoffed to himself. That was one reason why he'd always preferred taking the Porsche across the road bridge into town whenever he was by himself.

A sudden nostalgia washed over him, taking him by surprise. He'd miss his car, his flat and yes, damn it, he'd miss this bloody city. For a moment he hesitated, staring ahead at Saint Andrew's Cathedral and the glass-fronted building next to it reflecting the rush-hour traffic.

'Okay?' Alec was speaking to him and West realized he had stopped walking and was standing there like an eejit.

'Och, there's something I've forgotten,' West improvised rapidly. 'Look, you go on ahead. I'll catch you up. Okay?'

For a moment he thought that Alec was going to

question him further but the older man simply shrugged and walked on.

'Make mine a Tennent's!' Graham called after him, turning once more towards the office. He saw Alec's hand raised in acknowledgement.

It took an effort of will not to break into a run back to the office where his Porsche was waiting. His last night in Glasgow would not be spent sharing a pint with Alec Barr. No way. He had better things to do with his time.

Alec Barr sat frowning at the clock. He should have been here by now, surely? West hadn't turned up and there was no response from his mobile. Still the minutes ticked by and still the man sat on, sipping his beer and gazing into space.

Eventually he drained the pint and, with a heavy sigh, heaved himself to his feet and headed for the door. Ella would have his dinner ready, so he ought to be on his way home now anyway. He'd leave a message, though, just in case.

'Steve,' he caught the barman's eye. 'I was supposed to be meeting someone for a drink. Graham West. Tall fellow with dark hair. D'you know him?'

The barman shook his head in reply.

'Well, if he comes in tell him I waited till now. Have to get home. Can't stay here indefinitely,' Barr grumbled. 'That's nearly six-thirty. I'll be caught in the rush if I stay any longer. Rangers are playing at home tonight.'

The barman watched as the customer shrugged a

powerful pair of shoulders into his overcoat and glared around the room before thrusting the door open. He'd keep an eye out for his mate. Wouldn't like to be in this West fellow's shoes when Alec Barr finally caught up with him though, he told himself, polishing the spot where the pint glass had left a wet ring. The man who had just walked out didn't have the look of a guy you'd want to cross.

Joseph Reilly stood in the middle of the bridge and looked anxiously at his watch. The call had been made an hour ago and whoever had made it should be here by now. 'Something useful to you about Tony Jacobs,' the voice had told him. An educated voice that had held the sort of authority Joe hadn't heard since his schooldays, reminding him of big Eddie Docherty, the heidie at St Roc's. No names had been given and Joe hadn't expected any. His late brother-in-law had moved in a twilight world where shadowy figures had come and gone. Joe had put up with it for Shelley's sake: seeing her happy had been enough. But Tony had been another matter. Just being in the same room with the man had made his flesh crawl. Joe wasn't sorry someone had put a bullet in him. But Shelley was in despair and frightened now too. If this guy turned up with something substantial that he could take to the polis then maybe his wee sister would see her husband for what he had really been, a thoroughgoing crook. Okay, he was no saint himself, but Joe's brushes with the law were small beer compared to what Tony Jacobs had been up to.

A sound to his right made Joe Reilly turn. A man was walking towards him, swinging a case of snooker cues. He grinned at him and the grin was returned by a diffident sort of smile.

'Okay, pal?' the man put out his hand and Joe felt its grasp cold within his own sweating palm.

'Aye, what the—?' Joe's bewildered question was cut off as the man pulled him close and a pain seared through his chest. He heard a voice yelping in agony. Then everything went sideways and he was falling, falling through space until the dark water came rushing up to embrace his flailing limbs.

On the south side of the river the man with the snooker cues walked with a jaunty spring in his step. It would never pay to look as if he were running away from anything. He even stopped once to light a fag, throwing the match spinning away towards the river. Smiling to himself, he imagined the sizzle as it hit the water. One moment alight then instantly snuffed out. Like that bloke. He shook his head. Maybe he'd find out the man's name in the papers tomorrow but that didn't bother him. It was just a name, wasn't it? Just another job. If he hadn't done it someone else would, he told himself with a shrug of his shoulders. He continued his walk along the pavement, past the boatyard and beyond until he came to the gate into Riverside Gardens. They were waiting.

The man did not even look behind him as he strolled towards the red car. The easy bit was over, he thought. Now the hard bit was about to begin.

George Parsonage took less than eight minutes to reach the body below the bridge. There was the usual cluster of onlookers peering down with uniformed officers, keeping them back as best they could. There hadn't been time to set up a police cordon yet, by the looks of things. George rowed hard against the strong current, his arms a mere extension of the rhythmic beat of the oars. He could see the body floating several yards away from the suspension bridge, still in mid-stream.

Slowly he approached the lifeless shape, a lifetime of experience heightening his caution. One wrong move and the man's body could be engulfed by a wave then sink deep below the murky surface. It was over in a matter of seconds, the swift dip of the hull and one mighty heave lifted his cargo inside the safety of George Parsonage's sturdy craft. For a moment he let the oars rest in their rowlocks as he examined the man in the bottom of his boat. Blood mingled with water sluiced from his side, a darker patch staining his suit. George shook his head briefly then glanced upwards. Something bad had happened up there and the sooner he took this fellow into the van waiting by the quayside, the better.

Above him several pairs of eyes watched as he rowed back towards the city, the dark shape of a corpse at his feet. Already the people were moving away as the officers began their questions. They'd just been passing. Hadn't seen it happen: didn't want to be involved.

DCI Lorimer's face was grim. Through the viewing screen he watched as Dr Rosie Fergusson made that first incision into the man's flesh. The naked corpse lay under the lights, a case for the pathologist's scrutiny. He was no longer a human being, Lorimer thought, merely a collection of bones, flesh and fluids. Lorimer tried to concentrate on Rosie's voice telling them what she was doing to Joseph Reilly's cadaver. He listened as she talked about the wound in the man's chest.

'Measure this, will you, Dan?' she asked her assistant. 'Boat-shaped wound here. So we've got a blunt and sharp edge to whatever weapon caused this.' Her latex-covered fingers pushed the lips of the wound together. 'Still got to see now how deeply it penetrated,' she muttered, half to herself.

Lorimer watched with his customary fascination as the pathologist sought to interpret the injury that had proved fatal for Shelley Jacob's brother. One deep plunge with the weapon was all it had taken. Then that shove over the edge of the suspension bridge. Why had the killer not simply left him there to die? Had he wanted to make sure his victim would never recover? And had this been a random act of violence in a city too well renowned for its knife culture? Nothing seemed to have been taken from the victim; his wallet had still been inside the jacket pocket when George Parsonage had pulled him out of the river. But somehow he doubted that this was sudden and unpremeditated. He felt certain that Joseph Reilly had been taken out by a hired killer. Lorimer stared at the body. It was as if some statement was being made. Everything seemed to be revolving around the river: Jacobs Betting Shops on one side, Forbes Macgregor's palatial offices on the other. And Jennifer Hammond had lived right on the water's edge, he reminded himself.

Lorimer nodded. He couldn't yet see a pattern in all of this but he sure as hell knew somebody who might.

Solly sat up straight, listening intently to the news item on the radio.

'The body of a man was taken from the river Clyde in the centre of Glasgow earlier this evening. He had been fatally wounded. Police have asked for any member of the public who may have witnessed the man's fall from the suspension bridge to come forward.'

The psychologist stroked his luxuriant beard thoughtfully. Was this too much of a coincidence or was the killing of Tony Jacobs's brother-in-law linked to any of the other murders? No. There were too many little strands beginning to tie together for this not to be part of a pattern. And the choice of the river as a locus was once again an interesting feature. The riverman had told him all about the suicides and attempted suicides: the folk who had cursed him upside down for giving them back another chance of living in whatever hell they'd been in before thrusting themselves over the edge. But the

309

riverman had never encountered an episode of murders like this, not in all the decades he'd been patrolling the waterways.

Tomorrow that young pop singer would be in Glasgow helping Lorimer to gain more of an insight into the death of Duncan Forbes. Until then the psychologist would continue to study his maps and make more red lines across the meandering blue of the Clyde.

The car radio had finished relaying the main headlines including the fate of Joseph Reilly. His relationship to the dead bookie had been mentioned, too. These journalists weren't stupid, the man told himself as he waited patiently for the red Vauxhall to appear. The briefcase full of money lay on the passenger seat. He'd pass it over and go home. End of story. End of fuss.

The man flexed his fingers through the black leather gloves. He'd taken every precaution. No trace of him would ever be found. Even the car he sat in could not be identified as his.

It was all over in minutes, the briefcase handed over and the car door slammed. Then he was driving away from the darkened quayside. His skin tingled under the latex mask and he tore it off before he reached the main road. It was just another item he'd have to discard before he reached the sanctuary of home. He pressed the unfamiliar button to let down the window and flung the green mask away from him, watching briefly as it landed among other rubbish lining the embankment. A smile flickered at the corners of his mouth.

They hadn't been expecting to see the Incredible Hulk pass over their money and their astonished reaction had caused him a moment of unguarded delight.

CHAPTER 44

D CI Lorimer closed the front door quietly behind him. The darkness in the hall told him what he already suspected: that Maggie was fast asleep. It had been one of those long days when one event tumbled hard on the heels of another. A killer was out there somewhere while Joseph Reilly was lying stiff in the mortuary.

Lorimer didn't believe in coincidences. They all knew a pro had been hired to take out Tony Jacobs and he suspected the very same thing had occurred today. As he tiptoed up the stairs he recalled the angry scene back at HQ. Nobody had minced their words about this latest killing in broad daylight. It was a total slap in the face for Strathclyde Police. Reilly may well have had things to add to the background of the murder of his bookie brother-in-law. Maybe this would end up being one of these unsolved cases that the new unit would investigate in years to come. He fervently hoped not, at least while he was still senior investigating officer.

The bedroom was in thick darkness when Lorimer crept in but gradually his eyes became accustomed to the gloom and he made out Maggie's shape under the duvet. Leaving his clothes on the floor where he stepped out of them, he slid his naked body in next to hers. Maggie moaned softly, feeling the chill against her skin, so he wrapped his arm around her and pulled her closer, letting his fingers caress her breast. She gave a sigh and snuggled closer, but whether she still slept or was half-awake, he couldn't tell. Lying there in the dark, feeling her warmth was enough for now.

'Any luck?'

'Aye, thank God!' DS Wilson sighed and rubbed eyes that were reddened from lack of sleep. 'We got a description of the assailant. Good witness, too. Picked out one of our likely lads. Guess who?'

Lorimer shook his head.

'Dougie McAlister: Shug's younger brother. Would you believe the cheek of it? And him banged up for the bookie's killing.'

'Runs in the family then,' Lorimer said wearily. 'You'd think they'd have more savvy.'

'Aye, well there's a warrant out for his arrest but nobody's seen a thing. Or so they say.'

'Who's telling the worst porkies then?' Lorimer asked.

'His old mum, for a start. She swears her boy was

innocent of it all. Butter wouldn't melt et cetera, et cetera.'

'Kind of overlooking his older brother's confession to the Jacobs murder, isn't she?' Lorimer's sarcasm was palpable.

Wilson shrugged. 'She claims no contact in the last twenty-four hours, but our boys don't believe her.'

'Aye, well, opinions aren't going to find that wee toerag. Bring her in if you think it'll do any good.' Lorimer sighed. Mary McAlister was as much a villain as her errant sons. She'd been a madam in her younger days, letting her boys rampage around the city while she coined in the proceeds of her activities. Now she was a hardened old woman. They'd be wasting precious resources interviewing her at this point.

'Second thought.' Lorimer flapped a hand at Wilson. 'See what you can find out from Shelley Jacobs. That incident the other night brought her brother Joseph storming round, demanding we authorize police protection for his little sister.'

'Looks like he was the one needing it,' Wilson remarked. 'Any results from the post-mortem yet?'

'Just the cause of death. The blade went straight into his lungs. He'd have been dead before his body hit the water. No other results yet from forensics. Don't expect any either,' he added gloomily.

His ringing phone was the cue for Alistair Wilson to leave.

'DCI Lorimer.'

'I'm standing outside Graham West's flat,' Solly's voice came over clearly. 'There appears to be something of a problem.'

'He's what?' Alec Barr raised himself up from the chair, his face a picture of disbelief.

'Mr West seems to have disappeared, sir,' Detective Constable Cameron told him. 'Dr Brightman and DCI Lorimer are both at his flat now. Could we ask you some questions, sir?'

Barr clamped his mouth shut. A mere nod sufficed to show his compliance with the police procedures. At a sign from the detective constable, a uniformed officer closed the managing partner's office door. Cameron motioned for the man to sit down again.

'When did you last see Mr West, sir?'

Alec Barr glowered at the two men opposite his desk. The tall Lewisman watched the expressions flit across the man's face, wishing he could see into his thoughts. Something wasn't right, that much was certain. Instead of concern, Barr seemed to be beside himself with fury.

'Yesterday!' he snapped. 'We left the office together and that's the last I saw of him!' Cameron took in the fists clenching and unclenching as the man continued to glare at them. Barr opened his mouth as if to add something, thought better of it and closed it again. Cameron's raised eyebrow did nothing to encourage him.

'You're quite sure of that, sir?'

'Of course I'm sure! We left together then Graham

315

remembered something he'd left in the office so went back to fetch it. Then I went home.'

Cameron nodded. 'Thank you.' He wrote something into his notebook then looked up again. 'He was expected in the office this morning?'

'Damn right. Had someone waiting down in reception for over half an hour. We could lose an audit client because of this!' Barr exploded.

So that explained it, Cameron thought. That was why the managing partner was cursing West's disappearance. He frowned. Dr Brightman had been quite specific on the telephone. Graham West had agreed to see him at nine-thirty this morning.

'And this appointment was definitely meant to be today?'

'Yes! West's secretary had booked a client in for ten o'clock. When nobody had turned up by ten-thirty we tried to call him at home.'

'And there was no reply,' Cameron finished for him.

Barr nodded.

'Have you any idea where Mr West might be?'

Another glare shot across the table, but Niall Cameron was impervious to dark looks and waited patiently for a response. He used Lorimer's trick and stared at the man as impassively as he could.

'No. I have no idea at all,' Barr murmured. 'He should have been here. Have you looked to see if his car's still there?' he added.

'These matters are all in hand, sir. Perhaps I could

speak to some other members of staff, beginning with the other two partners?'

When Alec Barr rose from his chair this time, the detective constable could see small beads of sweat clinging to his upper lip. Whether he wanted to reveal it or not, Alec Barr was showing some genuine anxiety over the disappearance of his partner.

'Where else did you go?' Lorimer asked the psychologist.

'Round the river-side of the building to look up at the front windows, then back here,' Solly replied slowly, gazing into space as if he were repeating these steps in his mind's eye. 'It was the bin bags that gave him away, of course,' he added.

'Hm.' Lorimer sniffed. The three large bin bags had been left outside West's front door by a pair of ornamental bay trees. But West, or someone who had been in his house, had dumped the black bags right on his doorstep. Lorimer had picked through them with gloved hands, finding a selection of expensive men's clothing stuffed carelessly into every bag. It had given him something to do until the search warrant had arrived.

Now the two men and one uniform were painstakingly going through Graham West's luxury penthouse flat, looking for clues as to where he had gone.

Lorimer gazed out of the huge picture windows that looked over the Clyde and beyond to the city. Far below there were cormorants roosting on old mooring posts next to the ancient slime-covered jetty. From his vantage point high above the river, he could easily make out the Glasgow Science Tower and the hills beyond as the river curved westwards. To his right lay the City Inn and the Crowne Plaza Hotel, both dominated by the black silhouette of the Finnieston crane. Below, on the northern bank, lay apartments designed to resemble barges, their paintwork picked out in Cambridge blue. The mossy walls below revealed different shades of greys and greens like geological strata licked by countless tides.

As his eyes roamed over the areas bounded by the river, Lorimer spotted the police helicopter flying down towards the city. Another team was busy at work.

Graham West evidently favoured the minimalist modern look, two leather recliners his only concession to comfort. One wall held a serious-looking stack of hi-fi equipment. A quick recce round the house showed them the whole place had been wired for sound. His collection of compact discs and DVDs were neatly arranged in alphabetical order next to the stainless-steel sound system. The main room was a long rectangle, one end containing a glass and chrome table with matching chrome chairs, a curving panel of pebbled glass squares leading directly to the front door. It didn't take much imagination to see that the man had kept a tidy house; even the magazines (mostly sports issues) were stacked into a W-shaped metal rack.

A huge painting took up nearly the whole wall to the right of the window. Lorimer exhaled slowly. It was an Alison Watt, an original, not a mere print. Either West had had the good fortune to purchase before the artist's meteoric rise to fame or he'd been earning some serious money. Lorimer sighed enviously. Who'd want to leave something as beautiful as that behind?

'Let's see his bedroom.' The DCI turned on his heel and made for the upper level. The narrow staircase led him to the top storey of the building, the layout a mirror image of the rooms below. But that was where the similarity ended. By contrast to the pristine lounge, the place was a shambles. Drawers had been turned out, their contents allowed to lie where they'd fallen. The sliding glass doors of the wardrobe in West's bedroom were pushed to one side, empty hangers testifying to a deliberate escape. This wasn't a missing person's job, Lorimer told himself. This was something far more interesting.

'What d'you reckon?' he asked as Solly joined him. 'Has he done a runner?'

The psychologist didn't answer. He was looking around the man's bedroom, eyes taking in goodness knows what.

'Well?' Lorimer persisted. 'He was expecting to see you, wasn't he?'

Solly nodded, still regarding the various items scattered around the room.

'So if he wanted to make a getaway, and we don't know this for sure yet, why would he have appointments with you and a client in his office at almost the same time?'

'He knew he wouldn't be here, if that's what you're getting at,' Solly murmured. 'These meetings were only a smoke screen, I suppose.' He paused, one hand on his beard, stroking it thoughtfully. 'Wonder when he actually left,' he went on. Solly walked over to the unmade bed and slid his hand across the rumpled sheet. 'Cold.' He nodded to himself. 'But did he sleep here overnight, I wonder?'

'Barr seems to have been the last person in his office to have seen him,' Lorimer continued. 'We'll do a door-to-door in the building,' he added, turning to the uniformed officer who hovered in the doorway. 'And tell the caretaker to keep his mouth shut meantime. We don't want him jumping to the wrong conclusions or, worse still, talking to the press.'

'Right, sir.' The officer walked back to the lounge and moments later they heard his voice as the order was relayed down the line.

'West was due to come in and see us today,' Lorimer said. 'I wonder if that put the wind up him,' he mused. 'And perhaps he wasn't too keen to meet up with you either.'

'We can't assume that's the reason he left so suddenly,' Solomon replied. 'If it was indeed so sudden,' he added thoughtfully.

'What're you thinking?'

'This mess.' Solly waved a hand at the chaos around the room. 'Look at the lounge.' He walked downstairs, the DCI trailing in his wake. 'Not a thing out of place.'

He ran a finger over the wooden bookshelves. 'See?' Solly held up his hand and Lorimer did see. There was no tell-tale smudge of grey dust.

'So you think he made a deliberate mess in there? Wanted us to think he'd left in a hurry?'

'Such a hurry that he had time to bag up his clothes?' Solly asked, a smile hovering about his lips. 'My guess is he expected someone to take them away before I arrived. Why would he leave them there for us to find?'

'Who'd take a pile of his clothes?' Lorimer frowned.

With a shrug of his shoulders the psychologist continued to smile. 'That's one thing you're going to have to find out, but I'd hazard a guess that he was expecting an earlier visitor. The caretaker, perhaps?'

'But why bag up stuff in the first place?' Lorimer asked. 'And it wasn't rubbish. Some of these clothes had designer labels.'

'A social conscience? Letting them be resold by Oxfam, perhaps?' Solly mused. 'Maybe this will tell us a little more about Mr West,' he added quietly to himself.

An hour later Lorimer had seen enough. The caretaker, a nervous-looking middle-aged man, was sitting in a glass-fronted cubicle on the ground floor. He looked up as the three police officers approached and slipped off his stool, wiping his hands on the hem of his brown dustcoat. Lorimer saw that one side of the man's face was badly swollen and his eyes were pink-rimmed.

'Sir, this is Mr Johnston.' The PC introduced the man and Lorimer nodded briefly.

'You weren't here when we arrived,' Lorimer began.

'Naw.' Johnson touched his lip, looking apologetic and scared at the same time. 'Had tae go tae the dentist's,' he explained slowly, his words slightly slurred. 'Been up all night with toothache. Said he'd take me first thing. An abscess,' he said, indicating his right cheek painfully. 'Wis supposed tae go up to Mr West's,' he added.

'Oh? Any particular reason for that?' Lorimer asked, his professional expression concealing an eagerness he dared not show.

'Wanted me to take some o' his things to the Accord Hospice shop,' Johnson muttered.

Lorimer and Solly exchanged looks, the latter raising his bushy eyebrows over eyes that twinkled with child-like delight. The psychologist had got it in one.

'Did he specify what time you should collect them?' Lorimer asked.

'Oh, before breakfast. Said they had to be taken away early.'

'What usually happens to the household rubbish?'

'Outsize rubbish is supposed to be left down in the garage, the rest goes down a shute. I collect it every day,' the caretaker replied.

'So he could have taken it away himself?'

The man shrugged and mumbled, 'S'pose so.'

'When did you last speak to Mr West?'

The caretaker thought about this for a moment. 'Yesterday. Well, last night, really. About ten o'clock. That's when he asked me to see to them bags. I'd taken a couple of paracetamol and gone to bed but couldnae sleep for this tooth.'

'Was it customary for residents to call you out of office hours?'

Johnson shrugged. 'No' really. Usually they'd leave a message if they wanted me to do something particular.'

'So it was odd that Mr West asked you to do this for him?'

'Well, I suppose so.' Johnson looked from one man to the other, clearly unhappy and wondering if he were in some sort of trouble.

'When did you actually see him last?' Solly asked.

Johnson turned to the psychologist. 'Well,' he glanced back at the detective chief inspector as if seeking permission to continue, 'it wis durin' the night. Jist efter wan o'clock. It wis the noise that made me look out.' Johnson paused before continuing. 'I saw his Porsche leaving the driveway and turning towards Govan.'

Lorimer and Solly exchanged glances. Govan led away from the city. Where had he gone? And why make such a thing of appearing to have left in some haste when it was clear he'd been prepared to leave all his business suits behind him?

'I expect you have a note of his car registration?' Lorimer asked smoothly.

'Yes, sir,' the man replied, turning back into the tiny

cubbyhole that served as an office and flicking open a blue notebook. 'Here it is. G21 WST.'

An hour later Lorimer knew where Graham West had gone. His car had been sighted on the M8 and it hadn't taken too much wit to check the airport and find the silver car sitting on the second floor of the multi-storey car park. West had taken a BA scheduled flight to Heathrow and Customs had cleared him for an onward flight to Singapore.

'What now?' Solly asked, only to receive a black look from the DCI. Lorimer was fuming. Could they possibly issue an international warrant to stop the man from leaving Singapore airport? They had to have *some* sort of reason to arrest him. Without that, Graham West was free to come and go as he pleased.

'Just because he's skipped the country doesn't give us the right to assume he's guilty of any criminal act,' Lorimer seethed.

'And is he?' Solly murmured.

Lorimer smacked his fist hard against the palm of his hand. 'Well what the hell's he running away from if he's innocent? One of his clients is shot by a known hit man, three of his colleagues end up dead, or at least that's what he thinks, then Joe Reilly makes a fuss and ends up with the fishes.' Lorimer looked fit to explode. 'So don't tell me West's sudden disappearance has nothing to do with all that! The man's guilty as sin!'

Solly remained silent, his eyes fixed on a spot in the

middle distance. If he disagreed with the senior investigating officer he wasn't saying. But his very silence seemed to infuriate Lorimer.

'For God's sake, Solly, surely you've got some kind of handle on the man by now? He's rolling in money. Just look at the car, the fancy penthouse and that . . . that Alison Watt!' The painting seemed to be the final straw for the DCI. Solly could see that such a work of art being in the hands of a suspect upset him. The accountant's lifestyle certainly suggested a source of income well in excess of what even someone in his position could earn.

Solomon Brightman had given a lot of consideration to Graham West. It was a disappointment that he had not been able to meet the man that morning for there were things he'd like to have asked, reactions to questions he'd have noted with due care and attention. But it was too late for regrets. What he had to do now was to examine the bigger picture of the river to see if West might indeed have committed those crimes.

But Solly couldn't help feeling uneasy about the profile of a cold-blooded multiple killer. It just didn't fit with the image of a man who cared enough to ensure that his old clothes were taken away to a hospice shop.

CHAPTER 45

A lec Barr watched as the police constable carried the plastic bags full of paper shreddings. That was the fifth trip he'd made from the machine room. He felt the wetness of his hairline and took a handkerchief from his top pocket, wiped the offending perspiration away, then crushed the pale-lemon silk into a ball in his fist. If they should find anything . . .? For a moment as he pondered the situation, Barr found himself wishing for the familiar face of Duncan Forbes. The man's presence would have been reassuring right now, he thought ruefully. Everything had gone wrong since Duncan's death, everything.

He had made a decision that morning to continue with the day-to-day business of Forbes Macgregor; if they were seen to be operating as normal then that would inspire confidence in the staff as well as showing those policemen that the accounting world didn't stop during an investigation. But if things got out of control the Institute might become involved. The Institute of Chartered Accountants had the power to put a stop on their practising certificates which would effectively close down their operations, even on a temporary basis. To stop functioning in the international market would spell disaster. Reputation in this business was everything. Barr ground his teeth. He'd play all the cards he possibly could to keep the partnership afloat. The London office had already been notified (albeit with a watered-down version) of what was going on. The deaths of personnel could not be covered up in any case. The sad accident of a senior partner was now a full-blown murder investigation with two more unexplained deaths following. Peter Hinshelwood was flying up later today. The irony was not lost on Alec Barr. The London partner's last act before retiring might be to make a statement to the press. God! It could be as bad as the Enron disaster when a multinational firm of accountants had collapsed.

Barr had had the press onto him that morning. Some bastard had told them that Graham West was a murder suspect. As a fellow partner, what comment had he to make? Barr had given a one-word reply and slammed down the phone. But he couldn't evade them for ever. Sudden tears of rage smarted in his eyes. Peter would take over as soon as he arrived. Would there be anything he could do to limit the damage? His gaze wandered over to Catherine's room. Maybe she could still be of use. He stared hard at the door. It was worth a try at any rate, he told himself.

Detective Constable Niall Cameron came out of the interview suite, high spots of colour on his normally pallid face. Turning to the young woman at his side, he thrust out his hand.

'Thanks for all of that,' he told her. 'It was good of you to break your schedule to come back up here.'

Cindy Heron raised her eyebrows in surprise. 'But someone died!' she exclaimed. 'Surely that's much more important than me having a day off between gigs?'

'Wish every member of the public thought like that,' Cameron told her, letting go of the girl's hand. He walked her to the front door where Josh Scott, her manager, was waiting. They'd interviewed him too. Now all that remained was to collate these statements and see if there was anything positive to add to the investigation into the death of Duncan Forbes.

Cameron watched the girl link hands with her manager and walk towards the waiting car. Her hair shone in the sun as she turned to see him standing there and the smile she gave him made his cheeks redden all the more. As he stepped back into the shadows of divisional HQ, Cameron gave himself a wee shake. To think he'd just interviewed Cindy Heron, *the* Cindy Heron. She'd been nothing like he'd expected, just a young girl really. A bit intense given the reason she'd been there, and much nicer in an ordinary pair of jeans and a T-shirt than her fancy stage outfits. Cameron smiled to himself. It would be a good story to tell in time, but right now he needed to go and write up this report or Lorimer would be on his back.

*

'Two men,' Lorimer mused, reading over DC Cameron's report. 'They both give a good description of them, even though it was dark. Oh,' he added, reading on, 'their window was above one of the street lamps on the cycle path. That explains it.' He glanced at Cameron who was sitting across the desk from him. 'And you showed them the CCTV footage?'

'Yes, sir. And they both claim that one of the men was Duncan Forbes.'

'And the other?' Lorimer read on. 'Ah. Tall and dark. Athletic build . . . already by the railing as if he was waiting for somebody . . . was supporting Forbes and guiding him towards the bushes.'

'They both thought Forbes was going to be sick and that his companion was helping him,' Cameron added helpfully.

'Yes, so I see.' Lorimer's face was expressionless, his lips one thin line of concentration. Then he looked up suddenly. 'This other man,' he said quietly, 'could it have been Graham West?'

Cameron uncrossed his legs and straightened up. He'd been waiting for the chief inspector to put that question to him.

'Yes, sir, it could. There's no sign of him leaving the hotel later on. The only sighting we have of West is when he walked out of the side door of the hospitality suite a few minutes before Duncan Forbes.'

'On his own?'

'Yes.'

'And did the CCTV show him returning to the hotel at any time?'

'No, sir, it didn't.'

Lorimer's mouth twitched slightly at the corners as if he wanted to smile. 'Right. Thanks, Cameron, and well done. This is going to push things forward just the way we want, if we're in time,' he added to himself.

Graham West lay back against the leather seat and relaxed for the first time in days. It was all going according to plan. He'd cleared out everything that would link him with the whole sorry mess. Once the plane landed in Sydney he'd melt away into the crowds, just another back-packing tourist. His hand went to the place where he'd put the new passport and he felt its shape against the thin cotton of his shirt pocket. He would start a new life over here as Ray Easton. A bit of a joke really, that new name, and convenient enough for the guy who'd forged it. He closed his eyes and thought of the surf swirling up on Bondi Beach. Not long now and he'd actually be there, free as a bird.

'Singapore?' Iain MacKenzie, the Fiscal, asked. He'd never encountered a request like this before. Once, when a tourist had been found dead in Thailand he had had to arrange with the tour company to liaise with an English coroner to bring the body home. Such matters were way outside his jurisdiction.

'Maybe we'd better wait till he's arrived in Australia.

At least that's still a Crown Colony,' he remarked wryly.

Lorimer nodded, checking the time on his wall clock. West's plane had left London at six-thirty this morning and was due to arrive in Singapore at nearly nine o'clock GMT. A fairly brisk turnaround of two hours meant the ongoing flight to Sydney would arrive by mid-morning tomorrow, though that would be late evening Australian time.

'See what you can do at your end, Iain. Mitchison's been on to the Home Office this morning already. We're waiting to see what transpires,' he said, mimicking his superintendent's voice. He sensed the grin on MacKenzie's face as he put down the phone. The Fiscal was a good sort. He'd pull what strings he could to make an arrest at Sydney airport, but would they be in time? And, a small voice not too far from Solomon Brightman's measured tones asked him, was Graham West really their killer?

It was lunchtime so Malcolm was quite within his rights to leave the office at Carlton Place, though he felt as if he were sneaking away from the turmoil behind him. He'd managed to avoid speaking to Alec and Catherine so far with all the comings and goings of the morning, which had been made easier by the fact that they'd been closeted together for the last hour. Uniformed officers had been combing the place and looking at various pieces of documentation. He didn't want to be around when Peter

Hinshelwood turned up, but that might not be an option. He hailed a passing taxi and stepped in.

It was a cheek, really, to take a cab for such a short distance and he'd been given the customary glower by the taxi driver, but Malcolm was past caring. His stomach ached with a dull, constant pain. Was the thing growing inside him? The image of a fleshy carbuncle taking up space in his abdomen was almost as bad as the pain itself. He walked along Buchanan Street, no real destination in mind. It was an old habit to wander along the pedestrian precinct to find a good eatery. A sour smile crossed his face. He hadn't eaten lunch for weeks now.

He'd gone as far as the entrance to Nelson Mandela Place when the lights stopped him and he waited placidly with the other pedestrians for the crossing signal.

'Wait for the wee green man,' he heard a woman's voice just beside him. Turning, Malcolm saw a little fair-haired boy, face raised expectantly at the red light, his young mother holding his hand, smiling down at him. The boy glanced back at her then stared again at the light, willing it to change.

Memories flooded back then. He remembered waiting at the crossing with his own mum. Green Cross Code, that's what they'd called it. Standing there, Malcolm could hear her voice, see her face, as his earnest expression took in all that she told him about waiting for the 'wee green man'.

When the light did change, he crossed over in a daze, reluctant to let go of the image. Instead he stopped outside the Tron Church, watching the mother and child disappear into the crowds leading to the underground station. A sharp twist in his belly made him stifle a groan and hold onto the railing beside him for support. If he could just sit down somewhere. A glance at the church showed him it was open for the mid-week lunchtime service. 'Come Unto Me All Ye That Are Weary And I Will Give You Rest' proclaimed the poster outside. Well, he was weary, that was for sure, and he could do with a rest. Malcolm slipped inside, taking a leaflet from a woman who was handing them out as the worshippers entered, and sat to one side, grateful for the cushioning that covered the hard Presbyterian pew.

It was a relief to close his eyes when the service began. Others around him stood to sing a hymn that was unfamiliar to him but Malcolm sat on, feigning prayer. Then the reverberations from the organ faded into trembling ripples and he heard feet shuffle beside him.

'Let us pray,' the man at the front began, his voice echoing around the walls of the huge church. For a moment Malcolm opened his eyes to glance at the minister. His eyebrows rose a little as he took in the plain grey suit and dark tie. Not a minister, then? Or did they simply not bother wearing their robes for a mid-week service? Malcolm didn't know. He'd never been a Sunday school kid and hadn't bothered with any kind of organized religion. Keeping the image of the man's silver hair bowed in prayer, Malcolm closed his own eyes again and listened to the words.

He joined in at last, mumbling the Lord's Prayer under his breath, then sat back and listened as the man began his homily.

'Today I am going to talk to you about love and judgement. *God's* love and *God's* judgement,' the man said, firmly stressing the words. 'What does John tell us in chapter three verses 17 to 21? "For God did not send His Son into the world to condemn the world, but that the world might be saved through Him." And listen to what else he tells us: "He who believes in Him is not condemned; but he who does not believe already stands condemned. And this is the reason of this condemnation – the light came into the world and men loved the darkness rather than the light, for their deeds were evil."'

Malcolm suppressed a whimper. It was only because he'd loved Lesley and the girls. That was all. Where was the sin in that? But a dark shadow was falling over his mind as the preacher continued.

'We've all sinned in some way in our lives, but it will never be too late for repentance. Remember the thief on the cross beside Jesus? He left it almost too late, but the Saviour promised that he would be with him in paradise. So you see, friends, that God's love is great enough for any sinner. And John goes on to make this clear. "Every one whose deeds are depraved hates the light, and does not come to the light, but his deeds stand convicted. But –" and this is what I want you to take away from

334

here today "– he who puts the truth into action comes to the light, that his deeds may be made plain for all to see, because they are done in God."'

There was a pause. Malcolm stared at the silver head of the man, seeing its shape change into a shadow, a trick caused by the light suspended above. He could still see its image when he closed his eyes for the final prayer. He felt emptied, somehow, as if these words had cleaned away all his anguish. Had the repentant thief felt like this? He was under a death sentence too, after all. Malcolm clasped his hands together tightly as the prayer began.

'Father, forgive us for all our sins. You know how often we let you down, both by the things we do and by the things we leave undone.'

Malcolm listened as the voice continued, a gentle yet commanding tone that was some sort of conduit to an unseen God. He was letting the listening congregation know what was right and what was wrong as well as speaking to the Almighty on their behalf. Was that what prayer was? Apologizing for things done and things left undone? Things left undone, things left undone . . . The words drummed into Malcolm's brain as if a record was stuck and he couldn't nudge it forwards. The words of the prayer continued but he couldn't hear them. All he could hear was a booming in his ears – things undone – over and over again. It was true, he told himself. That's what his sin was. He'd left things undone. He'd taken the coward's way out, thinking that it wasn't so bad.

But it had made just as much difference in the end, hadn't it?

Malcolm was only aware that the service had come to a close when the person to his left said 'Excuse me,' in a polite voice and he stumbled in his haste to leave the pew.

Once out in the street, the brightness of the sky tore at his eyeballs and he stood looking upwards at the white clouds and the rays of sun streaming behind them. Dashing the back of his hand against his eyes, he felt the wetness of tears. How long had he had been weeping? He looked up at the dazzling midday sky, totally unaware of the strange looks in his direction from passers-by. All he could feel was a sense of peace emanating from somewhere inside him and the knowledge that forgiveness was not too late. That, and the sudden joyous realization that there was a cessation of pain inside his poor body, gave Malcolm Adams hope and a sudden courage.

Now he knew exactly what he had to do.

CHAPTER 46

The blue lights of the police car were flashing a warning to any vehicles that might come suddenly around the corner of the road. Two officers stood beside the battered white car, one looking along the road for signs of an ambulance. The guy was still alive, he'd felt the pulse beating strongly enough, but the injury to his head looked pretty nasty.

'What d'you reckon? Will you tell the boss what really happened?' the other officer stood up from where he had been crouching down at the open door of the damaged car.

'Got to. Can't see why not, anyway. Fellow tries to do a runner when we ask about his out-of-date tax disc. What were we suppose to do? Let him go?' The older of the two men gave a shrug. 'He'll be okay. I've seen worse. Anyway, let's have a dekko before anyone else turns up.'

The cop standing against the car's rear door looked

doubtful but did nothing to prevent his neighbour walking round to the passenger door. It gave a metallic screech as he wrenched it open. The entire side of the vehicle had crashed against the cliff wall before coming to rest in the middle of the road.

He stretched out his hand and opened the glove compartment. Maybe there'd be some documents to show just who the driver was. But when he pressed the button to let down the lid, he stepped back in amazement as the plastic bags tumbled onto the floor.

'Here! No wonder he tried to scarper! See this lot?'

'When are they coming in?' Solly asked.

'West was meant to be in at three o'clock so that gives us a bit of time. Adams and the woman were scheduled for after four but I had Barr down for one o'clock. Originally,' Lorimer said with a bitter twist to his mouth.

'Originally?'

'He's called off till later this evening. His London boss has arrived on the scene, apparently. No point in giving him more grief than he needs.' Lorimer shrugged.

'How did he sound?'

Lorimer paused. His conversation with the managing partner of Forbes Macgregor had been short. He had begun to insist on the three partners appearing at the pre-arranged times but Barr had been equally insistent. He had a quality of authority that Lorimer admired. They were both doing a job to the best of their ability; they both had staff to consider. In the end he had acquiesced to Barr's request. He had enough on his plate as it was. He'd already resigned himself to being here for the rest of the day and well into the night. Maggie would understand.

'I said,' Solly repeated slowly, 'how did Mr Barr sound when you spoke to him?'

Lorimer shrugged. 'Okay. Not harassed or upset, if that's what you mean. He was trying to organize things at his end. Sounded as if he runs a pretty tight ship, that man,' Lorimer commented, looking at Solly. 'Why d'you ask?'

Solly spread his hands and grinned disarmingly. 'Just wondered. He didn't strike me as the panicking type either.'

Lorimer was on the point of asking Solly more when the telephone rang.

The psychologist watched as the creases between Lorimer's eyes grew deeper. Then the policeman's face cleared and he slapped his open hand against the pile of papers on his desk.

'Gotcha!' he exclaimed, rising from his chair.

'What—?'

'Come on, I'll explain as we go,' Lorimer answered, taking his jacket off its peg behind the door.

It was not the first time the two men had sat side by side at a hospital bed, a uniformed officer by the door. The patient lying within the curtained cubicle groaned as he opened his eyes.

'Well, well. What do we have here? Thought you'd gone over to annoy the boys and girls in Argyll and Bute, Eddie. How come you ended up here?'

The man on the bed squinted up at Lorimer. His head was swathed in white bandages with another wrapped round his jaw. He opened his mouth to speak then closed it again, his reddened eyes flicking across at Solomon. 'Who's he?' the words came out hoarsely.

'Never mind that, Eddie. What were you doing with all that gear? And, more to the point, tell me about this.' Lorimer waved a long slim notebook in front of the man's face.

'Oh, Christ!' The man turned his head to one side in a groan of defeat.

'G21 WST. Familiar number, Eddie?' Lorimer read the license number off the notebook and grinned down at the man in the bed. 'Mean anything to you? Customer in a Porsche. Surely you wouldn't forget him in a hurry?'

'Don' know a thing,' Eddie replied.

'No? Well, it might come as a shock to you, Eddie, but we do. You'd been supplying something to the owner of this car, whose name and details we have right here.' Lorimer patted his jacket pocket. 'So why not do yourself a favour and tell us exactly what you were supplying him with.'

The man in the bed licked his lips nervously.

'Come on, Eddie, this isn't just about supplying.' Lorimer's tone was quiet but held a hint of menace. 'We're conducting a murder inquiry here.'

The man's eyes opened wider and he glanced again at the bearded psychologist who nodded gravely.

He gave a huge sigh. 'All right. Might as well tell you. Punter wanted a quantity of Goop.'

Solly caught Lorimer's eye and frowned.

'Goop. GHB,' Lorimer explained. 'Gamma-hydroxybutrate to give it its Sunday name.' He smiled down at the man beneath the bedclothes who seemed to have shrivelled up under the chief inspector's blue gaze. 'Isn't that right, Eddie?'

'Aye,' came the resigned voice from the depths of the hospital sheets. ''S right.'

'That explains a lot,' Lorimer told Solly as they made their way out to the hospital car park. 'West gets hold of GHB, drugs Forbes and tips him into the Clyde. Later on he doses Jennifer Hammond the same way, only gives her so much that he kills her,' he continued grimly.

'Why?' Solly stopped beside Lorimer's car. He had one hand on the door handle, his expression puzzled. 'I can see *how* he came to do it. The couple who spotted them from the Crowne Plaza Hotel seem to confirm that.'

'Plus he's done a runner to the other side of the world,' Lorimer reminded him.

'Yes, yes.' Solly sighed as though Graham West had let him down in some way. 'It's just—'

'What?'

'West's profile. It doesn't fit with that of a cold-blooded

multiple killer,' Solly told him as he eased himself into the passenger seat.

'Well, profiles have been known to be wrong before, Solly,' Lorimer told him shortly. 'And it's our number-one priority to get hold of West before he disappears.'

Catherine Devoy applied the scarlet lipstick to the brush and bent forward towards the washroom mirror. The face reflected back at her stretched its lips and held them in a rictus as the woman stroked an outline then filled in the shape, a blood-red bow starkly contrasting with her pale complexion. With a sigh that held just a trace of a sob she leaned back and let the brush fall with a tiny clatter, her hands gripping the edge of the countertop. She couldn't do this, she really and truly couldn't. For all Alec had cajoled and promised, Catherine felt a sense of sheer misery well up in her at the thought of facing the police. They were trained to notice things: she'd seen it on television, how they played good-cop-bad-cop with people in the interview room. What if they tricked her into saying things she didn't want to say? How would she answer them if they asked her about Duncan?

The woman in the mirror stood up straighter and gave her dark hair a reassuring pat. She'd encountered dozens of difficult clients over the years, dealt with cases where grown men and women had shrieked abuse at her for simply telling them what the law required and how they must make reparation to their creditors. She'd taken a pride in being on the side of the angels all those years ago, so what had gone wrong? The face that looked back at her was older, hardened with lines that told of sleepless nights rather than laughter. What had she to laugh about now? Her familiar world was about to be broken into pieces unless . . . ? Unless she told the story she had so carefully rehearsed. But could she carry it off? The dark woman staring at her lifted her chin a fraction as if in challenge. Yes, she could do it. She hadn't come this far to let a few policemen spoil everything.

'Miss Devoy's in the interview room, sir,' WPC Irvine told Lorimer.

He raised his head, 'Still no sign of Mr Adams?'

'No, sir. Shall I try his office?'

Remembering the London partner, Lorimer nodded briefly. Adams was probably still ensconced with his bosses. Still, it was bloody annoying. He'd had the instructions to be here at the same time as the Devoy woman.

'Oh, and tell him I want him over here, will you?' he added, rising from his seat with a sigh. He felt as if he'd been glued to that chair for the last hour listening to Mitchison warble on about Home Office procedures. If he'd just get on with it and stop trying to be so wrapped up in rules and regulations they might get somewhere. Graham West was winging Singapore and they were no nearer to finding a way to intercept him at his journey's end. So far, not a lot had been found in either Forbes Macgregor's offices or in the betting shop's riverside headquarters: plenty of bags of shredded paper, though, which had raised not a few eyebrows. That old chap in Human Resources, Adrian Millhouse, had admitted that there was about a year's worth of shreddings stacked in the machine room, and, no, the bulging plastic sacks hadn't been there at the start of the week. DC Cameron had already taken statements from other members of staff who had confirmed this. As he strode along the corridor, Lorimer wondered what Miss Catherine Devoy would say when he asked her opinion about West's sudden disappearance.

Thinking back to his first visit to the offices by the river, Lorimer recalled Jennifer Hammond. He stopped outside the door of the room for a moment, conjuring up the leggy redhead's flirtatious smile, the way they'd linked arms to cross the road. That such scintillating life should be snuffed out! He took a deep breath to bring the spurt of anger under control then turned the handle and entered the room.

Inside, three pairs of eyes turned towards him but Lorimer ignored the psychologist and the duty officer, turning with a smile and outstretched hand to the slim woman sitting on the edge of her chair.

'Miss Devoy, thank you so much for coming in today,' he said and took a seat opposite her.

Catherine looked up at the tall policeman with surprise. There was no trace of anything other than pleasant courtesy in his manner. He might have been one of her associates coming in to discuss the wording of a legal document. She sat back against the hard wood of the chair and clasped her fingers lightly together. This was going to be fine, just fine.

'You are one of Forbes Macgregor's associates?' Lorimer began.

Catherine inclined her head. 'I'm one of the partners,' she corrected him.

'Ah,' he replied and smiled at her. 'Sorry.' Then, just as she was beginning to relax, he added, 'An equity partner, I suppose, not salaried?'

Catherine frowned. 'Of course!' she snapped. 'But what's that got to do with anything?'

Lorimer inclined his head a little. 'Maybe nothing, but you would stand to lose a great deal if the firm were to collapse, wouldn't you?'

Catherine felt as if someone had pulled a plug inside her, draining away all her reserves of energy. She had to keep it together. She had to. Forcing a lightness into her tone, she heard herself reply, 'Oh I don't think that's ever going to happen, Chief Inspector. We're a well-respected firm, you know, with offices all over the globe.'

'Really?' Lorimer asked. 'Even in places like Australia and Singapore?'

Catherine frowned. What on earth was he getting at? 'Well yes, since you ask. In fact,' she lifted her handbag onto the table and opened it, searching for her diary, 'you can see for yourself,' and she handed it over to Lorimer who glanced at the Forbes Macgregor logo but did not make a move to take it from her. 'See,' she insisted, flicking over the pages till she came to the firm's international directory, 'we've got offices everywhere.'

Lorimer took the diary, gave it a cursory glance, and handed it back without a word.

'Do you have any idea where your partner Graham West has gone, Miss Devoy?'

'None at all, Chief Inspector,' she answered him, her eyes deliberately meeting his own.

'So it would surprise you to know that he has left the country?'

'What?' Catherine Devoy sat up suddenly.

Either she was genuinely surprised or she was a damn good actress, Lorimer thought, wondering obliquely what Solly was making of this.

'Yes. We wondered if he had spoken of his intentions to you or to anyone else.'

The woman shook her head slowly and deliberately. 'No. He did not.'

'So the first you knew of his disappearance was when he failed to turn up for work this morning?' Lorimer almost hesitated. This morning seemed like the day before yesterday, so much had happened in the past few hours.

'That's correct,' she replied, her gaze still concentrating on him.

'Why d'you imagine he's taken off like that, Miss Devoy?' Lorimer leaned back and swung gently in his chair, his tone easy and conversational.

'How should I know?'

'Well, you're his partner. Don't you all have inside knowledge about one another?'

Catherine Devoy shrugged, her eyes sliding away from his at last. 'Not about personal things, no,' she said.

'But you do know about Mr West's business affairs?'

'Of course,' she replied.

'So you would know that he had been taking out large sums of money from his partnership account?'

The woman's open-mouthed silence told him all he needed.

Lorimer nodded again. 'Perhaps you didn't know everything about Mr West after all?'

Catherine shook her head. 'Perhaps not,' she whispered.

Lorimer smacked his hands onto the edge of the desk suddenly, making her jump. 'Miss Devoy, we have reason to suspect that Graham West is guilty of killing Duncan Forbes and Jennifer Hammond.'

There was silence while they watched the woman's reaction. For a long moment she did not move or make a sound, her expression frozen. In disbelief? Lorimer wondered.

Then she swallowed hard. 'Chief Inspector, why on earth would Graham do something as terrible as that?' Catherine's voice was low but steady, her gaze once more on the chief inspector's face.

'I thought perhaps you might be able to tell me,' he countered lightly.

'Well,' she replied, her eyes suddenly hard, 'you thought wrong.'

'You don't think he was capable of murder, then?'

For a moment she looked away, thoughtful, then she gave a sigh. 'Who can tell what a person is capable of, Chief Inspector?'

'Indeed,' Lorimer replied.

'I think,' Catherine Devoy began slowly, 'that if Graham had been embezzling from the firm we would have known about it before now.'

Lorimer regarded her with interest. There was something about her manner that told him she was thinking on her feet. Had she really been unaware of West's massive withdrawals?

'The sums involved were pretty large. We found that he had transferred them to an overseas account,' he continued, blessing those of his team who had been quick to uncover these financial details. They would know soon enough exactly where it was.

'May I see these transactions, Chief Inspector?' Catherine Devoy asked, reaching again for her handbag and drawing out a slim spectacle case as Lorimer opened the file and pushed the relevant papers across the desk.

For a minute there was silence in the small room and Lorimer could hear the sound of traffic outside the building: cars turning from the main road and the rumble of a passing lorry. Then the woman drew off her rimless glasses and laid them on the table between them.

'This has nothing to do with Forbes Macgregor,' she

began. 'If Graham was making payments, then it was to a personal account.'

'Maybe one he'd already set up?'

'Perhaps,' she admitted. 'But it's not against the law to transfer your own money from one account to another.'

'How do you know it's his own? The sums are huge,' Lorimer protested.

Catherine Devoy smiled sweetly at him. 'But Graham West is a very wealthy young man, Chief Inspector. What's wrong with that?'

Lorimer sat back suddenly. He had no answer to that. Maybe she was right. Perhaps West had inherited money, invested it quite legally. After all, he was an accountant. A frown crossed his face as he changed tack.

'Could you describe his relationship with Duncan Forbes?'

The daylight was fading as Lorimer and Solly stood at the window, gazing down across the city rooftops. Catherine Devoy had left the building an hour before but this was Lorimer's first chance to speak to the psychologist alone. They'd found out very little from the woman. West seemed to be a charmer, 'Bit of a playboy' was how she had put it, and he'd enjoyed good relations with everyone in the firm. No animosity had been shown between the late Duncan Forbes and his younger, high-flying partner. He'd been popular with all the staff, too, and big things had been expected of him in the future. But now? The woman seemed genuinely puzzled as to where he'd gone and why. Part of Lorimer wanted to believe her.

'What d'you make of her, Solly? Think she's telling us the truth?'

The psychologist's eyes twinkled behind his horn-rimmed glasses. 'Well,' he began in the non-committal manner that infuriated Lorimer, 'I *think*,' he stressed the word, 'that Miss Devoy is hiding something.' He paused before continuing, 'I also had the distinct impression that she *was* ready to say something to you, but that your line of questioning took her by surprise.'

'How?'

'It was the way she came into the room, actually. She was ready, prepared. Her manner seemed quite relaxed and she held herself as though she were about to make some sort of pronouncement.'

'But she didn't.'

Solly shook his head, 'No. Pity, really. I'd have been interested to see what fabrications she was going to tell us.' He raised his eyebrows at Lorimer as if to invite a response.

The chief inspector merely sighed. 'Well, maybe you're right, but it hasn't got us much further, has it?'

'And Mr Adams hasn't turned up yet either, has he?' Solly looked towards the door, as if expecting their next interviewee to walk in at any minute.

'No, think it's about time we found out why, don't you?'

*

'Hello?' Lesley Adams picked up the telephone and listened, her hand going to her mouth as the voice at the other end identified himself as an officer of Strathclyde Police.

'Malcolm! What's happened to him? He hasn't come home!'

'Mummy! Where's my book?'

'Not now, sweetheart, not just now.' Lesley shushed the child, clinging onto her chubby fingers as if they were a lifeline.

'But Mummy—'

'Mummy's on the telephone, darling. No. No, I told you he's not here,' Lesley returned to the voice asking for the whereabouts of her husband. 'He should have been home hours ago.'

Alec Barr gave a huge sigh of relief as he swept away from Glasgow airport. Hinshelwood was gone at last. He'd given a brave version of West's disappearance, sticking to the depression theory. It was a reasonable card to play, after all. With three of his colleagues dead, how must Hinshelwood have felt? West had no parents or wife to go home to, he'd said. And, besides, these sorts of illnesses were hard to spot, weren't they? If Peter Hinshelwood was convinced, he didn't show it. But at least he'd tried to sell the idea to his London colleague, Barr told himself, revving into the outside lane as he left the slip road.

He was about to head for the city when his mobile

rang. A quick flick of the hands-free button told him who was on the other line.

'Malcolm,' he began, 'how did it go?' Barr's voice was hearty, encouraging.

'Alec, I need to see you.'

'Sure, sometime tomorrow?'

'Now! It has to be now, Alec,' Adams raised his voice. There was no mistaking the tone of desperation.

'But I'm on my way to police headquarters, Malcolm,' Barr protested.

'I need to see you now!'

There was a pause as Barr thought hard.

'All right,' he said at last. 'I'll see you in our usual place. Fifteen minutes max. That do you?'

There was no reply, just an audible intake of breath before the phone went dead.

CHAPTER 47

It was midnight. The curtains were still undrawn against the gathering darkness. Tomorrow would be the first of May. When she was little, her mum would laugh and say they should wash their faces in the dew and they'd be pretty for the rest of the year. It was a joke, really, that old wives' tale, but Lesley had always wanted to creep out in the dawn light and wipe the moisture from the wet grass across her cheeks, just in case.

Where was Malcolm? she thought desperately, for the hundredth time. This had never happened before. He wasn't one of the drinking and carousing types that she read about in the Sunday papers, those men who seemed to live such unpleasant lives of clubs and pubs where sexual adventuring was the norm. Malcolm would never – she bit her lip to stop the tears coming again. Where was he? She'd wanted to phone Mum earlier, just as a comfort, but her older wiser self stopped her hand lifting the phone. It would be selfish to worry her mum.

There was nothing to worry about, was there? Yet, a little voice suggested unkindly, turning her bowels to water.

When the telephone rang, Lesley Adams jumped as if she'd been stung. Stumbling away from the window, she grasped the phone and pressed it to her ear.

'Hello? Malcolm! Is that you?'

The voice on the other end of the line was unfamiliar and Lesley sat heavily on the edge of the bed, expecting the worst, expecting this to be the police telling her that Malcolm was dead.

But as she listened, Lesley Adams sat up straighter. The voice was telling her things that she could never have believed, things far, far worse than the sleazy goings-on outlined in any colour supplements. That Malcolm had been involved . . . She couldn't imagine her gentle husband being mixed up . . .

'What do you want me to do?' Lesley whispered at last, gripping the phone so tight that her fingers hurt.

With a sigh, the voice at the other end told her.

Lorimer lay awake staring into the darkness. Beside him Maggie moaned softly, dreaming about something she'd forget by morning. Unlike his wife, Lorimer always remembered his dreams but as yet he'd not even managed to fall asleep.

Adams had never shown up. His wife had been hysterical, they'd said, and Lorimer had initiated a discreet search for the man. He thought of Adams, he'd been the quiet one of the four. A mere stick of a man, his fair hair thin against a cadaverous skull. But his face had softened with pity, Lorimer remembered, when he'd asked questions about Duncan Forbes and Jennifer Hammond. Pity and grief, he thought, striving to recall the details of that meeting in Carlton Place. Yes, that was it. He'd appeared quite stricken, in a silent sort of way.

They knew little about Adams as yet. It seemed he was a family man whose wife cared enough to break down and beg the police to find him for her, to bring him home. None of that day's searching had turned up anything unsavoury about these Forbes Macgregor partners. They were as clean as the proverbial whistle, but the masses of shredded paperwork suggested that someone had gone to a great deal of trouble to make this so. Tomorrow he'd have the fingerprints off both sets of bags; those at the offices and the ones West had left outside his flat. If they matched, as Lorimer supposed they would, then their hunt for the fugitive would intensify.

Alec Barr had been helpful in that respect. He'd seemed reluctant to part with the knowledge that West had been suffering from some kind of depression. It was an old-fashioned reaction, to speak about mental instability in such hushed tones, but that was exactly what Barr had done. The man had seemed weary, and Lorimer couldn't blame him. Trying to hold on to the remnants of his world must be hard, yet Barr had maintained a dignity that the senior investigating officer admired. He'd looked grim, as if fearing the worst, and had answered all of Lorimer's questions with a directness that he'd found refreshing after the clipped responses he usually had to listen to. When asked what he thought was going on, he'd sounded genuinely perplexed. It was a nightmare of someone else's making, Lorimer thought. Barr would be losing sleep right now, just like the rest of them, trying to figure out what West had done, why he'd done it, and what would happen to his firm once all the facts were uncovered.

And more would be, Lorimer thought with a yawn, when tomorrow finally came.

She heard a baby's cry, sharp and insistent, as she sat bolt upright in the bed. But as her eyes became accustomed to the darkness, Liz Forbes was only aware of her own breathing. There was no baby in the house; Janey and the family had gone home. It must have been a dream, Liz decided, lying back against the pillows. The night air was cool in their bedroom and the linen curtains moved as a breeze blew in. Duncan had always liked an airy bedroom and she'd become accustomed to the night sounds over the years. There were always noises from the garden: trees soughing in the wind, their resident owl deep within the adjoining woods and, sometimes, the bark of a fox.

Along the corridor Philip would be sleeping. His room was far enough from his parents' bedroom to ensure complete privacy for them both, yet just to know he was in the house was comfort enough. Lately he'd dropped hints about maybe having to move away, if the search for work took him further afield. Liz had forced an under-standing smile while aching inside. Of course he must make a break for independence. Of course she must let him go his own way, but it was doubly hard to imagine him gone and being left alone in the family home.

If only, she thought again, if only she could be sure that Duncan had been faithful to her. Her heart told her it was so but the voice in her head, a voice that sounded like the author of those malicious letters, kept insisting that he had strayed. He'd been seeing another woman. Was it true? And if it was, then perhaps somewhere in this city she would be lying awake too, restless with the questions that seemed to have no answer. Who had killed Duncan? And, for God's sake, why?

'Solly?'

'Hm?'

'Come to bed, darling,' Rosie mumbled sleepily, her hand at her mouth as she stifled a yawn. 'It's after two in the morning, can't that wait?' she protested to Solly's rounded back. He had been sitting there hunched over his computer, when Rosie had finally given up and headed for bed. There was no reply so she ran a hand across her tousled hair and shuffled back to the dark-ened room next door. Well, she had to have a steady hand for tomorrow's PMs and a good night's sleep was called for. Whatever her darling was up to, he'd tell her in time. Graham West's disappearance had galvanized the lot of them into action, but she still had the routine of daily deaths to attend to. Not every cadaver that was pushed into her post-mortem room would turn out to be a murder victim. And, thankfully, not every one had engendered such complications as that of the late Duncan Forbes.

Solly hardly heard the living room door close as Rosie left him. He was gazing at a chart he had constructed. It showed the river Clyde from the area beyond the Science Centre, then the curves of its winding course twisting into the city and away to Glasgow Green where the riverman lived. George Parsonage had impressed him as a man who held himself in readiness for any sort of tragedy. He could be at the scene of an accident in minutes. What kind of life must he have, on call at every hour of the day and night? But then, Solly mused, he had been born into that way of life and seemed to have inherited a sense of duty to his fellow man. How different was the mentality of the killer! Whoever had dispatched Joseph Reilly had not a shred of compassion in his soul. And Jennifer Hammond? Duncan Forbes? Was anyone lying awake tonight, their conscience burning with the acid of remorse?

Solly's eyes took in the river with its meandering shape and those black circles dotted around its banks. That was where Forbes had been fished out of the water, a stone's throw from the Crowne Plaza Hotel; that was Jennifer Hammond's flat overlooking the river and, between them both, caught on a curve, Graham West's penthouse. Solly recalled the view from the man's home: he would have been able to see everything up and down the river from that position. Jennifer Hammond's view was more restricted but one could make out the Kingston Bridge with its never-ending traffic and catch a glimpse of the silver spire of the Science Centre's tower. He let the cursor take the map further east until he saw the circle that signified Carlton Place. It was just beyond the George V road bridge. Anyone could take a walk along there and disappear into the maelstrom of pedestrians in the heart of the city. Clyde Street was minutes away, then Argyle Street another short walk. Solly had dismissed any notion of a boat: West's own craft was moored in Kip Marina, way down the Clyde. The boats lying at the edge of the river were restricted to ferrying punters up and down to the shops at Braehead, he'd discovered, or out into the open waters beyond the estuary.

It all pointed to West. Then why should he be sitting here in the wee small hours, gazing at a computer screen as if it would somehow tell him something to the contrary? Was he simply looking for difficulties, as Lorimer had suggested? But, try as he might, the psychologist could not rid himself of the belief that Graham West was running away from more than the retribution that would come from being found guilty of murder.

CHAPTER 48

It was a morning straight out of Chaucer: '... as fresh as is the month of May,' she whispered to the still air. All it needed was the young squire himself to come riding out of the mists. This May morning was sweet indeed with a fragrance lifting off the long grasses and a haze in the air that promised a hot day to come. Maggie crumbled the remnants of last night's scones onto the bird table, shivering slightly in her flimsy dressing gown. Her ankles were wet with dew and she'd need to discard her slippers on the doormat or risk footprints all over the kitchen floor. But it was nice being out here before the day began. She hugged her arms tight around her chest, listening as a blackbird poured out his song from somewhere in the shrubbery. Their garden was overgrown and neglected, a haven for birds and wildlife, but a point of raised eyebrows from their more fastidious neighbours. Maggie always blitzed it during the long school holidays in a passion of guilt, then forgot all about it for much of the year.

Today she had several free periods since the seniors were on exam leave. It would give her time to catch up with the mountain of administration that had accumulated in her classroom cupboard. A real tidy up was needed there too, she thought to herself, glancing ruefully at the thistles swaying in the breeze. Then she stood quite still as a flash of red and yellow caught her eye: a goldfinch alighting on a clump of teasels, making the spiky plant bend under its tiny weight. Maggie watched intently, wishing her husband was up and about to see the wee bird but she had left him slumbering soundly. Poor soul, she thought. This case was taking its toll on him. If only he'd been promoted to superintendent, then maybe his caseload would have lightened a bit. But he'd have worked just as hard, a small voice scolded her. And Jo Grant would still have been in his team. She'd done nothing about that overheard telephone call, or the note in Bill's pocket. A sense of foreboding that she recognized as sheer cowardice had kept her from uttering any questions to her husband. Since her homecoming he'd been more than attentive. And these fevered nights of lovemaking were surely at odds with a man who was having an affair with his colleague?

The finch flew off and Maggie watched its bright wings until it was out of sight.

'Fresh-firecoal chestnut-falls, finches' wings,' she quoted softly to the garden. The poet-priest had had an eye for the tiniest detail. Maybe she'd give *Pied Beauty* a whirl with the new third years after exam leave was over, show them one of her bird books.

With the bird's departure came the sense of awakening and a need to begin her day. She'd put the kettle on, take Bill a cup of tea. Then his day could begin too, she thought, and with it the urgent hunt for the man they believed to be a killer.

Lorimer drove into the car park with one eye on the lines of vehicles. Good. He was in before Mitchison. That was something at any rate. He'd speak to Iain MacKenzie before anyone else. A quick glance at his watch told him it was eight o'clock in Sydney. West's plane would still be in the air. They had two more hours to arrange a welcoming party, if they could.

He sprinted up the steps two at a time and strode along the corridor to his office. One of several notes on his desk told him what he didn't want to know: no authorization had yet been given to stop Graham West from entering Australia and continuing to wherever he might choose to go. The note was marked with the time: six-thirty this morning. Maybe things would have progressed since then, he thought, grasping his phone and tapping in the Fiscal's number.

'Good morning.' Iain MacKenzie sounded cheery. 'Don't suppose you've heard yet, then?'

'What? Good news, I hope?'

'Aye, you could say that. We've got cooperation from

the Sydney police. They've arranged for officers to meet West's plane. They've got a good description of him.'

'Right,' Lorimer replied shortly. 'You'll keep me posted?'

'Naturally,' MacKenzie's voice betrayed an excitement that Lorimer suddenly realized he didn't share as he shut his mobile.

What was wrong with him? Why this sudden feeling of deflation? They'd arrest the man, return him to the UK and then have him up to face the charges here in Glasgow. So why wasn't he sharing Iain MacKenzie's jubilation?

Lorimer sat back and leafed through his notes. Malcolm Adams was still missing and an overnight search had proved fruitless. Alec Barr had cooperated as fully as he could, to Lorimer's way of thinking. Catherine Devoy had been questioned but, according to Solly, she was keeping something from them.

Solly. The fly in the ointment. As usual the psychologist had given him some disquieting moments. All that stuff about the bags of designer menswear for a charity shop.

Lorimer picked up the other notes lying on his desk. They'd confirmed the fingerprints on both sets of plastic bags belonged to the suspect, and there was something more: several sets of West's prints had been identified from the ones lifted from Jennifer Hammond's bedroom. It all looked neat and tidy. West appeared to be in the frame for everything. But what had happened to Adams, and, while he was at it, what was the latest news on their other 'missing person', Michael Turner?

For a long moment Lorimer stared into space. That's when it had all begun: the night of Turner's going-away party. He looked up suddenly, a new light in his eyes. Maybe he'd been seeing this from the wrong angle all along. That night had been overshadowed by Duncan Forbes' murder, but perhaps they should have focused on the young man who had been the centre of attention hours before. Turner had flown to New York, leaving behind him a girlfriend who didn't seem heartbroken by his departure. He'd also left behind the man who had been something of a mentor to him by all accounts, but who was dead before that night had ended. What had they found out about Turner? A young man with lots of partnership potential, Barr had told him. Going places, he'd said. Well he'd gone places, sure enough, but where they were remained a mystery.

What if . . . ? The thoughts rumbled around his brain as Lorimer considered the man who had flown into oblivion. What if he'd been seconded to America for some other reason? Maggie was always banging on about incompetent teachers who ended up in highly paid administration posts away from the chalk face. What if Turner had been sent away? Had that thought occurred to any of them? Lorimer played around with the idea. The more he thought it over, the more it made some sort of sense. They had only Barr's word for it, after all, that Turner was going to have made an impact on their

American counterparts. Duncan Forbes, who had known the young man best of all, was no longer here to confirm that statement. But had they even thought to ask anyone else? Had he made the fatal mistake of deferring to the authority of the Forbes Macgregor partners? Maybe it was time to ask more questions about Michael Turner. And this time he'd be asking people who had no reason to tell him anything other than the truth.

'Good morning, Chief Inspector.' Adrian Millhouse shook Lorimer's hand and the DCI motioned for him to sit down. Millhouse had responded immediately to his call, Lorimer noted with satisfaction.

'This is just a chat, Mr Millhouse,' Lorimer began. 'Confidential. No hidden cameras.' He grinned, relaxing as the older man smiled at his joke. 'I'd like to ask you some questions about Michael Turner. Now,' he lifted a hand to stop Milhouse from uttering any sympathetic platitudes, 'it's a warts-and-all picture I want you to give me.'

'Certainly.' Millhouse shrugged. 'Whatever I can do.'

'First of all, were you surprised at Michael Turner's promotion?'

Adrian Millhouse stared at Lorimer for a long moment then nodded. 'No, not at all,' he replied. 'It came as no surprise to hear he was going away to Kirkby Russell. We all thought that.'

'When you say *we* do you mean all of the staff?'

'Well, most of the ones I talked to. And being in human resources I get to see plenty of them.'

'So what was the general opinion of his promotion?'

For a moment Millhouse looked thoughtful. 'I was surprised he went overseas. It was felt he was good partnership material for the Glasgow office. Duncan had more or less said that Michael would be his successor. Such a waste of talent.' Millhouse shook his head.

Lorimer nodded silently. That confirmed his own suspicions. There had to be a reason for getting rid of the young accountant. They were still keeping up the idea of Turner's death even now that NYPD had confirmed the young man had made contact with them. The US police had agreed to complete secrecy over Turner's existence meantime. Still, it smote his conscience to hear Millhouse speaking in hushed tones.

'Shouldn't speak ill of the dead but I felt Michael was a bit out of his depth,' Millhouse went on. 'With Jennifer, I mean.'

'Really?'

'Well, he took it a lot more seriously than she did.' Millhouse sat back and bit his lip. 'I hate to say it but Jennifer had done the rounds with plenty of them in the office, if you know what I mean.'

Lorimer nodded. His initial impression of the woman had been of her flirtatiousness. She'd been unable to resist trying out her undoubted charms even on a senior officer from Strathclyde Police. Jennifer Hammond had been a dangerous sort of woman and somehow her death seemed inextricably linked to the men in her life.

'Who else in Forbes Macgregor had she been seeing?' Lorimer asked.

Adrian Millhouse sighed deeply, 'Well now,' he began and started to count off names on his fingers. Lorimer listened intently.

'Graham West,' Lorimer told Solly on the phone. 'It comes back to him time after time! He'd had an affair with Jennifer Hammond right before she was supposed to be seeing Michael Turner. According to Millhouse, she'd screwed just about every eligible man in the office at one time or another.'

'What about Duncan Forbes?'

Lorimer frowned. 'That was the funny thing. Forbes seems to have disliked her. Tried to have her sacked more than once for her behaviour.'

'So why wasn't she sent packing?'

'It was Alec Barr who intervened,' Lorimer told him. 'Millhouse reckoned Barr had a soft spot for her.'

In the ensuing silence the DCI could imagine Solly's eyebrows raised in disbelief. And he'd be right to have doubts about the senior partner's motives. Had Barr also been one of Jennifer's paramours? He recalled the woman's bedroom done up like a high-class tart's boudoir. But she hadn't been a stupid woman, far from it. She had known whose telephone call had alerted the police to the body floating in the Clyde. Without that impassioned plea for help there would have been nothing to show that Duncan Forbes' death was anything other than a sad accident. Yet, for some reason, Jennifer Hammond had chosen not to reveal the caller's identity. Why? And who had closed her mouth for good? All at once it seemed to be of the utmost importance that they knew the whereabouts of certain key players on each of those nights.

The woman who answered the door looked up at him nervously. Her gnarled hand was on the chain, ready to take it off if Lorimer proved to be the person he claimed to be.

'Mrs Barr?'

The woman nodded, taking her time to read his warrant card thoroughly. She had every right to be cautious, Lorimer told himself. An older lady like herself was vulnerable to all sorts of conmen who might call during the daytime.

Satisfied that he was indeed DCI William Lorimer, Ella Barr admitted him to her home.

Twenty minutes later Lorimer emerged from Barr's house, three cups of tea and a piece of homemade fruit loaf inside him. Ella Barr had given him something to think about, though whether she was aware of that fact was highly doubtful. No, Mr Barr had not returned home after the party for the young man. And, no, he had not been at home for those other two nights. Alec had been away on business. He was away on business such a lot, she'd told Lorimer proudly, the handle of her porcelain teacup gripped between bony fingers. Looking at her, Lorimer reckoned the woman must be at least fifteen years Barr's senior. In stark contrast to the redhead who had led them all such a merry dance, Alec Barr's wife was every inch the lady with her carefully permed white hair and cashmere crew-neck sweater. Even her pearls looked real. A quick glance around the drawing room while she was fetching them tea had told Lorimer a great deal. The place was an antique dealer's dream. Collections of ivories vied for pride of place with three Fabergé eggs; every piece of spindly-legged furniture was upholstered in pale silks to match the drapes hanging from the oriole windows and the carved shelves were simply littered with the sort of Chinese artefacts he thought he'd only ever see in the Burrell Museum. The place was not so much a home as a magpie's repository, a fabulously wealthy magpie, at that. Again, he couldn't help contrasting the room with the mock-oriental pleasure palace that had been Jennifer Hammond's bedroom.

That took care of Alec Barr for the moment, now he had to find out exactly where the other partners had been on the two nights when murders had taken place. Like Graham West, Catherine Devoy lived alone but was there anyone who had seen them coming and going? Had anyone bothered to check? Lorimer fumed to himself as he turned the Lexus away from the avenue that led to Barr's front door. Any moment now West's plane would be landing.

*

The plane skimmed the tarmac with hardly a jolt and the rush of brakes roared in his ears. From his position next to the window he could see the modern campanile of Inchinnan Church and the gentle curve of the hills to the west. A huge sigh heaved from his chest. God, but it was good to be back home in Glasgow! The few possessions he had were stowed in a canvas carry-on bag in the overhead bins, but he would sit quietly until all the other passengers had left their seats. That was what they'd told him to do. He wondered if she would meet him at arrivals. It was a long time since he'd seen her, but maybe he'd still recognize her. With a strange smile on his face, the passenger on flight 206 continued to look out of the window and marvel that he had managed to come so far and survive so much.

It took ages for the plane to clear. Graham West responded to the beautiful woman's smile with a cursory nod. The girls at Singapore Airlines had catered for his every whim, but for once he had barely noticed their feminine charms. His mind had been on other things.

He looked warily at the officials in fluorescent jackets at the mouth of the corridor, then averted his eyes. It wouldn't do to draw attention to himself. Keep your head down, he told himself. He'd bought a cheap baseball cap at Heathrow Airport and now he pulled the peak forward so that the lower half of his face was obscured. Just look like any other weary traveller.

Now the queue of people was moving forward towards

Immigration Control. He could feel his shirt sticking to his back. A large stain of sweat would easily be seen, but so what? They'd been travelling for a day and a half: loads of other passengers would be just the same. That was the secret: to be just like everyone else. The queue inched forward and Graham could hear the mumble of voices answering questions. Suddenly he grinned as the memory of an old joke came to him:

'Any convictions?' The Australian immigration officer asks.

'Didn't know they were compulsory,' replies the new arrival.

Well, he certainly had no previous convictions and neither had Ray Easton. But as he came closer to the barrier that separated him from the area beyond, he felt a sense of unease.

'Passport,' the man said.

Graham West handed it over, sweat now trickling between his shoulder blades.

The man looked at him for a shrewd moment then said, 'Just remove your hat, please.'

West took off the baseball cap, staring as the officer compared him to the face in his photograph.

He swallowed hard then touched his stubbled chin. 'Haven't had time to shave yet,' he commented, trying to raise a feeble smile.

The man handed him back the passport and flicked a hand in the direction of the baggage carousels. 'Next!' he called out, the man before him already forgotten.

West walked forward, every step taking him closer to freedom. He'd done it! He'd actually done it! Breathing a huge sigh of relief he replaced the baseball cap on his head and looked for any sign that proclaimed 'exit'.

People around him were pushing trolleys piled high with baggage and heading for the double doors that would take them out into the arrivals area. He slipped easily between two middle-aged men. Camouflage, he warned himself.

Then they were out, into bright sunlight pouring through the windows and a noise of voices talking, shouting and whooping as passengers were reunited with long-lost friends and relations. He could see the doors to the street and imagined a waiting line of taxis.

'Mr Easton?' a voice at his shoulder asked.

Graham whirled around. Two uniformed policemen stood there, unsmiling.

'Would you mind coming with us, sir?'

'They've got him!' Detective Constable Niall Cameron burst into Lorimer's room just as the DCI hung up his jacket. 'We heard from Sydney just now and they've taken him in for questioning. They say it's just a matter of time before he's sent back to Glasgow!'

'Good,' Lorimer replied, trying his best to look pleased. It had been a long case with so many twists and turns that the team would view this with huge relief. So how would they feel when he asked them to probe a little deeper into certain areas?

'Ask everyone to assemble in the muster room,' he told Cameron. 'Five minutes.'

When the door closed, Lorimer drummed his fingers on the desk. What the hell was he meant to say to them? That Dr Solomon Brightman felt West's profile was all wrong for that of a serial killer? That he himself had some weird sort of intuition that things were not as straightforward as they seemed?

When the telephone rang Lorimer ignored it for several moments, then picked it up.

'DCI Lorimer,' he snapped, then his face changed as the caller on the line identified herself.

'There's been a new development,' Lorimer told the assembled officers. 'Graham West has been picked up by the police in Sydney and it looks very much as if we'll have him back here within two days.'

The cheer that went up was silenced by his raised hand.

'There's something else,' Lorimer went on, his voice sombre. 'I've just had a call from Mrs Lesley Adams.'

All eyes turned in his direction.

'She's bringing someone else in to see us shortly.' Lorimer looked round the room at the expectant faces. 'Michael Turner has just arrived back in Scotland.'

Solomon Brightman alighted from the taxi outside police headquarters. It was less than half an hour since Lorimer's call. He had handed his lecture notes to his eager Scandinavian assistant, thrown on his coat and scarf and made for University Avenue. A taxi had arrived in minutes.

Solly nodded as the receptionist handed him his security badge then looked around him. There was no sign of any excitement here at any rate. That would change as soon as he went upstairs to CID, he chuckled to himself. Voices behind him made him turn around. A dark-haired woman and a younger man were approaching the reception desk.

'I'm Mrs Adams,' he heard the woman say, her voice breathy with nerves. 'And this is Mr Turner,' she added, permitting herself a smile in the man's direction.

Solly stood quietly, studying the pair. Lesley Adams was a small woman, petite, like Rosie, but without his fiancée's warm shapeliness. This woman was all angles, her high cheekbones and slim dark-suited figure making her appear brittle. The expression on her face was haunted and Solly could see by the dark circles below her eyes that she hadn't slept. Michael Turner, on the other hand, was gaunt but relaxed. He might have been an athlete fresh from a training session: Solly suspected that his wiry frame belied a hidden strength. He wore a pair of ill-fitting chinos and a checked shirt that looked like thick American cotton. A glance at his shoes told Solly the rest. Birkenstocks, the US students' favourite footwear. Wherever Michael Turner had been for the past few weeks, his luggage hadn't travelled with him.

*

'Havenae hud any breakfast?' the voice of the woman behind the counter accused him. 'Cannae huv that, son,' she scolded, dishing up eggs, bacon and black pudding with gusto.

Sadie looked at the row of people standing in the canteen. Lorimer had brought them in with a brief explanation that his companions would have tea but could this young man be given one of her breakfast specials? The wee woman looked as if she could do with a good feed an' all, but she just asked for some tea. Lorimer had taken a plateful of Danish pastries onto his tray, she noticed. Dr Brightman would have one too, she supposed, but yon man never seemed to notice what he was eating. Always away in a dream, they psychologists, Sadie told herself. Nae in the real world. Well, the laddie looked like he was happy with a 'Sadie special' at any rate, she thought, folding her arms in satisfaction as they trooped towards a table in the corner.

'That better?' Lorimer grinned as Michael Turner wiped the last of his egg yolk with a piece of bread.

'Wonderful,' he sighed. 'Thanks for that. I thought I'd be taken straight into some interview room and grilled for hours.'

'Is that what they did in New York?' Solly asked.

Michael turned his attention to the man with the thick dark beard. 'Not really. They were surprisingly quick about things. Asked me all about what had happened, of course, but they seemed to know the man who had kidnapped me.' He made a face. 'Sounds silly, doesn't it? Kidnapped. Like something out of a children's story.' He paused to swallow some tea. 'I think it won't be long before they catch up with him either.' He shrugged. 'Just a few hints they were dropping. Anyway my passport and other things were returned to me after they'd spent half a day finding out I was who I said I was.' A sudden yawn caught him unawares and he blinked and smiled ruefully.

'So,' Lorimer began slowly, 'the US police sent you back home? Just like that?'

Turner nodded. 'I was told that a report would be sent to Strathclyde Police in time but that I was to contact you as soon as I came off the plane.'

'But you called Mrs Adams first,' Solly reminded him gently.

'Yes,' Turner frowned. 'Actually I called to speak to Malcolm, but . . .' he trailed off as Lesley Adams bit her lip.

'Yes. That was good of you to bring Mr Turner in to see us so promptly,' Lorimer told her, 'but I think we can let you go back home now.'

Lesley Adams opened her mouth to speak but Lorimer shook his head. 'We'll let you know as soon as there are any developments about finding your husband,' he told her. 'Being here is no help either to you or to us. What if he should contact you at home?' he added. The woman sniffed and swallowed, holding back tears that would undoubtedly spill the moment she was on her own. 'You must remember what we agreed, Mrs Adams. Not a word to anybody that Michael Turner is here. And alive,' Lorimer warned her.

The debriefing was almost over and Michael Turner could soon be taken away to catch up with some sleep. That whole episode in the man's life would be bizarre were it not for the events that had taken place here in Glasgow.

Now they had been able to fill in some of the blanks. Turner hadn't known about Duncan's death; he'd been on a plane out of the country before the news had reached his other colleagues. Jenny's death had affected him most, he admitted. She'd been with him at the going-away party, but hadn't spent all night with him. They'd had a few hours in bed together before she'd returned to her own flat and he prepared for his journey to New York. The first he'd known about the murders was when he'd spoken to Malcolm Adams, shortly before his escape. He'd been shocked, of course he had, but getting out of that place was the most important thing then. It was only later, when that farmer had taken him in that he'd been able to make some sense of it all.

JJ had lived there with his family years before, the farmer had told him. A bad lot, the Jacksons, and young Jimmy had been the worst of them all. Old man Jackson had been shot one Saturday night. Sheriff was sent for but Jimmy, or JJ, as he called himself, just vanished clean away. Hadn't seen him since. Family had left one by one, the old lady dead and gone. Old house had been left just as it was until the day that vehicle had rolled off the highway. All this the farmer had told Turner and retold it to the local police who had driven Michael back from Alabama to New York. Nobody had said so in as many words, but Turner had enough hints to guess that JJ was already on the NYPD's most-wanted list.

Now Lorimer probed a little more deeply. Why had Turner been seconded to the New York branch of their accountancy firm? Why not someone else? It had proved an uncomfortable few minutes as Turner reluctantly admitted his surprise at being chosen for the New York posting when he had anticipated promotion within the Glasgow firm. And the business with JJ? He'd assumed the man was a major thief, trying to access Forbes Macgregor's bank accounts. Had a ransom been put up for him? Lorimer shook his head and watched as the young accountant's face became puzzled. Then why had he been captured? And what had been going on with the transfer of money from Graham West's account?

'Maybe you can answer that for me,' Lorimer told him. 'Cast your mind back to the time before you left. Was there anything untoward going on in Forbes Macgregor? Anything that might have been behind Duncan Forbes' murder?'

Michael Turner looked lost and weary. So much had happened to him and jet lag was obviously not too far away.

'Think!' Lorimer urged him. 'Was there anything you knew about? Anything that wasn't common knowledge?'

A sudden light came into the man's eyes at that and he raised his head.

'Duncan said that,' he told Lorimer. 'Those were his very words. "Don't let this become common knowledge, will you, Michael?"' Turner gazed beseechingly at the DCI. 'I didn't tell a single soul, truly I didn't!'

'What was it that he asked you to keep so secret, Michael?' Lorimer asked, his blue eyes fixing on the man.

Michael Turner shrugged, 'Nothing really. Just a routine sort of thing. Thought I should let Duncan know that there was an aberration in one of our client's audits. Funds had been transferred to deposit accounts then moved on immediately.'

Solly frowned. 'What's wrong with that?'

'It's a typical hallmark of money laundering,' Lorimer told him.

Turner seemed to wake up at that moment. 'That's right. We have a duty to report it. I decided to tell Duncan and that was the last I heard of it.' He looked at Lorimer intently. 'I never thought any more of it. Duncan said he'd take care of things, besides . . .' he trailed off, an expression of horror crossing his face. 'Oh, my God! *That's* what happened!'

'What, Michael? For goodness sake, what happened?'

'It was Jacobs Betting Shops,' he faltered. 'They were part of an international consortium; if they were laundering huge sums of money and Duncan found out about it, no wonder someone wanted him dead.'

'But wouldn't Duncan Forbes have told his other partners what was going on?' Almost as soon as the words were out of his mouth, Lorimer rose from his seat. The answer to that question was the key to this whole case. Elizabeth Forbes had told him something had been on her husband's mind. Now he knew exactly what that something was. His thoughts racing, Lorimer left Turner in the care of police liaison and summoned up the troops.

CHAPTER 49

'Try the offices first. Devoy and Barr should be there. Bring them both in.' Lorimer was grim-faced as he issued orders to the team. There was still no trace of Malcolm Adams.

'Cameron, you and DS Wilson get officers down to each and every one of Jacobs' betting shops. I want every bit of computer hardware seized now! Tell Iain MacKenzie he's to issue a warrant!'

Niall Cameron had looked astonished. Nobody, but nobody, told a Fiscal what he was to do.

One by one his officers left for their different assignments until only the dark figure of Solomon Brightman remained, standing thoughtfully in a corner of the room.

'Well?' Lorimer glowered at the psychologist. 'What now?'

Solomon pushed himself away from the wall he'd been leaning against. 'Now we wait.'

'Wait? What do we wait for?'

'To see what they say. Barr and Devoy. One of them isn't going to tell you the truth, the whole truth and nothing but the truth.' He grinned suddenly, pulling an imaginary forelock. 'And,' he added, 'I'd love to be a fly on the wall when we tell them about Michael Turner.'

'Oh, I think we can do better than that,' Lorimer told him.

'Oh, no!' Catherine Devoy was looking out of the window at the street below.

'What is it?' Alec was at her side in two strides. There below them were three police cars blocking the road, officers already climbing the stairs to the office.

Catherine looked up at the man beside her, willing him to take control as he always did, but all she saw was a mask of impotent fury drawn across his features.

'Alec?' she faltered, grasping onto his sleeve. 'Alec, what—?' but her words were lost in the snarl that issued from his mouth as he shook her off.

'Stay here!' he commanded. 'Say nothing. D'you hear me? Not a word!' Then he turned from the window and disappeared down the corridor.

Catherine ran out of her room then stopped as her PA looked up in astonishment. This wouldn't do. She couldn't chase him all over the office. It wouldn't do at all.

She retreated and closed the door. It came to her then that Alec wasn't coming back. She was on her own. Catherine drew a deep breath and exhaled slowly.

Hadn't she always known it would end like this? Any remaining fantasies she might have had about a new life with Alec dissolved at that moment. She would remain here and await the police who were no doubt swarming over the building already. What she had to do was like an exercise in damage limitation, she thought wildly. It was imperative that she took control of herself and maintained what vestiges of dignity she could muster. But what about Alec? What was he doing?

Alec Barr leapt down the fire escape to the cobbled area below. His breath came in sharp, short bursts. If only he could make it to the car park then he'd elude them.

His feet slipped and slithered on the metal rungs as he turned the final corner and jumped to the ground. Heedless of what was going on in the offices above him, Barr ran along the lane to the underground car park they shared with the adjoining offices. For once he was grateful that they did not have a basement car park of their own. A quick flick of the remote and the huge metal doors began to open. Slowly, slowly they rose, Barr cursing them under his breath, then at last he shot through and headed for his silver Jaguar.

The noise of the engine roared in the hollow echoing space as he rounded the bend that would take him out of the building and into the street. He prayed that no police car would be blocking the exit. A quick glance told him that the way was clear and he stepped hard on the accelerator, narrowly avoiding the kerb as he took the corner into the next street.

His hands gripped the steering wheel tightly as he negotiated another bend and took the road leading towards the other side of the river. The afternoon traffic slowed him down and he dropped into the inside lane. He'd have to hide the car somewhere and proceed on foot. They'd be looking for him: they'd know his registration. All these thoughts whirled around his brain as Barr left the main thoroughfare.

Alec Barr had baulked at the thought of taking the life of a fellow human being. He'd often wondered how on earth anyone could do it.

Now he was beginning to find out.

'I'll ask you once more, Miss Devoy, where is Alec Barr?' Lorimer wanted to thump the table between them, to jolt the woman out of her hard-faced complacency. He glanced over to the uniformed officer who was standing by the door and gave him a nod. It was time, he thought.

The woman continued to stare at the floor as if she were trying to blank out everything around her: Lorimer, Solly and DS Wilson, who were regarding her with ill-concealed impatience. It had taken them three-quarters of an hour to achieve precisely nothing. Now they had to play their trump card.

Solly watched her face as Catherine Devoy looked up at the man entering the room. Wordlesssly she rose to her feet, her cheeks drained of colour and then she slumped back into her chair, her mouth open.

Standing there in the doorway, Michael Turner looked from one person to the other, an expression of bewilderment on his face.

'How could you do this?' the woman whispered, staring at Lorimer as if he were somehow responsible for making the dead come to life again.

Looking at her, Lorimer saw the sudden change. She appeared older now, her white face a mask, those scarlet lips no longer the badge of a strong, confident woman but something painted on, making a mockery of the person she wanted to be. And he felt a surge of pity. Was she one more victim in this tangled web?

'Let's start at the beginning,' Lorimer said at last.

All that pent-up energy had gone out of her now and she sat, arms limply by her side, following Michael Turner with her eyes as he left the room with a uniformed officer. He would soon be in the observation room adjacent to them, watching and listening.

'Miss Devoy,' Lorimer's voice brought her attention back, 'tell me how it all began.'

'It was when Duncan showed Alec those papers,' she said listlessly. 'He was so concerned to do the right thing.' She shook her head as if trying to clear away some distant memory. 'The right thing would have brought the firm crashing round our ears. We'd been dealing with Jacobs' people for ages.'

'By dealing I take it you mean money laundering,' Lorimer said.

'Yes,' she muttered reluctantly. 'Then there was a proposition from another chain of bookmakers. Jacobs wouldn't countenance it.' She shrugged. 'His death didn't come as a total surprise. These sort of people can be very persuasive, Chief Inspector.'

Lorimer stared at her. They'd known about the contract killing of one of their clients yet had said nothing at all. What had motivated them? Greed or fear? But the woman was talking again, the words flowing now like a dam that has burst its banks.

'Made some good money out of that business, too. Then Duncan comes in like a knight in shining armour wanting to inform the London office that something wasn't right. It would have meant ruin for us all,' Devoy insisted, as if Lorimer should surely understand. 'Good old Duncan was prepared to make that sort of sacrifice but we . . . chose a different option,' she said heavily.

'We?' Lorimer prompted her.

'All of us. Graham, Alec, Malcolm and me.'

'Go on,' Lorimer told her. 'Tell us exactly what happened.'

They listened as she described how West had obtained the drug, she had made sure it was put into Duncan's drink at Michael's going-away party and then West had led Forbes over to the edge of the water and pushed him in. Michael's party had been the ideal

386

opportunity. They'd got rid of Forbes and their contact in New York would see that Michael was taken care of, she told them. Then things had started to unwind.

'And Adams? Where did he fit into all of this?'

'Oh,' she said, 'Malcolm was persuaded to take the money and keep his mouth shut.'

'So where is Adams now?'

A mere shrug of her shoulders told the DCI that Catherine Devoy didn't know and cared even less.

'Alec Barr,' Lorimer began slowly. '*You* made him do all of this?'

Her eyes widened in astonishment. 'What? You really think that?' Then she began to laugh, a dry harsh sound that ended in a sob. 'My God, he really fooled you too, didn't he?'

Lorimer frowned at her.

'You think *I* influenced *Alec*?' Her smile trembled on the verge of tears and she looked down, fumbling in a pocket for a clean, folded handkerchief. Then, as if drawn back by Lorimer's blue stare, she continued. 'It was his idea from the beginning. He set up all our accounts, made the running to these bookmakers, everything. He was like a . . .' she paused, trying to put her thoughts into words, 'like a pioneer. He thought of it all, even down to the last detail. How we would spike Duncan's drink, how Graham would make it look like an accident.'

Lorimer looked at her hands twisting the handkerchief round and round. 'Have you any proof that Barr was behind it all?' he asked.

For a moment she stared at him then her gaze dropped. 'No,' she said in a whisper. 'He made sure nothing could touch him, didn't he? We were all in his power, all of us.'

'But how could you have agreed to kill Duncan Forbes?' Solly interjected. 'He was your friend. You were godmother to his son.'

Catherine Devoy opened her eyes wider and looked at him as if seeing the psychologist properly for the first time. 'Yes. Yes I was, wasn't I? Good old Aunty Cath. Always there when she was needed.' Her voice sounded hollow, only a trace of bitterness left. 'And all the time I thought they were laughing at me. Poor Catherine. Nobody there to love her. Well, they were wrong, you know. They really were. I *was* loved. Alec loved me for years. Just because he wouldn't leave that dried-up stick of a wife—' She stopped suddenly as if realizing for the first time how long she had deluded herself, the mistress whose aspirations are never more than insubstantial dreams. Her jaw hardened. 'Liz Forbes thought she had it all. Nice house, nice kids, perfect husband. Well, why should *she* be so happy? And why should Duncan take it all away from me?'

'Those letters . . . ?'

She nodded silently, her head drooping once more, lips quivering.

Lorimer had seen remorse before, but usually it was tinged with self-pity. As Catherine Devoy's hands covered her face, he felt certain that the tears beginning to flow were ones of shame.

388

'Duncan Forbes was never unfaithful to his wife, was he?'

'Duncan?' She choked on his name, then shook her head and sighed. 'No. He was the perfect husband, wouldn't look at another woman.'

'Not even you?'

She looked back at him, her eyes dark with unfathomable sorrow. 'Especially not at me, Chief Inspector. Nor at any woman who tried to fling herself at him.'

'You mean Jennifer Hammond?'

She nodded.

'Please speak for the tape, Miss Devoy.'

'Jennifer tried it on with everyone. Duncan hated that. And she didn't like being spurned.'

'What exactly was her part in all of this?'

'Jennifer? Didn't you guess?' She looked at Lorimer curiously as if nothing could possibly have eluded the man who was unravelling her very existence.

'She knew who tried to telephone us about Duncan Forbes,' Lorimer replied evenly.

'I nearly blew the whole thing sky high with that call. If it hadn't been for Alec—' she bit her lip.

'Alec Barr was with *you* that night?'

'Yes,' she admitted. 'He was waiting at my flat after the party.' She paused and looked into the middle distance. 'Alec wanted to celebrate. But how could I? Duncan was out there somewhere in the water, cold, alone. I couldn't bear the thought of no one finding him. So I tried to telephone.'

'But why did you consent to murdering Duncan Forbes in the first place?'

Catherine Devoy's voice dropped to a whisper. 'We had to do it. Alec said it was the only way.'

'And you spiked Duncan's drink?'

'Yes. Only, Jennifer saw me do it. She thought we were having a bit of a laugh. The idea of Duncan seduced by a date rape drug was too good for her to miss.'

'And did *you* kill Jennifer Hammond?'

Devoy's head came up, here eyes meeting his own and before she spoke he knew what her answer would be.

'Yes.' She nodded, turning her head away from Lorimer's commanding gaze as if from a bright light that was hurting her eyes. 'She was sniffing around Alec,' she mumbled, 'knew too much for her own good. I told him we should have got rid of her straight after the party.'

'And why didn't you?' Lorimer's tone was dangerously smooth.

'Couldn't keep his hands off her, could he? Said he had her under control.' She glared at Lorimer, a sudden anger making her clench her fists. 'What a fool!'

'So what made you change your mind?'

'Oh, it was when she tried a spot of blackmail. Not a clever move, that,' the woman added, nodding more to herself than to the men in the room. 'Not a clever move at all.'

'Catherine Devoy,' Lorimer began, 'you are charged

with the murders of Duncan Forbes and Jennifer Hammond.' He continued reading the charge, watching her face as she tried to swallow down her emotion, eyes widening with a sudden apprehension.

'Take her down,' Lorimer commanded at last.

They watched as the duty officer laid hands on the woman to march her out. She sidestepped at her touch then, realizing the inevitable, bowed her head letting them lead her away.

Lorimer glanced over at Solly and sighed deeply. 'Let's get out of here,' he muttered, shuddering involuntarily as though the woman's presence still lingered like a draught of chill, malignant air.

Outside the room, Michael Turner was waiting for them. Lorimer put his hand upon the young man's shoulder. 'I can't believe it,' Turner whispered. 'They didn't want me to work for Kirkby Russell at all. It was just a ploy to get rid of me. They had it planned all along.'

Lorimer sat down beside him. 'Yes,' he said grimly, recalling the woman's confession. 'They only wanted you out of the way. Tipping another accountant into the Clyde would have seemed too obvious, so they came up with a different scheme. Wonder how they came in contact with JJ?' he mused. 'Must have had dubious contacts through the international consortium who wanted to take over Jacobs' bookies,' he said, almost to himself. 'Sorry you had to find out like that,' he added, patting Turner's arm.

'It's just such a shock to know that people you worked

with – people you trusted – could do such a thing! I mean JJ was supposed to have me killed as soon as I arrived, wasn't he?'

Lorimer nodded. 'Yes, he was. But that old sin, greed, got in the way.'

'Lucky for me, wasn't it?'

'Yes,' replied Lorimer shortly. It had been nothing short of a miracle that James Jackson had decided to go out on his own. Bits of information had filtered through from the US police since Turner's arrival. The man found in the woods with Michael Turner's ID had turned out to be someone long suspected of being behind many contract killings in New York. He'd been sought after by NYPD for years. Jackson had undoubtedly made the execution to effect his own getaway. From being a hired killer, he'd decided to take a chance and cash in on the whole scam for himself. Blackmailing Graham West would have been just the start of it. And he was still out there somewhere, on the run.

Lorimer stood up at last, 'Look, you're free to go, but I'd rather you stayed here until we bring Barr in.'

Turner nodded and heaved a sigh. 'Yes. I will stay.' He smiled and shook his head wearily. 'Besides, where have I got to go? Unless my flat's still up for sale.' He laughed weakly.

'Good man, I'll have one of my officers look after you,' Lorimer beckoned WPC Irvine across to where the young man sat, head resting on his hands.

*

Solomon Brightman looked at him silently, waiting.

Lorimer put up his hands. 'Okay, your instincts were right. West didn't kill them all.'

Solly nodded. 'I never saw him murdering a woman. It didn't fit his profile.' He paused, a habit that still irritated Lorimer. 'I couldn't work out which of them had taken it upon themselves to kill their colleagues. None of it seemed to add up until now.'

'And we still don't know what's happened to Malcolm Adams,' Lorimer reminded him.

He turned to face the window that looked over the city. Was Adams out there somewhere? Well, there was only one course of action to take now. It was time to close the net on Alec Barr. He couldn't have gone far; his Jaguar had not been spotted on any CCTV cameras leaving the city. Devoy had given them all the information she could about where he had gone, which was not much. He'd told her to keep her mouth shut, but that was before the ghost of Michael Turner had walked into the room and destroyed her nerve.

'Sir,' a uniformed officer broke into Lorimer's thoughts, 'we've picked up Dougie McAlister.'

'Right, Mr McAlister, let's have it all. And I *mean* all,' Lorimer told him, his blue eyes boring into the man's face.

Dougie McAlister was a smaller, more washed-out version of big brother, Shug. He lacked the older man's hard-edged experience, Lorimer guessed, looking at the eyes flitting from one person to another as he tried to avoid contact with the chief inspector on the other side of the table. He was on something too, by the looks of him. Not something that had instilled any confidence, however.

'It wisnae me, Mr Lorimer,' Dougie began, his voice a nasal whine. 'It wis this man . . .'

It was over in less than half an hour. Dougie McAlister had been the runabout for The Pony Express, a rival firm of bookmakers that had wanted to muscle into Tony Jacobs' empire so badly that they were prepared to kill to get what they wanted. With no evidence and no information from big brother Shug, who was currently serving time for the murder, the police had been hard-pressed to find the brains behind it all.

It had taken all of Lorimer's self-control not to laugh out loud at the image of the Incredible Hulk handing over Dougie's payment. Still, it was one of several leads they'd have to follow up. And with Forbes Macgregor being the financial adviser for both sets of bookmakers, Lorimer had no doubt they'd find plenty to keep their fraud boys busy.

CHAPTER 50

George Parsonage watched as the well-dressed man struggled with the padlock. His curses and the way he wrestled with the door spoke of someone in a panic. George looked on with mounting curiosity. These old sheds that bordered the water had been closed up for years. Any day now and another bulldozer would flatten them to make space for more of the luxury flats that were marching down the length of the river banks. Few old structures remained these days. The riverman's own blue-painted boathouses lay opposite his home across a sward of green, cropped grass, metal hulks that kept the weather out and the seventeen vessels safely under cover. His racing boats hung suspended from hooks on the beams; the trolleys to take boats over to the other side of the weir were always near the massive front doors. Today George had been busy with his latest sculpture, a figure of a rower for a friend's birthday. But he'd stopped what he'd been doing and lifted his safety visor as soon as the call had come to pull a kiddie out of the water.

Now he was making his way back to where he'd left the trailer, a heaviness upon his spirit. The wee lad had only been trying to fish a football out of the water when he'd tumbled in. And this time it had been too late to save him. To distract himself from such thoughts, George stopped walking and watched the man disappear into the shed.

The sounds of distress that followed made him reach for his mobile.

He dialled the number, not needing to scroll it up. It was one he knew off by heart.

'Get me DCI Lorimer,' George whispered.

Alec Barr pushed the body on the floor with his foot. It gave a groan as his toe made contact with the man's belly. Malcolm Adams gave a muffled yelp of pain.

'Not long now. Soon put you out of your misery,' he told the figure lying on the ground. 'We're going for a little ride, you and me,' he said, heaving the man to his feet.

Adams was bound and gagged. His slight frame was nothing to Barr who slung him across his shoulders and carried him out across the narrow strip that divided the shed from the river. With one almighty effort, Barr threw the man's body from him into the swirling waters. It landed with a splash and he watched it with satisfaction as it floated outwards into the current.

'What the—' he grunted as a hand shoved him aside and sent him sprawling across the stony bank. He was aware of a second splash of water as a man dived into the river and headed towards Adams. Picking himself up, Alec Barr began to run back up the towpath, away from the water's edge, away from the scene unfolding below him. This wasn't meant to happen! Where the hell had that guy come from?

Cursing, Barr turned into the main road and ran back towards the footbridge that would take him across the river and into Govan. Once there, he'd flag down a taxi.

The sound of police sirens made him look up. One car had already screeched to a halt. A tall figure that he recognized emerged from the vehicle and began shouting at him to stop, but Barr was running across the bridge now, running and running as if his life depended upon it.

The river below him swirled menacingly from the force of the swollen current. He could hear footsteps clattering behind him and, looking up, he saw two uniformed policemen waiting at the far end of the bridge.

'Give it up, Barr,' Lorimer yelled. 'It's over!'

Barr whirled around, baring his teeth at the man who was gaining on him, one step at a time. He snarled in response. He'd not be taken like a cornered beast.

In one quick movement he vaulted the railings and threw himself into the waters below.

Lorimer reached the middle of the footbridge just in time to see the man's body tossed by the racing currents. He watched, aghast, as Barr flailed against the might of the river and then disappeared in a wallow of white foam.

The riverman was always careful when taking bodies out of the water. One slip and they'd be gone, sinking into the river's murky depths. This one was heavy, waterlogged and weighed down by death. They'd do a post-mortem. It was the routine thing to do, as well as being a legal requirement, but George Parsonage knew what the cause of death would be. Call it suicide, if you like, he thought as though he were addressing the pathologists at Glasgow City Mortuary.

He barely gave the body of Alec Barr a second glance as it lay in the folds of his boat. He knew this man's story. He'd taken the easy way out, as many before him had done. Lorimer would fill him in with the details in time, no doubt. But for now as he rowed back to the van waiting on the shore, he could content himself with his own part of the story.

At least he'd saved one man's life today.

CHAPTER 51

The face that looked down at him was like an angel's, Malcolm thought as he drifted back to consciousness. But it was a face wet with tears, although the smile was all sweetness. Behind her, he was aware of other figures, other faces that he seemed to know, but it was on Lesley's face that he chose to fix his gaze.

'Oh, Malcolm,' was all she said, but in those two words he knew what a fool he'd been. There was no reproach, no condemnation, just love. He tried to smile back and sit up, but the pain drove him down again to the bank of pillows under his head. Somewhere he heard a nurse speak and the other people in the room disappeared, leaving him alone with Lesley.

'I'm sorry,' he whispered, 'so sorry for everything.'

'But why, Malcolm?' Lesley was shaking her head. 'Why did you get mixed up in all of that?'

'Didn't want you to be left . . . without anything,' he murmured, every word a stab in his chest.

'All I ever wanted was you.' Lesley was crying again, and now he was aware of her hand in his, squeezing it tight. He tried to respond but the tiredness overwhelmed him and he began to drift back into that blessed sleep.

With an effort Malcolm gazed up at his wife and smiled.

'I love you,' he said, the words faint in the air between them, before he closed his eyes and let the darkness take him.

Lorimer closed the door as he left the room.

'At least Malcolm Adams will never be charged with conspiracy to murder,' he said to the man beside him. 'That's one thing his poor widow will be spared.'

'Yes,' remarked Solly, nodding into his beard, 'Lesley Adams, she—' Solly stopped for a moment and a frown passed across his face. 'I had a feeling,' he paused mid-sentence, then looked up at Lorimer whose blue eyes were searching him intently. 'A feeling as though something had passed between them in that room. Something that was sustaining her. I find it hard to explain.'

'Try me,' Lorimer offered.

'Something in her expression before he died. Did you not notice that?'

Lorimer shook his head and continued to walk down the hospital corridor. Life, death: it was a mystery that never failed to amaze him. Adams had been drawn into this whole sorry mess through the simple fear that he'd leave his family all the poorer, knowing he'd been living on borrowed time. But their lives, and the lives of so many others, would never be the same again.

He sighed. 'Catherine Devoy's statement seems to ring true now. Alec Barr was her Svengali, right enough: the brains behind the corruption beginning with their money-laundering schemes.'

'What made them do it?' Solly asked.

'Jacobs' string of bookies offered too much temptation for them.' Lorimer shook his head. 'But for Michael Turner's observant eye and Duncan Forbes' honest intentions, they'd probably still be at it.'

Lorimer turned into the main corridor that would take them out of the hospital. He felt the sudden need to breathe some fresh air. A feeling of lightness washed over him as he thought of a place that would fill his nostrils with fresh sweetness. Perhaps it was time to come clean and tell Maggie exactly what he'd been up to.

The table in the corner was set for two, the white napery and crystal glasses sparkling against the candlelight. Carefully he drew out one of the chairs, ushering the woman beside him to sit. As his hand brushed hers, he smiled at her quizzical expression.

'What's all this in aid of?' she asked at last. 'Something special or is it just to celebrate the end of the case?'

Lorimer sat opposite, smiling still. 'I've something to tell you,' he began then, as Maggie's face showed alarm, he laughed. 'It's nothing bad, don't worry! Here,' he said, and passed a manila envelope across the table. 'It was meant to be a surprise for our anniversary but I thought you deserved to know about it now.'

Still puzzled, Maggie pulled out the stapled pages and studied them. The first page showed a colour photograph of a white cottage nestling beside a curving bay. The description below told her that this was Leiter Cottage on Fishnish Bay, Mull.

'We're going there for three weeks,' Lorimer said. 'I'm owed extra leave and I thought we could go right after you stop school for the summer.'

'This is brilliant!' Maggie was turning the pages, skim-reading the details. 'Where did you find it?'

Lorimer laughed. 'Belongs to Jo Grant's aunty. I know you wanted a quiet place somewhere like that. We've been trying to keep it a secret from you for ages so it would be a surprise.'

'It's that all right,' Maggie replied. And if her tone held more dryness than the moment afforded she wasn't going to tell him why. Sudden tears filled her eyes and she bent down to fish in her handbag for a hanky. How could she have been so stupid? Silly, idiotic suspicions. An over-active imagination after all, just as her old mum would have said if Maggie had told her.

'Hey! No need to get all weepy. It's not such a big deal.'

'But you *never* do surprises,' Maggie protested from the depths of her handkerchief.

'Well, maybe it's time I did,' Lorimer answered. 'Stops me becoming too predictable.'

Maggie reached for his hand across the table. 'Know what?' she told him, 'I like predictable.'

Epilogue

The gravestone faced the hills. Carved into its granite surface were the words, 'Beloved husband'. Liz saw them through clear eyes today. Now the time for weeping was over and she could remember Duncan with all the affection in the world. A small wind blew the grasses in a field beyond the cemetery, making her look up at the clouds scudding past. Was he there, somewhere, just beyond her sight? As she gazed past the headstone she imagined his voice calling to her just as he'd called every day after work. 'Liz? It's me. I'm home.' And somehow Liz Forbes knew that Duncan was at home in her heart and that her memories would no longer be tainted by uncertainties.

Acknowledgements

I would like to thank the following people for their help in researching this novel and making it come to pass in many other ways:

George Parsonage, for his unique insight into the ways of the river Clyde and for sharing so many of his experiences; Dr Marjorie Black for her unfailing help in checking all things forensic; the late Superintendent Ronnie Beattie; Marjory MacKellar, Douglas MacKellar and Arthur Hedley for letting me use their riverside properties; Nick Stimson, duty manager of the Crowne Plaza Hotel, Glasgow; my husband for his expert knowledge and for his huge support throughout; my agent, the wonderful Jenny Brown and to Caroline Hogg and the team at Little, Brown, especially David Shelley for his faith in me.

Now read an extract of Alex Gray's
next gripping novel featuring DCI Lorimer

Alex
Gray
PITCH
BLACK

THE *SUNDAY TIMES* BESTSELLING SERIES

PROLOGUE

When the car rounded the corner of the road, she gasped. Up until now the cliffs on either side had masked the skyline so she was shocked by the streak of orange like a gash across the horizon in front of her bleeding from the blackness. It took all her concentration to keep the vehicle from veering towards the sheer wall of rock on her left. A quick glance showed how near she'd come to clipping the kerb and she shuddered as the wheel turned under her grip. The slimy walls glowed with sudden reflected light; she'd been close enough to see tiny plant fronds uncurling from the cracks that ran up and down the cliff side.

It was better to slow down a little, let the fright of that panicked swerve subside before she dared take another look.

A huge sigh rose from her chest and she felt the tears prick under the sore places of her eyelids, which she'd rubbed constantly during the drive north. The reassuring hum of the engine and the straight road ahead gave her courage to turn her head a fraction.

Now she could make out dim hills, darker shapes against the ink-blue sky with its burgeoning shafts of dawnlight a beacon of hope.

Mornings had never felt like this before.

Here was a new day beginning and with it the excitement of a million possibilities. It was like the first day of creation, newly-minted, given to her as a gift. All the other mornings of her life seemed to have begun with despair.

Her fingers were numb from gripping the steering wheel so tightly and she flexed first one hand then the other, slowing the car down so she could take peeks at the sky and the water. There was no artificial light here, just cat's eyes reflecting the full beam as she tried to keep to her side of the narrow road. Few vehicles had been travelling south on the opposite lane and her car seemed the only one taking this night-time route away from the city, so she gave a start when the lorry's shape appeared in the rear-view mirror. It rumbled behind her and she slowed down to let it pass. There was a swish of tyres and then the flanks of the lorry passed her by like a looming grey shadow. She watched it move away from her, then it cut back into the left lane after a decent interval. The sudden flash of the lorry's hazard warning lights thanked her for allowing it to overtake. She opened her eyes wide in surprise; when last had she been shown such courtesy? That it should be here in this lonely place and from an unseen stranger was surely a good omen. She must be on the right road.

Now the sky was lightening even more and pale grey clouds merged into the yellow patches above the horizon's rim.

A bird flew past, slowly winging its way inland, making her suddenly aware that there was life outside this cocoon of engine noise and road and gears. Just up ahead there was a black and white pole indicating a parking place, and she drove in and stopped.

She gave a half-turn to the ignition and rolled the window down, letting in a rush of cold air, then breathed deeply, closing her eyes for a moment against the gusts of wind. It was quiet but not silent. The first sound she heard was the lapping of water against the edge of the shore, like a living creature trying to break free from the deep masses that threatened to hold it back. She listened, mesmerised, then heard another sound, a peeping bird somewhere out of sight in the bushes, then an answering call further ahead. Straining her eyes did not help; the birds were invisible in this early light. The cool air chilled her skin and set her sneezing. A quick rummage in her jacket pocket found only used and still-sodden paper hankies so she sniffled instead, then rolled the window back up. There had been no time to look for her driving gloves before the journey so she tucked her fingers up into her sleeves to warm them, the way she'd done as a child.

A memory of her mother suddenly came back to her.

It had been one of the days when she'd been brought home from school. The day had started out badly at home with a sore throat and difficulty eating her porridge, then became worse when no one had taken her seriously and she'd been forced out, to make the cold walk down to the bus stop. The shivers had begun as she'd sat wedged between a man in a big overcoat and a woman with sharp elbows; the only seats left on the bus were the bench seats facing the exit. Each time the doors of the bus had sighed open she'd been exposed to the cold air and had felt trickles of sweat against her flesh.

Later her mother had fetched her home with cuddles that she knew were born of remorse. She'd tucked her hands into Mum's coat pockets then, sitting on her knee as the bus trundled back out of the city.

Now Mum was long gone and her own children were simply memories of what might have been.

On the brightening horizon she could make out the colours on the distant hills, tweedy browns and greens with darker patches that told of clefts where waterfalls might run. She glanced at the fuel gauge. It was nearly empty. It was not a road she knew well but there must be a filling station at the next village. A signpost not far back had indicated it was only sixteen miles away. *Then what?* a little voice asked. She had no answer, just the knowledge that she had taken the only way she could. A bed and breakfast place, probably, once she had travelled further north. And it would be wise to take out more money from a cash machine if she could find one. After that she'd have to think about the long-term future. But not yet, not just yet.

Turning on the ignition, she released the handbrake and let the car roll back on to the road. The fresh air had woken up something inside her, a feeling that had become lost through all those months and years. How long had she been recoiling from that voice and those hands? Trying to avoid the blows and the weight of fear that had smothered so much of the woman she used to be. Now she felt like a girl again, a young, wild thing, free of any responsibilities with the whole world still to savour.

It was not yet tomorrow so there were still some hours before she needed to make her plans. So far, escape had been sufficient. What was behind her could be dealt with in time. His body would still be lying where she had let it fall. The blood would have congealed by now, and rigor would have stiffened his limbs. She had left no traces to tell a story, of that she was certain; nor were there any friends or family to come around enquiring about her. Perhaps there would be a call from the club in a few days, or maybe the smell of a decomposing body would alert a passing stranger. And if *she* should be found? If tomorrow brought questions and blame, then what would she do?

There was no easy answer. It was something she would think about later. Once the sun was high in the sky and the road had taken her into the wilderness. She yawned suddenly then felt her chest relax, her hands lighter on the steering wheel as the road disappeared under the twin beams. Shadows all around still shrouded the world.

Everything would be fine. It was not yet tomorrow, after all.

CHAPTER 1

The man trained his binoculars on the bird, his heart soaring with the sea eagle as its white tail feathers came into view, huge wings hardly moving, floating upon unseen currents of air. He watched the eagle fly into the distant haze until it was a mere speck, and then let his glasses fall with a sigh of pleasure. What a sight to see on their last day!

They'd decided to picnic in the Great Glen, making the most of the fine weather that had blessed their three-week holiday in Mull, and Lorimer had been scanning the skies hopefully all afternoon. Now he had that sighting and it was a treasured memory he could take back with him to the city.

'How many pairs are nesting this year? Did that fellow say?' Maggie asked him, her hand resting lightly on her husband's arm. Her gaze still followed that dot on the clouds, imagining the bird seeking some prey to take to its growing chicks.

'Gordon? He reckoned they had five pairs out at Torloisk this year. But nobody said anything about sea eagles over this way. Golden eagles, yes, but not these boys,' Lorimer replied, looking down at Maggie's earnest expression with a smile. 'Anyway, how about some food? I'm starving.'

Maggie wrenched her gaze away, thoughts of eagles fading as she looked down at their unopened hamper. It had been a good idea bringing it with them on holiday, especially to a self-catering cottage. Mary Grant had left the basics to start them off, but the old lady knew they'd want to stock up with local produce and so had left a list of suppliers from Craignure to Tobermory and beyond. It had been fun buying eggs and fresh vegetables from farms that were off the beaten track, finding other places of interest like the ancient stone broch while they were at it. Secretly Maggie suspected that was exactly what the old lady had in mind when she'd left the names and locations of out-of-the-way farms and crofts. But the main town on the island, Tobermory, had been the real treasure trove for picnics. Now Maggie unwrapped some rolls and handed one to her husband.

Lorimer leaned back against the grassy hillock and sighed. 'What a day. Imagine seeing that before we go home!'

Maggie, her mouth full of spicy chicken, nodded in agreement. It had been the perfect last day. Even the midges had left them alone for some reason: maybe it was that small wind stirring the bog cotton and bringing a scent of myrtle wafting towards them.

'Happy?'

She swallowed and smiled, nodding again. It had been a wonderful holiday, just the two of them exploring Mull together from their base at the cottage. They'd been content to live without the intrusion of radio, television or even newspapers; a real escape from the world outside. Even the West Coast weather had been kind, with almost no rain save an occasional nightly shower that had sprinkled the grass and kept it green. Tomorrow they'd pack up and catch the ferry from Fishnish then drive the long way round, making the most of their journey home. But for now they could bask in the sweetness of the Mull air, banishing any thoughts of returning to work.

Lorimer lay back against the soft, rabbit-cropped grass and closed his eyes. It had taken the Detective Chief Inspector days to unwind, to forget that last, protracted murder case and now he was perfectly at peace with his world and his wife. In a matter of minutes his head tilted sideways and he began to snore softly.

Looking down at him, Maggie felt a tenderness that she had almost forgotten. How she loved this man! Yet there was an ache, a longing that sometimes surfaced. She thought again of that sea eagle carrying food to its chicks. That would never be her lot in life, she told herself. As a school teacher, Maggie had plenty of contact with kids and she was glad to leave *some* of them at the three-thirty bell. But there were others she'd have taken home in a minute, satisfying an empty space that she sometimes acknowledged to herself.

Maggie let her gaze wander over the hills and the ribbon of single-track road winding below them. They were so lucky to have had such a time here. What was she doing becoming wistful at what she couldn't have, when she should be grateful for all that life had given to her, she scolded herself. Then she looked back at her sleeping husband. He'd been such fun to be with these last three weeks. It was a shame it was coming to an end, but maybe there wouldn't be too much going on back in the world of Strathclyde Police. Or was that too much to hope for? After all, crime never seemed to take a holiday.

The cottage door closed with its now-familiar creak and Lorimer turned the key in the lock. Putting it carefully behind a lichen-covered stone where Mary Grant would find it, he picked up the final bag and strode towards the car where Maggie was busy sorting things into the boot. He took a last look at the whitewashed cottage and beyond: the gardens ran all the way down to the boat shed then petered out in clumps of reeds and small pools down by the shoreline. He and Maggie had scrambled over thrift-strewn rocks, stopping sometimes to look for seals out in the curving bay or listen to the seabirds' raucous delight as they dived for fish. Once, Maggie had whistled at a lone black head, coaxing it to swim nearer to shore, and it had, curious to find the source of her music. They'd been rewarded with a whoofing bark then the seal had turned over lazily and disappeared beneath the dark blue water.

Lorimer took a last look at the Morvern hills basking in the sunshine across the Sound of Mull, a patchwork of yellows and greens that Maggie had tried to capture in watercolours. These three weeks had rejuvenated him, made him forget any evil that stalked the city streets. Under canopies of late night skies he had held Maggie close and gazed in wonder at the myriad stars and planets scattered across the heavens. Was there some hand at work in all of that? he'd wondered. On such nights it was not hard to believe in an almighty creator. They'd basked in the silence of the place, though by day it was full of birdsong, mainly the different species of warblers whose ubiquitous dun colouring made them nigh on impossible to identify without binoculars. And sheep, he reminded himself with a grin as a lone black face skittered along the cottage road, a panic-stricken *baah* emanating from deep within its throat. He was feeling fitter and leaner; every day they'd walked or climbed, every night he'd slept soundly, no anxious dreams disturbing his rest.

As they rounded the corner away from the bay, Lorimer heard Maggie give a small sigh. Taking her hand in his, he squeezed it gently.

'Maybe we could come back here next year?' he suggested and smiled as she grinned in pleasure at the thought.

A queue of traffic was waiting by the pier when they arrived. The ferry was usually right on schedule, they'd been warned, and space on this smaller craft was restricted.

'What's up?' Maggie nudged her husband and nodded towards a uniformed officer who was walking slowly down the line of cars, noting something on his clipboard.

'Maybe he's looking for that rainbow trout you guddled from the burn!' Lorimer joked. Maggie had tried catching fish with her bare hands after they had spent one interesting night staring out at the bay as silent poachers laid their illegal splash-nets at the mouth of the burn. They'd watched, entranced, at the pantomime being played out under a full, silvery moon. Mary Grant had hinted at such goings-on, telling how the local policeman always had a good sea trout for his dinner: a sort of reward for turning a blind eye. The fishing rights to the bay were quietly ignored by many of the locals, she'd told them. 'Better they get them than the seals!' she'd insisted.

Curious in spite of himself, Lorimer opened the car door and walked towards the policeman.

'What's up?' he asked, recognising the man as PC Gordon Urquhart, one of the team from the Royal Society for the Protection of Birds' Eagle Watch. They had been privileged to stay in the hide with the man for a whole morning, watching as the adult bird fed its growing chicks.

'Ach, there's been a report of some egg snatchers in the area. We've got their registration details but we have to check all cars coming on and off the island,' he explained. 'Not quite in your league, Chief Inspector,' the man grinned, recognising Lorimer.

Lorimer was about to reply but the familiar sound of Gordon's two-way radio made the policeman step away from him. He watched the other man's expression deepen; this was surely some business that far outweighed egg thieves?

As the island cop turned back in Lorimer's direction he was met with a pair questioning blue eyes.

'We've got some real trouble on our hands now!' he groaned. 'Got to pick up a woman coming off the next ferry,' he explained.

'Not an egg stealer, then?'

'No,' Gordon replied then stared at Lorimer as if seeing him properly for the first time. 'More in your line, sir.' He turned away and nodded at the car ferry making its way from Loch Aline.

'Looks like she's killed her husband.'

Check out Alex Gray's new instalment
of the DSI Lorimer series . . .

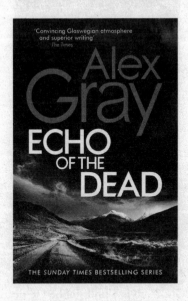

After a stressful winter, DSI William Lorimer is
enjoying some time away from Glasgow. He and
his new friend, Daniel Kohi, have retreated to
the wilds of the Scottish Highlands to unwind.
But what awaits them is far from a holiday.

Despite its troubled history, the mountain village
of Glencoe is now a popular resort, famed for its
close-knit community, its breath-taking scenery and
the warm welcome it offers weary travellers. So it's
particularly shocking when two bodies are discovered
in quick succession on the nearby peaks . . .

With a potential serial killer on the loose, Lorimer's
Major Incidents Team are drafted in from Glasgow.
It's clear that a dark secret lurks beneath the wild
beauty of this place. But will Lorimer manage
to root it out before the killer strikes again?

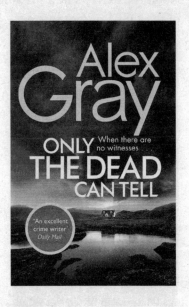

When Dorothy Guildford is found stabbed to death in her home,
all signs point to her husband, Peter. The forensic psychologist is
convinced there's more to the case that meets the eye but Police
Scotland are certain they have their man.

While DC Kirsty Wilson searches for evidence that will put
Peter away for good, she is shocked to discover a link with a vast
human-trafficking operation that Detective Superintendent William
Lorimer has been investigating for months. But before they can
interrogate him, Peter is brutally attacked.

With one person dead and another barely hanging on, the clock is
ticking for DC Wilson and DSI Lorimer. And the stakes grow higher
still when one of their own is kidnapped ...

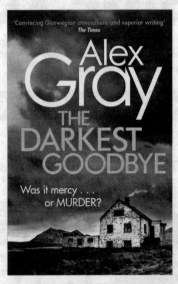

'Convincing Glaswegian atmosphere and superior writing'
The Times

Alex Gray

THE DARKEST GOODBYE

Was it mercy . . .
or MURDER?

'Brings Glasgow to life in the same way
Ian Rankin evokes Edinburgh'
Daily Mail

When newly fledged DC Kirsty Wilson is called to the house of
an elderly woman, what appears to be a death by natural causes
soon takes a sinister turn when it is revealed that the woman had
a mysterious visitor in the early hours of that morning – someone
dressed as a community nurse, but with much darker intentions.

As Kirsty is called to another murder – this one the brutal execution
of a well-known Glasgow drug dealer – she finds herself pulled into a
complex case involving vulnerable people and a sinister service that
offers them and their loved ones a 'release'.

**Detective Superintendent William Lorimer is called in to help
DC Wilson investigate and as the body count rises, the pair
soon realise that this case is about to get more personal than
either of them could have imagined . . .**